Ghost

KARI NICHOLS

Ghost

First Edition

ISBN: 978-0-9906123-5-3   (Paperback)

ISBN: 978-0-9906123-7-7   (MOBI)

Edited by Melissa Harlow

Proofread by Traci Craft (http://www.craftreads.com)

Cover design by Kari Nichols

Author photograph by Cottonwood Studios (http://www.cottonwoodstudiosworldwide.com)

Signet design by Nadine Pau (http://nadinepau-stock.deviantart.com/)

Title font by Tomasz Skowronski

Name/Chapter font by K-Type

Handwriting font (Caterina) by Richard Kegler

Handwriting font (Leo) by Denis Kegler

Handwriting font (Mother) by Colin Kahn

Handwriting font (Thomas) by Kevin Richey

For more information about Kari Nichols, please visit:

www.KariNichols.com

For Melissa.

I couldn't ask for a better friend or editor.

I will forever owe you for the amazing things you've done for me.

THERE ARE NO MISTAKES, NO COINCIDENCES. ALL EVENTS ARE
BLESSINGS GIVEN TO US TO LEARN FROM.

-ELISABETH KÜBLER-ROSS

PROLOGUE

SHE HAD NEVER BEEN so terrified in all her life. She had known tragedy, loss, and trepidation. But the sorrows of her past seemed like a small splatter of paint, accidentally spilled on an otherwise-perfect painting, compared to what now stretched dauntingly before her. Everything in the past had happened *to* her ... without her consent. But this—this she was choosing.

She knew it was the right choice—he had convinced her that the consequences of staying would be dire. But for all the wisdom in his advice, she still felt a twinge of fear in her stomach.

She stepped aboard the ship and stole a quick glance backward. She felt as if she were a prisoner being released after a lifetime locked in a cell—alone, scared, unsure of how to live outside the boundaries of her familiar cell and bars. She had survived the difficulties of her former life—surely the hardships of the life ahead could not rival those of her past.

One step at a time, she told herself in a small, terrified voice. She turned back to the ship and breathed a heavy sigh. She could not look back again, could not dwell on her former life, could not question the decision she had made.

As the ship set sail, she gazed toward the sea—toward the life that lay ahead. She wished she could paint the moment to capture the depth of her emotions. The vast, frightening sea that sprawled before her would be beautiful if only she had a way to capture the vision. *There is no turning back now,* she thought as a tear escaped from the corner of her eye. *There is only what lies ahead.*

ONE

Milan, March 1466

CATERINA FOLDED her clothing as quickly as possible. Her heart felt as if it was beating out of her chest. She had waited for this trip for months, and now it was finally here.

It had been nearly two years since she last saw her dear cousins. And to spend a full year with them, in Paris of all places, brought almost more joy than she could bear. Her mother and father agreed that once she turned twenty, they would permit her to travel to see Simona—who was one year older than Caterina—and Paula—who was three months younger. And because of that promise, her family had been forced to live with a two-year-long countdown to her twentieth birthday. She was grateful for her March birthday. If her birthday was any earlier in the year, her parents would not have allowed her to travel because of the cold air. But with spring just around the corner, they agreed she could travel with extra coverings on her feet and hands and a blanket to wrap around her body while she rode.

"Your friends will arrive at any moment!" her mother called from downstairs. She moved more quickly now—desperately trying to finish packing her things for the next day's journey before her birthday celebrations began.

"I'm almost ready!" Caterina called back.

"There," she said to herself as she placed her last garment in her luggage. "You are ready to go."

As she descended the stone staircase into her family's large gathering room, her mother, father, and three older brothers were already assembled, waiting for her. Her mother blubbered, but she forced a smile and reached toward Caterina.

"Oh mother!" she said as they embraced, and the two began to cry. "We were supposed to save our tears for after the party, remember?"

"I know, I know," her mother said as she pulled away from Caterina's embrace and wiped both their faces.

Caterina looked around at her family's expressions of grief. This trip would be a difficult separation for all parties. Her brothers—Filippo, Giovanni and Ludovico (whom she called "Ludo" because "Ludovico" had been too difficult for her to say as a child)—had always taken care of her as if she were a fawn on shaky legs. She had lived her life determined to show them she had outgrown her spots . They made sure she was happy at all times and went out of their way to provide her with every comfort and convenience. She could not imagine having brothers more loving than hers.

Caterina had not always thought of them so fondly. Three years earlier, she had learned from one of her close friends that the reason no gentlemen called on her was solely the fault of her brothers. They made it very clear to the young men in town that none were worthy to stand beside her. She still remembered her brothers' amused faces as she stormed into the dining room that evening and cried to her father and mother about how unfairly her brothers had treated her. Her father told her that although it *seemed* unfair, her brothers' judgment was absolutely correct. The conversation ended with her father congratulating his sons on their actions, while her mother scolded the men and consoled her weeping daughter.

Caterina was the daughter of a conte and contessa. And she was sheltered. She had always known as much. She was sheltered from the pain of a broken heart—no men courted her. Sheltered from the wildness of foolish young women—her parents were very strict about what manner of company she was allowed to keep. Sheltered from the disapproval of any elders—her upbringing and conduct were always of the highest degree. She was taught from a young age to always do the right thing, no matter what others thought. And she was not displeased to have been brought up in such a way.

No one who met the family could have anything unkind to say about them —they always behaved with a propriety fit for the company of a king or queen.

"Happy birthday, Caterina," her father said as he kissed her cheek. "I have a present for you to take with you on your journey, but you will have to wait until after your guests have left."

Caterina squealed in delight—she had assured her family that the only gift she wanted was the yearlong trip to see her cousins. But what young lady would disapprove of a gift? *None,* she thought.

Her friends soon arrived, and the birthday celebrations began. The families in attendance were some of the richest Milanese families. First came the Abramo family, with their daughters Nicolosa and Piera. Then came the Viscontis with their daughter Mella and their son Giuseppe (who would have been happy to attend any party simply to stare at his sister's beautiful friends, but was always quite cheerful when visiting Caterina's family because of his closeness with Filippo). Next, the Rosso family came with their daughter Isotta. And finally came the Brunettis with their five daughters: Tullia, Lisabetta, Cecelia, Diana, and Vittoria—who was Caterina's closest friend from the time she could walk.

As soon as all her guests arrived, the party began with a five-course meal, complete with laughter, stories and wine. Once everyone was incapable of eating another bite, Caterina's guests moved back into the gathering room. The fathers, of course, stayed in the dining room with their glasses of wine and conversations about their businesses and vineyards. The mothers congregated in the corner of the gathering room next to the fire.

Everyone was in high spirits, asking Caterina about her plans for the journey and her year in Paris. Caterina was unsure whether she was prepared for the journey itself—one month spent on horseback was enough to distress any lady. But she was unquestionably excited to spend the following ten months in her cousins' company. She was also eager to hone her painting abilities under the tutelage of her talented uncle. Uncle Giovanni was an accomplished painter who had been commissioned by a French nobleman to fill his home with artwork. She planned to spend hours watching him labor in order to take notes of techniques she had not yet learned.

Caterina's friends made her promise she would write to them as often as she could manage, and though she would much rather paint, play the pianoforte, or sing than write letters, she faithfully swore to write whenever a moment could be spared.

As Caterina's friends lamented over the events she would miss, she could not help but look around the room where she had spent many hours with her family. The gray stone floors covered in fine tapestries, the large fireplace in the corner, the walls filled with paintings of landscapes and family portraits—she would miss every part. She needed to take one last stroll around the home before retiring to her room for the night—she wanted to study every room in the house to ensure she would not forget a single detail while she was away.

As the party came to an end, Caterina hugged each of her friends firmly, and tears were shed by every feminine eye. Goodbyes were long and mournful, but at long last only Vittoria was left before her.

"Caterina Galli—how am I going to survive without you?" Vittoria choked out with a sob.

"I will write you of all my journeys. And I will send you paintings of the home and city so you can feel as if you are there with me," Caterina promised.

"I shall never have to depend on my sisters more than this next year, I am sure," Vittoria said with a backward glance toward her four sisters. "But I will bear it as best I can."

"I love you as a sister, Vittoria," Caterina said with one final embrace of her closest friend.

Once the last guests departed, the family sat down in their parlor.

"I believe some good will come of this trip," her father began. "I know your uncle and aunt have made arrangements for you to be comfortable during your stay in Paris. Their home is not as large as you are accustomed to, but I am sure they will make every comfort available to you."

"If at any moment you should decide you would like to return home, you need only write and we will send a manservant straightaway," her mother assured her.

"Sister," Filippo—her eldest brother—began, with a look of consternation on his face, "you may be twenty years now, but you are still our baby sister. Your brothers will be exceedingly cross if we hear reports that you are flirting with men in Paris."

Caterina rolled her eyes and heaved a sigh of frustration. She had long been aware of the plain image she saw whenever she viewed her reflection. Though she carried herself with elegance and grace, she did not often garner the attention of young men who were more engrossed by obvious beauty. Her curly auburn hair contrasted displeasingly with her pale skin. Her round face and large nose and forehead were often points of distress in her life. Her one comfort was that her eyes were tinted a pleasing golden-brown and had a nice shape. Though her family told her time and time again how beautiful she was, she often found herself wondering how her parents—handsome as they were—could have produced such an unremarkable daughter after three very good-looking sons.

"You know you will hear no such news, brother. I am traveling to France to see my cousins and increase my skills in the arts. Not to find a suitor. And if I return with reports of a man, then no one will be as surprised as I," she said with a small laugh. Her family shook their heads and continued to warn her of the evil kind of men that would be lurking in French society.

"Save yourself for an Italian," Giovanni said. "At least then we'll know he is from good blood."

Her father and brothers were soon off to bed. They knew that Caterina and her mother wanted some time alone on their final night together.

Her mother had been a picture of composure throughout the party and family discussion, but Caterina knew exactly what to expect once the men left for the night.

"Oh Caterina! What am I going to do without you?" her mother sobbed as she threw her arms around her daughter's shoulders. Caterina did not know how she would bear the separation either.

She and her mother were inseparable. As the only daughter in the family, she bore the delights of shopping, singing, sewing, and playing music with her mother. But the thing they loved most was painting together. They rode into the plains where they could find the best views of the mountains, and there they would paint from dawn 'til dusk. Other days they would paint her father's vineyards. But no matter where they were, they would sing and talk cheerfully whenever they were together. As a child, Caterina's mother had watched diligently while her brother—Uncle Giovanni—learned the art of painting. She brought her knowledge into motherhood and taught Caterina a great many things. Every spring, summer, and fall when Caterina's father made trips to their second estate in Florence, they would accompany him in order to view the masters at work in the city square. And upon returning to their home in Milan, they would apply their findings to their own creations. The art that covered the walls of the Galli estates were regularly replaced with new works by the mother and daughter. Their passion for art was insatiable.

"I know it will be difficult, mother. But I'm excited for the opportunity to go to a new place and meet new people! And I will be able to learn new skills that I'll show you once I come back. You know Uncle Giovanni is working on that grand fresco right now—that's something neither of us has worked with before. Do not despair. The time will go by quickly. I am determined that it will," Caterina said with a smirk.

Her mother kissed both her cheeks and sent her off to bed. But instead of heading directly to her room, Caterina took one last stroll through her home.

She walked through each room, lighting them with her small candle, admiring the way her mother decorated the entirety of the home. She took a moment to pass through her father's library simply to smell his leather books—she knew she would miss that smell. She walked out the back of the home to see how perfectly the moon struck the garden one last time—she had painted the scene more than she cared to admit, but failed to sufficiently capture the moonlight in all its brilliance. As she retreated back into the house, she chose to make one final stop before retiring to her room. She strode to the small prayer chapel in the back corner of the home and set her candle down to pray.

"My holy Angel Guardian, ask the Lord to bless the journey which I undertake, that it may profit the health of my soul and body; that I may reach its end, and that, returning safe and sound, I may find my family in good health. Do thou guard, guide and preserve us. Amen."

She decided one prayer was not enough for the situation at hand. Her mother would be terribly lonely in the coming year and would need comfort.

"Dear Lord! Make mother remember, when the world seems cold and dreary and she knows not where to turn for comfort, that there is always one spot bright and cheerful—the Sanctuary. When she is in desolation of spirit, whisper to her troubled soul that there is one Friend who leaves not—One whose love never changes—Jesus on the altar. Amen."

When she finally returned to her room, she found a small package wrapped on her bed. "My present!" she whispered excitedly. She had forgotten about the gift in the enjoyment of the evening, but could not wait any longer to know what it was. She tore the paper carefully away and sat down on the bed as she admired the offering. On the paper lay a simple gold ring with the tiny imprint of these words around the inside- "La gioia della nostra vita"- "Our joy for life." Tears dripped slowly down her cheeks. Her father could not have chosen a more perfect gift. She would cherish it forever.

TWO

WHEN CATERINA awoke the next morning, the house was in full preparation for the journey. Jacopo, one of her father's most trusted manservants, would take her as far as Auxerrois, near France. There, her uncle would send his own servant to retrieve her, and Jacopo would return to Milan. Caterina's brothers had put up a fight when her father announced a servant would be accompanying her on the trip rather than her brothers, but with Filippo and Giovanni in training to assume headship over the family business and Ludo in his final year of study at the university, there was no other choice. The brothers interviewed every servant in their home and every worker in their vineyards to find the best man for the job. Jacopo was the unanimous choice.

Caterina's mother affixed to her face the brave and determined look she had worn during the party the previous evening. They had cried enough tears the night before—today was a celebration of the year to come.

"Are you ready?" Caterina's father asked her carefully—he did not want to induce more weeping from his daughter and wife.

"Yes, father. I have everything," she replied with a large smile as she held up her hand for her father to see the ring.

"Do you like it?" her mother asked with hopeful excitement.

"Oh mother. I love it! You and father know my simple tastes. It suits me perfectly," she said as she admired the way the ring fit comfortably onto the third finger of her right hand. "While I am gone, I will never take it off," she said with a quick kiss on both her parents' cheeks.

"I'm happy you like it," her father said with a small grunt. He tried his best to remain emotionless at all times, but with Caterina—his only daughter—he had trouble accomplishing that feat. Whenever he was trying to smother a bout of emotion, he made the oddest face accompanied by a grunting sound—which, though he thought the sound small and discrete, was an announcement to all who heard that he was doing his best to choke down his tears.

"Jacopo," Filippo called as he walked to the man who would be taking care of Caterina for the better part of the next month, "I trust you are fitted with weaponry?"

"I have two knives on my person, my lord. And a sword readily available beneath my saddlebag," Jacopo responded politely.

As Filippo continued his interrogation, Ludo sneaked up behind Caterina and whispered quietly, "Give me your hand, sister. Tell no one you have it. Mother and father would think it unladylike, but we have decided it's necessary for your safety." He kissed her cheek as he pushed a linen-wrapped bundle into her hand and bid her farewell.

Filippo had apparently been watching the exchange from the corner of his eye, because as soon as Ludo gave her the package, Filippo finished his interrogation. Caterina shoved the package into her saddlebag and pretended to check the saddle's security. She said her final goodbyes to each family member before mounting her horse. Her brothers came over to secure her footings and remind her of the evils of French men. Before her departure, Filippo leaned in closely.

"Wear it always," he said with a solemn look on his face. Caterina smiled and held up her hand so Filippo could see the ring her parents had made for her. His head shook slightly, and she followed his eyes to the saddlebag where the package Ludo had given her was hidden. "Promise me, sister," he begged with a crazed look of intensity.

"Always," she whispered earnestly with a small nod of her head.

Her brothers backed away from her horse, and the family waved and yelled their goodbyes. Caterina's stomach churned in excitement and fear for the year that would follow. She knew not what the journey would hold for her, but she fervently hoped it would change her life.

THREE

Italy, March 1466

THE FIRST DAY of the journey was tiresome. Caterina had ridden horses her entire life. But to sit on a horse for eight straight hours proved difficult. She shifted her seat often to keep her bottom from becoming bruised. She prayed to the Virgin Mary that her skin wouldn't become raw and blistered, though she thought it very likely over the coming weeks.

As Jacopo made sleeping arrangements at a small inn for their first night, Caterina finally took a moment to withdraw the package her brothers gave her. She tucked it into the small bag she had compiled for her first night and followed Jacopo into the inn. After a hearty dinner of stew and bread, they were led upstairs to their rooms. Jacopo said a quiet goodnight and retired to his own room, leaving her to look over her room alone. The room was tiny—barely large enough for the small bed and wooden table which sat next to it. The bed, made of rough wood, was covered with a bit of straw for padding. Only a thin piece of coarse linen would lie between her body and the straw. *This will be interesting,* she thought with trepidation.

She sat on the uncomfortable bedding and pulled the linen-wrapped package from her bag. The package was no larger than her hand, and she hurriedly untied the leather string that held the package together. As the linen fell open, she saw a small knife wrapped in leather strips. The knife itself was about seven inches in length—the blade only three of the seven. But it was a thinner blade than she had seen before. The shape was just like her brothers' knives, and the handle was exactly the right length and width for her hand to fit around comfortably. The handle was wrapped in twisting leather that allowed her to hold the knife securely. Her brothers were always looking out for her safety. She smiled at the idea of owning her very own knife. *But how am I supposed to wear this?* she thought with some confusion. Filippo had made her promise to *wear* it always. She gathered the leather strips from the linen and realized it was a holster of some kind. The blade fit securely into a leather pouch that had been crafted specifically for her small blade. The pouch had loops through the sides which, Caterina realized after she studied it for a few moments, were designed for the leather string (which they had used to tie the package together) to be fed through. She pushed the leather through the loops and found that it was the exact length necessary to tie around the handle of the knife to keep it securely in the holster. She picked up the tangle of leather strips and arranged them in several different ways. The strips were each sewn into place, connecting with the other strips of leather at very specific points. She turned the contraption around and around in her hands before grunting in frustration.

"Why could you have not shown me what this is before I left?" she said, exasperated with her brothers. "You had time last night! How am I supposed to wear this?"

She removed her overgown and tried—with much frustration—to put the contraption on fifteen different ways. *I swore I would wear it! How am I supposed to wear something when I have no idea how to put it on?* She decided to sleep and try once more in the morning.

But when the morning came, she enjoyed no such luck. Fortunately, she had slept soundly. Her journey the day before was so tiring that once she lay in bed, she immediately fell asleep. She tucked the knife back into the linen and placed it into her bag as she dressed. She had mentally prepared herself for a month without the conveniences of her home, but had not expected to miss them this severely after only one day. She combed through her knotted hair and braided it as best she could without a mirror. She washed her face with the stale water the innkeepers provided her and joined Jacopo downstairs for breakfast. Apparently they would be eating more of the previous night's stew. *I know I come from a comfortable home, but I did not imagine people ate the same food for dinners and breakfasts. Maybe they wish to give us hearty food to keep us strong for the journey ahead,* she mused as she ate.

Conversation the day before had been lacking. Jacopo, a man of twenty-seven years, had served her father faithfully from the time he was a boy. And his father had served the Galli family before him. Jacopo was selected to act as Caterina's guide on the journey because of three things: he was able to adapt to any situation without becoming stressed, he showed the utmost propriety when interacting with any female, and he was young enough to maintain the strength and stamina that such a journey would demand. He was accustomed to laboring in the vineyards, carrying heavy objects, and riding long distances to do errands for Caterina's father. He was a silent person, not necessarily unpleasant; but out of respect, he would not even look in her or her family's direction unless one of them was addressing him directly. Her family had watched him grow from the time she was a toddler—he began working her father's land when he was only ten years of age. He was scrawny as a child, always unkempt, but a hard worker and a fast learner. Over the course of the seventeen years he worked in the vineyards, he grew tall and well-built in stature. His hair transformed from tight, unruly, blonde curls into beautiful, loose blonde waves. His eyes were so deeply brown that one could have mistaken them for black if they glimpsed his face too quickly. His skin was deeply tanned from his long hours of work in the vineyards. He was not displeasing to the feminine eye, but his propriety would not allow him to look upon a woman for longer than a short glance. She had protested at her family's choice at first—Jacopo was not friendly with Caterina … or any woman for that matter—but eventually gave up the argument due to the numerous praises of his character and abilities.

"Today, you shall endure conversation," Caterina said apologetically. "I cannot ride this long without talking. I cannot do much of anything for such a long a time without talking," she said with a giggle.

Jacopo, looking confused and distressed at the demand, only nodded his consent before helping Caterina mount her horse and mounting his own.

Caterina was worried after a full hour of silence. She was determined to have Jacopo partaking in easy discussion by the end of the trip.

"Well," she began, searching for a topic of conversation, "do you have any family?" *There! Now he has to speak about his family. Well done, Caterina!*

"I do," Jacopo said quietly.

Caterina waited for further elaboration on the subject, but none was to be had. She rolled her eyes and began again.

"And do they live near our estate?" she asked

"About a mile away," he said.

"Tell me about them," she said, hoping Jacopo might speak more than a handful of words at one time.

"I have parents and sisters," he said abruptly, seemingly becoming more uncomfortable in his saddle with each word he spoke.

"Tell me about them," she said once more, her voice a little louder this time.

He let out what sounded like a small groan before speaking. "My mother and father live in a small house with my two younger sisters."

"And what do they do for a living?" Caterina coaxed him.

"My father has many health problems, and my mother and sisters tend to him. My wages support them," he said mechanically.

Caterina smiled with triumph. She now knew she could force him into speaking if she got him irritated enough. She would allow him a respite in conversation—she feared that if she pressed him too far, he might turn back for Milan and leave her on her own.

Every hour or so, she would question him again. She learned his sisters did laundry for another family in Milan, he loved working with the grapes in her father's vineyard, his mother and father were proud he followed in his father's footsteps at the Galli vineyard, and he had not made an offer of marriage to a young woman. When he talked about women, he blushed and turned his face away from hers, speaking softly. She took his behavior as a sign that there was someone he fancied and was determined to find out who.

"And who is the young woman who has captured your affections? Why have you not made her an offer?" she asked with a smug look. He could not escape her company, and he knew she was persistent enough to ask until she made him answer.

"Her name is Fiora. And she is a servant in your household," he said with a sad tone.

"Fiora! Oh yes! She is lovely. And very kind and useful. You two would make a smart match. Why have you not asked her?" she wondered.

"I … I am not full of eloquence as you are. I find it hard to say the right words when I want to. And when I'm near her, I only want to gaze at her. So I usually examine the ground in an effort to keep her from feeling uncomfortable from my stare," he said quietly.

"Oh Jacopo. You are respected by the entire household. My family and our house servants alike find you honorable. I think Fiora would enjoy your stares rather than scoff at them. You must promise me that upon your return you will do as your heart tells you—stare when you want, smile when you want, and speak to her when you wish to. You are twenty-seven years old. It is time for you to have a wife—and you would make my mother and father exceedingly happy if you married Fiora. Then you could stay at the estate together and raise your family there! Oh yes. That would be a desirable arrangement for everyone!" Caterina thought aloud. Jacopo was staring at Caterina with a bewildered expression.

"Everyone speaks about me with respect?" he asked, surprised by her monologue.

"Well of course! Why else do you think my family would have entrusted you with my care? They have a good enough opinion of you on their own, but my brothers interviewed all the household servants before deciding you were absolutely right for the job. No one had an unkind word to speak of you. You are officially the most trusted servant in the Galli home," she announced.

"Well. That's nice," was all he could say.

Caterina chuckled at his short reply but decided she had forced enough conversation out of him for the day. *The poor thing must always be this quiet. I suppose I will have to work on that, or dear Fiora will have no idea of his affections.*

Over the course of the next week, Jacopo became more willing to partake in discussion. She tried to subtly hint at ways he could start conversations with Fiora. She was determined to do as much good as she could for Jacopo while he was undertaking such a long and arduous journey for her sake. She spent each night in an uncomfortable bed in a tiny inn, but somehow she always slept soundly after a full day of riding. She tried her best to figure out the leather contraption each morning, but, to her dismay, the mystery eluded her. After two weeks on the road with Jacopo, she decided they were close enough friends that she could seek his advice on how to wear it. Before breakfast, she dressed and tiptoed to Jacopo's door.

"Jacopo?" she asked with a quiet knock.

"Yes, Miss Galli," he said as he opened his door with a startled look on his face. "Are you unwell?"

Caterina blushed. "I know it is inappropriate for me to do, but I must ask you for help. Will you please come to my room?"

Jacopo looked uncomfortable when he entered her room, but he followed her nonetheless.

"Stop fretting. I'm not going to ask you to do anything wrong. I swore to my brothers I would wear this unladylike contraption, yet I have absolutely no idea how to put it on! I've tried every morning without success since we departed. Can you tell me how to wear it?" she asked as she held the thing up for him to appraise.

"Is this what Ludo gave you while Filippo was asking me about my ability to defend you?" he asked as he looked carefully at the leather strips and turned them about in his hands.

"Yes," Caterina said, stunned that he had noticed the quiet exchange.

He held the thing up for her to see. "This part goes over your shoulders here. And you must slide your arms in here—I cannot help you do any of this of course. And the knife will sit ... in the middle of your chest. Try to fit it onto yourself," he said as he handed her the contraption and abruptly left the room and shut the door. "I'm going to stand right here, and you can ask me if you have questions," he said through the door.

Caterina expected him to be respectful, but he showed propriety in a way that she was sure she had not seen from another before.

"I thought that your brother did not trust me," he said softly through the door while she was fitting herself with the leather. "When he was asking me about my weapons—I thought it was proof that he did not think me suitable for the task."

"Not at all! You were a distraction for my parents. I think my brothers are worried about my uncle's manservant. They have not met him, and my uncle does not take great pains in selecting his servants the way my family does," she said as she secured the two pieces of leather that hung down on her side.

The leather fit perfectly over her shoulders and around her chest. It had pieces that securely wrapped around her back and sides. She realized the reason for so many pieces of leather was that she could barely feel any of them because of the way they were distributed around her upper body. Now that it was on her, she felt foolish for her inability to comprehend how to wear it. She was grateful that Jacopo made such quick work of the puzzle. She finished dressing and opened the door.

"Were you able to put it on?" he asked as he searched her shoulders for any signs of the harness.

"Yes. Thank you. And please never speak of this to my mother or father. But you can definitely tell my brothers about the trouble they caused me. And tell them I'll never forgive them for not showing me how to put the cursed thing on," she said as he grabbed her bag with a small laugh and walked with her downstairs.

The remaining few days of the first leg of the journey were much easier for the two of them. They talked easily with each other about their lives, plans and dreams. By the time they met Uncle Giovanni's manservant, Caterina knew she would always call Jacopo her friend.

The day they arrived in Auxerrois was a day of mixed feelings for Caterina. Though she was excited that most of the trip was completed, she was sad to leave her friend and scared of the manservant who would take her the rest of the way. Before they reached the meeting point, she stopped Jacopo.

"Thank you Jacopo," she said appreciatively. "I am grateful for your protection and your courtesy. And your conversation," she added.

"I, too, am grateful for your help. I know you simply wanted someone to speak with, but I have not before felt at ease conversing with a woman. I've worked hard all my life to provide for my family, so I haven't made time to practice speaking with females. I will not forget your kindness," he promised.

"I thought you would realize my intentions," she chuckled as his expression became confused. "I did that so you might find the confidence to begin courting Fiora. I hope you will think of me as a friend from now on, Jacopo. And when you ask Fiora for her hand, I pray you will ask my mother to write to me about it. I look forward to hearing about your future." He smirked at her confession and shook his head in disbelief.

"Well … I thank you for your efforts. They were successful," he chuckled.

When they arrived at the arranged location, Uncle Giovanni's manservant was waiting for them. He was a stocky older fellow who seemed too old to ride such a distance. But he was kind enough in disposition to give Jacopo the peace of mind to depart. He gave his name—Jean—but spoke only a few words throughout the duration of the trip. Caterina had engaged in enough conversation over the three weeks prior to sate her need for words. She realized she quite enjoyed the extended periods of silence, and was happy for the momentary quiet to think about the trip thus far and the year ahead.

The inns were the same every night. The food for most dinners and breakfasts was from the same pot. She had built up a sort of tolerance to the pain of the saddle, but still felt sore each morning when she awoke.

When at last they approached Paris, she was overwhelmed with relief at having never had to use her knife. Her brothers had been so fearful of the journey that they had equipped her with a weapon. But when she thought about it longer, she wondered if their fear was of Paris itself. *It is the biggest city in Europe,* she thought. Perhaps she would have cause to use it after all. She would hold true to the promise she had made—she would wear it every day.

Four

Paris, April 1466

THOUGH THE HOUR was late, Caterina began to notice lights on the road ahead.

"Are we in Paris?" she asked.

"On the outskirts, missus," Jean replied in a gruff voice.

She paid close attention to every building they passed. The city was far larger than any city she had previously visited. The homes were closer and closer together as they drew nearer the center of the city. She had never seen a city so well-lit after dark. People were still walking about as if it was the middle of the day, and loud parties were still in full swing. Caterina wondered if the Parisian citizens were celebrating something specific or if they always lived that way.

The streets were wide enough for an entire home to span. The buildings were very different from the ones in Milan and Florence. These were far more ornate on the exteriors, with many more windows. Caterina was used to Italian architecture—white and yellow stucco or red and brown brick with deep orange rooftops. But this city was built mostly of white stones with either curved or steeply-pointed gray rooftops—or at least she thought they were gray, in the dim glow of lanterns that lit the lane on which they traveled. She focused on the clothing styles of the Parisian citizens and noted that the fashion here was noticeably different. Women's chests were showcased more prominently, the sleeves on their gowns were more ornate, and the hats on women's heads were … strange. She suddenly felt glad for her inability to bring many clothes from her own wardrobe. She would have felt unfashionable and uncomfortable in her Italian clothing. She needed to go straight to the seamstress in the morning.

As soon as Caterina noticed the buildings were directly beside each other with no separation other than a small lane between them, Jean commanded the horses to a halt.

Her cousins rushed outside before she finished dismounting her horse. They were laughing and squealing and hugging each other for five full minutes before a single word of sense was spoken.

Uncle Giovanni and Aunt Agnella had already retired for the evening, but Simona and Paula were still awake to greet her.

"Father will likely leave for work before we wake up, and mother usually stays in her room until lunch. We will have the first part of tomorrow all to ourselves!" Paula exclaimed.

Simona and Paula had been planning the trip for so long that they already had the first full month of activities scheduled. They would visit the city center, picnic on the banks of the River Seine, go to a large market garden called the Champs-Élysées, worship Sunday mornings at the Notre-Dame Cathedral, and attend several parties and even a masquerade ball.

"Tell us everything, Caterina! What has happened since you last wrote?" Simona asked excitedly as she took Caterina to her room. Caterina looked around at the large, elaborately decorated room. It was not as grand as her own room at her family estate in Milan, to be sure. But after a month of sleeping in tiny inns on hard wooden beds, it made her feel as comfortable as if she were back in her own home.

"The trip was tedious. But I had a friend along the way to make it tolerable," she said as she began to pull her clothes from the luggage that had traveled with her on the pack horse. She had not packed as many clothes as she would need for the year, but her father had given her a large sum of money so she could purchase new things.

"A friend?" Paula asked, intrigued by the admission. "And who is this friend?"

"His name is Jacopo—he is a servant in my father's household. And he journeyed with me until we met Jean," she said with a smile. She hoped that

Jacopo had been able to ride home more quickly without her and her luggage.

"Jacopo, hmm? Should we be concerned about the nature of your friendship?" Paula asked in a wicked tone.

"No! Of course not! He is a servant, not a suitor. Good heavens, Paula!" Caterina exclaimed, shocked by the implication.

"Well, servants in this household are more accustomed to flirtations from the ladies of the house, I suppose," Simona said with a glare in Paula's direction. "But it is Paris. And in Paris, anything goes. Tout va bien—as our friends say," Simona smirked.

Caterina blushed and placed a hand on her chest where she knew her knife was resting. *Thank God for my dear brothers. At least I can defend myself if one of these Parisian men decides to come after me.*

"Do not think yourself in danger, Caterina," Paula assured her. "They won't flirt with a woman who …" she paused and sported a guilty look before carefully finishing, "will not even look at them."

Caterina felt flush with embarrassment. She knew what Paula was going to say before she stopped herself. *You mean they will not flirt with a woman who is as plain as I. Well I would not have them flirt with me at all*, she thought with a slight twinge of anger.

Simona looked at Paula sternly and let out an exasperated sigh. "Tonight, you must rest. I am sure you are ready for some good sleep in a comfortable bed. We will talk about our plans in the morning. One of the servants will bring you dinner right away."

Simona and Paula kissed Caterina's cheeks and hurried off to allow Caterina some peace and quiet. She was grateful when they left. She had always longed for the company of friends rather than solitude. But somewhere on the road from Milan to Paris, she had developed a love of peace and quiet. *The next ten months could be very interesting.*

FIVE

CATERINA'S FIRST morning in Paris was spent rushing around to all the best seamstresses. Though she knew her cousins could not afford the clothing at such fine shops, they were happy to at least be seen in them, giving their peers the illusion they were wealthy enough to purchase gowns from the lofty establishments.

She was happy to have her cousins around to teach her the latest trends in French fashion. Paula was adamant that she purchase the "robe déguisée"—which, according to Simona, meant the most desirable and current fashions available—but Caterina worried she was far overstepping her own modest tastes. By the end of the trip, she had purchased eight gowns from three different shops. All eight would be made in different colors, and two were even in patterns. She usually chose deep blues, teals, purples and reds for her gowns, but in honor of the latest trends, she was persuaded to choose two bright fabrics with patterns in the designs. A floral patterned red and orange silk gown with slashes on the elbows of the red sleeves would be her costume for the masquerade. She would be attending as a bird—the seamstress agreed to make a mask out of dyed red and orange feathers. The other patterned gown was mostly a deep green velvet with strips of brighter green and gold fabric down the front and sides of the gown. Gold laces would cross all the way down the outside of her arms and tie tightly around her wrists. All the gowns either had slashes all the way down the arms or on the elbows to show the sleeves of her chemise underneath. She had never heard of such a thing in Milan but was excited for the practical application of the extra movement the slashes would provide. The most casual overgown would be delivered in two days' time, but the others would be split into two deliveries—the first to be made at the end of the week, and the second at the end of the following.

"Caterina." Simona began quietly as soon as they returned to the house.

"You don't have to lend *any* of your new gowns to Paula. I've already told her it would be rude to ask since they are *your* gowns and not hers. But she knows you are too sweet to deny her the favor—so of course she will ask." Caterina snickered at Simona's warning.

"Fear not, cousin. I have predicted this very scenario and will happily oblige her. Just make sure you tell me which gown you would like to wear most so I can set it aside for you," Caterina said, still smiling.

It was obvious that Simona was upset about Paula's behavior. She drew Caterina into her room and shut the door. They sat side by side on the edge of the bed as Simona gathered her thoughts.

"You are far too kind to Paula, Caterina. She has grown wild since moving here. The men in Paris are openly flirtatious, and I worry that Paula's morals have been permanently removed from her thick skull. If mother and father knew how badly she acted at parties and around her friends, they would never let her out of their sight! She hasn't come out and told me directly, but I am convinced she has performed immoral acts with several men—servants even! Oh! I don't know what to do with her! Tell me, cousin. What should I do?" she asked as she threw her arms around Caterina's shoulders and began to sob.

Caterina did her best to console Simona. But Paula's behavior was unfamiliar to her. She had only ever surrounded herself with women of good repute in Milan and Florence. *I cannot advise her on a subject of which I know so little,* she worried.

"Perhaps we should talk to her together? But I need to see how she behaves in the company of others first," Caterina suggested.

"Yes! Yes, that may work," Simona said as she sat up eagerly and wiped the tears from her eyes. "Oh, thank you. I knew you would be able to do more than I can. She will not listen to me. Perhaps she will be open to hearing what *you* have to say."

Caterina was not hopeful about the matter. Paula was one of the most stubborn women she had in her acquaintance. But she would do her best.

The first sign of trouble came the next morning after breakfast. The cousins went for a walk on the Left Bank of the Seine and came across some of Paula's friends taking a stroll with their suitors. Caterina and Simona stood back in order to observe Paula's behavior from a distance. Caterina noted with despair that Paula flirted unabashedly with both of the gentlemen—though she was careful to wait until her friends looked away for a moment to offer her flirtatious gazes. Simona looked at Caterina with a bewildered glance, as if she was begging for confirmation of the inappropriate behavior. Caterina returned the look with a small nod, and Simona visibly heaved a sigh of relief as her mouth turned into a tight smile.

As soon as they left, Caterina took her younger cousin's arm and led her to a small patch of unoccupied grass.

"Here, Love. Let's sit and talk for a moment," Caterina said as she sat down.

The look of blissful ignorance shifted to discomfort as Paula saw Simona's expression.

"What is this?" Paula said angrily.

"Just sit, cousin," Caterina demanded in a tone that surprised both Paula and Simona. Paula sat without further argument. Her expression remained bewildered for several moments.

"Your behavior with those gentlemen was very peculiar. Were they not courting your dear friends, upon whose arms they were attached?" Caterina asked.

"They are courting, yes," Paula said, confusion covering her face.

"Poorly done, Paula. You have been raised to act like a lady. Your mother and father would be *disgraced* if they were to witness that kind of behavior. If you do not stop acting inappropriately, I will be forced to take this issue to your mother and father. And I believe it is their right to keep you from society if they so choose. I will not allow my *cousin*—whom I think of as a *sister*—to act in such a manner. It would be ill-advised for me to remain in a home with such a woman. And since I only arrived yesterday, I suggest you make the correct adjustments to your behavior so I am not forced to leave ten months ahead of my plans," Caterina finished in a hushed yet firm whisper.

Her cousins stared at her in surprise, their mouths hanging slightly open. Paula eventually managed a nod, but that was all Caterina needed to move on.

"Let us continue our walk. The wind from the river will do us good. We all need to breathe some nice cool air, and the April breeze is quite refreshing," Caterina said as she pulled both cousins to their feet and took their arms on either side.

Paula wanted to scream. Caterina was the one cousin she was always excited to see. She had been more excited for Caterina's arrival than she was for the masquerade at the end of the month. But no more.

Paula hadn't been flirting with her friend's suitors. She was quietly asking them questions about her own suitor—Nicolas Lieferinxe. She was madly in love with him and had been seeing him privately for weeks. No other man could compare.

He was tall and slender, and he came from a wealthy family of which she was sure her mother and father would approve. His blonde, wavy hair was always arranged in a way that made him look as though he had tried to fix it (though it was never quite right). His piercing blue eyes melted her heart every time he looked at her. And his smile was, in a word, breathtaking. She hoped she could introduce him to her family soon, but Nicolas was worried about his own family's reaction to the news that they were courting. He feared his parents would force them to end the relationship after realizing her low social standing and tiny dowry.

Paula had hoped to confide in Caterina about the pairing, but after the scolding she just received, she decided it would be best if she kept the news to herself until it became public knowledge.

Caterina led her cousins on a quiet walk beside the river for nearly an hour before Simona decided she was ready for lunch. Paula barely spoke a word after Caterina's speech and walked slightly behind Caterina and Simona in what Caterina decided must be a pouting silence.

Upon returning to their modest home, Simona thanked Caterina profusely. She had been pleading with Paula for months without hope. But at long last, she believed there would be a material difference in her sister's conduct.

Uncle Giovanni and Aunt Agnella were already gathered for lunch when the girls entered the dining room.

"Caterina! We are so happy you have arrived in Paris safely," Aunt Agnella said as she kissed Caterina's cheeks.

"How was your journey, dear?" Uncle Giovanni asked as he wrapped Caterina in a giant hug.

"It was long and wearisome," Caterina smiled as he released her. "But worth the trouble. I'm very much looking forward to watching and learning while you paint," she said as she took her seat at the small table.

During lunch, she observed her aunt and uncle's interactions with their daughters. Their family dynamic was very different from her own family. Aunt Agnella, whom Caterina felt sorry for because of her unfortunate name, had become exceedingly vain since leaving Milan. She had gained excess weight and was much paler than Caterina could remember her being. Her dark brown waves were braided into an intricate pattern on the crown of her head. Her face was covered in a white powder to prove to all who saw her that she was wealthy and had no need to venture into the sun. Caterina had thought it odd that her aunt stayed in her room for most of the morning, but she could now see her aunt was trying to perfect her upper-class look.

She turned her scrutiny to her uncle. He had lost a significant amount of weight since leaving Milan, and she could tell he was under a great deal of stress. Though he was ten years older than Caterina's mother, the brother and sister had been mistaken for twins on more than one occasion. Now, her uncle's face had developed many lines reflecting his aging—seemingly exacerbated by some outside force. His light brown hair had begun turning to gray on the sides of his head. His light blue eyes, which used to be the same brilliant color as her two eldest brothers' eyes, had faded to a dull gray-blue. He appeared much older than the last time she saw him; she became greatly worried for his health. *At least his hands have not changed,* she thought as she looked over his well-worn hands, still covered in paint from the previous day. She hoped she could spend each afternoon observing him at work. She not only wanted to learn from his advanced skills, but also desperately needed a respite from Paula's exuberance and vanity.

Simona had changed very little except that she had matured into an even more elegant lady. Her bright blonde curls still framed her pretty face. Caterina thought that her bright blue eyes and rosy cheeks would not have gone unnoticed among the gentlemen of the city. The only hindrance she could foresee was that Paula's flirtations may entrap the attentions of any man who saw the sisters together. She would have to think of a way to help dear Simona.

Caterina had not expected to come to Paris and dislike one of her own relations. She watched Paula talk tirelessly to her mother about fashion and handsome men and parties that they were to attend this week. Paula's transformation into an unladylike nuisance was partly to blame on Aunt Agnella. She encouraged the behavior. Paula had her mother's dark brown hair and her father's previously bright blue eyes. There was no denying the girl was a beauty, but the unnecessarily loud volume of her voice and laugh had already begun to grate on Caterina's nerves.

"Would it be possible for me to come to observe you each afternoon?" Caterina asked her uncle quietly, trying not to interrupt her aunt and cousin's conversation.

"You want to come every afternoon? Surely not, Caterina. You will have many other amusements to entertain you with your cousins," Uncle Giovanni said, matching her volume.

"The mornings before lunch and the evenings after dinner will be more than enough time spent with my cousins. And I promise to tell you if there are any afternoon events that I would not want to miss," she assured him.

"Then you are welcome. And my patron would be happy to allow you use of the paints and canvases I use for my own work. I know how much you and my dear sister enjoy painting together. Was she doing well when you left Milan?" he asked with a loving gleam in his eyes.

"Very well, except for the pain of having me here in Paris for a year," she answered with a small chuckle. She was grateful to have someone so like her mother to speak to during her stay in Paris. Her uncle and mother had been very close growing up—so close that her uncle was the person from whom her father had asked permission when preparing to propose. Uncle Giovanni had spent many hours asking questions about her father's intentions, work ethic, intelligence and affections before granting his blessing. She smiled at the idea of how that conversation might have gone.

"I have been looking forward to observing your work again. It has been too long," she said wistfully.

"That it has," Uncle Giovanni said as he bent to kiss her forehead gently.

As soon as they walked into the studio where Uncle Giovanni had spent the past two years, Caterina knew she was in heaven. The room was a large square with high ceilings—she thought maybe it would serve as a large dining hall for grand parties after her uncle finished his work. The entire east wall of the room was covered in a fresco of four angels weeping in the sky while the Holy Virgin held the crucified Christ in her arms. Though it was not yet finished, the scene nearly brought Caterina to tears. She marveled at how intricate the work was— her uncle could have been working only on this fresco since his arrival, considering the size and detail of the work. She glanced around the rest of the room and saw several other half-finished canvases awaiting attention. She walked to each and marveled at their complexities. One was of a battle, another of a husband and wife walking beside a stream with a grove of trees in the background, and the third was a portrait of a very ugly gentleman.

"That one is my patron," Uncle Giovanni said as he raised his eyebrows and made a distraught face. Caterina covered her mouth to keep the laughter from escaping. "He may not be handsome, but at least he pays well."

"Very true," Caterina agreed. "If you don't mind, I will simply watch you paint to glean whatever I can from your methods."

"I don't mind at all. Do what you wish. And if you feel inspired, all the materials you could want are right over there," he said as he pointed to the back corner of the room.

I think I will enjoy my time in Paris very much, Caterina decided.

SIX

DURING THE NEXT WEEK, Caterina's days were each the same—mornings spent with Simona and Paula, lunches with the whole family, afternoons watching Uncle Giovanni paint, and evenings spent at home. As soon as the delivery of Caterina's gowns arrived from the seamstress, Aunt Agnella announced plans for the family to attend two parties in the following week. Though Caterina was happy to observe how Parisian society operated, she was wary of Paula's behavior in public. Since the scolding, Paula had been reserved—if not slightly resentful and distant. She held her tongue unless she was around her mother. But Caterina knew better than to think Paula was reformed until she saw evidence of a real change in a public place.

The house was buzzing with excitement on the night of the first party. Simona had braids intermixed with her blonde curls—all tied up with a blue ribbon. She had a simple, dark pink, silk overgown with a v-front neckline and a blue belt that perfectly matched the ribbon in her hair. Her blue silk kirtle and the band of her linen chemise were exposed where the neckline dipped. A large gold cross necklace sat perfectly situated between her neck and chemise.

Paula's dark hair and a white ribbon were woven intricately into a braided twist that was pinned to the sides and back of her head. The ribbon made a band over the top of her head which contrasted nicely with her dark hair. Her silk overgown was a two-toned orange color with a scooped neckline and full sleeves cinched tightly around her wrists. A white belt wrapped under her breasts. The white ruffle of her linen chemise showed around the neckline of the gown. Her necklace was a thin string of white pearls. Caterina had to admit she looked lovely, but the outfit looked very expensive.

Aunt Agnella's hair was pulled tightly back into a bun and covered by a tall pointed fabric hairpiece that matched her ornate blue velvet overgown. Caterina did not like this "hennin," as her cousins called it, but it was apparently the most popular head covering in Paris. When her aunt added the ornate gold necklace to the outfit, she looked regal. It was becoming more and more of a concern as she watched the lengths to which her aunt and cousin were stretching to obtain societal acceptance. *No wonder my uncle looks weary. His wife and daughter are spending all of his money for their own societal gain!* Caterina realized with chagrin. *At least he has Simona. Surely she will keep her sister in check.*

Caterina wore a dark turquoise velvet gown with a v-front neckline and cream belt. Her cream silk kirtle with a matching turquoise and green floral design contrasted beautifully with her dark gown. A simple ribbon necklace with a single gold charm hung around her neck. She wore her hair up, tucked into a caul with only a few of the shorter curls falling by her face.

Though the family told her how beautiful she looked, she knew better than to get excited over her looks. She was plain. And she would be standing with her beautiful cousins. No man would even glance in her direction. She would be attending the party to merely observe societal differences between her own Italian culture and the French. She placed her hand on her kirtle to make sure the knife was still securely resting in its hiding place. Even if she never had to use it, it was a comfort to know it was available. She decided to include some sort of veiled thanks to her brothers in the next letter to her mother.

When the family arrived at the party—which was only a short walk from their residence—the festivities had already begun. Dancing and laughing and drinking were found in every room of the large house. Simona and Paula pulled Caterina along with them as they greeted each group of their friends. The Parisian friends were kind enough, though a bit self-important, in Caterina's opinion.

She watched Paula's behavior closely throughout the evening. Though the girl was still too flirtatious for Caterina's liking, it was significantly decreased from the first day she had seen the ridiculous behavior. She eventually stopped watching Paula and simply enjoyed the evening with new friends. She and

Simona stayed close throughout the night while Paula enjoyed other people's company.

"Nicolas!" Paula squealed as she rounded the corner to find her sweetheart waiting for her.

"Hello my love," he said as he grabbed her hands and placed a soft kiss on each. "You are late! I thought you would be here an hour ago."

"There's an extra woman in the house who has to prepare for parties now," she said with a roll of her eyes. Caterina had been watching Paula's every move since she arrived in Paris, just waiting for her to act inappropriately. It was grating on Paula's nerves and was forcing her to stay aloof around Caterina and Simona. This was not the way Paula had envisioned her cousin's visit.

"Are you all right?" Nicolas asked with a look of concern.

"Of course. I'm with you," Paula said as she led him to a back corner of the party, where they stayed together for the remainder of the evening.

By the end of the party, the whole family was exhausted.

"Where were you hiding tonight, Paula? I didn't see you for a full hour!" Simona asked on the short walk home.

"I was enjoying other friends," she responded quietly.

"Well that was a splendid party. I look forward to our next outing!" Aunt Agnella proclaimed.

The party three days later was much the same as the previous one, though the home was a bit farther of a walk from their own residence. Caterina only met a few people who had not attended the last party. She and Simona were once again left to themselves by Paula. But this time, Caterina paid closer attention to her whereabouts. There was one handsome gentleman in particular who seemed to captivate Paula's attention. She was surprised to see that Paula did not behave badly with the man. And though Caterina did not want to admit it to herself, she believed that there were a few young men who were somewhat flirtatious with her and Simona as well. *I am sure they only have eyes for Simona. She is far prettier than I,* she told herself. She was not opposed to the idea of being with a handsome man, but she had promised her brothers she would not find a man in Paris. She felt a strange sort of joy at having been asked to dance by three different gentlemen. Of course, the men each danced with Simona as well. Nevertheless, at the end of the evening, all three of the ladies were exceptionally pleased with how the party had unfolded.

"Who was that handsome gentleman with whom you were enamored all night, Paula?" Caterina asked as soon as they had returned home.

"I have no idea who you mean!" Paula said with false innocence as she retired to her room and closed the door.

"I suppose we shall have to make our own inquiries since she will not tell us," Simona said, determined.

"Yes we will," Caterina agreed quietly.

Paula was a confusing person. She did not have patterns and probabilities—only risks and possibilities. This part of the girl's character was what made Caterina uneasy. Paula was known to follow the whims of her heart with little or no thought of the potential repercussions. Caterina would not be at ease until she knew exactly who this new man was.

A fortnight later, on the day of the masquerade, the women had found out very little of the young man to whom Paula seemed quite attached. Paula had spent much of her time during those two weeks going on walks with friends—and Caterina and Simona were unsurprised to often happen upon Paula and her gentleman taking long strolls together by the Seine. Paula's friends were kind enough to watch from a distance, but the implication of a serious attachment was very much present.

Each time Caterina and Simona pressed Paula's friends for information, they acted ignorant of any knowledge about the man. The one thing they were willing to give up to the cousins was that his name was Nicolas. The cousins were determined to find out more about the man at the masquerade that evening.

As soon as Caterina emerged from her room, her aunt, uncle and cousins were transfixed. The red and orange silk gown looked incredible on her. The seamstress dyed a fine linen chemise a deep maroon color to show through the slashes on the elbows of the red sleeves. Her sleeves—which were bright red on the outside and lined with maroon on the inside—flared at the forearms and hung down at her sides like wings. On her white silk kirtle was sewn a pattern of red and orange feathers—stitched where the v-shaped neckline dipped on the front and back of the gown. Her mask was covered in feathers that faded from maroon by her nose to a bright cranberry color around her eyes to orange where the mask came to points by her temples. It reminded her of the way the sky looked at sunset. Her hair was tucked on the top and sides into a knitted, red, jeweled caul with the rest of her long curly auburn hair flowing down her back. Caterina had been excited to put the ensemble on when she first received it from the seamstress' shop, but the reaction by her family made her feel truly beautiful.

Paula was dressed in a deep blue silk gown with a square neckline, a light blue kirtle and belt and a matching bourrelet on her head. Her mask was deep blue with small gold gems around the edges of the mask. Simona wore a black velvet overgown with a plain, white, silk kirtle and linen chemise. Her hair was tucked into a simple black caul. Her black mask had silver gems along its top and bottom edges. Neither of the girls' costumes could be called remarkable next to Caterina's, but they were still attractive.

The masquerade was hosted by friends of Uncle Giovanni's employer. His art had begun to gain recognition amongst the nobles of Paris, and this party would serve as a way for him to be introduced to more wealthy patrons. After finishing his current contract, her uncle would likely obtain several more commissions in homes of some of the richest nobility in Paris. Caterina was excited for her uncle's success, but hoped the city would not continue to change her Aunt and cousin for the worse.

The party was held in a mansion on the right bank of the Seine. Everyone was dressed in beautiful costumes and masks. Caterina loved masquerades more than any other kind of party—it was the one time in her life when she felt she could match the elegance and beauty of any other woman. Without a mask, she dressed simply—she did not have the looks to wear an ornate gown with fine jewelry. But at a masquerade, she could cover her imperfections with fine clothes and a mask. Yes, Caterina *loved* masquerades.

Heads turned as she walked through the party. Every man admired her; every woman eyed her as a competitor for the men's attentions. Over the course of the night, she danced more than ten dances and was involved in many lively conversations. She could not decide if they included her because of her obvious wealth or if she was a genuinely agreeable addition to the discussion of the group. She told herself not to worry about the reasons and simply enjoy the momentary affections.

Three or four hours into the evening, Caterina realized that she had not seen Paula since their arrival. She quietly asked Simona whether she knew Paula's whereabouts, but her cousin only shook her head. They excused themselves from the group they had been standing with and set out on a mission. They searched each of the main rooms without luck.

"This is a *mansion*, Caterina. How are we going to find her if she is hidden away? It would be rude for us to search each room!" Simona fretted.

"Come. Let's look outside. We can search the grounds without being discourteous to our hosts," she said as she grabbed Simona's hand and headed out the front door.

They walked arm-in-arm to appear as if they were taking a leisurely stroll in the fresh April air. They did not want to appear distressed—if someone saw them acting out their present mental state, they would likely try to help. And if Paula was acting inappropriately, no one else needed to bear witness.

They rounded the corner of the mansion and walked down a small lane surrounded by beautiful trellises of vines. Though the lane was unlit by torches, the moon was full and gave light to the gardens. The farther toward the back of the mansion they walked, the more sounds they began to hear—sounds that Caterina desperately hoped did not involve her younger cousin. They rounded the corner into the park behind the mansion, and the women stopped in their tracks.

There they were—Paula and Nicolas—on a small bench between two shrubs. Paula was sitting on the man's lap kissing him passionately while his hands groped her entire body. Caterina wanted to vomit. Simona looked as if she might faint. Without saying one word, the women marched up to the couple, grabbed Paula by the wrist, and stormed away from the ill-mannered scoundrel. Paula tried feebly to pull away from them, but her surprise kept her from responding as vehemently as she might otherwise have done. As soon as they were inside, Caterina pulled them into an empty room near the front door.

"Are you out of your head?" Caterina whispered violently.

"Of course I am! I'm in love with him!" Paula, beginning to sob.

"I do not approve, sister. If he was respectable he would have introduced himself to mother and father before touching you like you are some kind of courtesan!" Simona said, appalled.

"It's not what you think! We have to … oh never mind. I don't care what either of you think. We're in love, and we will be married soon. I am bringing him to our home next week," Paula said indignantly.

"If you think for one moment we will not tell your mother and father everything that has happened tonight, you are very mistaken. And if you think they will allow your relations with that man to continue after what you have done tonight … well, you might actually be crazy," Caterina said angrily. She could not believe her cousin's improper conduct. Paula stood silently for a moment, trying to gather her thoughts.

"Don't tell them. We had to wait to be introduced as a couple. Please, Simona. Don't tell them," she whispered.

"We will tell them. And your behavior will hopefully be corrected soon. Or I fear we will lose you forever. This is for your own good," Simona said as she ran her hands over her dress to calm herself and turned to leave the room. Caterina left with her and allowed Paula to stay alone and contemplate her actions.

Paula's life was over. She could not believe what was unfolding before her eyes. Her mother and father were not strict, but they would be, at the very least, displeased when Caterina and Simona revealed her actions that evening. Paula couldn't believe the level of hurt she felt when she thought about Simona's involvement in the situation. Caterina's outrage was to be expected—she was a sheltered, plain girl who was brought up to always do exactly the right thing, even if it meant hurting someone she cared about. But Simona. Simona was different.

A few months after their arrival in Paris, Paula had walked in on Simona half naked with one of the household servants. Paula had been shocked by the break in character, but chalked it up to the Parisian lifestyle making an impression on her. Simona wept in Paula's arms over the incident. Of course, Paula promised never to say a word ... which is why she now felt the intense sting of betrayal from her sister.

Paula would never again trust Simona if she revealed what had happened with Nicolas. They were practically engaged! All that was left was to obtain permission from both sets of parents. Paula did her best to dry her tears before rejoining the party. She was thankful for the mask to cover her red, puffy eyes.

The rest of the masquerade held little amusement for any of the girls. They were soon ready to leave, and though Uncle Giovanni was happy to oblige, Aunt Agnella put up quite a fuss about the early exit. She continued her protests all the way home, but her words fell on distracted ears.

As soon as they were safely inside the home, Caterina and Simona revealed the full story of Paula's indiscretion. Aunt Agnella did not seem to take issue with the kissing, though she was upset that her daughter had been groped by the man. Uncle Giovanni, however, was furious with his daughter and with the young man. In a rage, he swore she would never see him again. As Paula ran wailing to her room, she looked at her sister and cousin as if they were the scourge of the world. Uncle Giovanni thanked the girls for their honesty and retired to his room, only to be glimpsed during the following few days when leaving for and returning from his work.

Aunt Agnella and Paula both kept to their rooms for the next week while they pouted and wept. Simona and Caterina had the entire home to themselves and made good use of their time together. They embroidered new cushions for the sitting room, sang and played the pianoforte in the drawing room, and painted together in the small garden behind the home. Caterina found Simona's company almost as soothing as her mother's. She wrote long letters to her family and friends, outlining her journey and the month she had spent in Paris.

"It is almost May!" Caterina said with astonishment. "I cannot believe it has been a month since I arrived."

"And what an eventful month it has been. I cannot tell you how much I needed your company. I do not have the constitution to put up with Paula's excitement all the time. You are much easier to be around," Simona said gratefully.

"Well I have enjoyed your company just as much. I miss my mother, but I must tell you that you have made the separation tolerable," Caterina said with a smile. "I do feel badly that Paula and my aunt and uncle are upset. I felt that telling them was the right thing to do. Was I wrong?"

"Of course it was the right thing to do. If she continued in that way, she would have sullied the family name. I would not have *my* reputation ruined because of *her* actions," Simona assured her.

When Uncle Giovanni emerged from his room each morning, he kissed Simona and Caterina on their heads without a word and left to paint. He did not come home for lunch for several weeks. When he arrived home in the evening, he once again kissed Simona and Caterina's heads before retiring to his room. Aunt Agnella often came to sit with Simona and Caterina while they were sewing or painting, but only spoke in response to direct questions. When Paula did appear, it was only to eat. She refused to even look at the two informers.

When she finally left the home after three weeks, Simona and Caterina followed her from a distance. Paula spoke happily to her friends, telling them she had been unwell but was now recovered from her previously dreadful state. Then she whispered with them for several hours. Simona and Caterina were wary of Paula, but could do nothing more than watch her. She refused to acknowledge their existence, and they were happy to keep their distance during this time of awkwardness. Once Uncle Giovanni returned to his routine of coming home for lunch, Caterina began to spend her afternoons painting with him again. Their conversation was limited most days and non-existent on the others, but the quiet didn't bother Caterina. Simona and Aunt Agnella kept a close eye on Paula in the afternoons. This routine held consistently until the morning of June sixteenth.

Uncle Giovanni left for the morning, only to return home in a panic one-half-hour later.

"No one is leaving this house. Tell the cook and the housemaids to go to the market outside of town and buy as much food as they can carry. Tell Jean to gather as much water as he can and store it wherever it will fit. And lock the doors. I'm going to nail the downstairs windows shut," he said quickly as he rushed around the house looking for a hammer and nails.

"What has happened?" Aunt Agnella squealed in a panic that echoed her husband's.

He stared at the three terrified women for a long pause before finally responding.

"Plague. Plague has entered the city."

SEVEN

Paris, June 1466

OVER THE COURSE of the following week, Caterina spent her days sewing, singing, and looking out the upstairs windows to count the number of carts that passed by the house. She decided, based on the size of the carts, each held between ten and fifteen bodies. Just that morning, ten carts had passed. Every other day that week, only one or two carts had passed. It was getting worse.

"There were ten in the last two hours," she said quietly to her uncle.

"I'm sorry you're stuck here, my dear niece. If your mother knew what was happening she would be inconsolable," he responded warily.

"Don't fret, uncle. There's nothing anyone could do to stop this. I'm here, and we are safely inside. That's all we have control over right now," she reassured him.

After another morning with yet another increase in the carts of bodies, Caterina resolved to stop looking out the windows facing the road. She and Simona did their best to keep the family's spirits high, but the boredom and inability to get fresh air downstairs began putting everyone out of sorts.

Usually in the summer, all the windows and doors would be propped open to keep fresh air moving through the home. But with plague running rampant through the city, all the downstairs doors and windows had been boarded shut. They prayed daily that the sickness would not somehow find its way through the upstairs windows.

Caterina now wrote daily letters to her friends and family to pass the time. She knew she would never send them—she wrote mainly of her fears and did not wish to scare those whom she loved. She longed to walk beside the river or picnic in a field. Summers in Paris were beautiful—the air was neither too hot nor too stuffy. But being cramped inside a home with no air movement made the summer excruciatingly unpleasant. She daydreamed of riding her horse with her mother and painting the mountains to the west of her home. She did not know whether she could abide the separation for another nine months.

The servants had been able to buy one full month's supply of food. And Jean was able to match their water supply to the same. After two weeks, most of the food had gone bad, and the grain supply had run low. After three weeks without any hope of the plague's retreat, Uncle Giovanni realized the servants would have to try to find more food and water. He gave Jean and the cook money and sent them on their way with strict instructions to avoid contact with anyone who looked ill, had discoloration on their hands, had skin too pink, or had a cough. The terrified pair headed out arm-in-arm. The whole family prayed they would not bring plague back with them. But Caterina prayed specifically for their safety. People could become desperate in a time of crisis, and desperate people often did horrible things to survive. She thought the servants were more likely to be attacked for the food and water they were gathering than to catch the sickness.

When the pair arrived home two hours later, they carried fresh fruits and vegetables, bags of grain, and several pails of water. They had begged a few of the local shop owners to open their doors—even stripping off their clothing to prove their skin was untouched by sickness. The animals around town were not to be eaten out of fear that they first carried the plague and may pass it on to the residents of Paris. The family would have to eat more sparingly for the next several days, but at least the food would be fresh.

Another week passed with more and more carts each morning. Caterina wept for the loss of life she daily witnessed. She had foolishly thought the plague would be short-lived. She now understood the seriousness of what was happening. Each day, she wondered if she would ever see her family again.

Paula could not wait any longer to see Nicolas. She crawled down from her second-story window and landed safely on the ground below. She prayed no one would see or hear her escape as she headed down the lane behind her house toward the nicer part of town where Nicolas's family lived. She breathed heavily as she ran, trying to make it to the Lieferinxe home without coming into contact with a plague-stricken person.

When finally she arrived at the home, she saw Nicolas sitting in his window, reading a book by candlelight. She heaved a pebble at his window and watched surprise cross his face as he looked down and saw Paula waving at him. A massive smile broke across his face as he disappeared into his room.

When his front door opened a moment later, he rushed out to where she stood, picked her up, and swung her around while showering her with kisses. Paula could not contain her laughter. She had not seen Nicolas for almost two months and had worried that his affections might have lessened in her absence.

"Oh, my love! I have missed you. I am exceedingly sorry for the night of the masquerade. I was foolish to think no one would see us," Nicolas said fervently.

"Do not fret. If we have to run away in order to be together, then so be it. I would give up anything to be with you forever," she said as he kissed her cheeks and forehead over and over again.

"Come in. I have told my father and mother about you, and they wish to know you better," he said as he pulled her toward his home.

Paula could not have been more pleased with Nicolas's parents. They were kind and welcoming—and not at all pretentious as she had feared. She sneaked out every night for a week to spend time with her future family, but she hoped her nightly visits would not come back to haunt her.

Before she returned home once more, she kissed Nicolas passionately on the lips and prayed that the Virgin Mother would protect him and his sweet family.

One month into the seclusion, Caterina awoke in the middle of the night to a strange noise. She thought she heard talking, but then she heard banging sounds through the walls. She was terrified that someone had crawled up the side of the house to sneak into one of the upstairs windows. She wrapped herself in a shawl, took her candle, and carefully tiptoed out of her room. The noises were coming from Paula's room.

"Paula?" she whispered at the closed door. There was no response.

"Paula?" she said a bit louder. Still no answer.

She slowly opened the door and looked around. Paula's room was quiet. Her window was open. And no one was in her bed. Another bang at the window told Caterina that she had correctly guessed at someone crawling up the side of the house. *What do I do? Should I wake the whole house? Someone has stolen Paula from her bed and is trying to come back in and steal more!* Caterina's head whirled in fright. Suddenly, a young female threw herself over the window sill and onto the bedroom floor. Caterina rushed to the person to help—though she knew it was stupid to help the intruder. Perhaps finding a weapon to threaten the girl would have made more sense.

There, huffing and puffing on the floor, was Paula. She looked up guiltily at Caterina while she recovered her ability to speak.

"What on earth are you doing?" Caterina asked, confused. A few moments later, Paula finally recovered enough to speak.

"I needed some fresh air," she answered sheepishly.

"You crawled out an open window and down the side of your home to get some air?" Caterina asked suspiciously.

"Yes?" Paula answered in a question.

"In other words, what you're saying is that you sneaked out of your window and risked everyone's lives to see Nicolas," Caterina, now yelling, accused her cousin.

"Keep your voice down! No one else needs to know," Paula fervently pleaded.

"You think I'm going to keep your secret? You've risked the entire family's lives! Could you be more selfish?" Caterina scolded.

The rest of the family rushed into the room—having been awoken by the commotion. Aunt Agnella hurried to her daughter to see if she was all right. Uncle Giovanni asked for an explanation—which Caterina quickly gave—while Paula cried into her mother's chest.

"You would rather see the man we forbade you from seeing and endanger your family's well-being than obey and live a long life? Fine. When the sickness has finally left Paris, marry the boy quickly," he said angrily, his chest heaving. "Because I will not abide you living in my home any longer. You have until the city is free of plague. Whether you are married, I care not. You obviously have no concern for your family's well-being, therefore I feel justified in no longer caring for yours. And if you leave this house again before the plague has left the city, don't you dare come back," Uncle Giovanni finished as he exited the room and went back to bed.

Paula continued to weep through the night while her mother held her. Caterina and Simona did their best to fall asleep in spite of the wailing, but the next morning, both admitted they had not slept after the quarrel. When breakfast was served, Paula did not come down. The servants took meals to her room, and the only person whom she would allow in was Aunt Agnella. The family was furious with the entire situation, but Uncle Giovanni had decided she was no longer his concern and acted as if she did not exist.

Two days after the incident, Paula began moaning that she was in pain. She had a fever and her neck and armpits were swollen and tender. No matter how they tried, Aunt Agnella and the housemaids were unable to bring her fever down. All their fears were realized—plague was inside the house.

A servant was sent to find a doctor, but the sickness was so widespread across the city, all the doctors in town were either busy with patients or were already deceased. The family prayed for Paula to recover, to no avail. Paula's fever was too high, and no amount of cool water on her skin helped lower her temperature. Her skin grew blotchy all over, and the tips of her fingers looked black. After only three days of sickness, Paula began murmuring nonsensically. And on the day that she died, she screamed for Nicolas before vomiting blood all over herself and falling into unconsciousness.

Aunt Agnella and Simona were inconsolable. Caterina did what she could to comfort them, but they stayed together in Simona's room, holding each other and weeping. Caterina frequently checked on her uncle, but he refused to cry for his daughter. She had brought plague into his home in direct disobedience to his wishes, and he reconciled himself to his imminent death.

Within a day of Paula's passing, everyone in the household fell ill. Uncle Giovanni's fingers were blackened from his knuckles to the tips of his fingers. Everyone had a fever which could not be relieved no matter what was tried. After the second day, the servants stayed within their own quarters because they were too ill to function in a caring capacity.

Caterina tended to her aunt and uncle in the morning, taking them the last of the bread and water. She checked on Simona, who was writhing in her bed, unable to speak. But by the afternoon, Caterina was too weak to stand. With her last bit of strength, she wrote a final letter to her family.

My dearest family,
I have fallen ill with plague and will
not be able to return home. I wish I
had the strength to write at length, but
I am very tired. I wish I could have

seen you all one last time. I still wear my ring every day. I still wear my brothers' gift every day as well. Thank you for being good to me all my life. I hope this letter finds its way to you. I love you forever.
Caterina

Caterina sealed the letter and wrote her family's name and location on the outside. She prayed that whoever found it would have it delivered to her dear family. She thought about each of their faces. Her father—serious as he walked throughout his vineyards. Her brothers—laughing as they fought over the last piece of bread at supper. Her mother—smiling widely as she painted a beautiful landscape in an open field. She even thought about Jacopo—whom she imagined would be happily married to Fiora. Tears streamed down her face as she envisioned their sorrow when they discovered she was dead … and as she realized her own grief at never getting to see them again. She blinked the last of the tears from her eyes, and decided it was time for her to rest.

She closed her eyes and drifted away.

EIGHT

Brussels, June 1466

"THIS IS RIDICULOUS," Thomas said quietly as he paced the floor of the chalet he and his brothers had been living in for the past two months. He was annoyed that instead of fulfilling contracts, he was sitting around doing nothing. He hated to be idle, and awaiting orders for another fool's errand was more than he could bear. He knew they would not find the elusive survivors of the next outbreak of plague—no matter how many centuries they spent searching. Surviving the plague simply did not happen.

"Calm down, Thomas," Sergius said in his soothing (and incredibly maddening) voice. "There are no contracts to be fulfilled. The political climate across Europe is placid for this brief moment, and you know our father rarely accepts commissions that aren't political. Even if there were kills to be made, you are the fifth of ten sons—most of whom have sons and grandsons. There are over thirty others just as eager as you to get their hands on a contract— myself included. Surely you must understand that father is simply trying to keep us from becoming bored. Pockets of plague are breaking out all over Europe. And so we go."

"You would take his side?" Thomas yelled at his brother. Thomas hated it when Sergius defended their father (who went by the name 'Priest', though he was far from resembling one). Sergius was always respectful—which was not an easy task when it came to Priest.

"Careful, brother. Do not take out your anger on me. You are upset with *father*, remember?" Sergius replied with a knowing look.

Thomas heaved a sigh. He supposed that it was Sergius's right as the eldest brother to be the reasonable one. Sergius's words had hit their mark and brought Thomas's frustration down to a manageable level.

"I am sorry, Sergius," Thomas said softly. "I know you speak the truth. I am simply baffled by our ceaseless searching when—in over eight hundred years— we have never once found evidence to support the activity. One would think that all the fruitless seeking over that span of time would be enough to put a stop to these missions," he said as he realized his voice had risen and he was once again becoming angry.

Thomas was generally as mild-mannered as could be. His ability to stay calm under pressure was one of the keys to his success as an assassin. No matter the situation, he could always adapt with ease to finish the job. He was one of the best in the Family, and everyone knew it. But when it came to feeling idle or being bested by another in skill, Thomas was not as successful. He enjoyed training the newest inductees to the Family assassins at Castello San Romolo—the Family castle—if he wasn't out fulfilling a contract. During training he felt useful, and he was able to show off his superior skills to the trainees. But Priest was determined to spread the duties around to all of his sons and grandsons. Therefore, Thomas, Sergius, and Samuel were making their way across Europe, searching every city where plague was rumored to be.

The door of their room flew open as Samuel—Thomas's youngest (and incredibly haphazard) brother—barreled through the door.

"Paris!" Samuel gasped, completely out of breath. "Plague has broken out in Paris. Thank God we have something to do."

Sergius cast a slight grin in Thomas's direction as he stood.

"Then to Paris, we'll go."

NINE

Paris, July 1466

WHEN CATERINA AWOKE AGAIN, she was startled by the sound of men's voices. She lay still, terrified to move, wondering if the men had come to dispose of their dead bodies or to loot the home of its valuables.

She wasn't sure whether she was dead or alive. She wiggled her fingers and toes in a slight movement, just to make sure she could. She felt normal except for a growling hunger in her stomach.

"You check those rooms, I'll check these," a deep voice said in Italian as Caterina heard footsteps ascending the stairs. She quickly pulled her sheet over her head so the men might think she was dead and move on.

"There's a dead male and female in here," another voice shouted. "And another dead female in this one."

Caterina took a slow breath to calm her panic as the footsteps neared her door. She could hear her heart pounding in terror and hoped the intruders would not be able to hear it as well. One of them entered her room and rustled some papers on the table next to her.

"Two more dead females," the man said with an annoyed sigh. "We've been at this for two weeks. If we were going to find anything, surely it would have been during the Great Plague."

"Not again, Thomas. Please. Let's go. We have more homes to search," the second voice said as the men descended the stairs and exited the house.

She paid no attention to the cryptic conversation she overheard. Only one thought filled her mind:

They are dead. All of them are dead.

Caterina allowed herself to weep for only a moment. Her aunt, uncle, and both cousins were dead. She was alive but did not understand how. Her stomach once again protested its emptiness. She moved carefully, stretching out her stiff body as she placed her feet on the floor.

Apart from hunger, I feel perfectly healthy. How is that possible? she wondered as she looked her body over.

She walked from room to room, mourning each of her deceased family while keeping her distance. After seeing her cousins' bodies, she realized that something was wrong.

Is it common for the bodies to be this decayed after such a short time? I am no expert on death, but even my dear grandparents looked better than that within a few days of their passing. Surely I only slept for one or two days.

An uneasy feeling began to grow in her stomach. She needed to get out of this house—out of Paris. She ran to the kitchen to find everything there was completely covered in mold. She returned to her room and tried to concoct a plan.

I have to rid myself of anything that touched the plague, she decided. She stripped off her sleeping gown and found a bit of stale water in her wash basin to rinse off her skin. She opened her luggage and found a gown and chemise at the very bottom. She thanked the Virgin Mary that it was a simple gown as she dressed herself. Now that she was alone and terrified, she praised her brothers again for their gift. She would have protection during her coming journey. And she would thank them again when she returned home.

She rushed through the house in search of coin and valuables. Most of the money her father had given her had been spent on gowns, but she still had a little left. The men that came through the house did not take a single thing of value. She was perplexed, but did not dwell on the oddness of the situation as she gathered any gold she could find. She hoped and prayed she would have enough valuables for the journey home. She stuffed everything of worth into a linen sack and readied herself for her escape.

She returned to the room where she had slept to retrieve the goodbye letter she had written to her family—worrying that if someone found it and delivered it to her family, they would suffer a great shock when they found her alive and well. But the letter was gone. *That is odd. Perhaps I did not write it. Maybe I dreamt I wrote it, in my feverish state.* She told herself no letter ever existed and tried to put it from her mind.

Caterina waited until dark to sneak out the back—she did not want anyone to see her emerge from a house full of the stench of death. She kept her distance from people to assure she would not infect them, but she needed to purchase food soon or she would starve. And it was necessary for her to purchase a horse so she could ride home to her family.

Once outside the city center, she relaxed a little. Within ten minutes, she found a small inn where she purchased several bowls of stew and a pitcher of water. She refused to go inside despite the multiple requests of the innkeeper. She would not even breathe in the man's direction.

"Please, sir. Can you tell me how long it has been since plague first struck the city?" she asked as she ate her stew.

"I believe it's been about a month and a half. Maybe more," the man replied.

"Are you certain?" Caterina asked as her head spun. That would mean she had been asleep for nearly two weeks!

"Absolutely. My brother came here the day it hit the city. We've stayed away from town ever since," he said.

"Thank you," she whispered, bewildered by the information she had learned. She had already been scared that the plague was somehow on her clothes and in her body, but the two weeks she spent unconscious left her with even more terrifying questions than she knew what to do with.

I will not infect anyone with this horrible sickness. I am determined to stay away from people no matter how desperate I become, she decided.

The innkeeper was able to direct her to a stable where she could purchase a horse. She thanked him and went straight there where she bought a large, strong horse with reddish-brown hair. She mounted it as soon as the purchase was complete and rode hard through the night.

When she stopped the next day, the sun was high over her head. She paid a woman in a tiny cottage outside a small town, and the woman gave her a loaf of bread, a bowl of soup, and a blanket to cover herself while she slept. The woman's daughter tended the horse while Caterina slept for a few hours. Despite the woman's protests, Caterina would not go near the woman or her daughter—she slept under a nearby tree and awoke as soon as her body allowed. She thanked them for their kindness, bought another loaf of bread, and rode on until evening.

Each night, Caterina found an inn or a home where she would purchase food for herself and care for her horse. She would go near no one for fear of passing on the illness to others. She made sure she rinsed out her own bowl and cup when she finished eating her meals, worried the sickness might be able to pass to anyone who touched the food she had eaten.

Every day she rode as far and fast as her horse could go. She carefully guarded her sack of valuables and tried to take care of herself and her horse as well as she could. Some days, she was utterly exhausted from the previous day's journey and could only travel a short distance. But after twenty-five tiresome days, she could tell she was nearing home.

Every morning of her trip she prayed for protection, strength and stamina. Every night, she prayed for undisturbed slumber and continued protection for herself, her horse, and what little valuables she had left. She started the journey with many pieces of jewelry and an abundance of coin. Now she had only her ring and three coins left—barely enough for one more day of travel.

As Caterina lay down on the hard ground for what she prayed was her last night of the long journey, a loud noise startled her. It came from the stable where her horse was resting, and the horse began to snort and stomp. Her hair stood on end, and she knew something was amiss. She collected all the courage she could find within herself, pulled the knife from its holster, and quietly walked into the dark stable. A clumsy movement to her left caught her eye as a man stepped into the light of the moon.

He was a skinny, tall man who appeared to be somewhere around the age of forty. The top of his head was bald while the sides were covered in long stringy hair. His beard was wild and unkempt. He smelled as if he had been sleeping with the pigs for months. Caterina was overwhelmed by the scent that affronted her nose—she thought she had become desensitized to horrid smells due to her own body and clothes reeking from the month-long journey without any cleaning. The man's left eye was fully open while the right eye was slightly shut. His clothes looked old, but mended. As she appraised him, he started moving toward her.

She held her knife straight out at him and yelled for him to stop. He balked for a moment to size up the threat before continuing to come closer. She yelled again and swung her knife to show him she would be willing to use it. The man let out a taunting laugh and began moving from side to side, smiling a cruel grin as he teased of his attack. Caterina was at first paralyzed with the fear of what the man might do to her, but she somehow found her courage and braced for the coming assault.

The man finally made his move toward her. He ran with his arms spread wide to capture her in his grasp, but she stepped to her right just as he was upon her and threw her body around to swipe at him with the knife in her right hand. The knife caught him and left a long, bloody mark across his lower back. He screamed in agony as he turned around to face her, now seething with rage. He hesitated a bit before he came at her again and grabbed hold of her left arm. She cried out in horror and swung her right arm around into his side. Her blade disappeared into his skin all the way up to its hilt, but he did not stop. He began grabbing at her hair and her dress. She pulled the blade out and swung again, this time striking him a little higher. After she sank her blade into his side a third time, he faltered for a moment before releasing her and grabbing at the wounds. She watched him in the dim moonlight that was seeping through the cracks of the stable. The entire side of his body was covered in blood. He stumbled backward a few steps before reaching out to grab anything he could to keep himself upright. His hands flailed as he fell to the ground, breathing heavily. He looked up at her and muttered the first and only words he spoke during the altercation.

"You killed me," he said as his breathing became more labored. She held her knife in a shaking hand, unable to move, unable to look away from his dying form. After struggling for a few more minutes, he finally closed his eyes and fell silent.

Caterina collapsed to her knees. She had killed a man. A man who was trying to do God-knows-what to her. But she had killed someone nonetheless. Tears began to flow steadily from her eyes, and sobs racked her body. She held the bloody knife tightly, fearful that if she let go of it for one second, another attacker might appear. She glanced down at her hands, which she realized were shaking so uncontrollably that she wondered how the knife was still in her grasp.

Something is wrong with them. Something is wrong with my hands. I know they shouldn't look like this, but I cannot remember what they normally look like.

She stared at them for some time before understanding—not only were they dripping wet, they were red. She let out a long shriek of terror when her mind finally recognized the red liquid as blood. She rushed to the horse's water trough and wildly scrubbed her hands and her blade free of her attacker's blood. When the only remnants of the blood were under her fingernails, she sat down to decide what her next course of action would be.

She shakily forced herself up off the ground and walked to her startled horse. As she approached the poor creature that had borne witness to the violent exchange, she could not remember how to mount or ride the horse. She rested her head against its side while she stroked its fur and shushed its snorts. She focused on the way her hand felt against the horse's shoulder. She felt the muscles tensing and relaxing as it shifted its weight from one side to the other.

She moved her hand in time with the rhythm of her shushes and could feel herself relax as the horse calmed. *You can do this. You know how to ride.* She mounted her horse, tucked her knife away in its holster, and raced toward her home. She left the bag with the remaining coins behind. She would not need them—she would ride until she reached her home.

Ten

CATERINA RODE all night and most of the next day before she crossed the border onto her father's land. She was starving and greatly fatigued when she finally dismounted, and her horse was nearly dead with exhaustion. Neither could stand. Caterina dropped to her hands and knees. She was weak, and her head felt so heavy that she could not even look up.

Several servants rushed to help her, screaming for more aid. Caterina shrieked as they neared her.

"No! Stay back! Don't come near me! If you come too close I will kill you!" she said with all her might.

The servants formed a wide circle around her at her threat. They whispered to each other, but no one knew what to do or how to help her.

"What is this commotion?" she heard her father yell as he rushed toward the crowd of servants gathered around her.

"This woman has just rushed to the house, fallen from her horse, and then threatened to kill anyone who comes near her. We don't know what to do," one of the housemaids said, frightened by the ordeal.

They do not know me. What must I look like if they do not even know me? Caterina wondered as tears rushed to her eyes. She used the last bit of strength in her body to raise her head to look at her father. His eyes were huge as he realized that Caterina was on the ground before him. The servants gasped, and a few women fainted. Her father rushed toward her, but she raised her hand and yelled for him to stop.

"My dearest child," her father said, clearly in anguish, "What has happened? Did you make the journey from Paris on your own? And why are you covered in blood?"

She took a moment to collect her thoughts.

"They are dead. They are all dead. Plague is in Paris," she whispered as someone lifted her from the ground and carried her toward the house. "No!" she feebly said as she tried to push away from the person holding her. "I will kill you," she gasped before passing out.

ELEVEN

Milan, August 1466

CATERINA COULD NOT find the strength to open her eyes. She lay on a comfortable surface for hours—or maybe days or weeks. Her mind was incapable of remaining conscious for more than a few seconds at a time. A man and woman spoke quietly nearby, but their words were jumbled in her mind as if she was hearing them through water. Someone fed her periodically, but she could not tell what the food was or who was giving it to her. She struggled in vain to rouse her mind.

When she finally awoke, Caterina looked around and discovered she was in her own room. The light coming through the windows told her the sun had just begun to rise for the day. The man and woman she had heard talking while she slumbered were lying side-by-side on a thin palette of blankets on the floor in the corner of the room. The door opened quietly as someone slid an empty tray of food out and a new tray of food in.

Caterina's head felt better, but she was still in a state of confusion. She tried to remember what had happened before she blacked out, but the memories were too fuzzy. In a sudden jolt, everything came back in a flood of memories: the plague, the attacker, her blade in a dead man's side, her relentless ride home. Everything. She gasped and sat up from the fear that overtook her mind. The people on the floor stirred awake as Caterina's breathing quickened.

"Why are you in here?" Caterina groaned in agony. They would surely die now. She had carried the plague to her own home, and now everyone here would die. She was no better than Paula.

The couple stood quickly and rushed to Caterina's bedside. Her eyes slowly focused on the man and woman—Jacopo and Fiora stood before her.

"We're here to nurse you back to health, miss," Fiora said gently, taking

Caterina's hand in her own.

"You cannot be near me!" Caterina cried as she tried to pull her hand away. Fiora's grasp was tight, and Caterina could not put any distance between herself and her kind servants.

"Caterina," Jacopo started, "we've been in here with you for a week. Nothing has happened. We've been feeding you and keeping an eye on your health. And neither of us has gotten sick in any way. You are not sick, or we would already be dead."

"But you don't understand! I *was* sick. I had the plague. I lay dying in my bed, and somehow, when I awoke, my body was no longer afflicted. And now I've brought it to my own home! How could you two have put yourselves in that kind of danger?" Caterina demanded, upset by their actions.

Jacopo and Fiora exchanged a small glance before Fiora spoke.

"Because we owe you our lives," she said with a smile.

"You … what? No. That's not true at all! How could you possibly think that? How could you be so careless with your lives? What if I am carrying the plague?" Caterina asked in hurried frustration.

"What I mean," Fiora started, "is that Jacopo and I wouldn't really be *living* our lives if it weren't for you."

Caterina stared at them in silent confusion for several moments before Fiora explained what she meant.

"Before Jacopo left on the journey with you, his eyes were always turned down, and all of us housemaids had decided he was disinterested. But *I* was not disinterested. I started working here nearly six years ago, and from the first time I saw him, I was in love." She smiled up at Jacopo with an adoration that made Caterina's breath catch. "I spent six years silently pining after him. I would watch him leave the fields every day, and I always tried to offer him food or water if I had any to share. But he never looked at me. I thought I would die when he was chosen to take you on your journey. To not see my Jacopo for a month! I thought my heart should break right out of my chest. But when he returned home, he was different. The first thing he did when he dismounted his horse was look me straight in the eyes. I thought I was dreaming. The next day, I was waiting for him when he left the vineyard. I offered him some bread and water, and he walked right up to me and smiled! I nearly fainted. On the third day he was home, I saw him walking outside after dinner, and I watched him pace back and forth for several minutes. I didn't move for fear of him seeing me and returning to his quarters. He turned and looked up at me with a red face. So of course I smiled at him to try to put him at ease. Next thing I knew, he faced me with determined look, walked straight up to me, and asked if he could walk with me around the property. I yelled "yes" right in his face—loud and fast. I was afraid he would change his mind. Then, of course, I was mortified, so I threw my hands over my face to try to cover my embarrassment. He grabbed my hands in his, held them tightly, and told me he had wanted to court me since the first time he laid eyes on me," she finished with the threat of tears in her eyes.

"When Fiora says we owe our lives to you, she means it. Neither of us were happy before you advised me to be forthcoming with Fiora. We were married two weeks ago. And as soon as we saw you on the ground, all bloodied and weak, we knew we should be the ones to take care of you. If we were going to die, at least we would die together," Jacopo finished.

"And we would be dying for the person who allowed us to find such happiness," Fiora added.

Caterina began to cry. She had fiercely hoped that the two would be joined together but had not imagined they would give her most of the credit for the union.

"I am deeply happy for you both. And I am grateful that you took it upon yourselves to nurse me back to health. But please do not think that you owe me anything. It is a joy simply to see you together. Your happiness is all the thanks I require," she said, gripping each of their hands firmly in her own.

"That is what you think, Caterina. But from now on, no matter what you need, you can come to us for help. If it's in our power, we'll do anything we can. I swear to you," Jacopo said fervently, as Fiora nodded vigorously in agreement.

"Thank you," Caterina whispered. They allowed her a few moments to recover before asking her questions about her unexpected return.

Caterina explained in detail what had happened at her aunt and uncle's house in Paris. She told them how she awoke to strange voices and how everyone else had died but her. A constant stream of tears flowed from her eyes as she relayed the story. She was still traumatized by the ordeal. But she omitted her attack and subsequent murder—in her mind, there was no way to escape the fact that she had killed a man. Her wish was that no one else would ever know her darkest secret.

"But why were you covered in blood?" Jacopo asked, protectiveness thick in his tone.

"I cannot explain," was all she would say.

Fiora appraised her with somber eyes. "Caterina. When Jacopo brought you up here and laid you on the bed, the entire household waited outside the closed door for me to remove your clothing and tell them if you were injured. You were *covered* in blood! And you had a knife in a leather contraption that I had to cut off of you in order to even check your body for injury. Please. Your family is desperate to know who the blood belongs to. Was it your cousins'? Or your aunt's or uncle's?" Fiora pleaded.

"It was not my family's blood. But I cannot tell you whose blood it was. You must not ask again." Caterina would not budge, and Jacopo and Fiora exchanged a worried glance before nodding their understanding.

The three stayed in the room for one more week before their quarantine was lifted. Caterina's parents sent for a doctor to sign off on their health before they were let out of the room. The doctor announced that all three were healthy and free of any sickness. Caterina thanked her servants again before they left, but she still feared that the plague lay dormant inside her body.

TWELVE

OUTSIDE THE ROOM, her mother, father, and brothers were waiting expectantly for the doctor's prognosis. As soon as the door opened and Jacopo and Fiora emerged with the doctor, the family rushed inside to see their beloved Caterina.

"My darling daughter!" her mother squealed as she rushed to embrace Caterina.

Caterina returned her mother's hug, though her thoughts were more centered on fear than any other emotion. *What if the illness comes back? What if I infect everyone in a few days? Or a week? I should not have returned. If they die, I will never forgive myself,* she thought as she wept into her mother's shoulder.

"Tell us how you feel and how you came here. What happened?" her father asked as he kissed the top of her head. Each of her brothers hugged her fiercely and kissed her cheeks. The worry on all their faces was as clear as the afternoon sun on a cloudless day.

"I'm home," she said as she sagged with relief and allowed her brothers to keep her upright. "I am alive, and I am home. Please do not make me retell the story. Jacopo and Fiora know what happened. I beg of you. I cannot relive it again."

"Of course my love," her mother whispered. "Bring her down to the sitting room," she said to Filippo before turning her attention back to Caterina. "We can tell you everything that has happened while you were away. There is much to tell!"

Caterina could see the pain of loss written on her mother's face. She was mourning her beloved brother's death even as she put on a smile for Caterina's sake. Caterina knew she would eventually have to talk about her time in Paris—if only to tell her mother how accomplished and favored Uncle Giovanni was as a painter. She sighed as she sat down with her family and pushed her thoughts to the back of her mind.

The rest of the day was spent in light conversation. Caterina's mother told her how Filippo had begun courting Mella Visconti. Caterina raised her eyebrows at her eldest brother in surprise.

"I received Giuseppe's permission before even approaching Mella," Filippo said quickly. Filippo and Giuseppe had been the closest of friends for as long as Caterina could remember, but Caterina could not remember a hint of attraction between her brother and her friend. He must have read her thoughts, because he quickly added, "I only realized her beauty the night of your party. She has grown to be quite an attractive lady." Caterina couldn't help but smirk at her brother's enamored expression.

"Then I am happy for you," she said quietly. The whole family looked at her when she spoke. She realized it was the first thing she had said since the conversation began. Her thoughts were numerous, but this was the first time there was any need for her input. It was obvious her brother was nervous to divulge his courtship with one of her friends, and her encouragement quickly relieved his distress. She heard Giovanni clear his throat nervously before speaking.

"There is something I need to tell you as well," Giovanni said as he looked at her with concerned eyes. Caterina could not imagine the reason for the perplexing look, but she nodded reassuringly for him to continue.

"I … I have also begun courting someone," he blurted out too loudly for the quiet room. Again, she nodded for him to go on.

"I will not pursue her further if you do not approve. But I must tell you I am very much in love."

"With whom?" Caterina asked, baffled as to why she would have the power to put a stop to his adoration of any woman.

"Vittoria," he said guiltily.

Caterina lowered her eyes and tried very hard to remember if she had seen any attachment between her brother and best friend before her departure to Paris. A small glance here. A smile there. But nothing that had given Caterina cause to suspect an attachment. She silently considered the revelation. Vittoria was a level-headed girl with a naturally sweet disposition. She had been Caterina's closest friend since they were four years old. They were like sisters —closer than Vittoria was to any of her real sisters. She was the kind of woman who could calm even the most hot-headed of men—and Giovanni certainly fit that description. The more she thought about Giovanni and Vittoria together, the happier she became. Vittoria would actually be her sister now! And Giovanni deserved a wife as kind and beautiful as her closest friend. A wide smile spread across Caterina's face as the joy of the happy union took root in her mind. She looked at Giovanni and let out a laugh of delight. Her family breathed a collective sigh of relief as Giovanni jumped up to hug Caterina in thanks for her approval. She now understood why he had seemed uncomfortable all afternoon.

"This is the best news you could have given me! I will finally have a sister whom I already love like a sister." She turned to Ludo. "Do you have any marriage plans I should know about?" she said with narrowed, accusing eyes. The whole family laughed as he threw his hands in the air and fervently denied any romantic attachments.

Caterina was grateful for the relaxed day. She was doing her best to keep her mind off of the plague that was biding its time inside her body. If she dwelt on it for any length, the happiness of being home hastily slipped away, and a dark, terrifying panic replaced her bright, sunny joy.

Dinner in the old, familiar setting was perfect. Her mother requested Caterina's favorite meal—roasted beef with vegetables and risotto. There were bowls of the family grapes, fresh bread, and nuts on the table as well. When Giovanni and Filippo walked in, there were two familiar faces trailing behind them.

"Mella! Vittoria!" Caterina squealed as she recognized them. She ran to embrace her friends—and soon-to-be sisters.

"Are you upset we're here for your first family dinner home? The boys insisted we come, but if you want us to leave so you can be with your family we understand," Vittoria said in one breath.

Caterina chortled at her friend's cautious behavior.

"But you, Vittoria, have always been my family. And from what I have been told, you are both already a part of the family—aside from an official ceremony," she said, still giggling.

Her friends blushed, and Caterina wondered if she had spoken too hastily. She quickly eyed her brothers and saw they wore approving smiles at her remarks. She hugged Vittoria once more, and everyone sat down for the meal.

It was easy for her to forget her troubles in the company of the people she loved the most in the world. As she ate, her family asked her carefully worded questions about her stay in Paris. They stuck to topics like weather, fashion, parties, food, and manners. Caterina was impressed with their ability to avoid the questions she knew they were longing to ask. She was grateful for their discretion, and for the first time in almost two months, she felt completely at ease. She thanked Vittoria and Mella for coming, and gave them each another embrace before her brothers escorted them back to their homes.

Caterina's mother took her hand and pulled her to the gathering room as soon as the door was shut. Caterina braced herself for the coming conversation. She had known her mother would have questions about Uncle Giovanni. They were close their entire lives, and Caterina owed it to her mother to give a full explanation of how Uncle Giovanni had died.

"I do not wish to pain you, Caterina," her mother began softly as she held tightly to Caterina's hand. Caterina knew what her mother needed to hear. She took a deep breath and began.

"I was enjoying my time in Paris very much. I spent my mornings with Simona and Paula and my afternoons painting with Uncle. He taught me so much. And he was quite renowned around Paris for his work. His frescoes, mother ... they were breathtaking! Everything was wonderful until ... let us just agree that Paula lacked the propriety of her older sister. She acted with very little thought of how others would see her. And her indiscretions grew more and more frequent over the duration of my visit. There came a point at which her behavior was so egregious that Simona and I had no choice but to tell Aunt and Uncle what had transpired. The house was in complete disarray for weeks! Uncle spoke to no one. Paula stayed in her room and pouted while servants delivered meals to her. My aunt stayed in her bed, mourning as if someone had died. Only Simona and I acted normally—but I suppose we were the least surprised of everyone in the home.

"After some time, we thought everything was back to normal. But that was when plague entered the city. Uncle boarded up the windows and doors—the servants gathered enough food and water for us to live comfortably for weeks. Even after the food was gone and the servants had to go out again, everything was fine. We were protected." At that point, Caterina looked up at her mother's face as she waited expectantly for the next part of the story. Her mother's sniffling was becoming more and more frequent. Her heart would break after hearing the story, but Caterina knew she needed to hear it. Caterina felt a little guilty for blaming the entire incident on Paula, but when everything was said and done, there was no one else to blame.

"Paula climbed down from her window to see her lover. She sneaked out from the home, and when she returned, I caught her. The house was in upheaval. And I'm sure you can imagine my uncle's reaction.

"But it was too late. She was infected and died only a few days later. My aunt and uncle became ill soon after, and Simona and I caught the sickness in our attempt to care for them. I wrote you a letter, lay down for what I believed was the last time, and fell asleep. When I woke up, I was perfectly healthy. And I was terrified that I might still carry the plague. I gathered anything valuable I could find, changed into clothes that were untouched by sickness, and left the city. I purchased a horse and rode home as quickly as I could." She looked up at her mother's heartbroken expression and tried not to appear miserable at having just retold the second-most horrible event in her life. She could never reveal the first.

Her mother engulfed her in a tight hug. Caterina's eyes flitted around the room as she noticed her father and brothers were listening to the retelling of her misadventure. The four men's faces were plastered with anger.

"Paula died," she said quietly. "There is no one else to blame."

She watched as her words wound their way into their minds. There was no one for them to exact vengeance upon. The responsible party was gone forever.

"I wish you had never gone," her mother said, still crying into Caterina's shoulder.

"As do I," Caterina agreed solemnly.

THIRTEEN

WHEN CATERINA finally retired to her room for the night, her brothers slid in quietly behind her and shut the door.

"We know you used the knife, Caterina," Filippo whispered.

"Tell us why you used it, and we will finish what you started," Ludo said as if he were making an oath.

Caterina had no desire whatsoever to divulge her secret to them. She sat down on the bed and placed her hands over her face. If only she could scream without drawing the entire household to her room. She longed for a good, loud scream.

"I cannot tell you," she said, exasperated by their probing.

Her brothers remained so quiet and still that she had to look up to make sure they were still in the room. All three looked furious—not at her, of course, but at the situation.

"We didn't think you would need to use it," Giovanni said in a dejected voice.

Caterina did not think before the next words slipped from her mouth.

"But it saved my life. If I had not used it, I would be dead in a barn right now," she said, hoping to convey gratitude for the gift.

Giovanni began breathing harder (his face turning an interesting shade of red) while Filippo tried to calm him down. Caterina worried that her words were spoken too hastily. Ludo ignored his brothers, knelt before her, and took her hands.

"Then it truly was the best gift we could have given you. I could not bear a life devoid of my baby sister. I will thank God every day for delivering you back to us alive," he said ardently.

"Dear sister," Filippo began, "will you not tell us what happened? If there is *someone* upon whom we can exact our family's revenge, please tell us. I cannot sleep without the satisfaction of knowing the vagrant is truly gone."

Caterina wondered if there was any way she could word her response without giving up the fact that she had murdered a man. She closed her eyes for a few moments before responding.

"He is not a concern any longer," she said, keeping her eyes carefully on the floor.

Her words brought a sob from Giovanni's chest. All three brothers rushed to her, brought her up to her feet, and held her in a tight embrace between them.

They know what I have done, she thought as tears rolled down her cheeks. *They know, and they love me just the same.*

She was grateful for her brothers. They protected her from the wrong friends while she was growing up. They protected her from being taken advantage of by young men when she was a young lady. And they protected her from being killed by a drunken ruffian when she was an adult. Even now, they wanted to protect her from the pain of what she had experienced—and cried with her over the horrific incident.

As she fell asleep that night, she silently thanked the Lord for providing her with such devoted brothers. She asked that each would be blessed with a long life full of love and happiness. And she prayed that someday, somehow, God would forgive her for taking another's life.

FOURTEEN

CATERINA BEGAN each day by visiting the family chapel to beg God's forgiveness. After breakfast, she and her mother rode their horses, and in the afternoons they painted. She fell back into a comfortable routine with her family. Yet, the fear of what lay dormant within her body sullied her every thought with a dark fog—the kind of fog that kept her from fully relaxing into her old life. A fog that stained each happiness with dark spots of distress.

Caterina knew there was nothing she could do for her family if the sickness somehow broke free from her body, but she was not careless enough to think she could spend time in town. After several weeks, she realized her family had not asked her to make the trip into town for any parties or even for a casual stroll. Though gratefulness was the first emotion she felt, the more she thought about the situation, the more concerned she became. No one in her family had gone to any parties. No one had gone into town at all. What was happening? Before she left, not a week had gone by during which her family had not attended a gathering of some kind. What had changed? She needed to find out.

After dinner that night, she went to her father's library to find a new book to read, but she stopped outside the doorway when she heard her parents' voices inside.

"Everyone in town has heard what happened to her. They're afraid to be in our company. And despite our servants and future daughters-in-law remaining healthy, they refuse to invite us to any events. I don't think anything will convince them that we are well and that Caterina is unafflicted," her father said in an obvious state of distress.

Caterina was happy that the people of Milan were taking precautions. She couldn't deny the feeling that they were right to avoid her family. As a sense of relief washed over her, a simultaneous feeling of regret for her family's situation came to the front of her mind. *I should never have returned. My family will be forced to live as outcasts for the rest of their lives.* She knew how much her family loved to attend parties—almost as much as she did.

"Perhaps we should move to our estate in Florence. Filippo and Giovanni can stay here and take care of the vineyards. They can live here with Mella and Vittoria once they are married. Surely that would be agreeable. I worry that Caterina will not be able to adapt back to a normal life if she is not allowed to socialize regularly. She has changed. She is more … solemn. Her joy has been replaced by something sinister. It almost seems like she does not trust herself. I don't know what else to do," her mother sighed.

"I think that's a wonderful plan, my dear. We will talk to the boys in the morning to see if they are amenable to it. And perhaps Ludovico will want to come with us. He has no attachments here as far as I can tell, and I am certain he will be searching for a lady of his own now that his brothers …"

Caterina walked quietly away while her father spoke. She had not adjusted quite as well as she hoped. Her mother and father saw right through her smiles. She returned to her room, dejected. A new city. Perhaps that would help her mental state. But Caterina knew better. She knew what she truly was: a thief lying in wait for an unsuspecting victim. She shuddered once before forcing her worries to the back of her mind. Sleep would not come easily this night.

Fifteen

Two weeks later, everything was arranged. Caterina, Ludovico, and her mother and father were showered in hugs and kisses from Giovanni, Filippo, Mella and Vittoria. Vittoria and Caterina mourned together as they braced for yet another separation. And just as the group was preparing to set off on their week-long journey to Florence, Filippo placed a familiar-looking package in Caterina's hands.

"For good measure," he whispered. "It saved your life last time, so we had a new holster made for you. Just try not to need it this time."

Caterina could not help but smirk as she thanked her brother and kissed his cheek.

The trip was easy compared to Caterina's previous experiences. Nothing eventful came to pass. The family slept in the same types of inns as those she had grown accustomed to on her way to Paris. The trip was over so quickly, she was genuinely surprised when they arrived on the outskirts of Florence.

It had been nearly a year since she last saw her Florentine home, and the moment the city came into view, her spirits soared. The brilliant sun was setting over the rolling green hills and familiar orange rooftops. The Duomo towered over the city in all its glory, giving peace to those who viewed its beautiful façade. As her horse's hooves clacked on the city's cobblestone streets, she closed her eyes and breathed in the stillness of the moment.

This is precisely what I need, she thought gleefully. *A change of scenery and a life where no one knows or suspects what lies within my body. Surely I will be able to relax here.* She knew her thoughts were more wishful than truthful, but perhaps, here, she could wake each morning without the menacing thought of the plague within.

She glanced at her mother with a real smile affixed to her face. Her mother seemed to heave a sigh of relief when she observed Caterina's expression. The woman looked somehow lighter—less burdened.

Yes, Caterina thought. *This is what my entire family needs.*

Leo sat, staring at the blank canvas before him. Since he began his apprenticeship under Verrocchio, he lacked the inspiration he had always felt as a peasant. His life was more luxurious now than it was in his first thirteen years of life. Without the comforts of toys as a child, he had developed an insatiable imagination that, he thought, would rival the most ingenious of persons. The works of art he produced from that imagination secured his present apprenticeship under Verrocchio.

But the posed subjects he painted each day in the workshop were uninspiring. Subsequently, he felt his recent work was lackluster, at best.

"You need to learn the technicalities of painting, Leonardo. You are not here to be inspired into creating masterpieces. You are here to train your hand, your mind, and your eyes to see beyond the subject. You must learn to capture the light, the shadows, the emotions of every scene. Only then will you be excellent," Verrocchio told him over and over again.

But as he stared at the perfectly proportioned woman who sat before him against a backdrop of black, Leo wished he could paint something mythological or holy. Surely an angel or a beast could capture his excitement in the way that his imagination had held his mind captive when he lived as a peasant.

"You must begin to paint," Verrocchio said, annoyed that Leo still had not picked up a brush. "The only way your talent will grow is if you paint every day and hone your skills. If you do not work, no one will ever know the name 'Leonardo da Vinci'."

Leo nodded as he quickly grabbed a brush and started painting the outline of the woman's nose. Though he was younger than his fellow apprentices, he was determined to work as tirelessly as needed to accomplish his goals. *They will soon enough*, he snarled back in his mind.

SIXTEEN

Milan, April 1467

THOMAS PACED back and forth in the small room he had purchased at the inn outside Milan. He hated contracts like this.

"Surely this isn't necessary," he said with distress thick in his voice.

"I don't understand you," Paulus began. "You are restless and tiresome when you have nothing to do, but as soon as you receive a contract, you fret and pace the floors like you're doing something wrong. You make no sense to me."

Thomas grunted as he sat down roughly on the hard bed. He knew his older brother was right. This was the first contract he had received in over six months, but assassinating a woman was never on Thomas's list of "favorite things to do". In fact, he dreaded it. Whenever he was given a contract on a woman's life, he spent hours reminiscing about his mother and wife. He couldn't understand why anyone would want to rid the world of a precious female.

Thomas's mother had been a beautiful and mysterious lady. His father never told Thomas or his brothers where or how they met, and his mother rarely spoke more than a few words of wisdom or comfort. She died when Thomas was only fifteen years of age—while giving birth to Samuel. Thomas did not think of his mother often, but when he did, he could still remember her perfectly. Her olive skin was smooth, and she always wore her long, dark brown hair tied back in a leather strip. Her deep brown eyes were piercing, and her lips usually turned up at the edges in a slight grin. Her accent was indistinguishable—mainly Roman but with some other accent Thomas could not determine as a child (and he could no longer remember it with enough clarity to place its origins). He wished she was still alive so he could ask about her life before she met his father, but he knew better than to broach that subject with Priest. Even the slightest hint of his mother in a passing conversation sent Priest into a rage that might last for days. Thomas had come to grips centuries ago with the fact that he would never know his mother's story.

When Thomas met his wife, Aemilia, in the 8th century, she was breathtakingly beautiful. She was the daughter of a Roman noble, and after seeing her for the first time, he knew he would do everything in his power to acquaint himself with her.

His uncle, whom he only knew by the name "Saint", had sent him on a trip to pick up an important correspondence from a contact in Lavinium. He stopped in Rome to give rest to his horse (as he often did on any journey longer than a few hours). There, he saw a woman with long, black hair cascading down from the crown of her head in tight curls. Her dress was a lovely shade of pink that matched her perfect lips. Her skin was fair—he wanted so badly to walk to her and run his fingertips along her arm so he could know whether it was as soft as it looked. A few hours later (and a few coins poorer) he knew who she was, where she lived, and that she was not entangled with any suitors. As soon as he delivered Saint's correspondence in Lavinium, he returned to Rome to find Aemilia and take her as his wife.

He smiled as he remembered the first time she saw him. Her eyes openly appraised his size and build, but she tried to hide her admiration and play the role of a reserved woman. Unfortunately for her, Thomas had already seen the look in her eyes. In a matter of days the two were inseparable. Of course, she was terrified when he told her he was immortal (though after a few weeks of his pleading and doting, she finally came around). She remained by his side for the next forty years, but a terrible sickness overcame her and ended her life when she was fifty-seven years of age. She left Thomas childless, but he harbored no regret over their long and loving marriage.

He sighed heavily as he looked down at the contract in his hands. Dorotea Gonzaga was the wife of Galeazzo Maria Sforza, the horrid Duke of Milan whom everyone loved to hate. No one was surprised by the contract—Sforza's enemies seemed to grow by the hour. But Thomas would have been much happier to simply murder the duke himself rather than his poor wife.

"I think a poison should suffice," Paulus chimed in to break the silence.

"Poisons are detestable when it comes to women—they take far too long to take effect, and the suffering is unimaginable. Only a swift death will do. Perhaps I'll break her neck while she sleeps. I hate to see blood on a woman's body," Thomas said thoughtfully.

"Father doesn't care *how* you do it … just that you *do*. He's worried your spine has gone soft, and I must admit I've wondered the same," Paulus said in a taunting tone.

"You know that will not happen," Thomas barked back as he rolled his eyes. He was as happy to fulfill a contract as anyone in the Family. But where women were concerned, he could not imagine a time when he would feel easy about taking one of their lives. "Tell father it will be finished within the week. I need a few days to decide how it will be done."

"Excellent. Father is on his way home from Venice. He said the trip put him in much better spirits. You'll find us back at Castello San Romolo when you've finished with the scoundrel's wife," Paulus said as he left the room and shut the door behind him.

Thomas took a deep breath as he looked down at the contract again. *I'm sorry, Dorotea,* he thought as he closed his eyes and prayed that her death would be painless.

Seventeen

THE ARRANGEMENTS were made for Thomas's entry into Castello Sforzesco. He waited until there was news of a party at the castle, then he convinced a local nobleman there were rumors of thieves awaiting the unsuspecting party-goers outside the castle walls. The noble immediately became uneasy and begged Thomas to accompany him as a bodyguard. He told the man his name was "Giuseppe" and arranged the specifics for the evening. Thomas was astounded by the trusting nature of nobility. There was such corruption throughout Italy (and the rest of the world) that one would think the rich would be suspicious of everyone around them. But it was not so.

Thomas dressed appropriately for the role—nicely enough that no one would suspect he did not belong, but plainly enough not to be noticed by the people within the castle walls.

"Enjoy your evening, sir," Thomas said with a bow to the man he had accompanied to the party. Thomas had trouble remembering the names of the inconsequential people he used as pawns in his assassination schemes. The less he remembered of the details surrounding the kills, the less residual guilt he carried with him after he fulfilled each contract.

"Thank you for your services, Giuseppe. I'll meet you here when the party is over," the man said with a smile. But Thomas would be nowhere in sight at the party's end.

He made his way through a servant's entrance into the candlelit halls of the castle. He had no idea where Dorotea's room was, and would undoubtedly have to bribe numerous servants for the information.

After an hour of negotiating prices with a particularly clever cook, Thomas was taken to Dorotea's room to hide. He hoped the steep price he paid would keep the woman from revealing his location to the castle guard.

He sat nervously in the corner of Dorotea's room, hidden behind a large armchair. After the first half-hour, he decided he had trusted the right servant. He waited for only two hours and was surprised when he heard the room's door open. *These parties usually last much longer,* he mused, confused by her early arrival. A woman rushed in crying and sat on the edge of the bed, sinking her head into her shaking hands. The Duke of Milan rushed in after her and slammed the door shut behind him. Thomas watched silently as the scene unfolded before him.

"Are you trying to embarrass me?" Galeazzo screamed as he grabbed Dorotea's hands and roughly pulled her up to her feet. The woman let out a soft cry of pain. He slapped her across the face. "Would you like to experience real pain?" Galeazzo whispered with narrowed eyes and a maniacal grin.

Thomas wanted to kill the duke where he stood and comfort Dorotea, but he forced himself to remain hidden.

"No. Of course not, my dear," the woman said quietly.

"You are not the only woman I find comfort in. And you would do well to remember that I owe you nothing—you should be overjoyed that a duke would stoop to your level. You are only a duchess because of *me*. I will savor the company of whichever woman I please, and if you cannot enjoy my party, then you shall stay here in your room. Alone," he growled into her ear. He walked to the door to leave but stopped short and glanced back at Dorotea. "You must realize two things. One, I hold your pitiful little life in the palm of my hand, and I can end it whenever I wish. And two, you are nothing but a pawn in a game that I am winning." The woman nodded and kept her eyes turned to the floor until her husband left the room and the door shut behind him.

She collapsed to the floor and began sobbing. Thomas's heart broke for the woman. He wanted nothing more than to help her escape the clutches of her tyrannical husband, but his job was to kill her, not save her. Frustration filled his mind.

"Why must I endure this?" she softly cried. "Lord have mercy and take my life. I cannot live with his cruelty any longer. I have had enough."

Thomas felt his body move before he could stop himself. The woman looked at him with wide eyes, but she did not scream.

"I am here to kill you," he said quietly.

The woman's reaction was instant. She stood from the ground, rushed to him, and embraced him in a hug. She continued to cry, but her tears were joined by sobs of laughter as well.

"Thank you, Lord," she whispered as a prayer.

Thomas had never revealed himself to one of his targets before, and he was certain this was the first target who felt excitement for her coming death.

"Will you try to make it painless?" she asked as she pulled away and looked into his eyes.

"Of course," he answered quickly. "I've brought you a sleeping tonic that will send you into a deep slumber. Only then will I end your … misery."

She poured a goblet of wine from the pitcher on her table and handed it to Thomas. He mixed in the powdered tonic and watched as she drank the glass quickly.

"Thank you. You've rescued me from a life of torment," she whispered as she reached up and softly placed her hand on the side of Thomas's face.

She put the goblet down, walked to her bed, and lay down with a smile on her face. Within a matter of minutes she was in a deep sleep. Thomas had mixed the tonic himself to ensure she would not wake, no matter the pain.

He thrust his long knife up through her abdomen toward her heart, twisted it once, and pulled it back out. Her breathing immediately grew uneven, but she did not rouse from her slumber. In a matter of minutes her heart stopped beating. Thomas was not used to experiencing sorrow over his kills, but as he watched the life drain from the young duchess, his eyes filled with tears he could not contain. He wished he knew who had hired him to assassinate the woman, but as with all Family contracts, Priest and Saint did not reveal the story behind the murder—or in this case, the mercy killing.

Thomas knew it was unwise to linger in her room. He bent down and placed a gentle kiss on Dorotea's forehead. "I am happy I could be of assistance," he whispered as he left her room and hurried away from the castle —which would forever be marked by this contract.

EIGHTEEN

THE YEAR WAS one of the busiest Thomas had experienced. Though he was grateful for the influx of work—especially in comparison with the previous year's incessant searching for survivors of the plague—he was saddened by the nature of many of his contracts.

April marked the beginning of the onslaught with Dorotea's contract. Thomas was assigned to four more contracts in conjunction with his brothers or nephews during the months of May and June. At the beginning of July, he and Sergius were given a contract to murder Eleanor of Portugal—the Holy Roman Empress. The contract took months of planning. He and Sergius traveled to Austria, where she was residing, and became close with several of her servants. For two full months they studied the layout of the city and her residence. When it was time for her to die, they used poisoned wine. And though Thomas was upset about the painful death, there was no other logical way to kill her.

Shortly after they completed that contract, he received another to remove a heretical priest from service in Wroclaw, Poland. Felix joined him for the kill, and together they concocted a plan to murder the man without any bloodshed or evidence of foul-play (as were the terms of the contract).

Thomas always felt uneasy about murdering a man of faith, and he abhorred killing women. But it seemed such was his lot for this time in his life.

1468 marked an exciting time in the lives of the entire Family. There was always a buzz in the air when an assassination of a prince or king was offered to them, and Castello San Romolo was practically humming with the news of their most recent contract.

"Alfonso XII, Prince of Asturias. It will not be an easy task, but you will take care of it," Priest said to his sons and grandsons. Everyone gathered in the dining hall to see which of the Family would be the lucky recipients of the contract.

"Saint and I agree that five of you will be a satisfactory number to deal with the prince. Paulus will lead the group, and we would like Gregorius, Elias, Claudius, and Alexander to join him," Priest finished as grumbling broke out around the room.

Something isn't right, Thomas immediately thought. *Priest has chosen his most obedient sons ... not the best suited.* He glanced at Saint to see concern written on his uncle's face. He exchanged a worried look with Sergius.

"Do you know what's going on?" Thomas asked Sergius after the meeting.

"No. But Saint did not look happy. Perhaps he might enlighten us," Sergius replied.

They walked toward Saint's room in the east wing of the Family castle. Only he and Priest had their own rooms. Each of Priest's sons had been given a room of their own when they initially moved into the castle, while most of the rest of Family had stayed in the barracks beneath the winery. One particularly harsh winter in the 1340s brought the entire Family inside the castle, and after a few winter months it was decided that the change should be permanent. The twenty bedrooms inside the home easily housed the entire Family. Thomas and Sergius stopped outside Saint's door and knocked quietly.

"Enter," they heard from inside. When Sergius opened the door, they saw Saint standing over his table, looking at some paperwork.

"Would you like us to come back?" Thomas asked, worried they were interrupting Saint in the middle of something important.

"Not at all. Sit down," Saint said as he motioned toward the chairs opposite where he stood.

Neither knew where to begin or what to ask. They stayed quiet for several moments before Saint broke the silence.

"You want to know why I was distraught during the meeting and why Priest is sending his favorite sons to fulfill this contract."

The brothers were stunned, but both nodded for him to continue.

"The prince is only a boy—fourteen years of age," Saint said as he looked at their stunned faces. "You understand that this is the first commission we've accepted on a child's life. I reluctantly agreed to accept it due to Priest's absolute belief that we should take into account the overwhelming political implications surrounding the contract. But I made sure he knew I would not agree to more like this one. I also made it clear that none of his grandsons or great grandsons would know of the nature of the job. He chose your brothers because they are exceedingly devoted to Priest, and he knows they will not raise questions. If I am right about you, you two would not have gone through with it once you knew the boy's age," Saint said as he sat down and took a drink from the wine-filled goblet beside him.

Thomas could not contain his horror. *A fourteen-year-old boy on the cusp of manhood. Saint has made a grave mistake if he thinks the repercussions of this will not resonate for years to come.* He did not want to disrespect his uncle, but the grief that welled in his chest was almost too much to bear.

"Do you not see what this will do to us?" Sergius said in anguish.

Saint nodded slowly with a look of sadness in his eyes. "I had no choice in the matter. But I fear this will set a precedent that will change our Family forever."

NINETEEN

Florence, April 1470

FOUR YEARS had passed since the Galli family relocated to Florence, and in that time, a great number of changes had come to the family. Giovanni and Vittoria were married shortly after Caterina and her parents moved away, and Vittoria was pregnant with her second child in only two years. Their first was a boy, and Vittoria swore that their second would be a boy as well. A few months after Giovanni's wedding, Filippo and Mella were wed as well. Mella had just delivered her first child—a daughter—and Caterina's mother was beside herself with the joy of having grandchildren. Ludo found a beautiful Florentine woman named Gemma, and the two had been married for just over a year. Even Jacopo and Fiora—her beloved servants—now had a little family of their own. Fiora gave birth to a son three years earlier, and the boy spent most of his time in the company of Vittoria's son of the same age.

Caterina, along with her mother and father, made frequent trips to Milan to see her brothers' families. And though she had no romantic attachments of her own, Caterina was perfectly content with the life she was able to live. All the people she loved most in the world were in the center of her life. She rarely had time to think back to days once filled with trepidation and restlessness. Her past was truly that—a subtle yet distant reminder of another life long gone. And she did her best to keep it from her mind.

"I think I should find a place where I can spend more time studying the works of master painters," Caterina announced to her mother upon returning home to Florence from yet another trip to Milan.

"I think that's a wonderful idea. You have not been able to commit a proper amount of time to your art since the boys began having children. Perhaps you should see if there is any way to observe a workshop of one of the masters.

Wouldn't that be wonderful?" her mother exclaimed.

Nearly every time Caterina had been sad over *anything* in the past four years, she could see the weight of distress crush her mother's shoulders. And any time Caterina experienced a moment of joy or laughter, her mother's face was lit from within as if the very sun was hidden inside her, just waiting for a moment of happiness to release it from its human cage.

"I am sure the masters would not consider allowing a woman to observe or learn, mother," Caterina snickered. "But maybe I could work as a model for them. There is a great deal for me to learn simply by watching and listening," she said thoughtfully. She would need to travel into the city square more often in order to make connections with the local painters.

"I will see if any of our friends have commissioned paintings from the local artists. Maybe someone will make the introduction for you with little work on your part," her mother offered.

"Thank you, Mother. That is a lovely idea."

The next afternoon, Caterina sent up a quick prayer for guidance and made her way into the center of the city with excitement in each step. She immediately felt hopeful that the connection would be much easier than she had imagined.

Leonardo sat in the center of town with a blank canvas before him. After four years in Verrocchio's workshop, he no longer felt the longing for inspiration that he had felt as a young apprentice. Inspiration was all around him. It was in the way the sun reflected differently off the side of a home than it did off of the roof of the same dwelling. In the way a woman wore her hair. Even in the tiniest expression of sadness or delight on a child's face. It had taken him eighteen years to understand, but inspiration was in his own mind. He could create it out of the most mundane of details—he needed only to open his eyes to find it. And for the first time in his life, he felt as if he was an equal to most, if not all, of his fellow artists. His skill had grown to the same level as his dear teacher, Verrocchio. The man told him as much and invited Leonardo to help him paint several works of art.

Leonardo came up with grand ideas for his life beyond simply painting. His mind was nearing its peak of creativity with a brush. He daily wrote down ideas for creating new things. He wanted to study the body inside and out, to have a greater understanding of how it functioned. He wanted to learn how to build machines. He wanted to *fly*. He heaved a sigh. Today was a day for painting. And he knew Verrocchio would be disappointed if he returned to the workshop the following week without something to show for his absence.

He glanced up from his canvas to find his victim for the day's work. His eyes stopped searching when they found the corner of the bell tower, where he often found his gaze fixed. The intricate patterns of pink, white and green marble were mesmerizing. Depending on the time of day, the light hit that one corner in various ways that made him feel as if the stones were speaking straight to the depths of his soul. The lines and variances in the colors screamed for attention, but the oblivious passers-by never seemed to hear their colorful cries. He realized he was supposed to be looking for his next subject, and began searching the faces that passed his favorite corner of the bell tower.

And there she was. She was not a beauty like the women he painted so often in the studio against a boring backdrop. But she *was* somehow beautiful. Her hair was made up of reddish-brown ringlets all over. It was parted on the top of her head and pulled back into a snood. The curls were expertly pinned into place so that they framed her face in a pleasing way. Her face was full and her eyebrows thin. By her dress, he could tell she was a daughter of nobility, and it seemed as if she was searching for something—or someone—by the way her brows were furrowed. She was adorable. She was perfect. And she was heading straight for him.

"Hello, sir," she said with a curtsy. "I'm wondering if you can help me."

Leonardo was used to being ignored while he painted. The various workshops around the city and large number of painters throughout town made the profession so common that people rarely even glanced in his direction. Painters in Florence were almost as numerous as buildings.

"My lady," he said with a bow of his head, "I am at your service."

The woman smiled and craned her neck to peek at his work. Her face showed disappointment at the absence of paint on the canvas.

"I don't want to be an imposition," she began tentatively, "but I'm wondering if you have any need for a model. I would love to sit for an artist. But if you … if you don't need one … I don't want you to fear offending me by telling me so."

Leonardo was fascinated. It was obvious by her voice and expression that she was shy in nature, yet she approached him without hesitation. He wanted to understand how her mind worked—and in his experience, painting someone would unravel all of his or her secrets. He smiled and stood.

"How lucky for me then. You are just the person I was hoping to paint."

TWENTY

CATERINA REVELED in her sittings with Leo. She did not know who the artist was when first offering herself as a model, but after hearing his name, she was thrilled to serve as a subject for his artistic genius. The city had been buzzing about the young artist's work for some time, and he would have a wealth of knowledge from which she hoped to glean. But after three weeks of sittings, he still had not shown her his work. Initially, she had hoped to be able to see the painting at each stage to pinpoint his various techniques. Caterina did not yet know if she could reveal to him that she, also, was a painter. Most men in the Florentine culture would scoff at her desire to grow as an artist. But Leo somehow seemed different. One could only hope.

At the end of today's sitting, I will ask him for suggestions. Maybe he'll think I'm simply curious and give me advice. But either way, at least I'll know if he thinks a female painter is a ridiculous notion.

"Thank you again, Caterina," Leo said at the end of the day. "Would you like me to walk you home?" he offered.

"Yes, thank you." She was eager to have him critique her artwork, and on a leisurely stroll, she could question him gently without seeming like she was begging.

"Have you lived in Florence your whole life?" he asked as they left the workshop.

"No. My family has always maintained an estate here, but I grew up in Milan. My parents and I only moved here permanently four years ago," she answered.

"And what was the reason for the move?" he asked.

This stopped Caterina in her tracks. She had not been asked about the move before and was not prepared with an answer. Despite living in Florence for four years, she had unwittingly kept her distance from anyone who might ask her questions about her past. Her mouth hung open for a moment as she grasped for an easy response, but her mind would not function. *I survived the plague, and everyone in Milan thought I would infect them,* didn't quite roll off the tongue nicely.

"I'm sorry. You don't have to answer that question," Leo said quickly upon seeing her expression.

"No. No apology needed. I think my parents felt that I needed … a change of scenery," she answered with a smile she hoped would look genuine.

Leo nodded and continued the walk in silence. *Ugh. He knows there was something wrong with my answer. Why haven't I thought this through before?* she scolded herself. Several minutes passed in silence before Caterina decided to broach the subject of painting.

"I was wondering …"

"Yes?" he interrupted. It was clear he was searching for a new topic.

"Would it be improper for me to ask you about your paintings?" she said with as innocent an expression as she could muster.

Leo looked confused.

Why does he look confused? Why is it confusing that a woman would want to learn to paint from a master? Caterina thought in frustration.

"Why on earth would it be improper?" he asked.

Caterina breathed a sigh of relief. *He is confused by the question, not by my interest in painting! Thank the Virgin Mother.*

"You must know that the masters do not instruct women. It vexes me, but I have done my best to find ways to learn outside of workshops," she confessed.

"Really?" Leo asked with genuine curiosity. "Where have you been training?"

"Actually, my uncle was a great painter, and I studied under him for a few months. But he died in Paris during the plague," she said with her eyes closed. Every time she thought about her time in Paris, all she could see were the corpses of her dear relatives wasting away. She smelled the decaying flesh. *You must stop thinking about it!* she commanded herself. She ran a hand over her brow and found beads of sweat had formed during her nauseating flashback. Thankfully, Leo did not notice her struggle.

"Do you paint often?" he asked.

"When I'm not sitting for you, I paint daily," she confessed.

"That's wonderful!" he exclaimed. "Dedication is key to success. Could I see some of your work?"

Caterina agreed, but immediately regretted giving her consent. Her work was ghastly in comparison to his. She worried he would laugh at her and demand that, as an artist, she immediately relinquish all her paint brushes and canvases.

"Please don't laugh," she requested quietly before allowing him to enter her home. He nodded, his face once again covered in a look of confusion.

"You have a lovely home," he said with a smile. "And where is your work?"

Caterina tried to gulp down her fear, but her words stuck in her throat. She simply motioned with her outstretched hands toward all the walls within sight.

"All of them?" Leo asked in disbelief. He knew his voice had risen nearly an octave as he spoke the words, and Caterina's returning smile was evidence that she wanted to laugh at him. She was a serious person—more so than most women he spent time with. If she grinned, it was the equivalent to another person's smile. If she smiled, anyone else would be laughing. And he had not yet heard her laugh, but he imagined the inducement would have to be quite grand.

"Not all. My mother paints with me. She grew up observing my uncle's work, so I've learned through her as well," she admitted. "I'll show you which are mine if you would like."

"Yes, please!" he said enthusiastically. *I had no idea that my muse was this talented. These are better than most of my classmates' work! She definitely lacks certain techniques, but anyone who looked at her work would think she had studied her entire life ... and maybe she has,* he realized as he walked from painting to painting to examine each piece.

"Were you nervous to show these to me?" he asked in disbelief.

"Of course I was. Apart from my uncle, I haven't shown another painter my work. I assumed anyone with real talent would mock my attempts," she said with her eyes directed toward the ground.

"If anyone mocked you, they would be foolish. I know *many* painters who are paid great sums of money for far less impressive pieces. You have quite a talent, Caterina. You have no reason to be ashamed," he assured her.

As soon as he spoke the words, her face lit up like the afternoon sky. Her eyes were brighter, smile wider, and cheeks more flushed than he had seen on her before. If he was interested in female companionship, he might have even found her attractive in that moment.

"I like seeing you this happy," he admitted as he moved on to her next painting.

"Me too," she said in an almost-giggle, seemingly unable to control her joy.

He spent hours perusing her work, impressed by the sheer number of paintings covering the walls.

"This is only part of my work," she admitted. "The rest is at our estate in Milan."

"You surprise me, Caterina Galli. I thought you were simply an interesting face with a sweet temperament. But under your calm façade is the passion and skill of a crazed artist. I think I'll make you a permanent fixture in my circle," he said with a smirk. "Each time you begin a new work, bring it to me so I can see your technique. If I can help in any way, I will."

Caterina could not control herself. She smiled and giggled and threw her arms around Leo's shoulders. He looked stunned at first, but soon returned her hug and joined in, chuckling.

"Thank you," she gasped between laughs. She felt her eyes fill with the threat of tears, and she calmed herself back to her normal state before speaking again. "Thank you, Leonardo. I am grateful for your praise and your offer," she said evenly (which was her normal disposition).

"You are most welcome," he replied, mimicking her own calm, all the while hiding a smile.

She knew the conversation had transformed their relationship into a true friendship. She hoped she could someday return his kindness.

TWENTY-ONE

Rome, July 1471

"PLEASE DON'T MAKE me do this," Samuel pleaded as he dressed in the page boy's uniform Thomas had stolen for him. His eight-hundred-year-old youngest brother was dressed like a child, and Thomas was tickled by Samuel's appearance.

"As the shortest and youngest-looking member of the Family, it falls on your shoulders alone to complete this contract," Thomas said, smothering intermittent chuckles. Sergius stood beside him with his arms folded, clearly as entertained as Thomas, yet (as usual) more capable of containing his amusement. Thomas did his best to calm down by placing a hand over his mouth and lowering his gaze to the floor of the villa the Family kept for any extended stays in Rome.

Though the Family had rules in place which kept each member from completing a contract in the same area for fifty years, Rome was one of the few cities that was corrupt enough to warrant the Family owning a local property. Thomas couldn't remember a year in Family history that a contract had not been carried out in the city which Thomas and his brothers referred to as "the den of corruption." However, Priest and Saint did their best to keep the Family on a strict rotation in order to limit each assassin's exposure there.

"Do you want to go over the plan again?" Sergius asked as Samuel turned around, looking ridiculous. A single burst of laughter broke through Thomas's mouth before he cleared his throat and tried to play the chuckle off as a cough.

"I am dressed like a fourteen-year-old page boy. If you weren't choking on your laughter, something would be wrong," Samuel said as a smile crept across his mouth. Thomas and Samuel burst into synchronized guffaws while Sergius looked on, smiling.

Thomas appreciated Samuel's ability to poke fun at himself. Samuel had always been the clumsiest of the brothers. He constantly got into trouble while visiting brothels—he would drink far too much wine and tell the details of his latest contract to any courtesan who would listen. The Family rules dictated that everyone change their surname a few times a year to avoid accidental recognition, but Priest had paid off so many drunks and whores for their silence that Samuel made a habit of changing his name with each new contract he received.

Pope Paul II was Samuel's target. All the men in the Family had hoped for the opportunity to kill the loathsome fool. The pope maintained an unrelenting vendetta against the Jewish population, was constantly going back on the promises he made to his cardinals to first gain the papacy, and possessed an insatiable appetite for the company of young men. In a word, the man was a swine.

Priest threatened Samuel with his life when he received the contract—it was too important to the Family and the Church to be mishandled. One tiny misstep and Samuel might never receive another contract.

"Do you have your blade? And your secondary dagger?" Thomas asked, growing nervous for Samuel's mission.

"Yes, of course. I'm going to enter his chambers under the guise that I'm serving as his company for the evening. I swear to you, if I'm sodomized I will never forgive father," he said with a nervous chuckle. "I am not to look at him directly—just play the part of a coy child. And when he comes over to me, I'll take him down and break his neck. I will then carry him to his bed—which I'm still not certain how I'll manage alone—and make it seem as if he died in his sleep. Did I miss anything?" Samuel asked, exhibiting far more nervousness than his brothers.

"Samuel, you are far stronger than you give yourself credit for. And craftier. *I* believe you're ready," Sergius insisted.

Samuel crept through the hallways of the Apostolic Palace, hiding at even the slightest sound. He kept his head down so no one would be able to get a look at his face. He paid a drunken guard to disclose the security measures in place around the palace. Fortunately, they were minimal, and Samuel believed he could make it through most of the palace unnoticed.

Though his father believed he was an imbecile, Samuel had not once failed to carry out a contract, nor had he been discovered while in the act of killing one of his targets. He simply had a loose tongue when it came to alcohol and women ... and a tendency toward making tiny mistakes while planning for contracts. But his mistakes had not caused any permanent trouble for the Family—they simply cost a bit of money to cover up.

The window he climbed through was more difficult to scale to from the outside than he originally thought, and his outfit was ripped down the side from a particularly stubborn shrub. *Why does this pope have to be so reclusive?* he wondered as he rounded a corner. In front of the pope's quarters stood four Vatican guards. *You cannot be serious. Is there another way in? If I'm discovered, I'll be branded 'the Family fool',* he worried. A page boy walked up behind him right then.

"Can I join you?" Samuel asked in the highest pitched voice he could manage. The boy looked bewildered but nodded his agreement. Samuel grabbed several coins from his pocket and handed them to the boy. "When we arrive at the pope's door, you will turn back and go straight home." The boy looked from the coins in his hand to the odd page man-boy that stood in front of him before hesitantly agreeing.

Samuel heaved a sigh of relief, put his head down, and walked silently beside the boy. The guards barely noticed the two page boys walking by, and when they reached the door, the real page turned down another hallway and left without a second glance. Samuel opened the door and slid in as quietly as possible, locking the door behind him.

"Is that you, Lucha? I was beginning to worry …" the pope trailed off as he saw the larger frame of Samuel standing before him. Samuel kept his head straight down, terrified to meet the gaze of the pope he was about to kill.

"Lucha was ill. I've come to take his place," Samuel said, once again using the highest voice he could manage.

"Well you're a bit older than I prefer, but I suppose you'll do. Let me take a look at you," the man said as he began to circle Samuel.

Samuel felt the bile rise in his throat as the man walked around him, touching his arms and legs. *This is terrible. How could a young boy stand this behavior?* he wondered.

"You're quite muscular. How old are you?" the pope asked, beginning to sound wary of the new page boy.

"Fourteen," Samuel said unconvincingly.

The pope took a step back and started to yell for the guards to help him. Samuel swore, removed his knife from its hidden sheath, and clapped a hand over the swine's mouth. The guards pounded on the locked door, yelling to be let in.

"If you cry for help again, I'll slit your throat," Samuel whispered. "Tell the guards everything is fine, and you were startled by your own shadow."

"I'm sorry, men. I was startled by my own shadow," he chuckled as he cracked the door and peeked out. Samuel pushed the tip of his blade into the man's back to threaten him. "You can go," he assured them. The guards backed away, and the door closed once more.

"Walk to your bed," Samuel commanded.

"Oh? Are we going to have some fun? Is this why you've broken into my bed chambers?" the pope said sarcastically as he made his way toward his bed.

Samuel reached both his hands around the pope's face and whipped his head to the right, successfully snapping his neck. The pope collapsed, paralyzed but alive, and began moaning. Rather than landing face down on the bed, as Samuel had intended, he landed awkwardly on his knees beside the bed with his back bent in a horrible way and his head smashed against the small table that housed the pope's chamber pot. Samuel covered the pope's mouth with his hand, but he knew from experience the moaning could last for some time. He ripped a piece of his garment and stuffed it in the man's open mouth. *Please stop. Lord, please make him ...* Samuel stopped praying mid-sentence. He just murdered a pope. He thought it likely God didn't think very highly of him at the moment.

Samuel stepped back and surveyed the scene before him. *Well this wasn't my plan,* he thought with some distress. A knock at the door made him jump.

"Your Holiness?" a man called through the door. "Your Holiness!" he yelled, banging on the door.

Samuel panicked. *What do I do? What do I do?* He ripped the linen cloth out of the pope's mouth, and the moaning began again. The silence outside the door was terrifying.

"I am sorry, Your Holiness. So ... so sorry," Samuel heard as the man retreated from the door.

Samuel pushed the cloth back into the pope's mouth and sat down on the edge of the bed, needing a moment to recover from what could have been a life-ending incident. His heart was pounding, his hands shaking, and he could barely catch his breath.

The pope's breathing became labored, and Samuel heaved a sigh of relief, knowing the end was in sight. After a few minutes more, the pope was dead. Samuel removed the fabric from the limp mouth, twisted his neck back into a normal-looking position and decided to leave him where he lay. If Samuel tried to move him, the chances of the death looking natural were slim to none.

He cracked open the door to find an empty hallway. His outfit, now torn on the side from the shrub and at the bottom from the piece he removed to smother the pope's groans, now looked entirely unconvincing. He needed to get outside the walls of the Vatican without being noticed.

He crept through the corridors, ducking into doorways or behind curtains whenever he heard someone approaching. He was relieved when he made it back to his entry and exit window unseen, but he managed to rip the back of his outfit as he jumped down to the ground. He smothered the urge to roar in frustration.

Samuel walked quickly toward the gates and was nearly there when someone behind him called out to him to stop.

"Page! Hello there! Page boy!" the voice called. He stopped in his tracks, unwilling to turn around.

"Oh, there you are, brother," Thomas called from directly in front of him. Samuel heaved a sigh of relief. "You're looking tattered. We need to get you home or father will be worried sick," Thomas said as he threw his arm over Samuel's shoulders and walked him straight out the Vatican gates and back to their residence.

"What the hell happened to you?" Thomas asked worriedly, once they were safely inside the Family villa.

"He's dead, and I wasn't caught. They'll think he had some sort of seizure," Samuel said as he plopped down in a chair and rubbed the sides of his head. "It was horrible. And I am going to get astoundingly drunk tonight."

"Do you think he'll be all right?" Thomas asked Sergius as they stood over their snoring brother.

"I've seen him worse. He'll be fine," Sergius said without amusement.

The two of them bought him a variety of alcohol and made him stay inside their home to drink it. They feared what he might have announced about the contract if he had been so heavily intoxicated in public. After three days, the entire city was buzzing with speculation about the pope's death. Most people said he died of a heart attack, but a few whispers claimed he died while sodomizing a page boy. The rumors were close enough to the truth that Samuel would catch an earful from their father. But he *had* remained uncaught, and surely that must count for something.

"Father is going to be upset," Thomas said softly.

"Worse things have happened. It will be forgotten in a few years," Sergius assured him.

Thomas pulled a blanket over his sleeping brother's shoulders and hoped, rather than believed, that Sergius might be right.

TWENTY-TWO

Milan, September 1471

MONTHS PASSED, and Caterina's skills grew immensely. The direction Leonardo provided for her paintings was far beyond anything she had previously learned. Every brush stroke held purpose now. A simple line to which she would have paid little attention before, now created an entire landscape of emotion. The world was transformed. Every person, every blade of grass, every grape that hung from its vine—they were works of art which needed only to be captured by her brush. And the more she learned, the more she realized that it wasn't the world that had been transformed. It was she.

Leonardo's friendship reached far beyond her paintings now. He took her to his home and showed her his ideas and inventions. He dreamt most nights of new creations—and he functioned on very little sleep because the moment he awoke, he scribbled down everything he had dreamed. Unfortunately, many of his ideas involved fire or explosions. And it was becoming a weekly occurrence for him to lose most of the work he put into a new invention because of a fire in his work area. Caterina asked him, each time they visited with one another, how much work had been lost since their last visit. His answer was almost always, "Nearly everything." He was smart enough to keep his sketchbooks and journals separate from his inventions—he had learned the hard way not to keep them in his work space.

Leo was constantly asking Caterina to pose a different way in a different location with different lighting. He was never truly satisfied with his paintings of her, though she thought they presented her as much lovelier than she was in real life. And within a month of its completion, every painting he made of Caterina managed to be lost in flames with the rest of his creations. Yet he quickly made arrangements to capture her likeness once more.

Leonardo often attended Galli family dinners—her mother and father adored Leonardo. Caterina could see the pain in her mother's face when Leo spoke about his work—talking of workshops and commissions reopened the ever-present emotional wound of Uncle Giovanni's death. But at the same time, Caterina knew the conversation allowed her mother to feel intimately connected, once again, to the world of art.

Her parents regularly made passing remarks about what a beautiful pair Leonardo and Caterina would make. But Caterina was no fool. Though he had not spoken the words aloud, she was fully aware that his desires lay elsewhere. She viewed him as a brother. He joked with her in the same way as her brothers, often making fun of her or playing tricks on her. She cherished his friendship and hoped he would not soon have to leave Florence for a commission.

TWENTY-THREE

Florence, April 1476

THE GALLI HOUSEHOLD had barely awoken for the day when frantic knocking at the door sent everyone into a panic.

"I need to speak with Caterina. Please," Leonardo begged with a desperate sob.

Caterina threw a robe over her nightgown and rushed down the stairs as soon as the servant told her of Leonardo's presence. When she walked into the sitting room, she found her friend nervously pacing the room, his face dejected. She ran to him, grasping his shaking hands between her own.

"Tell me right now what is the matter. What has happened?" she demanded to know.

Leonardo stopped moving to look Caterina in the eyes. He shook his head slowly from side to side as tears began to form his eyes.

"We were so careful," he whispered. "I don't know what happened." His eyes glazed over as he stared out one of the front windows of the home.

"What do you mean?" Caterina asked, hoping he would continue. "Please. Let's sit down," she said, pulling him to the chairs situated next to the fireplace.

"Me and Saltarelli," he said as soon as his body touched the cushion of the chair.

"Oh." Caterina had known about Leonardo's love affair with Jacopo Saltarelli for years. She had not met Leo's lover, but she could usually tell when the two had been together—his temperament was decidedly more cheerful after one of their interludes. She also knew the lengths to which they went in order to keep their relationship a secret. The Florentine laws against homosexuality, while lenient for the most part, could put a man in prison or, at the very least, end his career if enough evidence was brought to the officials.

"Who would reveal such a thing?" she asked.

"I have no idea. But accusations have been made against three of my friends as well. Which leads me to believe they were made by another artist."

Caterina was furious. She had met most of the painters in the city. She spent quite a bit of time with the students from Verrocchio's workshop, and now she wondered if Leo's vast talents could have spurred a less-talented classmate to go to the officials with the accusations.

"Why don't you stay with us?" Caterina heard her father say from the doorway. She and Leo turned upon hearing the voice—and she realized both her mother and father stood there, wearing concerned looks on their faces. "We have more than enough room, and it would certainly keep the eyes of the officials away. We're a respectable family with a beautiful daughter. What more evidence would they need to stop pursuing the investigation?"

Leonardo collapsed into sobs where he sat, and Caterina ran to her parents to embrace them.

"What a wonderful idea!" Caterina exclaimed as she thanked her father for the generous offer. "Please say you'll live here," she said as she returned to her friend, who was slowly recovering from the impact of the offer. "At least until these accusations pass."

"I would be honored. You are too kind."

TWENTY-FOUR

Castello San Romolo, December 1476

THE FAMILY WAS in high spirits the week they received the contract to end the Duke of Milan's life. Galeazzo Maria Sforza was evil and corrupt, and even Priest (who rarely celebrated any occasion) was excited to see the man's life come to an end.

Felix, Gregorius, Elias, and Demetrius were assigned to the task, but everyone in the Family wanted to play a role in the contract's planning. Thomas was not allowed to physically participate in this contract. Only nine years earlier he had killed the duke's wife—Dorotea—in the very same castle. He was saddened by his inability to be involved for one reason alone—he wanted to see the light fade from the monster's eyes as blood flowed from Galeazzo's wounds.

"Our attention to detail is imperative. We have no room for error," Gregorius said solemnly. Gregorius and Elias were born minutes apart—and had been inseparable since. Neither was assigned a contract without the other. They were quite different in fighting styles and skill sets, which allowed them, as a pair, to be a singularly formidable foe. Gregorius was a master of knives and stealth, while Elias was a master of swords and firearms (though he was rarely able to display his talents with the latter). They were in charge of creating a large diversion for the crowds outside the church. The brothers wanted as few people to witness the duke's death as possible so rumors could be spread of the lie the Florentine populace needed to believe.

"You must wait until moments before the church service is set to begin. And take care that all three officials are present—if any one of them is away, all our planning will be for naught," Saint warned as he looked over the intricate plans once more. Saint was the Family tactician—there was no one Thomas (or anyone in the Family) trusted more with the formation of plans. Saint was somehow able to predict all the minor details that could possibly go awry during an assassination and come up with a contingency plan for each.

"Once we arrive in Florence, we will still need to steal the knives from the 'killers'' homes," Demetrius added nervously. There were three men in the Milanese court who were supposed to take the fall for the Duke's murder. There needed to be irrefutable evidence of their involvement, and Demetrius decided that using the men's personal knives would be the most convincing corroboration. He would be the one to actually stab Galeazzo with the knives—making the knife wounds seem as if they had come from four different people.

Felix was tasked with the job of gathering the three officials from *inside* the church while the duke was being stabbed by Demetrius *outside*. Once they were close enough to the body, he would make sure all three men were covered in blood before the masses spotted them. Demetrius had collected pig's blood in a sheepskin pouch from the animal that was slaughtered for the previous night's dinner. But his uneasiness over the role he would play was painted plainly across his sweaty face.

Sergius and Alexander would also travel to Florence to help spread rumors of what had happened once the deed was done. Everyone knew their roles. They were as prepared as they could be. And after two months of intensive planning, everything was in place for the assassination.

The morning came for the brothers to leave for Milan, but something nagged at the back of Thomas's mind. He didn't want to create any more stress for his brothers, but one detail in particular needed to be addressed.

"Demetrius," Thomas called before his brother mounted his horse. "I hope this will not add undue pressure on your role in this contract, but there is one last thing I must ask of you before you go."

Sergius watched as the crowd began to gather around his brothers. Gregorius and Elias were putting on quite a show for the churchgoers. The way they expertly flung insults at one another made Sergius question whether there might actually have been a dispute between the twins.

He turned around in time to witness Demetrius thrust the first knife into Galeazzo's abdomen. When he turned back to the crowd, he noted joyfully that no one had seen the stabbing occur. *This is working perfectly,* he thought triumphantly. He looked again at the duke in time to see the fourth knife enter his sagging body. Even from far away, Sergius could see the startled expression on the man's face. But in the next moment, it turned to horror. Demetrius had said something to the duke before turning away to leave the scene—and whatever he said had left quite an impact. Galeazzo collapsed just as Felix and three others (presumably the men who were to be framed) emerged from inside the church. Felix pulled out an animal skin and flung its contents over the distraught and confused men. Felix then disappeared around the side of the church.

Soon, screams were heard from people pouring out of the church, and the crowd watching Gregorius and Elias's fist fight ran to see what was going on. Sergius glanced toward his twin brothers, who nodded to him and quickly left the area.

Now everything falls to me and Alexander, he thought as he began making his way toward the church.

"Did you see what those men did?" he asked loudly as he pointed toward the three officials covered in blood. As soon as the words left his lips, the officials and their servants fled from the scene. "They stabbed him over and over again! It was horrible!" Sergius yelled loudly. He proceeded to make his way around town, telling and retelling the story to anyone who would listen. He paid town criers to spread the word and, after several hours, felt secure enough in the circulation of the story to head back to the room where his brothers were waiting.

"It is done," he announced when he walked in the door. The brothers cheered for the completion of such a complicated contract. They ate and drank and made up for the Christmas dinner they had missed at Castello San Romolo the evening before.

"Tell me, Demetrius," Sergius began. "What did you say to Galeazzo after you stabbed him? He looked rather dismayed."

Demetrius grinned and leaned in closely so only Sergius would hear his answer. "I said exactly what Thomas asked me to say. 'You must realize two things. One, I hold your pitiful little life in the palm of my hand, and I can end it whenever I wish. And two, you are nothing but a pawn in a game that I am winning.'"

Sergius smiled. Thomas had harbored hatred towards Galeazzo for nine years. He supposed the delivery of those words would give his brother some peace. Sergius bowed his head, thankful for the completion of the contract, and said in a quiet, relieved voice, "At long last, the villain is dead."

TWENTY-FIVE

Florence, May 1478

OVER THE COURSE of the two years that Leonardo spent with the Galli family, the charges against him were dropped, and his attachment to Caterina's family grew stronger than his attachment to his own. They set aside a room in the house just for his paintings. Conte Galli put his foot down when asked about bringing Leo's inventions and experiments into the home—apparently Caterina had revealed the destructive nature of his work. But shortly after he moved into the Galli household, Leo secured a workshop in the heart of the city where he could do as much work as he wanted with complete privacy. There he was able to continue to dream up new creations and tinker with his beloved explosions.

He and Caterina spent countless hours together, and her skills outmatched most of his classmates. He prided himself on being a magnificent teacher (but in his heart, he knew Caterina's passion for art and her natural ability had only needed a small push in the right direction).

Near the end of his second year living with the Gallis, the Medici family began to take great interest in his artwork. Only one month later, he received an invitation to move into the Medici estate. He accepted the offer but worried he would offend the Gallis' generosity with the move.

"Why are you apologizing?" Caterina asked emphatically when he told her the news. "What an incredible opportunity! Of course you must go."

The conte and contessa were equally as enthusiastic as Caterina. Leonardo promised to visit them often—at least one dinner a week. And just like that, his time living with the kindest family of his acquaintance came to an end.

Caterina knew she should not be desolate about the loss of Leonardo, but she had grown accustomed to their talks and strolls into the city. He was as much a part of her family as her own brothers were. And during the time under his tutelage, she had become an outstanding artist. She made a point to visit him at least once a week, but his new commissions kept him busier than she had expected. He continued his weekly dinners with her family for several months, but over time, they grew less and less frequent.

She missed her dearest friend.

TWENTY-SIX

Florence, October 1480

"CATERINA!" Leonardo exclaimed as she walked toward him. "To what do I owe this unexpected visit?"

The two embraced and kissed each other's cheeks. Though Leonardo had not spent much time with his friend since he had moved into the Medici household, he still thought of Caterina and her parents as his own family.

"I decided it was time for you to take a break from painting and go on a ride with me through the countryside," Caterina said with a smile. "You've worked yourself far too hard over the past few years. You are skin and bones, and your eyes have dark circles beneath them. You are well aware you need a break."

He knew she was right, but the lyre he had recently begun working on was too exciting for him to put down. And the Medicis were nearly as excited about his musical creation as he was. Not wishing to disappoint his patrons and friends, he had barely slept since beginning the project. And he often neglected his commissions in order to work on the musical contraption.

"All right. You win," he said to a satisfied Caterina.

She had prepared a picnic for their ride, and he was happy to escape from the city for a few hours.

They quickly caught each other up on the latest news and developments in their lives. Caterina's eldest brother had just become a father for the fourth time. Filippo and Mella's daughter was now an accomplished rider while their son was gaining interest in the arts. This made both Caterina and Leonardo very pleased. Ludo and Gemma were still without children—though it seemed they had no plans to add to their family any time soon. And Jacopo and Fiora's son had begun tending the Galli vineyards with his father—who was now the head caretaker.

It seemed that Caterina was always full of news concerning her family, yet had none of her own. *It is as if she is afraid to live her own life ... outside of her paintings, of course. What could be keeping her from finding a life of her own? She is a beautiful young woman with a good family and ...* Leonardo stopped in the middle of his thought. He was stuck on the word "young". *She looks very young indeed,* he realized. In the ten years since they had first met, she had not seemed to age at all.

"Caterina," Leo said with a solemn look on his face.

"What's upsetting you?" she asked.

"You have not ... since we met ... you've just," he stammered.

She giggled at his senseless words. "Come out with it, Leo. What's wrong?"

"You've not aged a day. In ten years. And I did not notice until now. How can that be?" he asked as excitement gleamed in his eyes.

Caterina's expression became grave. She had noticed the very same thing a few years earlier and hoped she was simply aging more slowly than others. But she knew it was not so. She was stuck. She couldn't be certain—because there was no proof of her theory—but after months of thinking over her situation, she now believed it was the plague that had changed her.

"Tell me what you're thinking." Leonardo demanded.

"I cannot. You will not believe me even if I tell you," she replied.

Leonardo's eyes narrowed before speaking. "You tell me right this second. Do not dare tell me that I won't believe what you have to say. Especially when you have not said anything at all."

Caterina took a deep breath and closed her eyes. Apart from her family, no one knew that she had contracted and survived the plague. She had hidden that part of her life away, never to be thought of or talked about again. Whenever she did think of it, the only memory she could recollect was of waking in a house full of her decaying relatives. The memory was enough to induce vomit. But at last, thirteen years later, she was going to confide in someone she knew she could trust. She had kept his secrets for years. He owed her this.

"In 1467 I was visiting my cousins in Paris," she began.

"And studying under your Uncle Giovanni, yes?" Leonardo interjected.

"Exactly. But while I was visiting, plague broke out in the city. We locked ourselves inside our home, but the sickness still managed to find a way in," she whispered as she remembered her dear cousin's actions that fateful night. She was astonished to find her memories of Paula had grown fond in the years following the incident. Paula truly thought herself in love, and she was willing to risk death to be with the man she loved. No matter how horrible the consequences of her actions, *that* was a love worth having … a love Caterina knew she was unlikely to find, under the circumstances.

Leonardo was captivated, unknowingly leaning closer and closer as she spoke.

"My cousin Paula was the first to fall ill. Then my Aunt and Uncle. Then all the servants. And finally my cousin Simona and me. When I finally lay down to die, I wrote my family a letter and closed my eyes to the world one last time. But I did not die."

Leonardo's mouth now hung slightly open. She could tell he wanted to ask her about the particulars, but he could not find the words.

"When I awoke, I was fully recovered. I had none of the symptoms of the plague. I was only hungry. But my aunt and uncle and cousins lay dead where they had been—skin gray and rotting away as if they had been dead for weeks. The smell was unbearable in the hot summer air." She stopped to wipe away a tear that escaped from her eye. "And I still see them like that and smell their rotting flesh in my dreams."

Leonardo reached out and pulled her close, wrapping his arms around her shaking body.

"You needn't talk about it if the subject is too difficult," he said softly as he stroked her hair.

"No. I need to tell you everything. I need to tell *someone* everything," she said as she calmed her breathing and began again. "I found clothes untouched by the plague, gathered all the valuables I could find, and set off under the cover of night. I purchased a horse and rode toward my family's home in Milan. I would not go near *anyone*. I would not go inside. If I purchased food, I ate outside and cleaned my own bowl and spoon. I even used ripped pieces of cloth to hold the utensils while returning them to their owners in the event the plague was somehow attached to my skin. I slept outside or in barns for weeks as I made my way home. On the night before I reached Milan, I was attacked by a man. Before my journey, my brothers had given me a knife to wear … a knife which I still wear every day beneath my gown. And I used the knife to stab the man to death. I murdered someone, and I have never spoken those words aloud," she admitted as sobs racked her body.

Leonardo held her tightly as she wept. She was grateful he did not flee upon her admission of guilt.

"When did you realize you were no longer infected?" he asked quietly.

"When I finally arrived at my family's villa, I was so covered in my attacker's blood that my family did not recognize me. Despite my protests, my family's most trusted servant and his wife took care of me until they were sure I was not infectious. After that, my family tried to return to our normal lives. But word had gotten out that I had come from Paris, and the entire city was in a panic that I would infect everyone with the plague. My parents made the decision to move right away, and we've lived here since. About two years ago, I realized I had not aged since returning from Paris. And when I thought about it more, I realized that I had not been sick a single day either. Something changed inside me. And I have no idea what to do."

Leonardo's mind swirled with hundreds of questions, but he knew, in that moment, he needed only to comfort his sweet friend. She confided in him the same way he had confided in her, and her secret would die with him. He knew she would eventually have to leave Florence. If rumors began to circulate that she was not aging, she would fall under suspicion of practicing witchcraft. And a long trial to uncover the source of her unnatural youth was the last thing Caterina needed. Right then and there, he decided he would do everything in his power to protect her.

Twenty-Seven

Florence, March 1482

Leonardo spent hours upon hours studying Caterina for anything that might prove a physical difference from other people, but everything about her seemed normal. Except, of course, that she wasn't aging or getting sick. He developed products for her to use on her skin that would help her appear older than she actually was. His obsession with helping his closest friend was causing him to neglect all his other commissions. The only piece of work that he could focus on for any great length was his silver lyre, which the Medicis were pressing him to finish.

Leonardo's new life plan revolved around giving Caterina a new start in a different city. The people in Florence had begun to take note of Caterina's youth —even with the application of paints to make her look more aged. He heard whispers of the Galli girl who used magic to keep herself young. Others thought she was given the gift of youth by God. But either way, people were growing suspicious, and Caterina needed to leave Florence.

The Medici family wanted to make peace with the Duke of Milan, and Leonardo's lyre was to serve as the peace offering. His plan was to ask Caterina to relocate with him in order to keep her safe while allowing her to remain close to her siblings. The only problem was convincing the conte and contessa that their daughter was not aging. According to Caterina, they were completely oblivious to any abnormalities in her and maintained the theory that she was 'so full of life that age would never catch up with her'.

"I want you to move to Milan with me," he told her during one of their now-daily walks.

Caterina stopped in her tracks. "What do you mean?" she replied quickly.

"I mean that you perpetually look twenty years old, and the people of

Florence have started to take notice. Your parents are in denial, and if you don't leave soon, you're going to end up in a long trial to decide whether or not you're practicing witchcraft. I don't want that for you *or* for your family. If you move to Milan, you already have family there, and I can help you stay out of the public eye." Caterina gulped at his low, dangerous tone.

"I know you're right," Caterina began timidly. "But the last time I left my mother and father, my life was flipped upside down. I'm not sure I trust myself to be apart from them," she admitted.

"Why don't we discuss it with your parents. But they need to hear everything—they must understand that your life will be in danger if you do not leave this city."

Later that evening, Caterina's parents were happy to see that Leonardo would be joining the family for dinner. Caterina's stomach was in knots over the coming conversation, but she fully agreed that it needed to happen.

"I need to speak with you," she said with urgency as soon as they were seated for the meal. Her mother and father looked at each other and then at Caterina with worried faces.

"What's wrong, darling?" her mother asked carefully.

"Leonardo has asked me to move with him to Milan," she answered.

"But he ... you're not getting married, are you?" her father asked as gently as he could.

A nervous giggle burst from Caterina's chest. "Of course not, father. You know that we are like brother and sister."

"Why then?" her mother questioned, showing signs of distress.

Leonardo took a deep breath before his words began to flow. "Caterina has not aged since coming back from Paris. Nor has she been sick even once. People are beginning to notice that she looks far younger than she should ..."

Caterina looked at her parents' reactions as Leonardo continued his discourse. She was surprised to find their expressions calm and knowing. *Perhaps they have not been as oblivious to my situation as I thought.*

"Then we will move back with you, and you can live with us," her mother said when Leonardo was finished.

"I don't think that will help. If she lives in our household, everyone we know in Milan will know she is back. We know almost as many people in Milan as we know here," her father quickly responded.

"How long have you suspected?" Caterina asked, wondering how it was possible that her parents were this calm about her condition.

"Well … we realized you had not been sick about two years after your return from Paris. But it wasn't until two or three years ago that we finally understood you were not aging at all," her father admitted. "We've talked to your brothers at length about this. We were worried you had not noticed, and none of us wanted to broach the subject with you because we did not want you to fret."

"I am thirty-four years old!" she abruptly yelled, quickly realizing her volume and lowering her voice. "I am not some fragile child that needs to be protected. Just because I look young does not mean I am. I have witnessed death and survived it. I have traveled great distances without help. And though I am unsure of how to proceed in my life, I am not afraid to face whatever comes next," she said.

Her parents and Leonardo stared at her. Caterina was not one for making great speeches. But she could no longer bear the idea of her family trying to protect her from the harsh reality of her life. If she was right about her physical state, she would someday have to witness the deaths of everyone she cared for. She would outlive her nieces and nephews. And suspicion would follow her wherever she went. She would not be able to stay in one place for a great length of time. Nor would she be able to make lasting friendships. She understood the pain her future would hold, and her family's coddling would only make her less prepared.

"Then you should go with Leonardo, and we will remain here," her mother said softly. Her father patted her mother's hand as she let out quiet sobs.

"I know, mother," Caterina said softly. "But we will see each other whenever you are in Milan.

Three weeks later, Caterina once again said a tearful goodbye to her mother. Fortunately, this separation was not as far as their previous one, nor was it as terrifying. Caterina's two eldest brothers, along with their wives and children, would be within walking distance. And Leonardo would be with her as well. Her mother and father promised monthly visits (which was already a regular part of their lives in order to visit their grandchildren), and Caterina felt as comfortable as she could within the strange life she called her own.

Once they were settled in Milan, Leonardo was surprised to find Caterina genuinely happy with her new situation. She spent much of her time observing Leonardo at work while he gave her tips on new brush strokes he was trying. He often asked her advice on how to capture light or shadow—she had grown into a master of their craft, and though she did not believe him, he often told her that he valued her opinion as much as she valued his.

When she stayed at home during the day, Mella and Vittoria either came by themselves to visit or brought their children along so Caterina could dote on her nieces and nephews. She often sewed new clothes for them in her spare time or painted portraits of them as gifts for her mother and father.

Though she rarely made visits to her family's estate just outside the city, when she did, she made a point to see Jacopo and Fiora. Her servants were as concerned about her as her own family, but they did their best to act like there was nothing surprising about her young appearance.

Her brothers regularly checked her knife, and often provided her with new knives (which would also fit correctly in her leather holster) and sharpening stones to keep her blades in perfect condition. Though she found ample amusement in their obsession with her protection, Leonardo noticed the serious gleam in her eyes that told him she was grateful for the added security.

Leonardo could see that Caterina was happy. His own work was much better than when he was in Florence. And for the first time in years, they were both able to live their lives without fear of their darkest secrets coming to light.

TWENTY-EIGHT

Castello San Romolo, 1483-1490

THE FAMILY continued to stay busy throughout the 1480s. Thomas was traveling here or there for his contracts—grateful that he was not assigned menial tasks or tiresome searches for plague survivors. Starting in 1483, Thomas was assigned a contract of importance every year.

In 1483, he assassinated Albert VI, Duke of Mecklenburg. The trip to the northern part of Germany took far longer than it should have, but he could only blame himself for that. His intense fear of horses put the idea in his head that at any moment, his horse might simply give up and lie down on him, thus crushing one of his limbs or killing him instantly from the impact. When Thomas was only four years old and first learning to ride a horse, the animal lay down in the middle of the lesson, breaking his leg and destroying his trust in the beasts. It was years before his father or uncle could convince him to get back on a horse, and the only reason he was willing to try at that point was because Sergius (whose opinion he valued above all others) told him it was of utmost importance. Ever since, he checked his horse thoroughly before each ride and stopped frequently to allow the creature to rest. He did not mind that his brothers teased him about the practice—he secretly knew he was saving the lives of his traveling companions as well.

A year later, he was commissioned with killing Ippolita Maria Sforza—Galeazzo's cousin—in Naples. Considering his extensive history with the Sforza family, Thomas happily carried out the kill (smiling while he poisoned Ippolita's wine).

In 1485, Thomas was given one of his favorite contracts to date. Pedro de Arbués—an official of the Spanish Inquisition—was seeking out practicing, and sometimes non-practicing, Jews who 'refused' to follow the ways of

Catholicism. Thomas, along with the rest of the Family, was tolerant of an individual's choice of religion above all else.

Though Priest lacked as a father in so many ways, tolerance was not one of his failures. Thomas felt certain Priest and Saint had been raised in a non-spiritual home. But Priest was so secretive about his personal history, no one knew where he was born or how he became immortal—except, of course, his brother, Saint. Unfortunately, Saint's lips were sealed as tightly as his brother's.

The Family had been taught the ways of the Orthodox church from before Thomas's birth, but he knew that practice had more to do with Saint than Priest. Saint held a service in the Family chapel at Castello San Romolo every Sunday, and everyone on the Family grounds attended out of fear of disappointing Saint. Though some in the Family were not inclined to practice any religion, they were each taught from the beginning of their lives to never mock or sneer at another's religious beliefs. It was one of Priest's central rules for his sons and grandsons. "Though you may believe one way—and know without question that your way is the right way—another person may feel just as strongly about their beliefs. It is not for you to judge if anyone else is right or wrong. It is for you to know what is in your own heart," Priest had said time after time. Priest no longer made those speeches to his grandsons and great-grandsons. The responsibility fell to Thomas and his brothers to continue teaching the new generations the old ways. He missed those moments with his father. More than he realized.

But the Spanish Inquisition—and many of the Catholic policies throughout Europe—were a thorn in the side of everyone in the Family. Sergius even caught Priest seeking out contracts for cardinals, priests, and even the pope. And if *Priest* was agitated in such a way, Thomas knew the church was even more corrupt than he previously thought.

When Priest handed him the contract for Arbués, he gave Thomas the specifics of the situation—something that rarely happened. A family in Zaragoza, the city in Spain where Arbués was carrying out his inquisition, had been accused on more than one occasion of practicing Judaism. They were being threatened with the loss of their property, their wealth, and even their lives if they did not renounce Judaism and turn back to Catholicism. The one problem with the threats was that the family had converted to Catholicism nearly ten years earlier and were still faithful to religion. It was only after the Inquisition began that they realized the extent of the corruption in the Catholic church and began to grow resentful of being forced to leave the Jewish faith. They desperately wanted to step out of Arbués's watchful eyes in order to continue living their lives without fear of punishment.

Thomas was thrilled to know the story behind the contract. He felt the excitement of any assassination much more when he knew *why* he was killing a target … especially one as evil as Arbués. Thomas was given his choice of brothers to join him in the task. He selected Demetrius (who was an expert with a blade) and Samuel (who could be guilted into performing nearly any duty to fulfill a contract) to accompany him to Spain.

On the journey to Zaragoza, whenever his brothers weren't complaining about Thomas's frequent stops, they were discussing their plans for Arbués.

"We should behead him while he sleeps," Demetrius suggested.

"We could always offer Samuel as a page boy and see if Arbués is inclined toward sodomy," Thomas said without keeping a straight face.

"For God's sakes, Thomas! Will you never let me forget that? I still have nightmares!" Samuel yelled, though he couldn't hide his smirk.

Thomas chuckled for a moment before growing serious.

"I think we should fatally wound him and leave him to die a painful death," Thomas offered, barely louder than a whisper. Both Demetrius and Samuel were unsettled by Thomas's suggestion, but neither could fault him for his line of thinking. To kill or persecute someone simply because they followed a different religious practice was abhorrent. Without speaking, both brothers nodded their agreement, and they quietly continued their trip.

Samuel stayed hidden in the corner of the cathedral to help in case he was needed while Thomas and Demetrius stalked Arbués to where he knelt. The cathedral was empty except for Arbués and the three brothers. When the first knife entered Arbués's body, he screamed in pain. But Demetrius covered his mouth and stabbed again—this time through his arm. Samuel watched silently as his brothers unleashed their wrath with their daggers. He was relieved that he did not have to participate—while he understood the necessity of the contract and his brothers' reasoning for acting so viciously, he did not like the idea of allowing someone to die slowly and painfully. Thomas and Demetrius were talented enough with their knives that they knew exactly where to stab in order to extend the process of dying. Samuel would have "accidentally" hit Arbués's heart if he had been one of the assassins. He let out a heavy sigh when they were finished—he was ready to be done with this contract.

Thomas was disheartened to find that the death of Arbués only agitated the other inquisitioners into taking more action. The family that had contracted Arbués's death were killed along with several of their friends and servants. But the satisfaction he felt in ending the life of such an evil man could not be overlooked.

The following five years were spent traveling around Germany, Belgium, and Poland. In Germany, he killed Jacques of Savoy in Ham and Rudolf IV in Lörrach. In Damme, Belgium, he ended the life of the Margrave of Baden. In Poland, he assassinated Stanislaw Kazimierczyk and the Casimir of Zator. Each time he received a new contract, he imagined its possible merits and motivations. After the contract Priest had accepted for the life of the fourteen-year-old Prince of Asturias, Thomas remained watchful of his father's actions. But thankfully, his worries had been for naught.

Upon returning to the castle, however, he felt a shift in the air. In the five years he had been away, an unwelcome darkness had taken root in the very foundation of Castello San Romolo.

TWENTY-NINE

Milan, April 1491

LEONARDO RUSHED home as fast as he could. The gossip around town had finally reached his ears, and he knew there was no time to spare. As soon as he burst through the door, Caterina's smile dropped. Her nieces, nephews and sisters-in-law stopped in their tracks. They knew this day would come.

"What happened?" Vittoria asked with urgency.

"The whole town is talking about the ghost of Caterina Galli. Someone saw you on the outskirts of town while you were painting and recognized you immediately. I guess everyone thought you were dead, but now the rumors have begun to circulate that you are either a witch or a ghost," Leonardo reported.

Caterina exchanged worried looks with Mella and Vittoria before her eyes turned toward the ground.

"I have nowhere else to go," she said in a choked whisper.

Mella and Vittoria clung to her sides to support her sagging frame.

"I thought we were being careful," Vittoria said as she hugged Caterina tightly.

Leonardo had been waiting for people to discover Caterina's true nature for years. He had concocted several contingency plans for her future in anticipation of this day, but now his planning seemed inadequate.

"When your parents arrive next week, we need to sit down and decide what we're going to do," Leonardo said abruptly.

All three women looked up at him, their faces serious, and nodded their agreement. In order to keep her safe, Leonardo would lose the company of his closest friend, and Caterina would have to give up everyone and everything she had ever known.

Caterina's family sat around her in their gathering room—the same gathering room where she had long ago spent her final night in Milan surrounded by friends and family before her fateful trip to Paris. Not a smile could be found. The only sounds heard were the occasional sound of a woman's sniffle or the clearing of a man's throat as he choked back emotion. Leonardo was the only person in attendance who was not technically a member of the family, though anyone in the Galli family would argue he was as much family as anyone there. As he paced the floor, Caterina followed his movement. One look at his face told her that plans were swirling in his mind for her escape from Milan. As he stopped moving and looked into her eyes, she saw his determination falter for a fraction of a second before he regained his composure and spoke.

"I've thought of three options for Caterina—none of which are ideal, and none of which am I content with," he said as he glanced sadly around the room. Everyone, including Caterina, was aware of the danger that lay ahead for her … regardless of where her next steps took her. "She can travel around Europe, accompanied by a servant, staying in each place for only a year or two before moving on to the next city."

Jacopo shot up from the corner seat where he and Fiora sat together. "I will take her if someone is needed," he said quickly while Fiora nodded her agreement.

"Absolutely not," Caterina rebutted firmly. "You will not leave your wife and children on my account. I forbid you to even think about it.."

He sat down slowly and smiled sadly at his wife. Though Caterina was grateful for the offer, she knew Jacopo and Fiora would be miserable with any separation longer than a few days. She couldn't live with herself knowing that she was the cause of pain for either of her beloved servants.

"There is no one else I would trust with her safety," Filippo chimed in and turned toward Jacopo, "and I could not allow you to leave your family *or* the vineyards. You are too valuable here." Jacopo blushed under the attention, and Caterina couldn't help but smile at his reaction.

"The second option," Leonardo began again, "is to hide her away in a villa somewhere in the woods where we would not be able to visit. But if she was isolated for the rest of her life, who knows what horrors her mind might concoct. I think we all want Caterina to live as close to a normal life as possible."

"I couldn't bear it if I knew you were all alone," her mother gasped between sobs. "This is difficult enough already, and if I didn't know where you were or how you were doing, I don't think I could ever be happy again."

Caterina knew her family well enough to know the truth of those words. None of the family would be amenable to this option—including Caterina.

"The final option—and least desirable—is one which I am hesitant even to speak aloud," Leonardo said softly.

Everyone in the room grew silent, awaiting the words Leonardo was desperate to keep inside. Caterina was nervous, but a little voice in the back of her head told her this final option would be best for her family.

"I contacted an old friend—someone whom I trust implicitly—who is preparing to journey across the open seas with an Italian named Cristoforo Colombo. He is determined to sail from Spain across the ocean to the Indies, and my friend assures me he can secure a spot in the crew for Caterina—as long as she is willing to dress as a man and work as hard as the rest of the crew. There have been brilliant and unique works of art pouring out of the Indies for years, but I have never known anyone to actually go there to study. I thought, maybe, if you traveled there, you could learn entirely new ways to paint. And maybe, in ten or twenty years, you could come back and teach me and your mother what you learn," Leonardo said with a forced smile.

Caterina's heart raced. She would not have to stay hidden away from the world, ever in fear of discovery. She could go to the Far East and live amongst foreigners. She could hone her craft. And maybe, someday, she could even return to her home … to her friends … to her family.

Her father and brothers erupted into loud conversations about the dangers of the journey and the unknown life that awaited her across the ocean. Her mother sobbed while Mella and Vittoria tried to comfort their wailing mother-in-law. Jacopo held Fiora closely as they watched the chaos with concerned eyes. Caterina realized she was the only one who felt this option was the answer to her problems. If she started over in a new land, she could live for at least ten years without fear of her immortality being called into question. She needed to speak up soon, or she might not have any say in the matter at all. She stood, feeling every ounce of fear drain from her body as courage took over.

"I will travel across the ocean to a new land. There, I will be able to begin again without fear of discovery. I will stay there and learn how they create their art. I will have *purpose*. I do not wish to hide somewhere in a forest, constantly in fear of being discovered … constantly in fear of losing my wits in the isolation. And I certainly am not willing to sit around here, locked in the house, just waiting for my family and friends to grow old and die. There is nothing for me here but pain and grief and fear." As the words rushed from her mouth, she wondered who had spoken them. Her family's faces showed surprise, yet they looked pained from the truth in her words.

Filippo's gaze was locked with Caterina's. "When does your friend leave?" he asked Leonardo without breaking his eye contact.

"In one month. He'll ride from Florence to Palos de la Frontera in Spain. They are supposed to set sail at the end of summer," Leonardo answered.

"And you are absolutely certain that your friend is trustworthy," Giovanni said as more of a demand than a question.

"Yes. He will protect her, and he will hide her true identity. He is unaware of Caterina's condition. He only knows she needs to leave Europe under disguise. And he was eager to help."

"Then we have a month to plan and train," Ludo chimed in for the first time. He was generally willing to let his father and brothers take the lead, but when it came to Caterina's well-being, he was more than happy to assert his opinion.

Caterina smiled slightly at her brothers' protectiveness. She was thrilled that they were going to train her—she had longed to learn how to throw a punch for years but hadn't found the courage to ask. Now she would learn how to use a sword and fight with her fists. *Stay focused on the exciting parts,* she commanded herself. *You will learn new painting techniques and become a proficient fighter.* She refused to look at her mother, who was in such a fit of sobbing that Caterina worried for the headaches she would later suffer. Her brothers agreed that Caterina would spend a good portion of each day learning to fight, running, and lifting wine barrels to gain strength and stamina. She would spend time under the sun to rid herself of the pale skin that elegant females were careful to maintain. There was much to accomplish in a very short time, but the men in her life were happy to drop everything to help her prepare. Jacopo would be in charge of teaching Caterina how to properly lift and carry heavy things—he had been working with the wine barrels since he was a small boy. Filippo and Giovanni would teach her how to fight with her fists, and Ludo and her father were responsible for teaching her swordsmanship.

Leonardo stood off to the side, looking miserable as the rest of the men discussed Caterina's training. She walked over to him and wrapped her arms around his waist in a firm hug. She was not one to show physical affection since her return from Paris all those years ago. She rarely hugged even her own mother. But in that moment, she wanted Leo to understand how grateful she was for the future he was providing for her. It was his idea and his planning alone that would allow her to live without fear for another ten to twenty years. He wrapped his arms around her and hugged her tightly, kissing the top of her head. There was no question about it—Leonardo was as much a brother to Caterina as her own flesh and blood. Without his friendship, the past twenty years would have been dismal at best.

"Thank you," she whispered as she held her friend tightly. "I do not know what I would do without you."

THIRTY

CATERINA WAS MENTALLY and physically equipped for the coming journey. For a solid month she trained—and did little else. Right after the decision to leave Europe was made, she moved back into her family's villa so they could help her prepare for her trip. She missed painting terribly, but knew she would be able to continue her passion for the arts in the Far East. Every day, she woke up and told herself to focus on the task at hand—when she allowed her mind to wander, she grew too emotional for her liking. Caterina spent hours studying the way her father, brothers and male servants walked and talked. She mastered a more masculine gait and deeper voice. Fortunately, she was not the kind of female to scream when she was frightened or faint at the sight of blood. She felt as prepared as one could to pull off the male persona she would become for the next several months. She decided to travel under the name "Matteo" and forced her family to refer to her as such whenever they addressed her. It was awkward for everyone at first, but as her time with them grew shorter and the urgency of her situation became more apparent, everyone in the household did their part in helping her.

The worst part of the entire process was that every time Caterina made eye contact with her mother, she watched her mother's mournful eyes fill with tears that always seemed to spill over no matter how hard she tried to keep them in. Caterina forced back her emotions. *They should not live with this kind of grief. I only hope that they will learn to live happy and fulfilled lives without me,* Caterina thought.

Leonardo watched as Caterina hugged her family and friends goodbye. She had grown hard over the past month. Her hair was cut short just like Jacopo's now, and the tan she had gotten from fighting outside made her skin look like a peasant's. Leonardo crafted several bindings for Caterina's chest—she needed to make sure her bosom looked no bigger than any normal man's chest. In addition to the bindings, Leonardo worked closely with Caterina's brothers to create a holster that would house multiple knives of different shapes and sizes. They landed on a design that allowed her to carry three knives on her being at all times—one on each leg and one right under her breasts. The challenge was creating a holster that would allow her to do the work she would be required to do comfortably. But in the end, Leonardo created a masterpiece—just as Caterina had said he would.

When it was Leonardo's turn to embrace Caterina for the final time, his mind became a flurry of thoughts and emotions. He didn't know how to convey his gratitude for her presence in his life.

"I …" he said as he choked back emotion.

"I know," she said quietly as a tear ran down her cheek. They had shared their deepest secrets with one another—secrets they would take to their graves. Leonardo knew he might never feel for another human what he felt for Caterina.

"I love you more than my own life," he whispered into her ear as he hugged her even more tightly. Her breath caught as she returned the fierce embrace. She did not say another word as she let go and kissed both of his cheeks.

She turned to look at each of her family and friends one last time. The longing gaze only lasted for a fleeting moment before it was replaced with a look of determination. She nodded once, mounted her horse, and rode away without a backward glance.

Once she was out of sight, an eruption of emotion overtook the entire Galli household. Sobs were heard by men and women alike. Leonardo knew the home would never be the same. They had just said their final goodbyes to the most beloved member of their family.

Leonardo couldn't take his eyes away from the place in the distance where Caterina disappeared. As tears continued to drip down his face, he felt in the very depths of his soul he would never see Caterina Galli again.

The trip to the coast of Spain was tedious, but Leonardo's friend, Prospero, was a pleasant companion. Caterina was well aware of the nature of the journey because of her trip to and from Paris, but in her newly-muscled body, traveling was much easier.

They arrived in Palos de la Frontera in the middle of July and spent the next several weeks familiarizing themselves with the rest of the crew. Caterina was initially nervous about her performance as a man, but Prospero assured her the crew was completely oblivious to her gender.

When the time came to set sail, Caterina felt the full weight of her decision. She thought of everything she had been through to arrive at this moment, and the emotion that rushed through her body was almost too much to contain.

Prospero boarded the ship with the rest of the crew while Caterina stood on the dock, looking up at the vessel that would carry her to her new life.

She slowly stepped aboard the ship and spared a quick glance backward. She felt as if she were a prisoner being released after a lifetime locked in a cell —alone, scared, unsure of how to live outside the boundaries of her familiar cell and bars. She knew how to survive the difficulties of her former life. Surely the hardships of the life ahead could not rival those of her past.

One step at a time, she told herself in a small, terrified voice. She turned back to the ship and breathed a heavy sigh. She could not look back again, could not dwell on her former life, could not question the decision she had made.

As the ship set sail, she gazed toward the sea—toward the life that lay ahead. She wished she could paint this moment to capture the depth of her emotions. The vast, terrifying sea that sprawled before her would be a beautiful painting if only she had a way to capture the vision. *There is no turning back now,* she thought as a tear escaped from the corner of her eye. *There is only what lies ahead.*

THIRTY-ONE

Castello San Romolo, August 1517

"YOU CANNOT BE SERIOUS, FATHER!" Thomas said in disbelief.

"Oh, I am perfectly serious," Priest answered with his eyes narrowed. Thomas knew this was a direct challenge to see how far he was willing to go to stand up for himself. He tried to calm his voice before speaking again.

"This is insulting," he said softly.

"And you cannot think of any reason I might have to give insult?" Priest asked with a feigned look of surprise on his face. Thomas's blood boiled. The man had become a tyrant.

Thomas had worried Priest might feel the need to retaliate. Since his arrival home in 1490, Thomas had been digging deeper into his own contracts and encouraging his brothers and nephews to do the same. He felt there was a need to keep Priest in check, and since there was no evidence of Saint taking a stand against his father, the weight of responsibility fell on Thomas's shoulders to draw attention to Priest's demoralization. If he was being honest with himself, he was surprised Priest had waited so long to retaliate.

"You have strayed from the principles on which you founded our Family! I only tried to show you where your steps have gone astray. Killing wives because their husbands think they *might* be having an affair and murdering children in retaliation for wrongdoings is *not* who we are! Surely you must see that," Thomas pleaded.

"I do not see that. Every contract I accept has its merits. And until you, your brothers, and my grandsons can see that I choose each contract for a specific reason, anyone who opposes me will have a similar fate to yours," Priest said.

Thomas could not open his mouth again without screaming profanities at his father. But he knew better than to disrespect Priest publicly. He had gone too far as it was.

As he packed his things in a large bag, Sergius and Samuel entered his room.

"'Tis not the worst that could happen," Sergius said quietly.

"You might actually enjoy it!" Samuel said enthusiastically.

Though Thomas knew his brothers were only trying to cheer him up, their words stung like alcohol on an open wound.

"A mercenary," Thomas growled. "A sell-sword. This is the first time any one of us has been contracted out this way. I feel like a whore—my actions dictated by some man who has the right to do whatever he wishes with me. And I, more than most of my brothers, feel strongly about what is right and what is wrong. You know there are things that I simply will not do. But if I do not fulfill the contract that Priest has set before me, I will not be welcomed back into the Family upon my return. This is a nightmare," he said, tasting the acute bitterness the words left on his tongue.

"I tried to convince him this is unnecessary," Sergius said. "But he told me the lesson is as much for me as it is for you."

Thomas was unhappy that his brothers were in danger of being hired out as mercenaries as well, but he hoped this one contract would put his father's mind at ease.

"Do not stir up strife while I am away. Do whatever tasks you are given, and we'll deal with anything that needs to be dealt with upon my return," Thomas commanded.

The Family gathered around him the next morning as he saddled his horse. Though he was not close with *all* of his relations, most of them shared the bond of brotherhood that came from centuries of life spent under the same roof. Everyone took turns wishing him luck and giving him a firm embrace. Everyone but Priest. As Thomas rode away from Castello San Romolo, he watched his father give a dismissive nod and walk back inside the home. Though the emotion Thomas felt the most keenly was anger, he could not help but feel betrayed. He needed to prove to his father that his opinions and convictions were worthy of consideration. But the only way he could accomplish that feat was by completing the contract and returning home with a new attitude. He would not fail.

THIRTY-TWO

Cádiz, Spain, September 1517

THOMAS'S TRIP to Spain took only a few weeks. He rode from Castello San Romolo down to Naples, where he hired a small vessel to take him across the Mediterranean. Once the vessel crossed through the Strait of Gibraltar, it was only a few hours until they reached Cádiz.

He had grown up listening to his father tell stories of Gadir (as the city was called long ago) and had wished to visit the city for as long as he could remember. The city was quite different than the exotic place his father had described, but though he was a bit disappointed, Thomas knew that was to be expected after the centuries that had passed. The inns and alehouses were filled with travelers—many of whom had just arrived from the Indies. The stories of the months-long journeys were harrowing at best, and Thomas found his stomach queasy just listening to the tales.

After three weeks, he was finally able to secure passage to Hispanola. Once there, he would purchase passage on yet another ship to end his journey in Santiago de Cuba.

The trip to the Indies felt endless. He found himself sick each day during the first week of the journey. Once the sea-sickness subsided, he spent most days helping the crew with their duties (as he could not stand to be idle). The captain was so impressed by his work ethic, he offered Thomas a job on the ship. Thomas graciously declined, informing the captain that his employer was eagerly awaiting his arrival in the Indies.

Thomas was grateful for the two days of respite in Hispanola. He was blissful to have his feet on dry land again.

By the time he reached Santiago de Cuba, he calculated the journey had lasted almost four months. He breathed a sigh of relief as he stepped off the ship onto the ground where he would spend the next several years.

Thomas found a small inn and purchased a room to spend a few nights. Though his employer knew Thomas was on his way, he had no solid time frame for the date of his actual arrival. Thomas knew he would need time for his body to recover from the feeling of rocking back and forth. *Once I feel as if the ground beneath my feet is stable again, I will go,* he decided.

Though it took him eight full days to return to normal, he could finally move about without giving off the impression that he was incessantly drunk. He took out his contract and found the location of his new employer: *La Oficina del Alcalde de Santiago.*

Thomas and his brothers had learned as many languages as possible over their nine hundred years of life. They mastered Latin and Arabic as children— Arabic was the language Priest used primarily, and Latin the language Saint spoke most often (though Thomas had never understood why brothers would use different languages). They learned Greek in their teens, and Occitan, Hebrew, Catalan, Spanish and Italian over the next several centuries. Once the Family contracts spread beyond the borders of Italy and the Papal States (due to the reach of the Roman Empire), they began rapidly learning languages wherever their contracts took them. Thomas was not certain, but he estimated he was fluent in twelve languages and proficient in at least another twenty. He made a point to study language at least a few times a week (and often found himself a devoted student in the long periods between Family assignments). He had most recently conquered the German language during his two-year stay in Germany. The Family now conversed predominantly in Italian (for the sake of their youngest sons), but conversation could often be heard in their original Latin or Arabic.

Thomas nervously approached the door of his employer's office and took a deep breath before knocking. He wondered what he would have to do for this Spaniard, and hoped the man had at least a semblance of a moral code.

"I am the mercenary you sent for," Thomas said in Spanish when the man opened the door.

"Oh yes! I did not expect you for at least another month. How nice that you have arrived early. My name is Hernán Cortés de Monroy y Pizarro."

Thirty-Three

Santiago, Cuba, October 1518

It HAD ONLY taken Thomas a few days to realize that his job was more as a bodyguard than a mercenary. He followed Cortés wherever he went, keeping an eye on whomever passed by. Cortés was more than capable of defending himself, but he had acquired many powerful enemies in his own rise to power. Fear alone persuaded him to hire a trustworthy bodyguard. One of Cortés's contacts in Spain had been the intermediary for the contract. Thomas was even given a room in Cortés's dwelling to provide an extra measure of security while he slept.

Cortés did not spend much time communicating with Thomas. Cortés spent most of his time hard at work behind his desk with his nose buried in papers. He wasn't unkind to Thomas (for which Thomas was exceedingly grateful), simply too busy with his own work to take an interest in the life of a hired hand. Thomas observed the man's behavior from a distance and quickly uncovered his strengths and weaknesses. Cortés was ambitious, well-liked (by those not competing with him politically), intelligent, and eloquent. Adversely, he was prideful in his accomplishments, over-confident that he would always succeed, unashamed about his endless philandering, and ruthless (sometimes even violent) to ensure his wishes came to fruition.

Thomas felt useless in the confines of such a worthless position, but he made the best of each day by learning Taíno—the language of the native people on the island who were enslaved by the Spanish settlers. He became fast friends with two young natives who served in Cortés's household, and after a few months of learning the basics, he asked that the two men speak to him only in their native tongue. Thomas often caught Cortés looking on in interest during his conversations with the slaves, but Cortés did not interfere.

Thomas spent the remainder of his time walking throughout Cortés's office and house (wherever Cortés was at the time) to check for potential threats. No matter where Cortés went, Thomas devised at least two exit strategies in case of an attack.

One afternoon, Thomas was walking around the exterior of Cortés's workplace when he heard a yell from inside.

"Thomas!" Cortés called from his second story office window. "Come in here now!"

Thomas set off at a sprint. He entered the front door of the building and ran up the stairs. He had not heard his employer shout before, and his heart raced at the possibility that he had failed at his duty. As soon as he opened the door to Cortés's private office, he was bemused. Cortés sat behind his desk with a massive smile plastered onto his face.

"I don't understand," Thomas said, slightly winded from his panicked race to an elated employer.

"Governor Velazquez has appointed me the Captain-General of an expedition to the mainland!" Cortés announced. "You are the first official member of the crew that will help me conquer another land."

Months passed. Cortés spent at least sixteen hours a day planning, gathering ships and crews, and drawing up plans for his coming expedition.

"Come over here, Thomas. I see your eyes searching my maps from across the room. Do you have something to add?" Cortés asked with a curious tone. Thomas had hoped he would be allowed to participate in the planning of the journey. It had been too long since he sat around the table with Saint and his brothers, devising strategies for one contract or another.

"I simply noticed that if you landed here first, you might find it beneficial to interact with a group of natives that have already come into contact with other Spaniards. It would add time to the trip, but you would be able to restock with fresh food and possibly find an interpreter," Thomas said quietly, worried that his suggestion would somehow upset his employer. He watched Cortés's eyes look back and forth from the path he had plotted to the list of supplies he had drawn up. The number of men he hoped to gather for the expedition was six to seven hundred, and he knew the fresh food and water would be depleted quickly if there were no amiable natives in the new land. Thomas hoped Cortés would see the merit of stopping first at the small island just off the coast of the mainland.

"You are very right, Thomas. We will need an interpreter. Have you any other suggestions?" Cortés asked, obviously happy to have a second set of eyes upon his plans. Over the course of the week, Cortés came to understand just how well-versed in strategy Thomas really was. He began asking for Thomas's opinions over even the most minute of details pertaining to the journey. The two were not exactly friends, but it was undeniable that in Cortés's eyes, Thomas was his closest advisor.

Meanwhile, Governor Velazquez began to grow worried about the level of respect Cortés would gain while undergoing the coming journey. Word spread quickly that the governor might replace Cortés to conquer the mainland himself. Cortés dismissed the rumors and continued to plan as if he would be leading the charge, but when word reached him that the governor had officially begun planning to strip Cortés of his commission to keep him from embarking on the conquest, Cortés and Thomas finalized their preparations with haste.

They were finally ready to sail on November 18, 1518. Thomas stood faithfully by his employer's side as Cortés looked over the readied ships in the harbor. The crews were boarded, the supplies stocked—everything was set for the trip.

Governor Velazquez and several guards rode hurriedly to the docks and dismounted. Thomas could tell by their expressions that trouble was afoot. The guards aimed their guns at Cortés, ready to fire at the governor's command (though Cortés seemed unworried and told Thomas to be at ease).

"Is this how you would part from me?" Velazquez yelled as he paced back and forth on the dock. Thomas was grateful Cortés was safely aboard a vessel, out of the reach of the furious governor and his guards. "You could not have been any more courteous in taking your leave," the governor said sarcastically. Thomas knew the governor could easily send ships after Cortés to bring the crew back. Cortés had disobeyed the governor's expressed wishes, and Thomas hoped Velazquez would not do anything too drastic.

"Oh! Governor Velazquez! I see you're here to send us off with your kind words," Cortés said cheerfully, ignoring the governor's statement. "But you see, time presses! And we are already behind schedule. Has Your Excellency any commands?"

Thomas coughed to hide his laughter as Cortés spoke. The governor's face was a dreadful shade of red, and Thomas thought at any moment the man might howl in frustration. But Velazquez held his tongue.

"If you've nothing to say, then I'll bid you farewell! And I'm sure I'll send word of the lands we conquer along the way," Cortés said with a smile and a bow.

Cortés gave the command for all eleven ships to set sail, and off they went with the governor pacing back and forth on the dock as they sailed away. Thomas could not take his eyes off the governor's figure. And when the dock was nearly out of sight, though he couldn't be certain, Thomas thought he heard a voice yell, "Cortés, you will go down in history as a mutineer!"

Thomas could not help but feel excited about visiting a new land. Most of his brothers had not been further than Europe, but a select few had visited Asia and Africa. The Family rarely went somewhere unless they were contracted to do so—and contracts were most often commissioned by the Europeans. The excitement Thomas felt was overshadowed only by the part of the journey where Cortés planned to conquer the native peoples. He hoped and prayed the journey would be peaceful, but the look in Cortés's eye told him his prayers were likely to go unanswered.

The first three months of their trip were spent hopping from place to place in the West Indies, gathering more ships, more men, and more supplies. Thomas was already sick of traveling before they even began their real journey.

When at last Cortés felt they had amassed enough men, supplies, ships, and weapons, they set sail for the small island of Cozumel—the stop which had been Thomas's idea. The bright blue water and sandy beaches mixed with the rocky shorelines were unlike any coastline Thomas had seen before. *Hopefully my prayers will yet be answered!* Thomas thought with a glimmer of hope.

Thirty-Four

Cozumel, Mexico, December 1519

CATERINA SAT in the corner of her small, stone home. She did her best to keep busy, but at the end of each day, she felt as if she had been idle. She gathered food for herself, sewed clothing and blankets, and checked her fishing nets. She made paints from crushed berries and leaves, and paintbrushes from feathers or animal hair (mostly from the foxes, as they were much more friendly than the animals whose fur looked as if they were wearing masks—those creatures too often stole food from her home).

When she first arrived in Kùutsmil, she was terrified, alone, and starving. The natives gathered her limp body from the tiny boat she had traveled in and brought her to their village—which was called Tantun. Though she was too weak to move her own limbs, the natives looked upon her as if she was the most terrifying being they had ever seen. Only one tiny, shriveled woman was brave enough to come near her. The woman said a few words while Caterina stared. Then, the old woman took a knife in her hand and pointed it in the direction of Caterina's heart. *Yes!* her mind had screamed. *Please, dear Lord, let this woman end my life. Let it be over.* The knife cut through the shreds of cloth that had previously been a shirt, and the onlookers' eyes widened when they saw the knives she wore in her leather holster. The woman removed the contraption, and Caterina wished she could yell out for her to give it back. The holster held not only her knives, but also the ring her parents gave to her long ago.

Next, the woman cut through the bindings Leonardo had made to conceal her gender from the rest of the crew—though, in the end, she had been found out anyway. When the natives saw that Caterina was a woman, all the men were quickly pushed from the room. Within minutes, the native women were bathing her, feeding her, and giving her water to drink. Caterina tried to smile to show her appreciation, but her exhaustion was too heavy to overcome.

After only a day of attention and care, Caterina felt her strength begin to return. The women brought her brightly colored dresses with the most beautiful embroidery of flowers and patterns. They returned her holster (Caterina was surprised to find they had removed nothing from it), helped her dress, and began to show her around the village. As she walked, she noticed several men keeping an eye on her every move. She once again felt as if she was the threat —a feeling she had hoped would be permanently gone from her life.

The village was incredible. The homes were constructed from stone, and massive stone structures reached into the sky. Caterina could not fathom how people could manage to build such a design (though she had heard rumors of similar structures existing in Africa).

After a week of recovery, something changed in the village and people began looking at her with fear. Caterina did not know what to attribute the change to, but she worried her welcome had come to an end. The old woman who had cared for her took her by the hand and began pulling her away from the village. No one followed them, and Caterina wondered if she should be anxious about what was coming. The woman stopped her and began speaking and waving her hands. Caterina had no idea what the woman was saying, but the message was loud and clear—*you cannot be in our village ... it is not for you.*

Caterina wondered where she was supposed to go—she did not know if the other natives in the region would be more hostile than this group—but she did not have to worry for long. The old woman led her nearly a mile from the village before veering off the main path. Buried inside the thick forest was a small, stone dwelling. It was completely hidden from sight, and Caterina could tell the woman was trying to protect her. Once inside the hut, Caterina saw that the old woman had brought blankets, baskets of food, and pots for cooking. There were beautifully designed clay pots filled with fresh water, and a mat was carefully placed in the corner where she could sleep.

Caterina's eyes filled with tears. She smiled and knelt down before the old woman, grasping her shriveled hands and praying she would understand the level of gratitude Caterina hoped to convey. The old woman seemed astounded at first, but soon grinned, barked out a few words, and abruptly left Caterina on her own.

That exchange had been twenty-six years earlier (if Caterina's tallies were correct). The old woman died only a few years after her arrival, but the natives —whom Caterina now understood were called the "Mayan" nation—were accustomed to Caterina's presence. She was still not welcome in the village— whenever she tried to venture into town she was met with horrified stares, or more often people running back to their homes to hide—but they knew she was not a threat to their existence. Once a week, a group of men and women would leave a basket of fruits and vegetables outside her home. Some days they would bring her a new dress or shirt. Caterina also spent a little time with the natives down by the river where she washed her clothes each week. She had learned enough of their language to understand basic words—the names of foods, clothes, animals, and buildings. But because of the care the natives took to keep their distance, she could not even speak their language in broken sentences. The one word she heard each time a native saw her was "ish-chel"—which she assumed was their name for her. After years of trying to figure out what the word meant, she decided that "ish" meant female. The other part of the word meant white. She heard the two words spoken separately on many occasions, but the combination was spoken primarily when they were looking upon her with wary eyes. Periodically, she heard other words in relation to her name, and she was fairly certain the words referred to her as an "apparition" or "spirit". The natives thought of her as a *ghost*.

Caterina looked down at her pot full of blood-red paint as she felt a shiver run up her spine. She had gotten lost in her thoughts and mashed the same berries for nearly an hour without realizing. Her hands were stained bright red.

She put down her small mixing bowl and took a deep breath. *You're all right, Caterina. You're alive and healthy. Alone. But safe.*

That night, Caterina's sleep was restless. The wind gusted through her home more violently than usual, and the moonlight was blocked by thick, dark clouds. She woke up each hour with the same nightmare: a blanket of darkness crept nearer and nearer to the shores of her home. An unearthly scream shattered the quiet of the night, and the entire forest quivered in fear. She pulled her blanket up close around her face and squeezed her eyes shut. *Please God, protect me from whatever evil is stirring this night.*

Caterina felt in the depths of her soul that something was coming. Something terrifying and dark was on its way to Kùutsmil.

THIRTY-FIVE

CORTÉS'S SHIP was the last to arrive on the small island of Cozumel. But by the time Thomas and Cortés set foot on the white sandy shores, the damage was already done. Two natives lay dead on the beach, and the fleet commander had made a small camp where hundreds of men were sitting around, doing nothing at all. Thomas swallowed hard when he saw the shade of red that covered Cortés's face.

"I told you to use utmost care in your dealings with these people!" Cortés growled at his commander (and anyone else in the vicinity). "We need supplies here! Not enemies! You are a fool!" he spat as he marched toward the forest, Thomas following closely behind. "You—come with us," Cortés said to the translator they brought with them from Cuba. He was not fluent in the Mayan tongue, but he had spoken with enough of them to be able to decipher a few basic words. "No one else follows us!" Cortés yelled without a backward glance.

Thomas had not heard Cortés so angry before, and he was happy to see the idiotic commander and crew receive a tongue lashing. Before the journey began, Thomas had tried to convince Cortés to send him with the lead ship in order to keep an eye on the crew. But Cortés placed too much faith in his fleet's commander—a faith that was now lost.

"I had no idea that I would receive a trusted adviser when I contracted your services. You're more than a bodyguard, Thomas. I hope you understand the gratitude I have for your input and help," Cortés said as they continued walking inland.

Thomas didn't know how to respond. He had been forced to take the contract under the impression that he would be doing mercenary work. He had dreaded the job all the way from Italy to Cuba. But after only a few months of carrying out his work, he realized he was actually enjoying the change.

"It has been a pleasure to work for you. I haven't done this kind of work before, but I have quite enjoyed my time here," Thomas admitted.

After a ten-minute walk, Thomas began seeing signs of civilization. He could hear leaves rustle in the forest as they walked—a sign that they were being followed and watched. Thomas could feel the hidden eyes appraising their movements. The interpreter followed closely behind Thomas but didn't seem to fear the locals (which put Thomas at ease). A few small huts made of sticks lined the path on their right and left. As the huts grew more numerous, the construction of the homes was more sturdy. Thomas was intrigued by the layout of the village.

A few seconds later, a large group of men came out and blocked the path. Cortés braced for an attack, but Thomas could see that the men were more curious than hostile about being approached by only three men.

Thomas appraised the men as they took their time drawing nearer. Every man in sight was tiny and deeply tanned in comparison to Thomas and Cortés. They were adorned in gold jewelry—with smooth, green stones affixed to many of the bracelets and necklaces. Two of the men's teeth had been filed into points, the gaps somehow filled with the same green stones. Another man had a completely flattened forehead—it was unfathomable to Thomas how it could have grown that way naturally. Several onlookers had horribly crossed eyes, and Thomas assumed the problem with sight was a widespread problem throughout this tribe. He realized the men were waiting for Thomas or Cortés to make the first move.

"Give them a gift," he whispered to Cortés.

The sound of Thomas's voice made Cortés jump a little, but he recovered quickly and removed a leather pouch full of colorful beads. Cortés had planned extensively for creating positive relations with the natives. He brought beads, ribbons, and buttons in bright colors to offer to each new tribe in exchange for food, supplies, and peaceful alliance. Cortés bowed as he held the pouch out toward the natives. The leader of the group stepped forward and cautiously took the pouch from Cortés's hand. He stepped back to his group and opened it, allowing each man to look at the contents. Words and nods were exchanged, which put Cortés at ease. The men still eyed Thomas with concern, and he knew he would need to assuage the natives' fears as well. He stepped forward, knelt on the ground, and offered up one of his knives. He always kept at least four knives on his person, and two of them were sentimental (he wasn't willing to part with the knife his father had given him as a child or the knife he stole off the body of the Lombard King he had killed in the 700's). The leader took the offering and smiled in return. Thomas and Cortés heaved simultaneous sighs of relief as the men began talking cheerfully and beckoning them to follow the natives into their village.

Men and women came pouring out of the stone homes with baskets of goods. Cortés's crew would have plenty of supplies when they left the island.

The leader of the village spoke with the interpreter about the goods that would be available for exchange. After only a moment, Thomas heard the interpreter's tone change—he wasn't sure whether it was surprise or panic, so he grabbed the knife on his side in case there was trouble.

"I think he says there is another like you here. Just up this path—he lives with a neighboring group of Mayans," the man said, astonished.

Cortés was thrilled that another Spaniard might be joining his crew—though they weren't exactly sure if the man was a prisoner or a guest.

"Can he join us?" Cortés asked.

"I do not know. It doesn't sound like the situation is hostile, but I don't understand these particular words," the man admitted.

Three hours later, Cortés gathered a crew of men from the beach to bring trading supplies to the Mayan village. They now had even more fresh fruits and vegetables for their journey, as well as extra cloth that several of the native women gave as gifts to the Spaniards. Cortés made the fleet's commander kneel before the Mayan leader and offer up several gifts—including the commander's own sword. After Cortés gave the commander several lashes with a switch, the natives appeared satisfied and at ease—even offering an invitation to the entire crew to stay in the village for a feast that evening.

The men were excited to feast and drink with the natives, and by the second hour of the gathering, only Thomas remained sober.

"They are bringing the Spaniard now," the interpreter told Thomas with a smile. He spun around to witness a tall, dark-haired man in Mayan clothing approaching the camp with a look of relief plastered on his face. He looked around for a moment before his eyes met with Thomas's. He took off at a run—Thomas was unsure of how to react—and when he reached Thomas, he threw his arms around Thomas's neck and began weeping.

"Are you Spaniards? Please! Tell me you are Spaniards!" the man choked out between sobs.

"These men are," Thomas said as he pointed to the rest of the crew. "But I am Italian."

"It does not matter! You can take me home! My family thinks I'm dead—you have no idea how it feels to live with that kind of knowledge. Completely detached from everyone and everything I know, believing I will be separated from my loved ones forever. My ship wrecked years ago—only myself and one other man survived. But he's a part of a Mayan tribe now and has no wish to return home."

Thomas was trying to process the onslaught of information the man was delivering. He spoke so quickly—so desperately—that Thomas's mind had to catch up during the short pauses the man took to breathe.

"What is your name, sir?" Thomas asked during one of the pauses.

"Gerónimo. Gerónimo de Aguilar. And I have never been happier than I am in this moment."

"Can you speak the language of the natives?" Thomas asked, excited about the prospect of what Gerónimo could provide for Cortés's mission.

"Fluently. I've lived amongst them for these past eight years. At first, they kept me as a prisoner, but once they realized I was a hard worker, they let me partake in daily life. I live in a hut on the outskirts of a nearby city. When a messenger from this village arrived with news of more white men, I took off at a run. I do not think anyone would dare stop me from joining your expedition," Gerónimo said with a wide smile, tears still streaming down his face.

Thomas smiled back at Gerónimo to reassure him.

"Do you know of any other natives or Spaniards that might want to join our expedition?" Thomas asked.

"I don't often leave my village. But I will ask the people here if there is anyone else," Gerónimo promised.

After a few more hours of feasting and heavy drinking, Cortés and most of his crew were passed out on the ground. The natives were still dancing and laughing, enjoying the festivities. Thomas watched Gerónimo talk with each of the leaders and several of the villagers throughout the night. When he finally returned to Thomas, his face was pale.

"What?" Thomas asked carefully. "What has happened?"

"They want me to tell you a story of … I don't know exactly how to translate the word. There are tales of a being that lives across the island. The literal translation is white, woman. They use a word that means 'apparition,'" Gerónimo whispered, his face still pale. "They think you are going to steal it from the island, and I guess some of them want the thing removed. But I would advise you to leave the apparition alone. It is unholy, and the people of the village where the entity resides regard it as a deity."

"I don't understand why this scares you. Ghosts are not real. Certainly there is nothing to fear," Thomas said, trying to reassure Gerónimo.

"They are real on this island. Before living here, I would have agreed with you. But now I have seen and heard things that are inexplicable," Gerónimo said urgently.

Thomas decided to let the matter rest for the evening. He would relay the story to Cortés in the morning, and together they would decide how to proceed. But for the rest of the night, no matter how much fun Gerónimo seemed to be having, a haunted look of fear cloaked his face.

THIRTY-SIX

CATERINA COULD TELL something was happening in the village. The last time the tribe was this agitated, a neighboring tribe attacked within a fortnight. She did her best to stay out of everyone's view—she had long since realized that the villagers seemed to blame her for their misfortunes. They were not unkind in any way, but the unhappy glances that she caught from one person or another were more than enough evidence of the blame that was placed on her proximity to the village.

They believed she was a creature of evil. And Caterina thought she might agree. Her longevity was born from something destructive and horrible ... did that make her destructive and horrible as well? No matter how many times she thought about it, she couldn't find a definitive answer.

One of the village leaders rushed to her hut the next morning.

"Ish-chel!" the man yelled as Caterina peeked outside to see what was the matter.

"You must stay hidden! There are men on the island that will try to steal you! The other tribes want to show the men where you live, but our leaders will protect you. Do not unleash your wrath upon the village. Stay here. We will bring you anything you need, but please stay hidden," the man whispered in his native tongue. He set a basket full of food on the ground, and he was gone as quickly as he arrived. Though she could not speak the language fluently, she had learned enough of it to understand the gist of any conversation. The man's words lingered heavily in the air. Caterina struggled to find a full breath, and her hands could not stop shaking.

You will be all right, she told herself. *Do as he said and everything will be fine.* But even as she told herself those words, she knew they were hollow. Her life was once again in danger.

Thirty-Seven

THOMAS RELAYED the events of the previous evening to Cortés as soon as he awoke the next afternoon. Cortés was more cheery than Thomas expected, considering the hangover his employer must have been dealing with. But Cortés —in a jubilant state—followed Thomas to the beach where Gerónimo lay sleeping.

"Welcome to the crew!" Cortés said loudly to wake Gerónimo, and anyone sleeping nearby, with a start.

Gerónimo jumped up and thanked Cortés for the kind welcome. Thomas could tell that Gerónimo was so grateful to be rescued from the island, he would happily take on even the most menial of tasks for Cortés. Fortunately for Gerónimo, he was invaluable as an interpreter and would likely spend all his time with Thomas and Cortés. After a brief conversation, Cortés and Thomas headed back to Cortés's tent so they could discuss the rest of the previous evening's events.

"There was one more matter," Thomas said hesitantly. Sailors were notorious for believing folklore, and Thomas worried that the presence of an apparition on the island would cause Cortés to push for a hasty exodus from Cozumel.

"Out with it, Thomas. I'm not inclined to make guesses at what you might say," Cortés joked.

"The people spoke of an apparition," Thomas said as he watched Cortés carefully. "A white female apparition."

"Really?" Cortés asked, his interest understandably piqued. "What did they say?" he wanted to know more.

"Half of the villagers want us to take it away, the other half seem more interested in worshiping the ghost like a deity," Thomas answered. He didn't know whether or not he wanted to see the apparition, but he was intrigued by the idea of trying to find it.

"I wonder if they're trying to scare us away. Perhaps they created the story to keep us from wandering around the island," Cortés said in a worried tone.

"It didn't seem that way," Thomas offered, but Cortés, lost in his own thoughts, didn't hear a word.

"But if that's the case, they may have something to hide," Cortés whispered with a nervous edge to his tone. "I want you to go out today—take whichever of the crew you need. I want to know if they're hiding something … and I feel certain you're the only one competent enough to find anything that might be well-hidden," Cortés said with a smile. "If there is an apparition, don't let it suck out your soul," he said with a playful gleam in his eye.

Thomas noted that Cortés was in an uncharacteristically good mood. Perhaps he should secure more alcohol to replicate the person Cortés became after a night of heavy drinking. Thomas let out a chuckle and said "good day" to Cortés.

Thomas spoke with Gerónimo at length to help him chart a course to the place where this "apparition" was supposed to live. He didn't want to take any of the crew along—he was capable of handling whatever was thrown at him, and he would be much happier without needing to look after someone else during the outing.

He set off to the place where the apparition supposedly resided and marked his path along the way so he could easily find his way back. The trip would take him at least two days—one day to travel to the village and another to search for the apparition and return to Cortés. He packed a bag filled with enough food for three days, and as he walked, he hoped he would not need more. The path between the villages was barely visible during most of the trip, and completely unmarked during the rest. At some points, the foliage was too dense for Thomas to find the sun through the trees. He worried he might have made a mistake in taking the trip alone, but he knew he could find his way back to his own camp if he became too lost.

After eight hours of trudging through the thick forest, he finally saw signs of a village. He walked carefully, searching for any indication of hostility from the natives watching him, but they were only curious. When he reached the borders of the village, he was met by several leaders—just as he had been met at the other village. He came prepared with gifts of colorful beads and leather pouches. He knelt and held them out to the leader—who was appeased by the gifts—and was welcomed into their village.

"Tantun?" Thomas asked as he motioned around at the village. He hoped he was in the right village, but his journey was more confusing than he had accounted for. When the leaders began nodding their heads and repeating "Tantun," Thomas knew he had found what he was looking for.

The men took Thomas on a tour of their village, speaking as if he could understand them, though he had no idea what they were saying. He kept a lookout for any signs of hostility or holy ritual (it had crossed his mind more than once that the natives might try to use him as a sacrifice to their deity), but just as he suspected, he found none. There were no dead carcasses lying in odd places, no strange symbols drawn in the dirt, nothing that seemed out of place compared to the rest of the village. But every time he thought he might ask about the woman—Gerónimo had taught him the word the natives used for her —a little warning in the back of his head told him it wasn't a good idea. He noticed that every movement, every glance, was being appraised by the villagers. He would not easily sneak away to search for the 'ghost'.

By the end of the evening, Thomas had seen the entire village, eaten a large meal, and been offered use of a small hut made of sticks on the outskirts of Tantun. He knew there would be men placed outside his hut during the night, but his senses were strong enough that he could hear when they were near or far. *I must wait until they leave for a short moment. I'm certain I can find evidence of this "ghost" if I'm able to search for it unwatched,* he decided.

He slept for a few short hours before awakening to the sound of footsteps leaving his hut. He stood from the mat where he had been sleeping and stretched out as quietly as he could. One peek outside the door told him there was no one watching the hut. They had waited until they were sure he was asleep before leaving his hut unattended.

Thomas left his bag of provisions next to his bed—he planned to come back as soon as he found evidence (or a lack thereof) of the "ghost". He felt foolish for even playing along with this ghost-hunt. He rolled his eyes as he walked out of the village in the opposite direction from whence he came. Once he was hidden in the forest just south of the village, he closed his eyes and listened closely. He heard the sounds of animals moving about. A stream flowed swiftly nearby. And something made a sound that sent the image of a ghost moaning in its deathly agony straight into his mind. Thomas felt a strange and foreign sense of fear run up his spine. A stab of doubt pierce his mind.

He pulled a knife from his side holster and began walking as quietly as possible toward the place where he thought the moan originated. He walked for some time and stopped once again to listen to his surroundings. He was much closer to the stream now, and it took nearly five minutes of complete silence for him to hear another sound from the "ghost".

Damn. I've passed by the sound, he scolded himself. *Or maybe there really is a ghost, and it has moved. Why on earth do you suddenly believe these stories? Calm down,* he told himself as he moved toward the strange noises once more.

He stopped every minute or so to listen for the ghost, and he found himself having trouble moving through the dense forest quietly. He often stepped on twigs and leaves that would crack and crinkle beneath his feet, and he worried he would be caught by the natives before he found the origin of the sounds he was searching for.

Suddenly, his foot fell on a worn path—a narrow, well-hidden path, but a path nonetheless. The moon shone just brightly enough through the trees that he could see the path as it twisted deeper into the woods. He crept at a leaden pace, checking for signs of danger each step of the way. After ten minutes on the winding path, a stone building came into view. The structure resembled the stone dwellings of the leaders' homes in the village, but it was so secluded in the woods, it was unlikely anyone would stumble across it unless they knew where it was.

How odd, Thomas mused. He looked around the outside of the home—it was definitely lived in. There were freshly-washed clay pots outside on a piece of cloth. There were clothes hung on the low branches of the surrounding trees. And a basket of fresh fruits and vegetables was carefully placed on the path about six feet away from the only entry into the home. A piece of cloth hung in the doorway to prevent the wind from sweeping through the structure. There were no windows on the front or sides of the home, and he knew it would be impossible to silently make his way around the back to check for other openings. Thomas wondered if the basket was an offering *to* the ghost from the person who lived in the home, or if the offering was from the natives for the ghost who lived within it. *I've never heard of a ghost living in a home. Maybe this is a hut for villagers who are sick? That would explain why the basket is placed far from the doorway,* he mused.

He crouched behind a small grouping of trees several paces from the dwelling, well-hidden from anyone who might come up the path or anyone inside who might peek out. He watched for hours, but no one came and no one left. The ghostly sounds from earlier were absent in a way that made Thomas think he might have dreamed them.

Finally, curiosity got the best of him. He decided to at least peek inside to know for sure if someone was there or if he had hallucinated the moaning.

He crept to the doorway and stopped for several minutes, listening for any sign that someone might be inside. He had trained his senses over the past centuries to be able to detect movement, breathing, and usually the number of persons inside a home, just by listening from the outside. The fact that the door was nothing more than a piece of cloth made it even easier for him to hear inside. After taking extra caution outside the entry, he could tell the inside of the home was vacant.

He gently pushed aside the cloth, still taking care to move quietly. He poked his head inside the dark room, only to realize he could barely see a thing. The moonlight was hardly bright enough to light his path under the thick trees … it could not find its way through the small doorway, and he could now see there were no windows on the back of the dwelling for light to enter. He stopped moving and held his breath once more—he heard nothing for a full minute (except the beating of his own heart). But when he finally heard a noise, it came from behind him. Something crashed over the back of his skull, and his consciousness was lost.

THIRTY-EIGHT

CATERINA'S HEART RACED as she looked down at the crumpled body on the ground. She wished she could see who this intruder was, but he was most certainly *not* a Mayan villager. The leaders had warned her that men were coming to take her away. She would not stand by while abductors came to steal her in the night.

Caterina gathered her strength and pulled him all the way into her home. Rolling him onto his stomach, she bound his hands behind his back with several strips of torn fabric. Then, she did the same to his legs and ankles. She thought she might have gone a little overboard with securing him but didn't want him to somehow slip away under the cover of darkness.

She was overwhelmed with gratefulness for the dream that woke her from slumber. A great predator had been pacing in the forest outside her home, just waiting for her to step outside so it could pounce. She had awakened with a groan but heard the tell-tale signs of a visitor as soon as she snapped to consciousness. *This man must be the predator from my dream,* she thought. *God must have given it to me so I would wake and be ready for his attack! Thank you, Lord!*

The rest of the night she sat up against the opposite wall, keeping watch over the intruder. Even though it was too dark to see him clearly, she pictured him looking grotesque and twisted—imagining he was the evilest man in the world.

When sunlight hit her face, she realized she had faded into sleep after all. She rubbed her eyes and yawned, but soon the memories of what had happened the night before rushed back to her. Her eyes shot open and her mind sprung awake as she looked across the room for her intruder.

No one was there. There were no signs of the broken pot, no remnants of the cloth that tied his hands, no marks on the ground where she dragged him from the doorway to the opposite wall.

Was it all a dream? she wondered. *Surely not! If it was a dream, I would still be asleep on my mat. I'm sitting where I sat after I bound his hands. How could anyone have broken free?*

She stood, feeling stiff after spending the night sitting up against the stone wall. She paced back and forth, worried the whole incident was a frightfully realistic dream. Caterina walked over to her food preparation area and sat down on the mat where she readied her meals and mixed her paints. She turned the situation over again and again in her head. *It definitely happened. Right? Yes. It happened,* she decided, gripping a knife in each hand (though she didn't remember pulling them from her holster). Her heart was pounding. She feared that she was no longer safe in her home, but if he hadn't killed her the night before while she slept, maybe he wasn't the evil creature she feared he might be. She heard footsteps on the ground outside and mentally prepared herself for another encounter with the stranger.

Thomas had awoken at dawn with a terrible headache. He couldn't believe someone had been able to surprise him with such a vicious attack, but he was quite curious to see who had been capable of such a thing.

He tried to move and found that his hands and feet were bound. *Oh, how perfect,* he thought humorlessly. Fortunately, the knife he always kept secured to his back was still there. He reached it without struggling too much and easily cut the bindings from his hands. Once his hands were free, he cut the bindings from his legs as well.

He looked up and saw that someone was sitting across from him. His heart stopped for a short moment until he realized the person was in a deep sleep—and that the person was a white female.

This is her! I've found the ghost! But she isn't a ghost at all. He crept closer to examine the woman. She held a knife firmly in her right hand—a knife that was clearly European-made. Her long brownish-red hair hung in tight curls all around her head, sticking out in several different directions. Her clothing was Mayan, but her skin was fair like an Italian. She wore a plain gold ring on her left hand—which was discolored by various shades of reds, greens, and yellows. *Strange,* Thomas thought as he stood over the woman.

He didn't quite understand what came over him, but the moment he was finished appraising her, he decided he hated the woman. If she had been prettier in looks, he might have forgiven her attack more easily. But as it stood, she was not. Once his feet had found the narrow path, he had gone to great lengths to approach the dwelling silently—there was no explanation for the woman expecting him other than ... *maybe she is a ghost.* No mortal had ever bested him, and only his most skilled brothers had been able to scare him—with great planning. He turned to look around the room—which was now filling with the dim light of dawn. He scanned the room for any signs that the woman might be unearthly, but he found no evidence to support the theory.

There was a mat in the corner that obviously served as her bedding—complete with leaves for cushioned padding underneath. Another mat in the opposite corner served as her area for preparing food ... and something else. He looked around the home and noticed that every inch of the walls were covered in paintings of vineyards and villas and horses and sunsets. They were quite good, though a little rough because of the porous surface of the stone. This woman had mixed her own paints and made her own paintbrushes to create this work of art.

This much work must have taken years. How could one so young do so much with this level of skill? The answer eluded him, and he decided he would stick around to ask her when she awoke. He gathered the fabric he cut from his hands and legs and picked up the shattered pieces of the pot that the woman had broken over his head in order to dispose of them outside. He wanted to eat some of the fresh fruits and vegetables from the basket outside so he would be at full strength when the woman finally woke up. He listened at the door to make sure no one was outside the hut before he exited, and only when he was certain he was alone did he walk out into the soft light of dawn.

The forest was magnificent in the morning sun. He stretched to loosen some of the stiffness which had developed from sleeping on his stomach with his arms bound behind him. He rubbed the back of his head and found that blood had dried into his hair where the pot shattered over him. He wished, rather than believed, that his headache would go away soon, but he didn't want it to sully the morning in this wild place.

The animals around him chatted away in the forest—birds sang joyful songs, bugs rushed about, and small animals chased each other through the leaves and into the canopy above. Thomas loved this untouched land. He loved that the Mayans lived *within* the natural setting rather than forcing nature to conform to their existence. *This is how it should be,* he decided as he looked at how the stone hut blended into its surroundings. He was not surprised that he had nearly missed it the night before—it would be difficult for someone to find the hut in bright daylight.

He ate a few bites of an unfamiliar fruit, but worried if any might be poisonous when raw—for though drinking or eating poison did not kill him or his family, it still caused them intense pain. He placed it back in the basket and crept through the dirt that covered the small clearing in front of the home. He didn't want to risk a repeat of the night before. He leaned his back against the front wall of the home, listening inside. He heard nothing but the bustling sounds of the creatures in the forest around him and wanted to yell for the creatures to be quiet. He wished he could look through a window to make sure the woman was still sleeping on the floor, but the windowless dwelling worked in the woman's favor. He wasn't sure how to proceed—he was unwilling to risk his skull being assaulted by another pot, but he desperately wanted to question the woman about her presence on the island.

He heard a noise right next to his head and he slowly turned to look toward the curtain. His eyes registered that there was an arm sticking out from the doorway, and less than a second later, he felt the gentle pressure of a blade against his throat. He flattened his body as closely to the wall as he could, and his eyes never left the doorway. The woman crept slowly from the opening, her hand holding the knife motionless against his neck while she moved. Her right hand also wielded a blade that she held at her shoulder's height (directly in line with his heart), ready to use at a moment's notice. She had pulled her unruly curls into a tie at the nape of her neck, and the look of ferocity on her face worried Thomas. *Surely the woman will not kill me without first asking why I am here,* he hoped. He remained silent, unwilling to give her knife any reason to score his skin. Wordlessly, she motioned for him to turn around—which he rapidly obeyed. But in the tensity of the moment, he turned too quickly, and the hilt of the woman's knife rendered him unconscious once more.

His eyes opened slowly. He registered that his hands and feet were once again tied. He reached for his knife, but this time it was nowhere to be found. Annoyance overtook his mind. Twice he had been bested by a mortal—a female mortal, no less. His pride was more than a little injured, and he *needed* to understand how this woman had managed to get the upper hand on him. He wiggled around until he was lying on his side, and he looked up into the face of the woman. *Maybe she is a ghost!* his mind screamed. That would explain how she had bested him. But in all the lore about ghosts, none of them required food to live—and she was currently chewing on a piece of fruit. He used the wall to work his way into a sitting position as the woman watched him with distrusting eyes. After quite a struggle, he was finally able to look directly into the eyes of the woman sitting in front of him.

"Who are you?" he asked quietly in Spanish. He could feel the blood dripping down the back of his head, traveling all the way down his spine. *I'm losing too much blood. This wound needs to be bandaged—soon,* he realized. The woman did not respond to his question. She just stared at him with an angry glare affixed to her face.

"Who are you?" he asked again, this time in Italian. Her face registered excitement as she squatted down to look at him more directly. She still didn't speak, and Thomas could feel annoyance rising inside his chest. "You do not have to answer me, but I am losing too much blood from the back of my head. I fear I might bleed to death unless it is bandaged," he said pleadingly. He was having trouble maintaining cordiality.

She jumped up with determination in her eyes and grabbed a few strips of the fabric she had used to bind his legs the night before. Apparently she had gone outside during his period of unconsciousness to see what damage he had done. She silently bent down and pulled his head toward her in order to see the wound. He heard her hiss through her teeth when she saw the cut, and Thomas hoped she wouldn't faint at the sight of blood. She rubbed a salve on the wound before covering it with a piece of cloth and wrapping another around his head a few times to hold it in place. She was so gentle and her hands so careful, he barely felt a thing. When she finished, she moved away from him and sat back down on the ground to more easily look directly at him.

"Thank you," he said in Italian again.

"You're welcome," she replied softly (also in Italian). Her voice was sweet and quiet—like music—but he didn't let himself enjoy the sound. He looked over her features in the light of day. She was not pretty by any means, but there was somehow an odd attractiveness about her. Her skin was perfectly creamy. Her cheeks were a beautiful shade of pink. Her hair—which had been brushed since he saw it in its disheveled state while she slept—was still wild as it framed her round face. Her amber eyes were an interesting shape. And when she moved, she carried herself with the grace of nobility, which Thomas found confusing against the backdrop of the wilderness. She was perfectly annoying. Under different circumstances, Thomas might have found her intriguing, but after the earlier bludgeoning to his head, *everything* about her was aggravating.

"If you untie me, I will leave you in peace and never come back," he said, frustrated that he had to plead to be cut free. He knew this was his fault—he was the one who had twice invaded *her* home. He couldn't tell if his aggravation was truly aimed toward the woman or if he was so upset with himself for being caught unawares that he was projecting his frustration on anyone nearby. He knew he was often guilty of taking out his frustrations with his father on his brothers. *This is different*, he told himself angrily. *She beat you over the head twice—knocking you unconscious. You have every right to despise her.*

"I don't believe you," she said, still glaring.

Thomas rammed the back of his head against the wall in frustration, then immediately regretted the lapse in judgment as a searing pain shot through his entire body. He had hit the wound directly and now felt dizzy from the impact.

"You can see I meant you no harm. I didn't hit *you* over the head or tie *you* up or try to take advantage of you. I was bringing in the basket of fruit from outside when you hit me earlier. Surely you can see the difference between a threat and a visitor," he said through gritted teeth.

"Why are you here?" she demanded with a crinkled forehead.

"I was exploring the woods, and I happened upon this place. I am a guest at the village, and I wanted to take a look around without anyone accompanying me," he lied.

"You're a terrible liar," she said as she took another piece of fruit from the basket next to her and started eating it.

Thomas glared at the floor of the home. *Why are you even here?* He asked himself. *You should have left this morning when you cut yourself free. What compelled you to stay?* He had no answer.

"If I was a native female and you stuck your head in my home, the men would cut it from your body. You were looking for someone—or something. And you won't convince me otherwise," she said with a knowing look that frustrated him even more.

"How did you come to this place?" he asked, hoping the change in conversation might ease his strain.

"I don't want to tell you. And even if I did, you would not believe my story," she said with a smirk.

Damn it! Why could she not be more accommodating? he thought as he narrowed his eyes at the woman.

"And you? Where did you come from?" she asked with a strangely hopeful expression.

"Cuba," he answered shortly.

"I don't know what that is," she replied quickly. "Where did you really come from?"

He didn't know why he felt compelled to give her a longer explanation, but he continued, "Before setting sail from Cuba, I came from Italy … just outside Florence."

The woman's eyes lit up. *She must also be from Florence. How strange! She doesn't look Florentine.*

"Are you from Florence?" he asked, upset that he was continuing the conversation at all. His deepest wish was to leave the woman behind and tell Cortés there was nothing of interest in Tantun.

"Florence and Milan. I was born in Milan, but I spent much of my life in Florence," she answered carefully.

Much of her life? Surely this woman is not older than twenty-five. And by the sheer scale of these paintings, she has been here for at least five years.

"What is your name?" she asked.

"Thomas." he replied, refusing to ask hers.

"Mine is Caterina," she offered after a short pause.

"Well, Caterina," he began, "I *swear* to you I am simply passing through this village and would love nothing more than to journey back to my shipmates on the north side of the island. If you'll cut off these ties and return my weapons, I'll be on my way."

A look of disappointment and wariness washed over the woman.

"But you haven't eaten," she said softly. "Surely you're hungry."

He was hungry. His stomach was screaming for nourishment.

"How about this—if you agree to stay for a meal *and* answer my questions, I'll cut you free afterward. I long to hear news from Italy. Please," she begged with a crazed look of desperation in her eyes.

He heaved a sigh, knowing his next words would give the woman too much enjoyment.

"Why not. I'll stay for a meal."

THIRTY-NINE

THE CONVERSATION with Thomas came more easily than Caterina had expected. Her Italian was a little rusty after twenty-six years of having no one to converse with. While she painted each day she "spoke" with Leonardo, imagining his critiques and jokes as he would have said them to her long ago. But without anyone *real* to speak with, her mastery of the Italian language had dwindled. After only an hour of conversation with Thomas, she felt as if she had fallen back into the familiarity of her native tongue.

She noted that Thomas was careful about what kind of questions he asked her, and she was grateful for his discretion. She also noticed that he had to think through his words before he spoke them. At times, she got the distinct feeling that she was an irritation and that he wished he could be out of her sight. Of course, she *had* hit him over the head and knocked him out ... twice. And he was still tied up, unable to eat without her assistance. So maybe irritation was a natural response. But it was *he* who had invaded *her* home. She knew she should be more upset, but having him to talk to was bringing her more happiness than she could remember having since she left her home. Occasionally he would show genuine interest in a topic and ask questions that required lengthy answers. She was confused by his mood swings, yet the joy she felt in conversing with a real person trumped her distaste for his odd personality.

She told him about the way she lived in Tantun, how she made her paints, and what her normal diet consisted of. When he asked how she had learned to paint, she told him that her mother and uncle had been accomplished painters and left it at that. He seemed upset when she revealed that she could not speak the natives' language, but he didn't give a reason for his dissatisfaction.

She tried to be reserved with the number of questions she asked, but her curiosity was difficult to curtail. She wanted to know what was happening in

Italy politically, religiously, and socially. She wanted to know about Cuba—a land of which she had never before heard. She wanted to know about the expedition of which Thomas was a crew member. She wanted to know how he came to join the crew. He glossed over the last question, but his answers to her other queries were enough to quell her curiosities for the time being.

After a few short hours, he insisted on returning to the village.

"I'm sure they're suspicious of my disappearance in the night. There's no way for me to communicate with them, but I hope leaving more gifts will put them at ease," Thomas chuckled.

"Will you come back?" Caterina asked sorrowfully. She feared that she might not speak with another Italian again, and it was such a comfort during the short time she had spent with him that she wasn't sure she could handle the emotional toll of losing her new Italian 'friend'—though that probably wasn't the right word for their connection.

Thomas's expression seemed conflicted. She could tell he didn't *want* to return, but she hoped he would be willing to oblige her.

"It is possible," he finally answered with an annoyed look in his eyes. She cut the ropes from his hands and feet, and he stayed quiet as he looked toward the doorway.

She felt relief wash over her at the possibility of another visit, and a smile that she could not contain took over her lips. She ran to the corner of the room where she had stashed his knives. When she returned, she held out all three of the weapons she had removed from his body after she knocked him out the second time.

"I can't believe I didn't take your knives last night. It was foolish to forget." She mumbled "they would be disappointed" as she thought about the chagrin her brothers would feel if they knew what had transpired the night before.

Thomas took the knives and removed the bloodied bandage from his head, handing it back to her with a grunted "thank you". The dark-haired, green-eyed man wanted nothing to do with her, yet there was something about him that felt deeply familiar. She felt as if he was a kindred spirit, and she longed to understand from whence those feelings came.

I cannot believe I said I might return. I should not have given her hope. She's obviously hiding something—a young Italian woman alone in the forest of a distant island is almost impossible to grasp. How did she come to this place? She is not to be trusted. Good God! I cannot believe she bested me twice! A female. If Sergius was here, he would tell me to temper my anger. And Samuel would no doubt tell me that if I would just bed her I would not hate her so much. Thomas laughed as he pictured how the conversation would unfold, then sighed as his thoughts drifted back to the present. He shuddered at the mere idea of bedding Caterina. There was nothing about her that appealed to him. She was plain and strange and … well, he thought she might be crazy. She had been far too happy to have a complete stranger invade her home.

He looked up through the trees to find the sun high in the sky—it was barely midday, and he had spent too much time with the mysterious woman.

As soon as he approached the village, he was met by several of the tribe's men who barked words at him which he could not understand. He pointed to his wounds and then at the woods. They looked at his head, examined his cuts, and led him to a hut where a healer sewed his scalp shut with thread and rubbed a salve over the sewed wound.

He spent the remainder of the day under the watchful eye of two terrifying armed guards who did not look away from him for a moment. He didn't care, though. He was enjoying watching the natives live life. It was such a pleasure to witness a tribe such as this in its daily routine. The men left with empty pots and baskets and returned hours later with their bounty of fruits, herbs and water. The women weaved clothes with painstakingly detailed effort, and the finished products were vibrant and beautiful. Children tossed rocks to each other and played games with which Thomas was unfamiliar. Everyone sang throughout the day, and Thomas was awed by the simplicity of their lives. At the end of the night, he was happy his thoughts had not drifted back to Caterina ... until he was trying to fall asleep.

I should return to Cortés and tell him the "ghost" is an insane Italian woman. She is useless to our journey since she has little understanding of the local language. I could be done with this, and we would be on our way. But I told her I might come back. WHY? Why did I have to give her any hope at all? I am not a liar. But I have no wish to see her again. He drifted off to sleep with the argument still raging in his head.

The next morning when he awoke, he tried (without luck) to explain that he had to leave. He took his bag, and began to walk in the direction of the camp where Cortés was awaiting word of his discoveries. The two guards followed him for some time before coming to a halt and watching him disappear into the forest. After he knew he was out of their sight, he stopped walking and turned the matter over in his mind. He was not being followed. He could return to his camp and tell Cortés that the "ghost" was no ghost at all. He could tell them that the woman was crazy, that she was under the protection of the natives, and that they should leave her alone and continue on their journey as soon as possible. But a voice in his head—that sounded eerily similar to Caterina's—told him he should stop deliberating and return to her home. He groaned, turned toward Caterina's dwelling, and trekked through the woods in order to reach it undetected.

He approached slowly, picking his feet up as he tiptoed down the hidden path toward her home. As he walked, he devised a plan of attack to surprise Caterina (and regain a little of his pride). He found a section of a large branch lying on the ground and picked it up. He readied himself, taking long, quiet breaths, and heaved the branch through the doorway, running quickly to follow it into the home. Caterina was waiting for him with a clay bowl full of fresh fruits and vegetables. She was smiling up at him expectantly as if she had known he was coming all along.

"Was that necessary?" she asked with a chuckle.

"How do you do that?" he demanded with furrowed brows, hoping she would answer truthfully.

"I have more keen senses than most. I can hear if someone is approaching with shoes on or with bare feet, if they are male or female, adult or child. I think I was a bit paranoid in the beginning, but I can usually hear someone coming from a great distance. I heard you pick up that branch," she answered with the hint of a smirk on her face.

He walked inside the hut, put his things in a corner, and sat down against the front wall of the home. Caterina brought a bowl of food to him, and he began to try each different item. These foods were wholly unfamiliar to him, and he enjoyed tasting the new flavors.

"The soft green one is my favorite—I call it 'yax', since that is the natives' word for 'green'. But the nuts and the round yellow fruits are wonderful too," she told him as she sat down against the opposite wall and ate from her own bowl.

"Do you not have names for the yellow fruit or nuts?" he asked.

"No. I don't know what they're called, and I don't know the natives' words for yellow or brown," she admitted.

The conversation came to a halt, and they ate in silence for a few minutes. But once Thomas had tried a bite of every different food, Caterina was eager to hear how he liked them.

"The nuts are delicious. And I like how creamy the yax is. The yellow one would make an excellent sauce, I think," Thomas answered as he began thinking of ways he could use the fruit in his cooking. Caterina seemed pleased that he was enjoying the food, and she smiled as they continued to eat.

Thomas didn't like the idea of spending more time with Caterina. The more he got to know her, the less insane she seemed. Her presence on this island was a puzzle he could not piece together.

If she isn't willing to tell me how she came here, maybe she'll tell me more about her home, Thomas thought in the silence of the room.

"What do you miss the most about your home?" he asked, immediately wishing he had not opened his mouth at all.

"Everything," she sighed. She stared down at her lap for a moment, her eyes glazing over. "I miss riding my horse with my mother. I miss painting with my friend. I miss playing with my nieces and nephews and talking with my sisters-in-law. I miss the way my brothers were over-protective of me, and how even after I was an adult, they still treated me like a child. I never imagined I could think fondly of that," she said wistfully. "I miss ... family."

Thomas could hear the emotion in her voice, and he didn't want to push her further. He puzzled over her statement about her brothers being over-protective. *If they were over-protective, how on earth did she end up here? Perhaps she ran away? But she said "even after I was an adult" ... that doesn't make sense. Maybe she journeyed here with a lover.* His mind raced with unanswered questions, but he stayed quiet.

"I have three older brothers—all of them married," she said, unprompted. "My family are the best kind of people—selfless, caring, thoughtful, and loving." She sighed again, and he could tell that this part of their conversation had come to an end.

"What is your favorite subject to paint?" he asked.

"Landscapes," she answered without hesitation. "Especially during sunrise and sunset. It's very challenging to capture the light correctly, because the colors of the sky change by the minute. At times, it took me a month to paint one sky. I would sit and wait until the sun was right where I wanted it, then I would paint furiously during that short period. One perfect sunset hangs in my parents' home. None of the others were good enough ... in my opinion."

Thomas couldn't help but smile at her answer. Her passion for painting was obvious. Caterina looked up at Thomas with a conflicted look and opened her mouth several times before she finally spoke.

"Do you have a wife?" she asked carefully.

"Not anymore," he said, as the memories of his wife crept back into his mind. "She died years ago. I have no children and haven't met another woman that I've found interesting enough to wed," he added.

She looked at him for a moment with an unreadable expression, and he immediately felt uncomfortable. That, combined with the lull in conversation, made him want to stand and leave.

"Do you like to go riding?" she asked with a glimmer of excitement in her eyes.

He heaved a sigh of relief that the conversation had taken a turn.

"No. Horses should *never* be trusted," he said definitively.

Caterina was taken aback by his response, her eyebrows rising in confusion.

"What in the world happened to you?" she asked, as a chuckle escaped her mouth.

Thomas was not amused by her laughter, but he felt obligated to instruct her on the dangers of horses while he had her attention.

"Do you know that if a horse is ready for you to be off its back, it will simply lie down—even if you are trying to ride it?" he said as he leaned toward her, hoping his expression showed the seriousness of the situation.

Caterina let out a full laugh now—which did not amuse Thomas at all.

"What did you do to the poor horse to make it lie down while you were riding?" she asked between laughs.

"Nothing!" he yelled. "They are evil creatures who do as they please even though they are supposed to follow *our* commands! If I must ride any great distance, I stop as often as possible to allow my horse to rest and drink. Who knows when it will grow tired of walking and simply give up? And what if it lies down and crushes my leg and makes me lame? Then I will have no way to walk and no horse to take me where I need to go! Vile, evil, untrustworthy creatures!" he spat. When he looked back at Caterina's face, he could not get a read on her reaction.

"I think you need to find a horse that agrees with you. Horses are wonderful pets—if they know you are theirs and they are yours, they are faithful to the end. My horse once kicked a boy who was pestering me. She could tell I was upset, and she kicked him right in the gut. But she was as careful as could be in all her dealings with me," she said.

"Maybe," he said with a grunt. Thomas liked the sound of *that* horse, but he thought it likely that Caterina's horse was the *exception* to the rule, as every horse he had encountered seemed untrustworthy even in the way they looked at him.

"Why do you carry only three knives though you have four holsters?" Caterina asked, abruptly changing the subject.

"I gave one of my knives to the leader at the village where our ships are docked—as a gift," he answered. "Why do *you* carry a knife? And how are you hiding it?" he asked, wondering about the knife he had seen her grasping while she slept.

"I always have three knives on my body. My brothers gave them to me. And they fitted me with a custom holster," she answered as she patted each of her knives where they lay against her body.

So she came here intentionally, with the blessing of her brothers? I don't understand what could have brought her here. At least they gave her a way to protect herself. I wonder if she knows how to properly use them.

"They sound like good brothers," Thomas said with a wistful look in his eyes.

"Do you have brothers?" Caterina asked, hoping she hadn't stepped into an area of discussion that would cause Thomas pain.

"I do," he answered with the hint of a smile. "Nine of them."

"Nine? That's quite a family! Do you have any sisters?" she pressed.

"No," he said with a tone of finality.

"And what do your brothers do? Are they adventurers to new worlds like you?" she asked.

"No. We all work for the family business. I'm apparently the only rebel," he said as he stared at the knife he grasped in his hands with an almost bitter look on his face. She couldn't understand the hidden meaning behind his words —and she wasn't sure she wanted to.

"Did your brothers teach you how to use those knives?" he asked as he looked up and met her gaze with a mischievous gleam in his eyes.

"Of course!" Caterina said as she stood to her feet. "I have unfailing precision with my knife. You pick the target, and I'll hit it every time," she said vehemently. "In fact, I'll bet I'm more accurate than you," she smirked.

She thinks she's more skilled than me? If I were a lesser man, I would show her just how insignificant her skills are in comparison with my own. The only other person that could exasperate him to such great levels was his father. *Calm down, Thomas,* he commanded himself.

"Why don't we have a little competition?" she offered.

Thomas jumped up and grinned, ready to show her just how talented he was with his beloved knives.

"You've made a terrible mistake, my lady," he said with a bow. "Prepare to be bested."

Caterina knew she was more skilled than Thomas. She had spent years alone in her home, throwing knives at various pieces of fruits and trees—and even living creatures at times. She decided to start with a large target for the sake of Thomas's ego.

"Let's first try to hit the side of that tree," she said, pointing to the largest tree outside her home.

Thomas nodded and smiled. "Ladies first."

She was happy to show off her skill, and her first throw landed squarely in the center of the intended target. She saw Thomas glance at her quickly before he threw his own knife. It landed only an inch from hers, and she knew he might be more formidable an opponent than she had expected.

"Let's try for this," she said as she pulled one of the green fruits from the basket inside her home. It was about the length and width of her small hand, and though she knew she would be able to hit it, she felt certain Thomas would be less successful. She had chosen the least ripe of the fruit so it would hold its shape when her knife struck its skin. She set the fruit on the ground in front of a tree much further away, hoping it would not roll too far when struck.

She readied her knife, keeping her eyes fixed on the fruit, and released the knife from her hand. The fruit took an odd jump as her knife pierced its side, and she and Thomas walked over to it to see what had happened. When she reached for the fruit and turned it over in her hand, she saw that Thomas's knife had struck the fruit less than an inch from where hers had hit.

Caterina looked at him, shocked that she had not seen his knife in the air beside hers, and took in the smug look that was plastered on his face.

"I'll admit, you're quite good," she offered.

"That was…" he stammered. "You didn't even notice that my knife traveled beside yours. That level of focus is unbelievable." She felt her cheeks flush with color as he continued. "Truly, you are quite gifted," he said begrudgingly. "But never allow your focus to detract from your awareness of surroundings. If I had attacked you while you were throwing that knife, you would be dead without having put up a fight," he warned. Her cheeks felt hot under the combination of praise and censure.

"Thank you. And I'll work on that," she responded in a small voice. She cleared her throat and decided to continue the competition.

"Let's aim for these next." She extended her hand, revealing tiny purple berries. The berries grew in the bushes around her home. She took a handful from the closest bush and pushed them into crevices between the pieces of bark on a nearby tree.

"We each have three berries. Whoever hits the most is the winner," she offered. He smiled with a gleam of excitement in his eye and nodded. "Gentlemen first," she said with a curtsy. He chuckled once and turned to face his target. He took a deep breath as he turned his knife over in his hand. He drew his arm back, holding it there only for a split second before hurling the knife at the first berry. As soon as it landed, Caterina rushed toward the tree.

"That's one for me," he said smugly.

Determination flooded Caterina's mind and body. She walked straight to where Thomas had stood, turned to her target, and released her knife. When it landed, the berry fell to the ground in two separate pieces.

"I guess we don't have to look closely to see you hit that one," Thomas said quietly. "You can go again," he suggested with an arm extended toward their targets.

She took much longer on the second throw but still hit the second berry. She only barely nicked the side this time—not the perfectly-centered hit she had made on the first. Thomas, too, hit his second berry, the look of self-satisfaction remaining on his face the entire time.

Caterina was determined to win this game. She had many more years of life to practice her knife throwing, and it was one of the simple pleasures she always maintained in this place of solitude.

"Your turn," she said as Thomas lined up his final throw. He drew back his arm, and as he released the knife, a curse slipped from his mouth. The knife struck the tree almost two inches higher than where the berry was wedged into the bark. Caterina's face lit with excitement. She was about to prove her exceptional skills to a man who obviously felt superior to her.

When her knife struck the center of the last berry, she jumped in the air and held back a squeal. She didn't want to alarm the natives—Thomas was worried they didn't want him with her, and if they found him at her home, she wasn't sure how they would respond. She thrust her arms in the air and giggled as she jumped around. Thomas looked amused and frustrated at the same time.

"Congratulations, Caterina. You are, indeed, better than I am with a knife. And that's really saying something," he said with another bow. He looked as if he wanted to laugh at her continuing celebration, but he held in the emotion. Caterina calmed herself abruptly, as Thomas pulled back the curtain for her to enter her home.

"I thank you for your conversation," he started as soon as they were inside. "And for crushing my ego," he continued with a bitter chuckle. "But I fear it is time for me to return to my camp. My employer is awaiting my report on Tantun," he said with a slight bow.

Caterina felt her jubilation drain quickly away. She did not know how to do justice to the words she wished to speak, so she opened her mouth and hoped they would come out correctly.

"I am grateful for your company. You have no idea how lonely I have felt for years. In the past two days I have felt more at home than I have in … too long," she said, nearly allowing "twenty-six years" to slip out.

"You are most welcome," he said as his expression softened.

"Will I ever see you again?" she asked as a flicker of hope flashed through her mind.

"I suppose it's possible," Thomas said as he grabbed his bag and walked out the door without a backward glance.

She watched him go until he passed through the thick foliage and out of sight. She worried that might be the last conversation she would ever have with an Italian.

FORTY

CATERINA LAY DOWN on her bed. Her smile stretched all the way from one ear to the other.

"Oh, Leo. I wish you could've met that man," she said as she closed her eyes and imagined her friend sitting against the wall next to her. In moments like these, she could almost feel his touch on her skin. She missed him nearly as much as she missed her mother. Unfortunately, no matter how hard she tried, her mind could not conjure the image of her sweet mother. But Imaginary Leonardo was as much a part of her home as were the paintings on the walls.

"I think you like him," Leo said with a wry look on his face.

"I think *you* like him," she countered back teasingly. But her emotions quickly turned serious. "I do like him. Not romantically, of course. But there's something about him that feels … connected," she admitted.

"Take care, Caterina. Don't let your heart break. He's only here as a stop along the way, and he'll soon be gone," Leo said sadly. "You may never see him again."

"But at least he was here—even for a short time. At least he's real," she whispered as the ghost of her friend faded away into her memories.

FORTY-ONE

THOMAS'S RETURN TRIP took only five hours because he had marked his path on the way to Tantun. He was ready to tell Cortés about the crazy Italian woman he encountered, and a part of him wondered if Cortés would ask him to go back and get her. *Maybe he'll want me bring her to the camp,* he thought with a strange mix of emotions. He certainly didn't want to make the journey back to Tantun. But he felt like she was stranded on the island, and he got the impression she might want to leave. *Maybe she'll join our voyage,* he thought with a stirring of hope in his gut. *Stop this! Her attitude of superiority is disgusting ... even though she beat me at my own game.*

The inner struggle lasted the entire trip back, and by the time he stepped onto the beach where Cortés was camped, Thomas was flush with anger.

"Good God, Thomas. What happened? You look furious," Cortés said with a furrowed brow.

"Well, I found your 'ghost.' But she's not a ghost at all. She's an insane Italian woman with incredible knife-throwing skills. I recommend we leave her alone and get off this island as soon as possible," Thomas spat.

Cortés let out a full laugh. "She really got under your skin didn't she? No, no. I think I'll have you bring her here. I'd like to see what makes her 'insane,'" he said as he continued to chuckle. "You look terrible. Rest for a few days before you go back."

Thomas had a new mission—*do your best to not kill Cortés.* He resented his employer for the first time. But a small, unwelcome part of him heaved a sigh of relief that he would have an excuse to find the missing pieces of Caterina's mysterious puzzle of a life.

For the next two days, every waking moment was spent feeling frustration over his time with the woman. He was angry about the broken pots. He was furious that he hadn't hit his third berry.

After only two days of rest, he could bear it no more, and on the third morning, he set off for Tantun. He found himself running at times during his trip, and he made the journey in only three hours. He carefully avoided the village in order to go straight to Caterina's stone home.

When he was sure that he was not being watched by the nearby natives, he walked down the narrow path to her home. He could see the circle in the dirt where the basket of fresh fruits and vegetables had been left for Caterina earlier that morning. He walked straight down the path to the opening of her home, not taking any care to hide his steps. He walked through the curtain, not pausing even for a moment. Caterina held knives in both hands, extended straight toward him.

"Yes, I know. You heard me coming," Thomas said with the roll of his eyes. Caterina chuckled and put one knife away, returning to slicing the vegetables she was going to eat for lunch.

"You don't understand how frustrating it is to be expected all the time. I'm not going to bother trying any more with you. Not even myself or my brothers have the ability you've somehow developed, and this is what we do!" he said, looking down at the dirt floor of the home with a tormented look on his face. Her expression morphed into an inquisitive gaze at his words.

"What? What is it that you do?" she asked with genuine curiosity.

"It's none of your concern," he said as he cleared his throat. No one outside the Family had any business knowing what they did for a living.

"I'm sorry I asked," she said as her face grew serious and she turned her eyes downward. She remained quiet, and he knew if there was any more conversation to be had, it would have to be his doing. He racked his brain for any question—any topic of conversation—but came up empty. They sat in silence, neither one willing to speak or even look in the other's direction. Finally, it was Caterina who shattered the silence.

"Why did you come to this island? Why did you come to Tantun?" she asked with an angry expression on her face.

"My crew stopped on Cozumel to resupply before we head off to conquer the Aztecs," he said quietly.

"Cozumel?" she asked.

"That is the Spanish name for this island," he explained, and she nodded in understanding.

"So why did you come back to Tantun?" she pressed, still angry. "Why did you feel compelled to visit this village at all?"

He breathed deeply before answering as his eyes finally met hers.

"For you."

FORTY-TWO

CATERINA'S HEART STOPPED. Thomas had just said he had come here for her. *Why?* She knew her expression must be awful because Thomas immediately began trying to explain.

"We heard a legend about a white, female ghost, and we thought it was either true or a made-up story to scare us from something else that the natives wanted to keep hidden. Of course, once I met you I knew you were not a ghost. I also knew *you* were the thing the natives were trying to hide. Why else would they put you in a dwelling in the middle of a dense forest with a hidden path?

"My employer wants me to bring you to our camp. He's interested in meeting you. I don't know what he wants to talk about, but I've been instructed to accompany you to our camp," he admitted sheepishly.

Caterina's head began to spin. Her emotional and mental soundness had become a source of great fear since she began her life of solitude in Tantun. She conjured up Leonardo to talk with nearly every day—sometimes more than once. She often found herself crying for no reason. She worried that she was slowly losing her mind. But Thomas's appearance made her feel like a normal person once more. His conversation reminded her of what it was like to talk to someone who actually talked back and to laugh with another person over something as ridiculous as throwing a knife at a berry. These were things Caterina had resigned herself to never experiencing again. She wanted to leap up and hug Thomas for making her feel human once more. She wanted to go with him to his camp. She wanted to have a nice conversation with his employer. But she felt a feeling of terror stir in her gut.

"It's been quite some time since I've spoken with anyone. I'm not even fit to be seen," she said as she worried about her disheveled appearance.

"What do you mean? You've been speaking with me. And you look just fine," Thomas said as the irritated expression returned to his face. Caterina sighed. She only wanted to understand *why* Thomas's employer would want to speak with her.

Maybe if I go, they'll take me back to Europe, she thought as hope welled within her for the first time since she had arrived in Tantun.

"All right. I'll go with you," she decided.

FORTY-THREE

WHEN CATERINA ASSURED him the natives were asleep for the night, Thomas led her to Cortés's camp. Each time he checked behind him to make sure she was still there, he was surprised to find her keeping pace through the dark, dense forest. She was much more formidable than her appearance implied. And when Thomas would normally have wished to take a short break, Caterina seemed so unaffected by the journey that he pushed onward, despite feeling winded himself.

"Do you trek often through the forest?" he asked, hoping his heavy breathing would not be noticeable.

"Oh yes. I have always loved being outside, and I feel the most alive when I'm in the midst of a great forest or field. I spent hours roaming absentmindedly through my father's vineyards. And I almost always painted out of doors before I came here. The fresh air and the hum of nature are some of my favorite parts of life," she said as her eyes glassed over. He worried she might start crying and tried to think of another question.

"Do you wish to return to Italy?" he asked abruptly before he could stop himself. He *needed* to understand why she was in Cozumel and how she had gotten to the tiny island.

"I do. More than anything. But it would be unwise," she said as her countenance fell once more.

"I don't understand why it would be unwise." Thomas could think of nothing that would keep her trapped on an island with natives whom she could barely understand.

"It simply is. I could not make you understand even if I wished," she said with a tinge of exasperation. She pushed past him and continued on as Thomas watched her hedge forward in the dark. He stayed behind her as she easily found each marker Thomas had left to find his way back to Cortés's camp.

They moved at a slightly faster pace than before, Caterina spurred on by her anger.

When they finally arrived at the camp, there were only a few drunken men still awake on the beach.

"You may sleep in my tent for the night. I'll stay outside and keep watch to make sure no one bothers you," Thomas said as he pulled back the flap to his small tent. He had dug himself a Thomas-sized hole in the sand where he could comfortably sleep without any unwelcome lumps of sand or shells to give him problems. He knew Caterina would mess up the work he had done, but she needed to sleep somewhere. He was resigned to the idea of starting over the next night.

"Thank you," she said as she slid inside and shut the flap behind her.

Thomas built a small fire next to his tent and found some uneaten food that the sleeping crew had left near another fire. There was a bowl of fruit and a small skinned animal just waiting to be cooked. He took them back to his small fire and started roasting the meat of the creature using a stick he had found near the edge of the forest bordering the encampment.

He allowed his mind to empty as he watched the flesh smolder and bubble under the heat of the fire. He absentmindedly picked up a fruit to take a bite, but before he put it in his mouth, a hand smacked the fruit away.

Thomas turned to physically reprimand the attacker—everyone in the crew knew better than to accost Thomas. Caterina knelt next to him, braced for the swing he might have taken at any of the crew.

"Why did you do that?" he whispered as he held back his fist.

"It's poisonous," she said with wide eyes. "It won't kill you, but you'll have terrible stomach cramps for days."

"Well … I appreciate that. For not letting me eat poison," he stammered, humbled by her intervention.

She smiled a little at his difficulty to find the right words and simply nodded her head in response.

"Are you hungry?" he asked as soon as he realized she was still kneeling next to him.

"Yes. I didn't think I needed to eat, but as soon as I smelled what you were cooking, I couldn't stop myself from asking for a bite. Good thing I did, right?" she said with that smirk on her face again.

With that little smile, in the flickering light of the fire, Thomas could see that she might actually be pretty … when she wasn't trying to act superior.

"Help yourself," he said as he held out the cooked piece of meat. She ripped off a small piece and took her time to chew it. They ate in silence, but Thomas kept finding his gaze fixed on her mouth or eyes. She was an enigma. And he wasn't accustomed to meeting people outside his Family who fit that description. The Family was always a provocative and terrifying mystery to those who learned the truth. But Thomas felt like there were so many hidden layers to Caterina that she might be even more intriguing than his own kind.

"What are you?" he asked.

She looked taken aback. He hadn't meant to actually ask the question. His mouth had betrayed his mind, but he wasn't sure he cared. He wanted so badly to understand who and what Caterina was—along with how and why she had traveled to Cozumel.

"I've had enough to eat. I'll try to sleep now," she said as she quietly climbed back into the tent and shut the flap once more.

Thomas lay down on the sand and closed his eyes. *I'll figure it out sooner or later.*

FORTY-FOUR

CATERINA AWOKE to sounds of men laughing and chatting in Spanish. It was strange to hear any sounds besides those of animals and leaves rustling, but to hear European voices was incredibly odd. She had slept next to the imprint Thomas made for himself in the sand—she knew he must have worked to make it fit his body and did not wish to undo his efforts.

She opened the flap just slightly and peeked out to see if Thomas still kept watch over her. *No,* she thought as she worried what she should do. A lone female in a camp full of men was never a good idea, but she had no idea where Thomas had gone. She sat back down in the tent and pondered her next move.

"Rise and shine!" Thomas said as the flap opened and his face appeared. "Did you sleep well?" he asked with a smile.

Caterina had no idea where this happy, caring version of Thomas had come from, but she didn't mind the change in his demeanor.

"Well enough," she answered as he handed her some fruit. "The sound of snoring men is not something to which I'm accustomed. But once you turned on your side, I slept better the rest of the night," she teased.

That got a small chuckle from Thomas, and Caterina was, once again, stunned by his mood.

"I'm taking you to meet Hernán Cortés. He's a Spaniard, but he speaks Italian fairly well. You'll like him."

Caterina followed Thomas closely, taking in the wide-eyed stares of each crew member as she passed. The silence was deafening in comparison with the boisterous racket she heard only moments before.

"Cortés. This … is Caterina," Thomas said as he presented her to his employer. The man that stood before her was much smaller in stature than Thomas—almost feminine by comparison. Cortés's angular face and balding dark hair were not very attractive to Caterina, though she didn't think he would necessarily be unpleasant in the eyes of other young ladies. She was confused by the clothes Cortés wore—his dress was inexplicably gaudy for someone on a mission to conquer a nation. Thomas's clothes were much more practical—plain, thick, and well-made. The sudden realization that she was comparing the two men surprised her.

"It is an honor to finally meet the 'ghost,'" Cortés said as he took her hand and kissed it. Caterina didn't know what to do with the gesture, so she simply said "thank you" and removed her hand carefully from his grasp. Thomas looked on without expression, and she wondered if his mind was otherwise engaged.

"So tell me, Caterina, why you are here. In Cozumel," Cortés asked as he motioned for her to sit on a small bench in front of his tent. Caterina could barely pay attention to his question. There were many western items in and around his tent—items that she hadn't seen for over twenty-six years. There was a table with a quill and paper. There was a small mirror. There was a comb for his hair. She glanced around in awe before Cortés cleared his throat in order to bring her mind back to the present.

"I'm here because I washed ashore and the Tantun tribe took me in," she said matter-of-factly. She wouldn't give up any more of her story, but she could see Cortés had more questions swirling around in his mind. She glanced at Thomas and found his expression eager to hear more, but when she remained silent, his face returned to its normal look of irritation.

"And *how* did you wash upon the shores of this island?" Cortés pushed.

"I'm sorry, but that's not a story I can reveal," she said as she continued gawking at the western luxuries scattered around Cortés's tent.

"Do you speak the natives' language?" he asked, obviously frustrated by her unwillingness to answer his previous question.

"I do. But not fluently. I understand about half of what they say."

Just then, another man in Mayan clothes walked up to the group and stared at Caterina in shocked silence.

"Ahh! Gerónimo," Thomas started. "This is the Mayan's 'ghost,'" he said with a snort of laughter. Gerónimo did not look amused.

"Ixchel?" he said reverently.

Caterina was unsure how he knew the Mayans' name for her.

"Yes. That is what the Mayans call me," she answered.

"But that's not possible. You're an apparition. You're a *deity*," he said quietly as he took a small step away from her.

"I am *not* a deity. The Mayans look at me like I'm a pariah every time something bad happens to the village. They don't even let me set foot *in* the village. If they thought I was a deity, don't you think they would want me to live in the village with them?" she asked, now upset by Gerónimo's implication.

Thomas and Cortés looked on with silent confusion. Caterina would have shared the expression if she wasn't so frustrated by the idea of being thought of as a deity.

"Of course they would be upset if you didn't protect them from bad things. You. Are. Their. *Goddess*. The temple at Tantun is dedicated to Ixchel—to *you*. The name literally means 'white goddess red goddess'. You are a white woman with red hair. I never understood before, but you *are* Ixchel. How is that possible? I heard stories of Ixchel when I first arrived nearly ten years ago," Gerónimo said absently, his mind wandering back to earlier days.

"I have no idea," Caterina said as she tried to change the subject. Her mind was still reeling from the villagers' goddess assumption, but at least she possessed a more clear understanding of why they acted terrified of her all the time. She knew she was harmless, but to them she was a powerful deity. *How curious.*

"What are you thinking of doing with the goddess?" Thomas asked Cortés with a slight grin.

"Are you stranded here?" Cortés asked her plainly.

"Yes," she answered quickly.

"Do you wish to return to Europe?" Cortés asked without ceremony.

"More than anything," she answered with excitement welling in her chest.

"I was actually asking Thomas, my dear," Cortés said softly.

Thomas sat up straight as he realized the implication of the question. His face was confused, but he looked a little relieved.

"More than anything," he answered, using her exact words.

"Well then, go. Take the girl home. You don't have the heart to slaughter natives, and I don't want your conscience following me around everywhere I go. I know this doesn't quite fulfill the contract the way it was specified, but I don't really care. You've gone above and beyond for me, and I'm happy to part from you as a friend," Cortés said with a hint of emotion in his voice.

"I am in a state of disbelief," Thomas whispered, apparently taken aback by the new development. "What brought this on?"

"It's something I've been tossing around in my head. I never quite felt right about your contract, and now I have a reason to release you from it. Escort the young lady home safely. Once you've returned her, your contract will be fulfilled. I'll write you a letter before you go that says I no longer require your services," Cortés said with a smile.

Thomas looked like he might jump up and scream. His face glowed with excitement, and Caterina couldn't help but feel she was glowing the same way. She was returning to Italy. *To her home.* She began allowing herself to imagine seeing her brothers and sisters-in-law, her nieces and nephews, maybe even Leonardo. She knew it would be unlikely that her mother and father would live to such an old age, but she hoped and prayed that they were somehow alive and well. She wanted to dance at a party. She wanted to ride a horse. She wanted to paint with real paints and paint brushes. Nothing could stifle the mood she was in. She did her best to contain her joy, but it was difficult, to say the least.

"I must return to Tantun to gather my things and tell the natives I am leaving," she announced as she stood to go.

"Good, good. Take Thomas and Gerónimo with you. You don't seem to have a good understanding of the language. Maybe he'll be able to explain you're not a real goddess," Cortés laughed.

Forty-Five

THE THREE SET OFF shortly after the conversation ended. Caterina wanted nothing more than to return to her small home, gather her things, and set sail for Europe. Thomas couldn't deny he felt similarly. If she had wanted to dawdle, he would likely have been upset. Cortés had released him. He was free to return home. Nothing could be better.

Cortés was right about Thomas not having the stomach to slaughter the natives—though his career was committing contracted murder, the slaughter of masses for the sake of staking claim on an uncivilized land felt utterly *wrong*. He wanted no part of it—and felt a little guilty about leaving Cortés and the crew alone during the coming journey. He hoped Gerónimo would step up in his stead and be the voice of reason with Cortés. Gerónimo harbored a soft spot for the natives and would hopefully try to keep relations peaceful for the sake of both sides.

Caterina walked as briskly as possible back to her home, and when the three arrived, the Tantun leaders were waiting outside her home. Everything became immediately tense, and everyone but Caterina grew defensive.

If they think I'm a goddess, I will act like a goddess. They're certainly not going to harm me, she decided as soon as she saw the armed leaders outside her home.

"I am leaving this place. I am grateful for the way you have treated me. You have taken great care of me," she assured them in a broken form of their language. The natives stayed silent as they listened to her words, but the looks on their faces were worried. "I will bless the village with many children," she desperately hoped she was conveying the correct sentiment. "I will keep you safe. But only if you allow me to leave with these men," she added.

The natives looked at each other and nodded to one another with worry on their faces. They each took turns stepping forward and bowing to Caterina.

"We thank you for your blessing," one said, and they backed away from her while continuing to bow until they were out of sight.

How could she have missed the fact that they thought she was a deity? She was confused by the natives' misunderstanding, but grateful that her "blessings" had assuaged the natives' fears about her leaving.

"I only need a minute to gather my things. Wait here," she said as she entered her home in Tantun for the last time.

She looked around at the walls covered in her paintings. She had spent years trying to mix the colors into proper shades and consistencies, and now she would travel back to a place where paints were easy to come by. She sat on the mat where she had spent hours mixing paints and preparing food. She would return to a life of servants and luxury when she made it back to her brothers. *How do I go back to that life?* she asked herself as an unexpected tear dripped down her cheek. Twenty-six years of solitude. Twenty-six years of self-sufficiency. *Will it even be possible for me to feel normal living in a civilized world?* she wondered, looking across the room at her bed made of a blanket stretched across a pile of leaves. She picked up the pile of clothes she had been given over the years from the Mayans and placed them in a bag she had sewn a few years earlier out of a torn dress. She grabbed her crude paintbrushes and thrust them into the bag as well. She looked around and realized there was nothing else—not one thing—she needed to take with her. The home itself with her paintings on its walls was what had made the home feel like *hers*. She knew that when she stepped outside the door and turned her back on this place, a little piece of her soul would stay behind.

The home where she lived for the twenty-six most difficult years of her life would be behind her forever. The tears flowed more steadily now, but when she walked outside, neither Thomas nor Gerónimo said a word. They followed her down the narrow path she had walked on hundreds of times before without so much as kicking up dust. She shed tears for the path that had become the walkway to her home. She shed tears for the stream that flowed nearby where she bathed and washed her clothes. She shed tears as the villagers bowed and cried at her departure. And as she walked away from Tantun, she squeezed her eyes shut and envisioned the sunset over her father's vineyard. She was going home.

FORTY-SIX

THEY BOARDED the ship which Cortés had arranged for them and headed to Santiago just three days later. During the short trip from Cozumel to Cuba, Caterina barely spoke. Thomas worried she was either sick or scared, but the look of calm that remained in her amber eyes told him he didn't need to fret about her health—physical or mental. He stayed close to her and kept her informed on the timing of their trip, but she only nodded when he spoke.

As soon as the ship docked in Santiago, they disembarked the vessel into the bustling city. Caterina looked and felt like a foreigner compared to the women who walked through the city in the latest European fashions. Passers-by stared at her untamed wildness with curiosity and confusion. The unearthly calm never left Caterina's eyes, though Thomas kept a close watch on her, wondering if she might have an emotional breakdown after the vast number of tears she shed while leaving Tantun.

Thomas immediately made arrangements for their passage on the next ship sailing to Spain. It would not depart for another five days.

He took Caterina to Cortés's empty home and tried to make her as comfortable as possible.

"Can I get you anything?" he asked, hoping to coax out some conversation. But when he received a single 'no,' he could tell something was bothering her deeply.

"I know I've only known you for a very short time, but you truly seem out of sorts. Surely there is something wrong. Can I call for a doctor? Do you feel ill?" he worried.

"I'm not ill, I assure you," she began quietly, but panic soon began to seep into her tone as her words flowed more quickly. "I'm never ill. I just feel as if this is a terrible mistake. I'm going to hurt more people than you can imagine by returning home. I thought only of myself in leaving Tantun. But my return to

Italy cannot possibly be joyful. I should go back as soon as possible to Tantun," she said, nearly in tears.

"I do not understand your situation, but there would be no way for you to return to Tantun now even if you wished. The ship we used for our journey here has already set sail to the mainland. Cortés's crew has left Cozumel for good. Still, I don't see how returning to Italy could possibly be worse than living a solitary life in a remote village surrounded by people you don't know and barely understand," Thomas said carefully.

"You're right. You don't understand my situation at all," Caterina said sadly as she walked to her room and shut the door behind her.

Thomas sat down, concern and frustration swirling through his mind like a vicious storm. Until they had begun the journey to Santiago, Caterina had been nothing but kind, excited and irritating. Thomas didn't know how this drastic change could have happened over such a short span of time, but he wanted to do his best to get the old Caterina back. *I didn't think I liked the old Caterina,* he observed. He didn't want to dwell on the change, so he, too, retired to his room for the night.

The two kept to themselves the majority of the time over the days leading up to their journey. They said very little during meal times, and even less in between. They were not rude to each other, simply reserved—neither one willing to start a conversation with the other. Thomas tried to think of topics he might bring up to prompt her to speak with him the way they had in Tantun, but every question that came to his mind seemed to somehow tie back to her family or her home—both of which, he worried, would anger her in her present state. So he commented only about the weather, their meals, and the kindness of the household staff. She smiled pleasantly and agreed with him each time he spoke, but he could tell she heard very little of what he said.

"When we arrive in Spain, I will accompany you back to Italy," he announced the night before their departure.

"What?" she asked, taken aback by the statement.

"You heard me. I'm returning to Florence anyway, and Cortés's instructions were to deliver you safely home. It wouldn't make sense for us to make the journey separately. I'll take you to Milan on my way home. And perhaps you can teach me how to properly ride a horse along the way," he smiled. She let out a small chuckle before her face became impassive once more.

"Thank you. It's really not necessary, but I welcome your company," she said as the room returned to its normal silence.

The next morning, Thomas knocked on Caterina's door just after dawn. When she opened it, he could see she had already been awake for some time.

"Good morning," he said, trying to gage her mood.

"Good morning," she answered with a curious expression.

"Your Mayan clothing will be a spectacle if you wear it on our trip home. I bought a few simple dresses for you from the seamstress' shop down the lane. I don't want the crew to have any reason to look at you as an oddity. Sailors are notorious for their ... indiscretions," he said as he placed a box of clothes at her feet.

"Thank you for your concern, but I had another idea," she said. "When I first came here, I was a member of a ship's crew. I cut my hair, bound my chest, and dressed like a man. I was thinking I could do the same thing to make the trip easier."

Thomas was aghast at the idea of Caterina working as a part of a ship's crew. She was so petite. So ... womanly. And, in his opinion, a woman should never *have* to do physical labor—especially as a ruse to hide her gender.

"I didn't secure us passage as members of the crew. I paid for us to be *passengers*. We won't be working at all."

"I won't know what to do with myself if I'm stuck on board a ship for this long without something to do," she said as she stepped away from her door and sat on the edge of her bed.

Thomas looked around the room and saw her bed was untouched. Two blankets from the foot of the bed had been removed and placed on the floor for

Caterina to sleep on. The Mayan clothes were folded in a pile on the small table next to the bed, and the clothes she had worn the day before were washed and hung over the open window sill. Thomas didn't know what to think of her behavior.

"How long were you in Tantun?" he asked as his eyes returned to her face, searching for a hint of the story that lay behind the curious woman before him.

"A long time," she answered abruptly.

"Caterina. How long?" he asked, now demanding an answer rather than asking for one. Caterina seemed indignant.

"I don't have to tell you. But I will *consider* telling you … if you tell me what you meant back in Tantun when you said 'this is what we do' after our knife-throwing game," she offered, looking smug.

Thomas knew he was treading on dangerous ground. If he told her the truth, she might try to flee. She might run to the authorities to report him and never want to speak to him again—which wouldn't work out if he was going to fulfill his contract and take her back to her home.

"I'm not sure you really want to know," he said with a warning in his tone. But his answer only seemed to spark interest in Caterina.

"But now you must tell me. I was stuck in Tantun for what seemed like forever. I had no connection with the outside world before you found me. I'm currently sleeping on the floor in a real house … in a real city … surrounded by people I cannot relate to any more. I'm about to have a panic over returning to a family that might not want to see me. And I … please. *Please* tell me something that will take my mind off of all this. Plus, we're about to embark on a months-long trip together … shouldn't we at least know a little about one another?" she begged.

Thomas thought about her words. She was on the verge of crying again. He still wasn't sure he should confide in her, but he wanted to do something … *anything* … to comfort the poor girl.

Father would quite literally kill me if I told our secrets to someone I barely know. Sergius certainly wouldn't approve—he waited until his wedding night to tell his wife the truth back in the 900s.

"I think your reasoning is flawed, but just like you said, I'll consider telling you … at some point. We'll be traveling together for months, so I'll have plenty of time to decide if you're trustworthy or not," he said, hoping his smug expression reflected the same one she had used earlier. "We should leave soon … don't want to miss our departure," he said as he turned and left Caterina's doorway.

FORTY-SEVEN

CATERINA ROLLED OVER on the piece of cloth she used as a bed and looked up at the wooden ceiling above. She grunted in frustration as she heard men doing work right outside her room. Two weeks into the journey and Caterina was already at her wit's end. She could not bear to sit idly by while others worked around her. She was staying in one of the ship's only private quarters. The ship had one large room of living quarters for the crew, a captain's quarters, and one additional room that was built for rich patrons to rent for the long trip across the ocean. Apparently, Thomas had paid a large sum to secure the room for her. Despite her protests, Thomas stayed with the crew in an uncomfortable hammock. Every morning at breakfast, she could see that he had slept poorly. She would rather he slept in the bed in her room than in a hammock surrounded by dozens of snoring sailors. She wasn't using the bed anyway. After twenty-six years of sleeping with only a thin layer of leaf-padding under a piece of cloth, the soft bedding was impossible for her to fall asleep on. She explained the situation to Thomas at least once a day, hoping he would change his mind and take the bed in the room, but all of her attempts were received with a roll of his eyes. He kept telling her, "You can't sleep on the floor for the rest of your life. Now is as good a time as any to begin sleeping on a bed again."

She made her way to the captain's quarters where she and Thomas dined. Thomas was there, where he always waited outside the captain's quarters. Each morning, he escorted her inside and pulled out her chair. He was the consummate gentleman. And when she looked at him, she held back a little sigh —he was the definition of 'an ideal partner'. He was evidently rich—which she assumed because of his ability to spend money on whatever he fancied. His deep green eyes shimmered—even in the dimness of night—and his dark brown hair always seemed to be perfectly fixed. His muscular build was like one of Leonardo's studies on the human body (which was obvious even though she had never seen him without his being fully clothed). He was serious, as a general rule, but when he found a reason to smile, the expression was breathtaking. Caterina wished she held even an ounce of the physical appeal that Thomas radiated—he would make a perfect husband for any woman.

But she didn't allow herself to reflect long upon those thoughts. She had lived in fear ever since Paris that she would infect anyone who might come into contact with her. And though she had proven plenty of times that the sickness did not transfer through the air, she was always careful not to share food or drink with others. If she were to cause the death of someone through her saliva, she would prove to be the monster that she had always believed she was. Yes. Kissing was completely out of the question. She would be alone for … the rest of her life.

"Good morning, Caterina. Did you sleep well?" he asked, same as every morning.

"Quite well," she always replied.

"On the bed this time?" he said in an accusatory tone.

She refused to answer every day and simply rolled her eyes and brushed past him. The soft laugh he produced made her smile, but she kept her back to him so he couldn't see it.

"We're eating cheese and biscuits for breakfast this morning. I hope that suits you both," the captain said with a grin. Caterina giggled forcefully, though she wanted to yell at the captain for the tired joke. Cheese and biscuits were what they ate every morning for breakfast, and she knew she would likely have to hear the captain's joke every morning for the next few months on the seas. Thomas looked at her with an accusatory glare...so she rolled her eyes and looked away, pretending to look around the cabin she had already memorized.

"Ah! My favorite again. How did you know?" Thomas said charmingly, probably to cover for Caterina's mood.

This was her breaking point. She could feel her nerves unraveling. She had woken up on the verge of a panic attack, and each moment since then made her even more frustrated. When she and Thomas finally left the captain alone after breakfast, he pulled her to her quarters and shut the door behind them.

"What is going on with you today?" he asked. She couldn't tell if he was more upset or worried.

"I *must* do something. I am going to lose my mind. I'll clean up after the crew at mealtimes," she offered.

"You know Captain Donoso would never allow you to dirty your hands aboard his ship," Thomas argued.

"Maybe I could clean the floors below deck?" she thought aloud.

"That's even worse, Caterina," he said, growing irritated.

"Wash the clothes?"

"No."

"Scrub the deck?"

"No."

"Assist the cooper?"

"Caterina!" he finally yelled.

"Thomas! I don't think you understand the direness of my mental state. I would man the bilge pumps right now if it meant I was able to do something with my time!" she yelled back as Thomas stepped away, shocked.

"That is disgusting," he said in a repulsed tone.

"I don't care. I am losing my mind. *Please* find me something to do. *Anything*," she begged.

"I'll see what I can do," he promised as he quickly left her alone in her room. She deeply regretted not sticking to her plan to dress like a man and join the crew on the trip home. She knew this would happen.

Thomas left Caterina, feeling incredibly sorry for her while being utterly incensed by her relentlessness. There was no chance the captain was going to let Caterina work on his ship. The captain was a proper man from good breeding.

It took him nearly an hour of convincing, but when the conversation with the captain was finished, Thomas felt a smug sense of satisfaction.

"You can help with the mending," he announced as soon as he reentered Caterina's room.

"Truly?" she squealed with a huge smile on her face.

"Yes. The crew's clothes and the sails. If anything needs mending, you'll be the one to take care of it. I had to tell Captain Donoso that you were losing your mind and needed some useful employment unless he wanted a madwoman aboard his ship. He wasn't happy to let you work, but I don't think he's willing to find out how serious your condition is."

Caterina threw her arms around Thomas's neck and hugged him tightly, letting out a carefree sigh. Thomas straightened immediately, not sure how to respond to her touch. It was the first time they had touched since she bandaged the head wound she gave him in her hut that first day. He backed away as soon as she released him from her grasp.

"Thank you thank you thank you!" she chanted joyfully as she spun around in the tiny space next to the bed. "I'll survive the rest of the trip now. You saved my life!"

For the next several weeks, Thomas watched Caterina do her mending each day. He kept an eye on the sailors, who were all becoming more brazen about their behavior with her. It didn't help that each time she spoke with them, the part of her that had once pretended to be a male sailor seemed to find its way to the surface. The men looked at her as if she was a shiny piece of gold—something they wanted not only to see more closely but to physically touch if the moment presented itself.

Thomas didn't trust a single one of them. He felt the urge to keep an eye on

Caterina at all times, but the knowledge that she was equipped with three knives and had excellent aim put his mind at ease … a little.

"You shouldn't worry so much. I already told you I was part of a crew on a ship once before. I can handle this. You're treating me like I'm a lady, but believe me when I say I haven't been treated like one of those for some time," she said with a chuckle.

Thomas didn't like the sound of that one bit. *Every woman deserves to be treated like a lady. How dare someone not treat her like a lady.* He told himself it was simply the way he was brought up, and that he needed to calm down. This was going to be a long enough trip as it was.

"I don't like the way they look at you," he said quietly while she sewed shut the rip in a pair of pants.

"Well I don't think they like the way you constantly watch them. It's not as if they're coming in here to court me. They bring me clothes to mend. I'm hardly the object of their desires," she chuckled.

But Thomas knew better. Caterina's unconventional beauty was beautiful. The fact that she would not stay idle while everyone around her worked was fascinating. The dedication she showed to even the most menial of tasks was astounding. The way she fixed her hair differently each day was mesmerizing. And Thomas caught himself watching her more and more. He did his best to serve as her bodyguard and nothing more, but he couldn't help feeling as if he was becoming attached. He didn't feel for her *romantically*, but there was something there … something he couldn't put his finger on. They often talked for hours about topics which Thomas never realized he enjoyed. One day, they spent an entire afternoon discussing proper care for a vineyard on a cold night. Another, they spent four hours talking about the merits of different lengths and widths of knife blades.

Thomas kept a proper physical distance from Caterina at all times, but she was such a joy to be around that he spent almost all of his time in her presence. He could see she held no interest for him romantically either, though he had to admit that his pride was more than a little wounded by her indifference. Most women at least looked at him appraisingly from time to time. But with Caterina, it was obvious she viewed him only as a friend. Not that he wanted to be involved with her romantically. She definitely wasn't his type.

Forty-Eight

"I HAVE A SURPRISE for you," Thomas said as he burst into Caterina's room with an almost-giddy bounce in his step. She could honestly say she had never seen him this way.

"I only have two pairs of trousers left to mend. Can it wait just a little?" she asked, hoping she could finish her work before he took her away for whatever surprise he put together.

"That's perfect. I'll set everything up and come back for you soon," he said as he raced from the room with a smile plastered on his face.

She had no idea what had gotten into him, but she looked forward to seeing what could produce this level of excitement.

There was a quick knock at the door, and Caterina put down the trousers she was working on. *Surely he doesn't think I'm finished already. He only left two minutes ago*, she giggled. When she opened the door, three of the crew stood before her.

"Hello gentlemen. How can I help you?"

Thomas was happy he would be able to bring Caterina a little piece of home. After breakfast, he had stayed with Captain Donoso when Caterina returned to her quarters to work.

"I understand Caterina's need to stay busy. I would not survive if I didn't keep myself busy each day," the captain admitted.

"How do you keep sane out here?" Thomas asked, genuinely curious about the man's incessantly jovial countenance.

"My favorite way is to play my violin. I play at least a little every day. I also read books. I love a particular series by Garci Rodríguez de Montalvo—it's a bit romantic, but the books are easy to understand. My mother gave me a copy of Utopia last time I was in Spain. It's a new book that's gaining all sorts of attention, mostly bad. But I can hardly read the thing. It was written in Latin, and my Latin is terrible," he chuckled.

"I try to pick up different hobbies from time to time to see if I enjoy them. Last month I tried my hand at painting—that was a horrifying disaster," the captain said with a shake of his head.

"Do you still have the paint? And brushes?" Thomas asked, feeling a hopeful excitement at the prospect of surprising Caterina with such an unexpected pleasure.

"Yes I do. They're in that cabinet over there. Why?"

After their conversation, Thomas ran straight to Caterina's room to see the status of her work for the day. She would have plenty of daylight to paint, and he knew she would be infinitely more happy painting than she was fixing torn trousers.

He set up the easel and canvas on one side of the quarter deck, out of the way of the sailors' work. The brushes and paints were set on a small overturned carton he took from the storage area below, and he borrowed a chair from the captain's quarters to allow for the greatest comfort while Caterina painted. The seas were calm with cloudless skies—he knew she would have a peaceful day for painting. He couldn't wait to see the look on her face when she realized what her surprise was.

After making sure everything was perfect (for the fifth time), he made his way to her room to see if she was finished with her mending. He wanted every part of this to be special for her.

He knocked three times on her door, but there was no reply. *That's odd. She was just here. Surely she's not off wandering around the ship.* He knocked again.

"Caterina?" he said loudly.

A muffled scream broke the silence on the other side of the door as Thomas's mind filled with crazed panic. He tried the handle of the door to no avail and began beating on it wildly to break through. He ran at the door several times, each time lowering his shoulder for a forceful impact. He could see the frame begin to give way, so he kept up the attack until he heard the wood crack all the way through.

The scene unfolding before him made his eyes glaze over with a blood lust he had not felt before. Caterina screamed and wept on the floor as one of the crew held down her arms and another sat on top of her flailing legs.

A third man was writhing on the floor next to them with a knife wound slashed straight across his neck. Thomas looked back at the man sitting on top of Caterina's legs and noticed a knife sticking out of his side. She had done significant damage to two of the attackers. *Good girl.*

Two of Thomas's knives had somehow already found their way into his hands, and within seconds, he cut open the throat of the vagrant sitting on top of Caterina. Thomas grabbed the third—very surprised—man by the throat with both of his hands and held him against the wall, effectively cutting off any air he hoped to breathe. The man's eyes bulged as he tried, ineffectually, to gasp for air. He pulled at Thomas's hands and pushed against Thomas's face until the fight left his body completely. Thomas's hands didn't release the villain's neck until he felt the last pulse of blood beat in protest. As soon as he was sure the man was dead, he dropped the limp body to the ground.

Thomas looked down at the crumpled body and saw a gash across the dead man's stomach—his insides spilling out onto the ground. *I didn't do that*, he thought as the haze of anger faded from his mind. He turned to see Caterina standing right next to him with her knife grasped tightly in her hand. Blood dripped from the knife, but Thomas couldn't tell where the man's blood stopped and Caterina's began. He stepped back to evaluate her health. Her dress was ripped up to her hip, and her leg and side were bleeding from knife wounds. He took a step forward, but knew better than to rush at her while she still held her knife. She had killed one man tonight and aided in the deaths of two others. Thomas couldn't help but feel proud of her strength.

"Caterina? You're safe now," he assured her while maintaining his distance. All he wanted to do was hold her in his arms so he could feel the life in her—so he could know for sure that she was all right.

When she looked up at him, her face was covered in tears, but she didn't look fragile.

"I know I am," she breathed. "I kept praying you would come back. I knew you would come back." She dropped her hand down to her side and Thomas stepped closer to wrap his arms around her. He was afraid of how badly she might have been wounded, but at the same time he was afraid to let her go. He knew he had arrived in time, but she would forever be traumatized by the attack. He was furious at himself for being oblivious to the threat. He should have been more careful—more vigilant—and this would never have happened. He screamed curses at himself in his mind for putting this lovely creature in any kind of danger.

"I'm sorry, Caterina. I had no idea you were in danger," he growled, as his eyes narrowed and his expression grew even more furious.

He wanted nothing more than to bring those three bastards back to life just to kill them again—but more slowly and painfully the second time around.

"I know. I know," she said as she wrapped her arms around him. He couldn't help feeling that she was trying to comfort him, and in that moment, he knew she would be all right.

FORTY-NINE

NEITHER CATERINA nor Thomas noticed the crowd that gathered outside her quarters during the altercation. But within minutes, everyone on board knew what had transpired. The captain apologized profusely for the actions of his deceased crew members while Thomas fretted over Caterina's wounds. Caterina tried to insist she needed to help the crew with their duties since the captain had lost three men, but much to her chagrin, neither Thomas nor Captain Donoso were amenable to that plan.

As soon as the bodies were removed and blood cleaned from her room, Thomas asked everyone for some privacy. Caterina watched as Thomas cleaned the needle she had been using to mend clothes in the flame of one of her candles.

"This is going to feel awful, but I don't want you bleeding to death under my watch," he said with a forced smile.

Until that moment, Caterina hadn't noticed that she was wounded at all. She looked down at her body and realized her hands and her dress were completely covered in blood. Her heart started racing as she thought about the similarities between this day and that night so long ago. She closed her eyes and saw all the bodies—past and present—lying dead on the ground at her feet. When she squeezed her eyes shut even tighter, she heard her own screams from earlier all around her head.

"No!" she whispered as her mind succumbed to darkness.

When she woke, Thomas was sitting next to her bed. He had fallen asleep holding her hand, his head resting on the bed next to her hip. His blood-splashed sleeves were rolled up around his biceps and his hair was still disheveled from the earlier incident.

She looked down and saw she was in a different outfit. *How did I change clothes? Oh my goodness. Thomas changed my clothes.* The embarrassment of the idea colored her cheeks, but she forced her mind to move onto more pressing matters.

She took a deep breath and felt a searing pain in her left side. She tried to make subtle movements with each part of her body in order to pinpoint where she was hurt. Her left side and right leg seemed the most painful, but she hadn't yet moved her left arm—she didn't want to wake Thomas from his nap. She moved her sheet out of the way and lifted the nightshirt she was wearing as much as she could. She saw a cut almost six inches long on her ribs. It was stitched shut expertly, and she smiled a little at how carefully the stitches had been made. The cut on her leg was much smaller in width, but she could tell the knife had found deeper purchase there. It, too, was stitched shut, and she breathed a little easier knowing she was alive and her attackers were dead.

When she let the shirt fall back to her body, Thomas jolted away from the bed, turning toward the door with his knife raised for a fight. The entire move was swift and silent, and Caterina felt a sense of calm flow through her when she saw his aggressive stance.

"Thank you," she said softly. He jumped at the sound of her voice and turned back to her. As quickly as his knife had come out of its holster, it was put away again, and he was sitting by her side once more.

"How do you feel?" he asked urgently.

"Surprisingly good. Did you stitch my wounds?" she asked, admiring the careful work.

"Yes. I wouldn't let anyone else in the room. I *won't* let anyone else in the room for the rest of this trip. But everyone knows to keep their distance from you. They saw ... what happened," he stiffened at the end. She could tell he was worried about her mental state after the incident. She hoped she could make him understand that she was all right.

"It's all right, Thomas. I know I killed them. Or I killed one of them. I think you finished off the other two," she said quietly. "Thank you. You saved me from ...." But she couldn't seem to find the words.

"I should have been here. You wouldn't … they couldn't have."

She shushed him softly and placed a hand on his cheek. She needed him to understand that she was going to be all right. She had recovered before—she would recover again.

"I'll be just fine, Thomas. Not right away, but soon," she assured him.

"You're in shock. When everything sinks in, I want to make sure you're still all right," he said vehemently.

Caterina took a deep breath as she realized what she was about to admit. She knew he would be a wreck, just waiting for her to break down, unless she told him what had happened so many years ago.

"This has happened before … to me," she started, unsure of how to continue.

"What? What do you mean?" he asked, his expressions turning deadly.

"What happened today. A long time ago, another man tried … and I killed him. I killed him, and I overcame the grief."

Thomas stood up and looked around. He looked as if he wanted to throw something or punch through a wall. He began pacing back and forth in the room, and Caterina worried what he might do.

"Do your brothers know what happened?" he asked, furious.

"Well yes, sort of. They don't know all the details. But what does this have to do with them?" she asked, confused by his question.

He knelt down by the bed and took both her hands in his. He was breathing more heavily than normal, and the look in his eyes was intense.

"How could they have possibly let you go—alone—across the ocean. They are senseless fools for allowing it—let alone *helping* you!" he said in a terrifying, hushed tone.

Caterina pulled her hands away from his grasp. She felt a surge of pain in her side as she did, and a hiss escaped her mouth. Thomas immediately calmed down and asked if she was all right.

"No. I'm not all right. You're judging my brothers—*my family*—over something you can't possibly understand. You don't get to have an opinion on the reasoning behind my leaving Europe." She crossed her arms and looked away from him. She didn't want to discuss it any further, and she knew there was no reason to divulge her secrets. He would be gone as soon as they arrived at her home in Milan, and she didn't need anyone out in the world telling people about her condition.

He stood silently for some time before turning toward the door.

"I'll be just outside if you need anything. I'm not sorry for being upset with your brothers, but I am sorry that I upset you," he said as the door closed behind him.

FIFTY

THOMAS STATIONED himself outside Caterina's room for the next several weeks. Their trip across the ocean would soon come to an end, but he still needed to deliver Caterina back to Milan in one piece. He had taken responsibility for her well-being when he was tasked with taking her home. He had failed to protect her once already. He wasn't about to let it happen again. No one was allowed to come near her room, and the only time he allowed Caterina out of her quarters was when she insisted she needed fresh air and sunshine—at which point he followed her around like a bodyguard.

The wound on her side healed within a matter of days, and she claimed the one on her leg was good as new. But despite her protests, Thomas remained doubtful that she was truly better—he had seen how deep her cuts had gone.

"Please let me check them again," he begged as he handed her breakfast one morning.

"Thomas. This is ridiculous. I'm telling you, I'm *fine*," she said with a roll of her eyes.

Their interactions were rocky—at best—ever since his comments about her brothers.

"Caterina. Let me do this. If it becomes infected, you could lose your leg," he pleaded.

She grunted in frustration and threw her hands up in defeat. She sat on the edge of the bed and lifted her skirt to where the wound had been. All he could see was a tiny red line that proved she had, in fact, been wounded at one point. He pushed gently on the place where the cut should have been open.

"Does that hurt?" he asked.

"Not one bit," she answered.

"You took out the stitches," he observed.

"The same day you took the stitches out of my side," she nodded.

"But … it was deep. I saw how deep it was. There's no way it should be fully healed," he marveled.

"I'm a very fast healer," she said as she dropped her skirt to cover her leg once more.

Thomas stood and left the room, pondering what he had witnessed. *She heals faster than any mortal I've seen. She once told me that she never gets sick. Her brothers helped her leave Europe. And she won't tell me how long she lived in Tantun. Is it possible?* He couldn't help but let his imagination run wild. But he knew he was crazy for even thinking it. Only men were immortals. He had known that for over nine hundred years. *If there were any female immortals, one of us would have found them by now*, he told himself as his thoughts returned to protecting her from harm.

Caterina was sick of being locked in her room. She felt like Thomas was over-doing this protection thing. She had spent weeks dealing with the emotional aftermath of the event and was ready to move on. Her physical wounds had been closed for a week, and her emotional ones were as healed as she thought they would ever be. She wanted to go back to mending clothes.

All this alone time gave her far too much time to think about Thomas and the way he protected her. He had choked a man to death with his bare hands to save her. A part of her wanted to just tell Thomas about her past and let him decide what to do with the information. She was going back to Europe anyway. She would need to move around for the rest of her life to avoid being found out. One more mortal knowing the truth couldn't really hurt, could it? She sighed and realized how foolish that thought process was.

She needed to get out of the room. She needed to do anything besides thinking about revealing the truth of her immortality to a stranger.

"Thomas!" she yelled as she opened the door abruptly. "I need fresh air.

Right this second."

"Are you all right?" he asked as he looked her over with worried eyes.

"Good God, Thomas. I am *fine*. But you can't keep treating me like I'm a fragile, wounded little girl. I'm as normal as I've ever been. And I need out of here."

Caterina walked up to the deck as Thomas followed closely behind. She leaned on the railing of the ship, looking out over the endless ocean. It had felt so threatening, so ominous on her voyage with Colombo. This journey felt better—almost as if the sea was welcoming her home. She breathed the fresh air and closed her eyes as sunlight hit her face. She envisioned the vineyards, just as she had left them. She saw Jacopo checking the grapes with his son as her nieces and nephews played nearby. They would be grown adults now, probably with families of their own. But she hoped they would remember her somehow.

"What was it?" she asked.

"What?" Thomas answered, obviously confused by the ambiguity of her question.

"What was my surprise going to be that morning?" she wanted to know. She had forgotten about the surprise before that moment.

He smiled, but she could see he was conflicted about something.

"Captain Donoso? Can you stay with the lady?" he asked as Caterina rolled her eyes. When the captain joined her, Thomas left with expediency.

"I'll be right back," he called without glancing back.

When he returned a few moments later, Caterina's heart took flight. As soon as she saw the canvas and easel, her joy spilled over, and she began to cry.

"How?" she asked as tears dripped down her cheeks.

"Our captain here had them lying around, and he wasn't using them. He wanted you to have them," Thomas said modestly.

"Thank you, sir," Caterina curtsied.

"It was my pleasure," the captain smiled and bowed slightly before returning to his quarters.

Caterina smiled as Thomas stood stiffly, wearing an awkward grin.

"Thank you," she said softly. "I know it was your idea, not his. This is an amazing surprise."

He only nodded in response, but she knew from the redness in his cheeks that he felt the depth of her appreciation.

She spent the next week on deck every day, painting the ship and the ocean. She was grateful for real paints in every color and paintbrushes not made from clumps of stolen animal fur tied to twigs. The joy she received from painting made her spirits soar. The loneliness of the past twenty-six years and terror from the present journey faded, and all she felt was the happiness of her coming freedom.

Fifty-one

THE REST OF THE TRIP flew by. Thomas was happy that Caterina's walls had come down a little with the presentation of the painting supplies. But things still weren't back to the way they had been before the incident. Their friendship was going to come to an end as soon as they parted ways, and Thomas wasn't sure he felt comfortable leaving her unprotected with brothers who allowed her to leave in the first place.

When their ship finally ported in Cadiz, he and Caterina said goodbye to Captain Donoso and found a room for the night.

"I'll go out tomorrow and hire a boat to take us to Naples," he decided.

"Oh," she said softly. "I thought we were traveling by horseback."

"God, no," he chortled. To think of traveling on horseback for that long—the horse would definitely try to kill him. But as he thought about it more, he realized the remainder of their trip was only one week on the boat and another week on horseback from Naples to Milan. If they traveled by land the entire way, it would take at least a month. *Maybe you should have thought that through before you decided on the boat.* His time with Caterina was drawing too quickly to an end.

The room he booked included only one bed, and since Caterina insisted she could not sleep on the bed, Thomas used it. When they awoke the next morning, they ate the best breakfast they had eaten in months—fresh bread, fresh fruit, and hearty stew. The food on the ship had progressively gotten more stale and disgusting. They savored each bite before heading out to find a boat for hire.

The ship they found was leaving that very day, and Thomas found himself wishing there was more time to waste before beginning the final leg of their trip.

"Are you all right?" Caterina asked, seeing the pained expression on his face.

"Oh yes, I'm fine. I only wish we didn't have to board another boat so soon. My body only stopped feeling like it was swaying in the last hour," he lied.

"Mine too," she agreed.

This vessel was quite a bit smaller than the ship they had spent the prior month aboard. The crew included only ten men, and Caterina and Thomas were given a small corner of the cargo hold as their living space.

"I'm sorry this isn't nicer," Thomas apologized.

"I promise, it's all right," Caterina chuckled. "I've spent years sleeping on the floor of a hut in the middle of the woods. This won't be a problem for just one week."

Thomas knew she was right and smiled at her attempt to lighten his mood. They would spend most of their time in their "room" over the next week. The deck was too small, and they would be in the way of the crew if they stayed above.

He stared at her as they sat side-by-side in the dim candlelight. She had asked him twice before what it was he and his Family did, and he hadn't felt comfortable enough to provide her with an answer. Here in the dark, with no one else around, he felt compelled to tell her the truth. She couldn't run and hide from him in the confines of the small vessel, and he felt he had proven he would protect her at all costs. *What would the harm be?*

In Cozumel, his feelings for Caterina were barely cordial. She attacked him twice, beat him at a knife-throwing game, and remained impassive about her past—proving she didn't care to know him any more than he cared to know her. But over the past month, her mysterious life had become more than just a puzzle he wanted to figure out.

As he looked at her face in the dim light, he felt his vision shift just slightly. It was like he had viewed a star in the sky night after night but only just realized its placement in an elaborate constellation. He saw in her face more beauty than he could remember seeing before. Nothing had changed in her appearance, but it seemed as if the blinders were removed from his eyes. He could finally see her for what she was—a beautiful, caring, insightful woman. He yearned to *know* her—not just know *about* her. But he knew if he wanted the truth about her past, he must first tell her his own secret.

"I'll answer your question. But you might never want to see me again once I tell you. If that's the case, I will still take you to your home to ensure your safety, but I will leave you with the promise that you will never see me again," he swore. Caterina looked at him with confusion written in her expression.

"What on earth are you talking about? What question?" she asked.

"In Tantun. You asked me what it is that I do. What it is that my Family does."

"Is it really that awful?" she breathed, wearing an excited smile.

Thomas chuckled at her enthusiasm. She was different than women of his previous acquaintance. She wasn't an emotional wreck over what happened on the ship. She was mentally stronger than most men he knew. And she was excited over the prospect of his career being terrifying. *She's an enigma.*

"Not ... awful. Umm. I cannot believe I'm going to tell you this," he sighed as he averted his eyes from her gaze. He ran a finger up and down the bridge of his nose and breathed deeply. He kept his voice low as he started to speak.

"Everyone in my Family—myself included—is an assassin," he whispered, watching her face closely.

She chuckled at first, thinking his statement was a joke. But the impact of his words sunk in as she read the seriousness of his expression. Her mouth opened slightly, and her brows furrowed. A hundred questions gathered on the tip of her tongue, but none found their way out of her mouth. She shifted her body away from him, pushing her back against the side of the ship so she could look at him directly without craning her neck. He watched as she appraised his weapons and his hands, as if waiting for him to grab a knife and stab her. But when he made no movement, her body relaxed a little. She sat silently for quite some time, looking this way and that, as she pondered his secret.

"Are you being honest?" she asked with an odd expression that Thomas could not interpret. He nodded once as she searched his face for answers to her unspoken questions. "Are you going to kill me?" she asked, still wearing the same expression.

"What? No! Of course not. Haven't I proven I would do anything to keep you safe?" Thomas asked, exasperated by her thought process. "If I was hired to kill you, you would already be dead," he said as a matter of fact. "And why would someone try to kill you? Did you do something? Is that why you sailed across the ocean? To escape something you did?" he asked in rapid succession.

She looked angry for a short moment but ignored his questions and continued with her own. *Interesting*, he thought. *Maybe her brothers were trying to keep her alive by sending her away.*

"How did your family become assassins?" she asked, pulling his mind back to the present.

"My father and uncle one day decided they wanted to train their sons to be assassins. I have no idea *why* they came to that decision, but I believe it had to do with the political climate of the age," he answered.

"If you're an assassin, who were you in Tantun to kill?" she said excitedly.

"I wasn't there to kill anyone. I was hired as a sort of bodyguard by Cortés. I advised him and made sure the politicians in Santiago didn't try to kill him. A lot of people hate that man," he said with a smirk. "Now it's your turn. How long were you in Tantun?"

"No. I'm still not going answer that. But I'll consider telling you ... someday. Now, will you turn around so I can change out of this dress? I'm not sure I'll ever readjust to European fashion again after spending so much time in Mayan clothing."

Thomas felt his cheeks flush with embarrassment as he turned around. He had opened up to her, and she returned the favor by telling him absolutely nothing about her story. *At least she isn't afraid of you. She didn't seem upset ...*

that has to mean something. Maybe she's putting on an act to make you think she's all right. But really, she barely even flinched.

When she announced he could turn around, he looked her up and down and felt his cheeks flush again.

"What's wrong? Did I do something wrong? Why are you looking at me like that?" she worried, checking each part of her body to make sure she was fully clothed.

"Nothing is wrong. You look like a noble. I mean, you've always carried yourself like nobility. But now you really look like one," Thomas said, struggling with his words.

Caterina looked at him in obvious confusion for a few silent moments.

"All right. Thank you?" she said as a question rather than a statement. After a few awkward moments of silence, she added, "I'm beginning to grasp that I'm actually returning home. I haven't quite come to peace with it. I'm quite nervous my presence won't be well-received."

"I'm sure your family will be ecstatic," he said, hoping to assuage her fears, but worrying he might be wrong. "But we still have a week on horseback once we arrive in Naples," Thomas said, trying to relieve her nerves.

"Right. Which I'm sure will be your favorite part of the trip," she snickered.

His mood plummeted. "Not likely," he spoke quietly. His only thought was that the next few days would likely be the last he would ever spend with Caterina.

FIFTY-TWO

Naples, Italy, August 1519

WHEN THEY STEPPED ashore in Naples, Caterina hoped and prayed that Thomas's strange attitude would finally change. Since the incident, he had been acting like an overprotective big brother—more specifically, *her* brothers. He hovered the way they used to and worried in the same manner. And on the trip from Cadiz to Naples, his mood was wildly inconsistent—he was happily talkative one minute and silently mopey the next.

Maybe he doesn't want to return to his family. Maybe he doesn't like the work he does. Or maybe he's simply fretting over the week he'll have to spend on horseback. That's probably it, she decided.

"I've purchased our horses," Thomas said nervously as he lead two beautiful gray mares toward her.

"Hello girls," Caterina whispered. She ran a hand over each of their noses and checked to see if their bodies were strong and ready for the week-long trip.

"I don't think either of these girls will try to lie down on you," she teased while she checked their hooves for cracks or sores.

"You say that now ..." Thomas said with a playful smirk—though she could tell he was doing his best to hide his fear.

After eating a small lunch of stew, they mounted their horses—Caterina made sure Thomas rode the larger of the two—and set off toward Naples. Caterina had forgotten how much she loved a good stew. She had forgotten how much she loved home-cooked meals in general. Her family always ate huge meals with at least three courses—usually four or five. She couldn't wait to experience that once more.

She glanced at Thomas and noticed his body appeared to be tense and uncomfortable in his saddle. His elbows jutted out to his sides with the reins held far too taut for the horse's comfort.

"Thomas! For goodness' sake! No wonder horses hate you. Loosen the tension in the reins, and relax your arms and your body. The horse can feel how uncomfortable and nervous you are—which makes the horse uncomfortable and nervous. She watched him try to relax as he let out some of the tension in the reins.

"More," she demanded. He tried to copy her technique, and after a few more moments of terror-filled glances, she watched the horse relax beneath him.

"Well that's different," he smiled. "You fixed my riding problems in five minutes. Wish I'd had you around a long time ago," he mumbled under his breath.

Caterina smiled at his appreciation. She was happy she could change his attitude toward horses. More specifically, she was thrilled she held enough influence over him that he would listen to her suggestions and change so willingly. She caught herself staring at him and quickly dropped her gaze, hoping he hadn't caught her.

Thomas wanted to drag out the last leg of the trip for as long as possible. He originally hoped that his discomfort on a horse would slow them down, but Caterina's adjustments actually worked. He felt far more in control, and his horse was moving at a more brisk pace. She looked exuberant, and he knew she only thought of returning home quickly. She didn't care one bit that he would leave her in Milan and likely never see her again. His mood became taciturn once more—as it had frequently been on the trip from Cadiz. He glanced at Caterina to see her look quickly away from him with an angry gleam in her eyes. *She looks as if she wants to get away from me as quickly as possible*, he thought, dejected. *Maybe she isn't amenable to my being an assassin after all.*

They barely spoke throughout the next three days. And when they did, the conversations were short and impersonal. They kept to general topics about the way each city looked, the style of clothing worn by passers-by, and the niceness of the weather. He thought that after everything they'd been through, they had moved past small talk, but apparently that was only wishful thinking.

Thomas desperately wanted answers about Caterina's background. But no matter what, Caterina brushed off his questions and flatly refused to give him the satisfaction of knowing. He was unaccustomed to others having such dark and private secrets. He hated that he was unable to uncover the reasoning behind her silence, and the emotional wall she had constructed between them was beginning to grate on his nerves. He *needed* to know why she was in Tantun—and he no longer had the luxury of time to find his answers.

He caught himself glaring at her from time to time, hoping she would see his expression and finally come clean about her secret.

The day of riding had been terrible. She caught Thomas looking at her angrily on more than one occasion, and her own mind was filled with unpleasant thoughts. There was no way to explain her family's ages to Thomas when they finally arrived in Milan. She had thought about it all day, and the only way she might be able to avoid telling him the truth would be to treat her nephews like they were her brothers and let him make his own assumptions. The other subject on which her mind was fixated could not be remedied. She knew Thomas didn't see her as a romantic interest, but even so, she worried her heart would break when he finally left. She had grown accustomed to his presence. Though his dedication to her protection was a bit overwhelming at times, she had to admit it felt nice having someone pay this much attention to her well-being. Cortés had arranged for Thomas's contract to end with her safe delivery back to Europe, but she knew Thomas would only believe the contract truly fulfilled when she was safe in her family's home. She didn't want to return home broken-hearted. The nervousness she felt over her brothers' reactions to her reappearance was already too much for her mind to wrap itself around. Adding a broken heart might put her emotions in a state of uncontrollable sorrow. *Maybe I'll have him leave me at my family's villa in Florence. Then I can make the trip to Milan on my own. That way, I can shed my tears over his loss before seeing my family. And then he will never know the age difference between myself and my brothers.* But that was wishful thinking. She knew Thomas wouldn't let her go anywhere alone—and she had already made the mistake of telling him her brothers were in Milan. Nothing could be done.

She would have to find another way to keep the truth hidden.

FIFTY-THREE

THOMAS WOKE UP the next morning determined to find out Caterina's secret. He barely slept an hour the night before because he couldn't stop thinking about her mysterious past. *She is intent upon not telling me, but I cannot function without knowing. She is going to drive me mad!*

The moment she emerged from her room, his determination dwindled into doubt. *Perhaps I have no right to know her reasons. She doesn't seem to trust me enough to think I'm worthy of knowing. I must show her I'm trustworthy. I need to show her that her protection means more to me than the fulfillment of a contract.*

But by the end of their fourth day of riding, she felt more distant than ever. His thoughts were filled with paranoia over her continued silence. He worried she would try to say a short goodbye at the entrance to her family's home, and he would be forced to watch her ride away without a backward glance. He wanted to meet Caterina's brothers. He wanted to talk with them at length to understand what had happened for them to send their sister across an ocean— alone. But he doubted he would have a chance to meet them at all.

"Are you all right?" Caterina asked, pulling Thomas from his unpleasant thoughts. He didn't know how long she had been staring at him.

"Yes," he said after some time. It took him a few seconds to remember what she asked.

"Good. Fine," she said in an awkward tone as she dismounted her horse and led the mare to the inn's small stable.

He could see that she was upset now as well, but couldn't understand what the problem could possibly be.

"Are *you* all right?" he asked carefully.

"I can see you staring at me. I know you've been watching me all week. Or glaring at me, if we're being honest. I don't know what you want from me!" she said, disappearing into the inn.

Thomas watched her shut the door to the small inn as his cheeks flushed with embarrassment. Was she truly oblivious to the purpose behind his frustration? He thought he had been quite obvious.

He tried to purchase two rooms for them in the tiny inn, but there was only one available. Caterina protested that she could sleep alone in the stable with the horses—away from him—but the very thought of it made his hair stand on end. It was still his duty to keep her safe—and sleeping in a warm bed while she slept in the stables was out of the question.

He felt badly knowing that she hadn't understood his frustration. *I must have looked like such an ass just glaring at her all those hours. I thought surely she could see through my anger. I thought ....* He was angry with himself for assuming she understood. Normally, in situations like these, he would project his anger onto whomever was near enough to feel his wrath. But he desperately needed to remain calm. It was essential Caterina hear his pleas.

As soon as they entered the room, Caterina took the blanket from the bed and made herself a pallet in the corner of the small room. She lay down facing the wall, and went to sleep without a sound. He couldn't seem to find the right words to break the silence, and by the time he was ready to talk, he could hear her breathing the deep breaths of sleep.

That's it. We're not leaving here until I've discovered her secret, he decided.

Thomas made sure he woke early the next morning. He was going to confront Caterina whether she liked it or not. He positioned the only chair in the room right in front of the door and sat down in it so she couldn't escape when she woke up. An hour later, she finally opened her eyes for the day, and Thomas braced himself for the coming discussion.

FIFTY-FOUR

CATERINA SLEPT soundly for the first time since arriving in Italy. She had found Thomas's proximity on the boat comforting while she slept. But since they began sleeping in separate rooms once more, she had been struggling with horrific nightmares. Somehow, simply knowing Thomas was in the same room kept the nightmares away. She stretched before standing, feeling every bit of the soreness from riding a horse after such a long hiatus from the activity. She stood slowly and turned to the door, expecting to see Thomas still asleep in bed. What she saw instead stopped her in her tracks.

Thomas was sitting in a chair, blocking the door, with a steely look of resolve.

"We're not going anywhere until we talk," he said impassively.

Caterina took a deep breath, walked to the edge of the bed, and sat down. She could not fathom where the conversation was headed.

"What do you mean?" she asked, looking him directly in the eyes. He averted his gaze from her face and shifted uncomfortably in the chair. After a few minutes of silence, he moved his chair to sit directly in front of her. When he looked up, their eyes locked, and she saw questions swirling behind his eyes once more. *Oh no*, she worried, finally understanding his strange mood swings.

"I *need* you to tell me why you left your family," he pleaded, in a desperate tone she had not heard before. "Tell me why you're afraid to return home. Please. Tell me what's going on," he begged, his voice and expression softening.

"I don't understand why you feel like you need to know," she said, hoping he had some sort of explanation.

"I need ..." he growled, and she watched him stop himself and take a few deep breaths to calm down before he spoke again. "I cannot sleep at night. I cannot think of anything else while we ride. I do not feel right with the prospect of leaving you with brothers who would willingly let you travel across an ocean alone. And if you do not tell me what sent you so far away, I will be plagued by the secret for the rest of my life. I am begging you to put me out of my misery and tell me *why*."

She knew he was telling the truth, and while she felt he was reacting a bit too dramatically, she felt his concern for her well-being more strongly than ever. His expression was pained, and his eyes showed fatigue. Maybe she could give him just enough of a reason for her exodus without telling him the whole truth.

"I left Milan to keep my family safe," she said slowly, watching confusion fill Thomas's eyes.

"Was someone after you?" he asked, his expression growing worried.

"Not yet, but they would have been if I had stayed," she answered as obscurely as possible. Thomas's returning expression announced he was not amused by her avoidance. His eyes grew hard, and she worried he was angry with her.

"Explain," he said sternly.

Caterina paused, unable to speak. But the ferocity in Thomas's eyes told her he would wait for as long as it took for her to answer. *He is between me and the door, and I don't think he'll let me out until he's satisfied with my answer. This is dangerous ... not only for me, but for him. I don't know how this could affect him. But he is an assassin. He has proven he will protect me at all times. Perhaps if he knows of my situation, he will decide to continue protecting me. That wouldn't be terrible.* She knew it was wishful thinking, but she sighed and gave in to his command.

"When we arrive in Milan, there are going to be some things you won't understand," she began. Thomas stayed silent. "My brothers are ... older."

Thomas's brows furrowed in confusion, but he didn't speak.

"They're going to be much older. Much. Umm ... I don't even know where to begin. It's going to take some time to explain everything," she said, unsure of how to proceed.

"I will sit quietly and listen until you've said everything you need to say," he promised.

She took a deep breath. *You can do this*, she told herself shakily.

"I ... I'm not a normal person," she tried to explain.

Thomas chuckled.

"I could have told you that the day we met," he joked with a smirk.

"No! That's not what I meant," she said, feeling a bit exasperated by his lightheartedness. He was forcing her to tell him her deepest, darkest secret, and he was joking about it?

"You promised you would sit quietly. Please don't joke with me right now. I'm having trouble enough as it is," she asked with her eyes turned toward the floor.

"Of course. I'm sorry," he said, reaching out awkwardly toward her before pulling his hand back. She looked up into his face and saw he was genuinely sorry. His eyes were practically begging her to go on with her secret.

"I ... I will never grow old," she said sadly.

"Of course you will. If someone is trying to find you and kill you, you can come with me. I'll keep you safe. And if they get too close, I'll kill them before they can even find you. You would never be in danger if you let me protect you," he promised fervently.

She felt her heart leap at his offer, but she once again felt the emphasis that he placed on her protection. Of course he would do whatever it took to keep her *safe*. He felt it was his honor and duty to do so.

"No! You don't understand!" she said, frustrated by her inability to speak the words aloud. It felt exceedingly strange, revealing her immortality to a mortal who would never be able to grasp the idea. She hoped he wouldn't assume she was a witch. She hoped he wouldn't kill her where she stood. She hoped he wouldn't look at her with fear the way she used to look at herself each time she saw her reflection staring back at her in a mirror. She stood up and began pacing the floor.

"I … cannot … age." She stopped pacing as she watched a strange expression flash across his face. His posture became immediately rigid, and he didn't say a word. The panic that welled up in her chest began pressing in on her heart. He remained silent, so she resumed her pacing and continued to explain. This time, when she opened her mouth, the words began to flow out rapidly. She knew she might only have a few minutes before he ran away forever. Whatever she wanted to tell him, *this* was the time to say it.

"I am seventy-three years of age. I stopped aging when I was twenty. I fled from Italy when people started noticing I wasn't growing older each year. I crossed the ocean with Cristoforo Colombo in 1492. I lived in Tantun for twenty-six years. There was a reason the natives thought I was a deity! I am *immortal*. And it's dangerous for you to be near me," she said as she realized her volume had risen and her chest heaved with exertion.

Thomas couldn't believe what he heard, but Caterina's fervor told him she was telling the truth. This changed everything. There was actual merit to their searching all those years for other immortals. And the fact that she was a woman made his head spin even more.

There are no immortal daughters, his mind protested. Priest bored that phrase into his head from the time he was a child. *No immortal daughters exist.* But standing before him was proof to the contrary. Physical evidence. This was an immortal woman. His blood raced through his veins.

"How? How and when did this happen?" he begged as he stood and his hands found her shoulders. He grasped them tightly, unknowingly clinging to her for support.

She looked at him with a bewildered expression, but she answered after only a slight hesitation.

"1466. In Paris," she answered sheepishly. He could tell she didn't want to explain further, but her answer was evidence enough. *Then it's true! My God! It's true! She's an immortal.* He heard laughter break through his lips, and his jubilation could not be contained. Without thinking, he swept Caterina up in his arms and spun her around.

"Put me down!" she yelled, now terrified. "You are mad!" she said as he obeyed, and she stepped away from him.

"I *am* mad. With excitement!" he said with a smile affixed to his face. Caterina still looked concerned, but he hoped his next words would put her at ease.

"I was in Paris in 1466," he said. Her expression was distrustful, but he knew he held her full attention. "I was there with my eldest and youngest brothers. We were searching the homes of the dead for survivors of the plague. The only problem was that we were only searching for men," he said with a laugh. "We have always believed that only men could be immortal. You see, in my family, we are *born* immortal—and we have never seen a female immortal."

The expression on Caterina's face could only be described as engrossed. She was hungry to hear more, but at the same time she was having trouble trusting his words. He continued.

"I was born in the year 625. I am the fifth of ten sons. My father was the first immortal—though none of us have knowledge of how and when he came to be that way. For years, we have searched through plague-ridden cities for survivors, but we have never found a single immortal ... until you. You survived the Parisian plague of 1466, did you not?" he asked, hoping her answer would confirm his conclusion.

"I did," she whispered as she sat back down on the bed, in shock.

Caterina's head spun. *Wake up. Wake up this instant. You are dreaming, and you will be devastated when you wake up and find that none of this is real*, her mind screamed. She did not awaken, and the possibility that Thomas was truly immortal began to sink in. She hoped he was not playing a cruel joke. She hoped he was not making fun of her, but his expression did not suggest mockery.

"You are serious," she said as a statement rather than the question she meant it to be.

"Completely," he said, still smiling from ear to ear. He sat down in the chair to face her once more. They sat, staring into each others' eyes. She watched Thomas's gaze move to her lips and back up to her eyes, and she had the distinct feeling he wanted to kiss her. The idea distracted her for only a moment from her confusion over an entire *family* of immortals existing, but every time he glanced at her lips, she felt a longing for him to lean over and place a kiss on them.

"You are over nine hundred years old?" she asked in awe. She couldn't imagine living for so long, but she realized it must not be quite as lonely when one was surrounded by an entire family who were also immortal.

"Yes," he said as his eyes drifted once more to her lips. "I cannot believe you are real," he breathed. Her breath caught in her throat as she lifted her eyes to meet his.

"And I cannot believe I am not dreaming," she whispered back.

They stared at each other in silence for some time before Thomas opened his mouth to speak once more.

"You must come with me. I want you to meet the rest of the immortals."

FIFTY-FIVE

THOMAS FELT as if his entire existence had been culminating to this point. If Priest had not been so reckless with the contracts he accepted, Thomas would never have spoken out against him. If he had never spoken out against the direction the Family was headed, Priest would never have contracted him as a bodyguard to Cortés. And if Thomas had never gone with Cortés to Cozumel, he would never have met Caterina—another immortal. A female immortal. A *beautiful*, female immortal. *This must be fate*, he thought with a smile on his face. *It's too fortuitous to be anything else.* Now that he knew the truth about her—and she knew the entire truth about him—he thought it might be time to make his intentions clear.

"We can arrive in Florence tomorrow. We'll stay there as long as you like. I know my brothers will be overjoyed to meet you," Thomas tried to mention casually. He knew she was eager to see her family in Milan, but Thomas doubted whether her brothers would even be alive.

Caterina seemed to be in a permanent state of shock. Her gaze flitted from Thomas's eyes down to his mouth then around the room every few seconds. Every time her gaze met his, he watched her cheeks grow a little rosier. He didn't think she was interested in him the same way he was in *her*, but he hoped he might have a chance now that she knew they were both immortal.

"I think I would like that," she finally said. "But I am quite eager to see my family again," she tacked on.

He heaved a sigh of relief that he had managed to secure at least one extra day to win her over. Previously, he was resigned to the idea that she wanted nothing more than to return home and be rid of him. Now that she agreed to come with him, he felt a sliver of hope that he might convince her to stay with him.

Thomas's heart leapt. He couldn't imagine the possibility of falling in love with someone who would continue living. The idea of handing over the entirety of his heart to a woman had been unimaginable only one day earlier. Even when he had married centuries earlier, he always knew she would someday die —and that knowledge made him unknowingly place a wall of protection around his heart. He had spoiled and adored his wife, but he never quite felt as if he could be completely honest with her about his feelings of heartache he felt each time he looked at her—knowing she would someday die. Thomas's excitement swelled as he thought about the possibility of holding onto Caterina for the rest of his life.

Caterina couldn't decipher her feelings. The range of emotions she felt over the new information covered everything from self-pity to exuberance. There were no words in her mind, only emotions. One minute she wanted to cry for the years she spent alone while other immortals were happily gathered together. The next, she wanted to laugh and twirl around while singing about the joy of having finally found another immortal—at having discovered she was not the only one in the world. There were too many questions she wanted to ask to focus on a single thought, so she stayed silently seated, hoping Thomas would announce it was time for them to mount their horses and ride toward Florence.

"Are you going to be all right? I know it's a lot to take in," he said as he leaned closer and his voice grew quiet. His expression changed into something she'd not seen before, and he reached out toward her as if he wanted to cup her face in his hand. But before his hand touched her skin, he quickly pulled away and lowered his eyes to the ground.

Caterina momentarily forgot how to breathe. *Why didn't he touch me?* She imagined what it would feel like for his hand to touch her skin. *Maybe it's possible that he feels something for me*, she hoped. She had never experienced what it felt like to be romantically involved with a man. She could not recall a single man flirting with her (except for the time she wore a mask at the masquerade ball in Paris). But who would count that? Not her, certainly.

He didn't make another move to touch her, and the embarrassed look on his face announced that he wouldn't soon try again. He got up from the chair and pushed it back to the corner where it belonged.

"We should be going if you want to make it to Florence tomorrow," he said without making eye contact.

"All right," she said quietly as she moved past him and headed to the stables.

Thomas was upset with himself for getting excited over a woman who clearly didn't want him. When he tried to touch Caterina's cheek, the look on her face had *not* been welcoming. It was a cross between surprise and disgust, and Thomas wasn't going to force himself on her. After the incident on the ship and her admission of a similar experience in her past, he didn't know if she would *ever* want a man to try to touch her again. He was ashamed for thinking she would be interested in him that way. But there were many questions he wanted to ask, and he hoped she would overlook his indiscretion and talk openly with him about her years as an immortal.

As soon as they finished a breakfast of stew and bread, they mounted their horses once more and rode toward Florence.

"What was it like when you woke up? Did you know you were immortal? Could you feel the change?" he asked one after another.

Caterina's smirk put Thomas at ease once more. *At least she doesn't seem angry*, he thought with relief.

"I had no idea my body was changed. All I knew was that my aunt, uncle, cousins and their servants were dead—and had been dead for much longer than I would have thought it possible for me to stay asleep. I believed I was still infected," she admitted as her entire body tensed.

"What did you do when you woke up?" he asked, hoping she would continue the story. He had never spoken with an immortal born from plague.

Caterina relayed the full story, down to the horrifying details of her attack. Thomas was engrossed. She rode across Europe by herself to return to her family. She slept outside—alone. She killed an attacker. *No wonder her brothers weren't troubled by the prospect of sending her across the ocean for her safety. She's a self-sufficient wonder*, he marveled.

"My family did what they could to make life normal, but it was impossible when everyone in Milan already knew I had returned home from a plague-ridden Paris. My parents and I moved with one of my brothers to our home in Florence. I met a painter there, and we became great friends," she said with a smile that Thomas didn't like one bit. She looked almost giddy when she said 'painter'. "He remained my closest friend until he helped me arrange a position in Colombo's crew across the ocean. Of course, we thought we were going to end up in the Far East," she chuckled.

"What made you leave the crew?" Thomas wanted to know.

"One of the other sailors discovered I was a woman, and I knew it was only a matter of time before something … unpleasant … happened—either for him or for me. It's a long story, but I ran away and ultimately washed up on the shores of Cozumel."

"Was I the first European you had spoken with since you left Colombo's crew?" he asked.

"Yes. And I thought you were going to be the last until Cortés said you could take me home," she smiled. Thomas realized her smile grew on him more and more—and each time he saw it, his desire to reach out and cup her face in his hands only increased.

"Can I ask you some questions now?" she said carefully. Thomas chuckled at her caution.

"Of course. From now on, I'm an open book," he answered with a smirk.

FIFTY-SIX

CATERINA ASKED HIM every question she could think of. How was he raised? Where was he born? What was his family like? How long and when was he married to his wife?

Each time he answered a question, another one immediately flew from her mouth. She was starving for information on the newly-found immortals, and the questions came to her mind faster than Thomas could answer them.

Thomas seemed happy enough to entertain her inquisition—for which she was incredibly grateful. She never once felt he was annoyed with her and didn't get the impression she had asked anything too personal (though she knew other people might have thought her prying too intrusive). He maintained a courteous attitude all day, and only stopped answering her questions when he needed to take a drink of water or relieve himself.

"What's the one thing that fascinates you most about mortals?" she asked, changing the direction of their conversation abruptly.

Thomas thought for some time before giving an answer.

"I suppose I'm fascinated by the utter neglect concerning the brevity of life. When you have a limited number of days on earth, each day should be lived to the fullest. Each moment aimed toward some purpose—some goal. I've ended many a wasted life in my field of work," he said solemnly.

Caterina never thought of mortality in those terms. But she supposed his extra centuries of life likely added to his wisdom. *What will I be like when I've lived nine-hundred years?* she wondered.

"How many people have you killed?" she asked quietly, hoping the question didn't cause offense. She had managed to keep that part of Thomas's life out of her head before now. But an 'immortal assassin' seemed a bit more ominous than a mere mortal one.

"Hundreds," he said solemnly.

Hundreds, she thought in sickened awe. She didn't know how to reconcile 'assassin-Thomas' and 'protector-Thomas.' She had witnessed his ability to make a swift kill on the ship, and she knew he was deadly with a knife. But in the short time she knew him, he had done nothing but comfort her, protect her, and bring her joy. Though he *had* broken into her home, the intent had never been malicious. There was no possible way she could label him a 'bad person' in her mind, even if he had killed hundreds of people.

"Were your victims corrupt?" she asked, hoping for an explanation of the high number.

"Not all. But most, yes. I once killed a man who murdered three of his own children and fed them to his dogs. That kill was particularly satisfying. Another time, I killed a man who beat his servant to death and threw the remains into a river. But whenever I am given a contract on a woman or a child's life, I consider walking away from my Family and starting over somewhere new.

"Your family should not force a lifestyle upon you of which you do not approve," she said, hoping she wasn't overstepping her bounds.

He let out a sigh. "I actually enjoy it—most of the time. The killing brings me immense pleasure when I know the bastard deserves death. It's only when the target is innocent that I can't stand the idea of fulfilling a contract."

Caterina could understand his reasoning. She had not enjoyed killing her attacker in the barn when it happened—it took years to erase the guilt she felt over murdering another person. But looking back at the situation, she was happy knowing someone capable of such evil was no longer roaming freely. She felt the same way about the sailors who attacked her on the ship. She was *happy* they were dead.

"I understand," she said as a look of surprise filled Thomas's eyes. "You feel as if you've rid the world of someone dangerous … someone who might do harm to innocent people. Yes, I understand," she said as she watched Thomas nod his head in silent agreement.

She wanted to hear more about his world, but her mind could not conjure another question.

After an hour of riding in silence, Thomas couldn't stand it any more. His answer to her last question left Caterina's eyes full of contemplation, and he worried she was trying to distance herself from him as the journey came to an end. They were only a few hours from his Family's castle, and the sun was beginning to sink in the sky.

"Shall we stop for the night at the next village?" he asked, hoping she would say 'yes'.

"How much longer until we arrive at your Family's home?" she asked in a strange tone—he thought she might actually be sad.

"A few hours," he answered quietly, hoping she would want to spend the extra night on the road.

"I would very much like to arrive there tonight," she said eagerly.

Thomas sagged in his saddle. *She wants only to meet the other immortals. I wish I could've prevented myself from becoming attached. I fear one of my brothers or nephews might capture her heart.* He couldn't bear the thought of losing her to another in his Family.

"Yes. If we ride quickly, we might even be able to get there before the sun has set," he said with as much false joy as he could muster.

FIFTY-SEVEN

Castello San Romolo, September 1519

AS THEY TURNED down the tree-lined path, Caterina saw a massive structure outlined in the dimly-lit sky.

"What is that?" she asked as she squinted her eyes to try to figure out what she was seeing.

"That's my Family's castle," he answered.

Caterina felt her hands involuntarily pull back on the horse's reins.

"Castle?" she marveled, suddenly nervous at the prospect of Thomas being royalty (or at the very least, impossibly wealthy) in addition to being a handsome, immortal assassin.

"We're not royalty … or at least not that I know of. My family's distant history is not known to any but my father and uncle. But as far as I know, I'm just a normal immortal," he chuckled, apparently amused by her sudden fear.

"But you live in a castle?" she asked in hushed awe.

"We built it in the 12th century. The contracts we accept produce a good bit of income. And there are quite a few of us. You have to understand that over the course of our lives, many of us marry and remarry dozens of times—producing quite a few sons to join in the Family business," he answered as lightly as he could.

"But you've only married once? And have no children?" she asked, hoping she understood him correctly. Her pulse raced as she felt jealousy rise in her chest at the thought of him being with *any* women—even women long gone. The smirk on his face made her blush, and she hoped the dimly lit sky would conceal her jealousy.

"That's correct. I have no children, and I was only married once. Though, I never quite felt like I could share my entire self with her. A part of my mind always reminded me she would someday die," he said with emotion in his voice.

She looked at him, feeling sadness for his loss. As much as she longed for Thomas to feel romantically about her the way she did for him, she wasn't heartless enough to ignore the pain he had suffered after the death of his wife. She remembered the castle ahead and turned toward it once more. A sudden, overwhelming nervousness made her feel as if she was choking. She was about to meet every other immortal in the world. Dozens—if not more—lived inside the castle ahead.

"Please don't leave me," she said, trying to steady her breathing.

"What? Why would I …" he faded out, his brows furrowed in confusion. "I'll remain at your side for the duration of your stay," he promised. "I will keep watch outside your door while you sleep … if that is what you wish."

Caterina wanted him to sleep in the same room as her, but she knew that was inappropriate to even think.

"No. I'm sure that's not necessary. If you trust your family, I will trust them as well," she smiled as she started down the path to the castle ahead.

Fear swelled in Thomas's mind—an emotion he was not used to experiencing (unless it was in response to riding a horse). *Should I trust my Family? I've never worried about bringing a woman here in the past. I know my brothers and nephews share the same respect for women as I. But none of us has brought home an immortal woman. Will they think of her as a threat? Or an impostor? Or a spy?* He knew beyond a shadow of a doubt that she would not reveal their secrets to any others, but would the rest of his Family believe him?

"These are the stables," he said as he guided their horses toward a large building. There were no less than thirty horses inside—telling Thomas that at least a handful of the Family were out fulfilling contracts. He looked around for Sergius's and Samuel's horses and spotted them in the back corner of the room. His heart leapt, and for a moment he forgot all his nervousness and simply felt joy over his reunion with his brothers after so many years apart.

Caterina apparently noticed the change, because she dismounted quickly and unsaddled her horse with a swift efficiency.

"Are you in a hurry to visit one of the horses?" she asked, turning back to Thomas with a smile on her face.

"No," he answered with a small chuckle at her ability to read him. "I'm in a hurry to see its rider. Those are my closest brothers' mares. I can't wait for you to meet them," he said as he grabbed her hand and led her toward the castle door.

Caterina hadn't expected Thomas to hold her hand. She momentarily forgot where she was—she could only think about the welcome pressure of his large hand covering hers. But as soon as they ascended the stone staircase to the massive wooden door, she felt the weight of what was about to happen.

They burst through the door to the most amazing aroma Caterina could remember having smelled in some time. He pulled her through a cavernous entry and turned to the right through an arched doorway. A massive chandelier of hundreds of lit candles hung over a giant U-shaped table. Thirty men—maybe more—sat around the table, laughing and eating a feast. There were a few women also seated around the table, but they were so slight in build compared to the men next to them that they were difficult to see. She tried to take in the scene before her, but awe was the only emotion her mind could conjure.

"Father. Uncle. Brothers. Nephews," Thomas said loudly.

The room grew silent as every pair of eyes darted in their direction. Caterina wanted to hide behind Thomas under their gazes, but she couldn't detect any hostility—only curiosity.

She searched each face, noting that every man appeared to be the same age as Thomas. He had mentioned in passing that everyone in his family stopped aging around twenty-seven or twenty-eight, but seeing a room full of men stuck in time felt odd. She had thought herself alone for so long, the family's mere existence was overwhelming.

"Thomas!" one man yelled as he jumped up from the table and ran to embrace him, forcing Caterina's thoughts back to her present situation. Others joined in the chorus of jubilation over Thomas's return, and he released her hand to hug each of the men who approached.

"You have returned," one man said, still seated at the head of the table. Everyone grew silent under the weight of his monotone words. It hadn't been a question—more like an indignant observation.

"Yes, father. Here is the paperwork from Cortés," he said as he pulled a document from his belt and presented it to his father.

Caterina could already tell she didn't care for Thomas's father. In three words, she felt as if she knew everything necessary to judge the man's character.

"And you brought back a woman? That surprises me most of all. I thought you would never marry again," he said in a bored voice.

Thomas was irritated by his father's interruption. He wanted to enjoy the company of his brothers for a few moments before needing to explain that Caterina was immortal. But it seemed he would not be given that pleasure.

"We are not married, father," he said as his mind searched for the next words to speak.

"So you are planning to be married here?" Priest asked.

"That is ... I didn't bring her here for that reason. We are not ...," Thomas stuttered, not wanting to say something that might make Caterina think he did not care for her romantically.

"How dare you bring her here!" Priest jumped up from his seat, pushing his chair away from the table. "Do you think this is a place where you can bring whatever whore you choose to bed for the night? Are you so quick to betray the entire Family?" Priest yelled.

Thomas's anger boiled over. He was not about to announce his feelings for Caterina in front of his entire Family without her having first heard them from him in private, but he was furious that his father was acting like an irrational fool in Caterina's presence.

"She isn't a *whore*, and you would do well to watch your language in front of the lady," he declared as calmly as possible under the present circumstances.

"Father. Please," Sergius pleaded as he stepped between the two men and glanced embarrassedly at Caterina. "Let Thomas explain before you jump to conclusions."

Thomas tried to slow his breathing. He knew his face was bright red with fury, and he would need every bit of self-control he possessed to keep his hands from reaching out to choke his father.

"We need to call a full Family meeting," Thomas said with authority.

"Oh yes?" Priest mocked. "And why should we do that?"

"For her," Thomas said as he pointed at Caterina—whose cheeks were now a bright rosy pink under the scrutiny of every man and woman in the room.

"What about her, Thomas?" Sergius asked, his eyes lit with interest.

Thomas chose his next words carefully—hoping to make the greatest impact on his watching Family. He took one deep breath and looked into Caterina's beautiful amber eyes.

"I have found the first female immortal."

FIFTY-EIGHT

THE ROOM ERUPTED while Caterina stood as still as possible. She wanted to run and hide. Everyone stared at her as they spoke, mostly with eyes full of confusion or disbelief. A few sets of eyes looked at her with longing—an expression that made Caterina nervous and uncomfortable. She knew she was a novelty, and the protective look on Thomas's face proved she was not imagining or misinterpreting the interested gazes. She glanced from person to person, hoping to find one set of eyes that were filled with kindness alone. She at last found friendliness in the eyes of the second man who had hugged Thomas upon their arrival—the same man who stepped between Thomas and his father to keep them from fighting. He looked at her with genuine kindness and interest. He smiled before walking over and grasping her hands in his. The room fell silent.

"When and how did you come to be this way?" he asked.

"She was …" Thomas tried to step in.

"Don't answer for her Thomas," the man commanded as he maintained eye contact with Caterina. "We need to hear her answer for herself."

Caterina swallowed the lump in her throat and turned to Thomas, hoping he would somehow assure her that answering was the right thing to do. He gave a quick nod, and she looked back at the man who asked the question.

"I was visiting my uncle's home in Paris in 1466. Plague broke out in the city. We all grew sick, and everyone died but me," she answered as loudly as she could muster (though it came out only slightly louder than a whisper).

"Amazing," the man said, still holding her hands. "And what year were you born?"

"1446," she answered, becoming more comfortable with each moment that passed.

"That makes you seventy-four years old, correct?" he asked.

"Yes," she said with a smile. Caterina liked this man. He was gentle and helpful. His voice even reminded her a little of her eldest brother's. She hoped others in Thomas's family were as courteous as this brother.

"I believe an official Family gathering is in order," he announced loudly as everyone silently nodded. Thomas looked smug, while his father continued to appear furious. He glared at Caterina as if she was a plague upon his home. She looked away, feeling her cheeks flush once more.

"You must stay here with us, Caterina," the kind brother said as he escorted her away from the large room. Thomas and one other followed closely behind.

"Where did you find her?" Samuel asked Thomas as they ascended the stairs quickly.

"Wait," Thomas barked out as he grabbed Caterina's hand and pulled her into his room. Sergius and Samuel followed and shut the door behind them.

"Caterina. These are my brothers Sergius and Samuel. You can trust them above anyone else inside this home," he said, hoping to convey the deeper message. He hadn't thought that bringing her to the Family home could possibly put her in danger, but he now worried he might have been mistaken.

"It's a pleasure to meet you," she said with a relaxed smile on her face.

"She was stranded on an island during an expedition. It's a long story, but I can tell you without question that she is an immortal," Thomas answered Samuel's previous question.

"Amazing," Samuel breathed. "A woman."

"I know. She really is amazing," Thomas agreed (accidentally) aloud. Though he quickly added, "It's incredible that an immortal woman really exists."

Caterina's eyes darted to his as he spoke, and he could feel her appraising his meaning. He changed the subject quickly.

"We need to keep her safe until the meeting. Who knows what father might do when he's in one of his moods. I can't believe she was met with such hostility," Thomas said, wishing he could understand the true reason for Priest's erratic behavior.

"He's been perfectly normal for months. After you left, he went back to being the regular, surly version of our father. But your return certainly stirred something inside him," Sergius worried.

"We can take turns watching the door. You are staying with us, are you not?" Samuel asked Caterina.

She looked surprised that he was asking her opinion on the matter, and took a minute to think over the question.

"I'm staying for at least tonight—unless you think it's unwise. I'm not sure what to think about the present situation. Am I in danger here?" she asked. Thomas could tell she was thinking aloud, but Sergius quickly chimed in.

"Not while we are watching over you. No one would think of laying a hand on you while you're with one of us. But I do not recommend running around the castle on your own until you become acquainted with more of the Family," Sergius said with a reassuring smile that seemed to put Caterina at ease. "I'll take the first shift," he added.

"Can you give us a moment alone?" Thomas asked his brothers as they shuffled out the door quietly.

Thomas turned to Caterina—who looked like she might fall over at any moment—and put his hands on her shoulders.

"Are you all right?" he asked as he searched her face for signs that he should back away.

"I suppose. I think I'm in shock. I didn't imagine that happening quite so dramatically. Does your father think I'm a threat?" she asked, still processing the eventful evening.

"I have no idea. But everyone is going to want to question you … which is why we're holding an official Family meeting. Your existence is unfathomable, and everyone will want to ask you about your life and how you came to be. You only have to be as open with them as you want. Do not feel pressured to reveal anything you are uncomfortable sharing," he assured her.

"That sounds fine," she said softly, her eyes still holding a steady look of bewilderment.

He wanted nothing more than to kiss her right then and there. He wanted to take her in his arms and tell her she would be all right as long as he was near. He wanted to ask if he could stay the night with her.

"I think I should try to rest. I'm exhausted, and I can't think clearly enough to process what just happened," she said as she ran a hand down her braided hair.

"That's a good idea," Thomas agreed as he watched her fingertips play with the curled end of her braid. He took a step toward her and watched her eyes widen at his proximity. He towered above her tiny frame, but their eyes stayed locked as he looked down into her beautiful face.

"Goodnight," he said softly.

Caterina's breath caught, and if he wasn't worried about overwhelming her, he might have kissed her.

"Goodnight," she breathed, barely audible as he walked out of the room and shut the door.

FIFTY-NINE

THE NEXT DAY, Caterina was ushered around the grounds of the castle by Thomas—except for short periods of time when Samuel or Sergius would momentarily step in. She felt like she was under the same constant protection that Thomas had provided during their trip from Tantun. He eyed everyone as if they might be a potential threat, sizing up each man for any possible attacks. But as hours passed, she watched Thomas's posture and countenance begin to relax.

She enjoyed watching Thomas in his home environment. When they first met, he was in her land. On the way to Italy, he acted only as her protector. She liked seeing him interact with his brothers and nephews. She felt she was glimpsing a side of Thomas she had not yet seen.

"Is he always this protective around you?" Samuel asked when Thomas was out of earshot.

"What, this? This is the most relaxed he's been since we met!" Samuel looked at her incredulously before reading the sincerity of her words. He let out a guffaw. Thomas's head jerked up from where his attention had been, and he walked over to see what caused their merriment.

"Is Samuel telling you stories?" he asked suspiciously.

"Not at all. I think most of your family is afraid to look at me, let alone tell me stories," she said with a smirk as Samuel coughed out another chuckle.

"At least *she's* not afraid of you. Goodness knows you've terrified the rest of us," Samuel said with a hard jab to his brother's side. That seemed to ease some of the tension in the room, and Caterina once again saw another layer of Thomas's protective behavior come tumbling down. The more his walls came down, the more enamored she became with him. He was really charming. And his interactions with his brothers and nephews felt very much like the interactions her own brothers had with one another. She felt more at home with this family than she had felt since leaving her own home. The pang of longing to see her brothers was growing.

"Can we make the trip to my home tomorrow?" she asked Thomas later that evening. She watched as a new emotion washed over his face—if she was flattering herself, she would have thought it was pain.

"Yes … of course it would be better if we waited one extra day. The Family meeting will not be for another several weeks, but Priest needs to see that you are not trying to run away without his examination. He is … sensitive to certain behaviors, and in his present state of insanity, you are better off allowing him to see you are not a threat first-hand. If you wait just one extra day and get to know a few more of my brothers and nephews, he will be far less likely to act out. I hope you understand. We will still have plenty of time to spend time with your family, though," he said carefully.

Caterina was no fool. He was letting her know that his father currently deemed her a threat. She now had no choice but to be present for the family meeting—which didn't terrify her the way she thought it might terrify someone else. She wanted to meet all the other immortals in the world. She liked knowing she was not alone in her condition. The mental transition from being the only one of her kind to being one of one hundred was only too easy to make. She welcomed the knowledge with open arms—or more accurately, ran to the knowledge crying tears of joy and relief.

"I understand, and I have no quarrel being present for the meeting—if that is what is required for me to know about your existence," she said, hoping to accurately convey her feelings on the issue. Though she wasn't thrilled at being labeled a threat by Thomas's father, she was more than willing to spend the time to prove him wrong—especially if it meant prolonging her days in Thomas's company.

He walked her back to her room for the evening as she tried to make small talk to lighten the heaviness of their previous conversation.

"Should we walk the vineyards tomorrow?" she asked as lightly as possible.

Thomas nodded in agreement, astounded by Caterina's attitude in the face of his father's insanity. Thomas had tried to give Caterina as much distance as possible since arriving at his home, but his affection for her had only grown to new heights. She seemed so at ease in her interactions with his brothers and nephews that it felt like she was made to be a part of his Family all along.

He did not know if she would be willing to stay at his side for all eternity, but the thought alone broke his self-control.

He lifted a hand to cup her chin, and she inhaled slightly at his touch. He leaned down to kiss the soft pink lips that he had desired to kiss for so long, but she turned her head and took a step away.

"No," she whispered as she covered her down-turned face with both hands.

Thomas felt devastated for a short moment. Then anger and confusion swept through his body. He took a step away from her, unable to find the words to ask her 'why?'. His mind began to blacken with anger as he felt the rejection more and more keenly—she was so upset by his advance that she couldn't even look at him. He picked up the closest object his hand could find and hurled it across the room. Caterina screamed in surprise as her head jerked up and her eyes darted toward the shattering clay pot. She looked back and forth between Thomas and the broken clay several times but did not say another word.

Thomas yelled, angry at himself for his childish outburst, as he turned and stormed out of the room, slamming the door behind him. He saw Sergius and Samuel rushing toward him to help, but their worry turned to confusion as he brushed past them without a word. He needed to leave the castle immediately.

He walked past a crowd of his brothers and nephews who were discussing Caterina's existence, and headed straight through the front door. The moon shone brightly above—it was a cloudless night—and Thomas decided to take a long walk to clear his mind.

She rejected you—she does not want you. You've known that for a long time. But you made a fool of yourself and tried to kiss her! He scolded himself relentlessly as he walked. He didn't pay attention to where he was going. He knew the Family's land as well as he knew every curve and line of Caterina's lovely face. With each step, his anger over his rash behavior only grew. *You know what happened to her in the past. She probably hates men in general— especially men who try to touch her. How could you?*

By the time he made it back to the castle, the sun was rising in the East, and he was dead on his feet. He went inside and headed to his room without thinking—his mind was as exhausted as his body. Without undressing, he walked straight to his empty bed and lay down. His mind shut off as soon as his head landed on the soft surface.

When he woke up, he groggily looked toward the window—there was no sun in the sky. He changed his clothes and washed off the stench of the past few days. As he tossed cold water on his skin, an alarm went off in his brain.

I left Caterina here. In this room. I tried to kiss her right there, and then I stormed outside and left her here. And when I came back, there was no one outside the door, and the room was empty. Where is she? he thought with panic. He hurriedly finished washing his body, threw on a clean set of clothes, and ran to Sergius's room first. His knock was unanswered, so he barged into the room only to find it empty. He ran to Samuel's room and found it vacant as well.

"Samuel? Sergius?" he yelled as he made his way down the stairs in the dark. No one seemed to be awake, and he was beginning to wonder if he was dreaming.

"They left last night," Saint said quietly, as he approached holding only a candle. "After you stormed out the front door, Samuel and Sergius escorted Caterina out to the stables, and the three rode away together. None of them said a word to the rest of us. We just watched as they rode off. Of course, your father wanted to send a few of the boys to bring them back. He doesn't trust that girl.

But I convinced him to let it be for the time being. Do you have any idea where they would've gone?"

"Her family's villa in Florence?" he said aloud, but worried they might have traveled to Milan without him. "I have no idea where they are," he answered, frustrated by the fact that he had not asked about the specific locations of either home.

"You should go back to sleep. The sun will not rise for another two hours. And if you do not know where they are, you certainly won't have any luck finding them in the dark," Saint said as he turned and walked away.

Thomas begrudgingly returned to his room and sat on the edge of his bed. Nothing would put his mind at ease until he could see Caterina to apologize. He had scared her away. He would hate himself if he never got a chance to apologize for his outburst. He could not rest until he found her.

SIXTY

CATERINA WANTED to leave the castle immediately after Thomas's attempt to kiss her. She was surprised he even tried—she always thought he had seen her as a *cause* rather than a *woman*. He protected her fiercely and never even hinted at an attraction. She wanted so badly to let him kiss her in the heat of the moment, but her reasoning and will-power outweighed her desire. She thankfully turned her head at the last minute. *I could have killed him!* she thought, terrified that she almost allowed him to kiss her. *If I still carry the disease that changed me, who knows what it would do to another immortal.*

While she fought back the tears she wanted to sob, Sergius and Samuel hesitantly agreed to take her to her family's nearby Florentine villa. She hoped the home would be empty (as it usually was during the harvesting of the grapes at her family's vineyards in Milan). Thomas's reaction to her rejection was far more intense than she expected—and the shattering pot had scared the wits out of her. She sighed deeply at the ache she felt in Thomas's absence. He probably hated her now, but it was for his own good. Better he live out the rest of his immortal life without her than risk contracting the plague from her kiss and dying a miserably painful death.

In the blackness of night, the stars and half-moon did little to light the empty villa. Just as she had expected, everyone was away, likely preparing for the harvest in Milan. She lit the candle that always sat in the front entry when no one was home. Without thinking about Samuel and Sergius, she hurried up the stairs to her old room, leaving them alone in the dark entry. She felt as if it had only been a matter of days since she last walked the familiar path. She entered the room, expecting to see some difference. But it remained untouched —exactly as it had been when she lived there so many years ago. She smiled, knowing that her mother had kept it for her in case she returned.

"Caterina?" Samuel called from below. Caterina walked downstairs to her escorts, embarrassed by her lack of hospitality.

"Here are candles for each of you," she said, lighting one for each man. "Would you like to sleep in my brothers' rooms?"

Sergius exchanged a glance with his brother, and both simultaneously answered, "No."

She felt a pang of sorrow in her heart. They reminded her too much of the way Thomas had protected her while she slept. She fervently wished she could somehow *know* if her kiss would affect Thomas's health. But she would not risk his life for the sake of her own selfish desire.

"My father's library is just through there. And though there won't be much food, the kitchen is just down that corridor. If you don't mind, I need some rest —the physical toll of the journey seems to have caught up with me." She still couldn't believe she and Thomas had only arrived at his family's castle the night before.

The brothers said goodnight, and Caterina returned to her room and lay down on her old bed. She fell asleep doing her best to think only of her family —not of Thomas's angry departure.

The next day, Samuel and Sergius spent the sunlit hours with her, asking questions about her family and upbringing. They only asked questions about her immortality if she brought it up. She found herself only wanting to ask them about Thomas, but she pushed down her desires and continued to answer the brothers' questions.

"What exactly happened last night? If you don't mind me asking," Samuel finally said during dinner.

"I don't really know," she lied but immediately felt awful for it. "That's a lie. Thomas tried to kiss me." She waited for the brothers' reactions, but both looked uncomfortable with her answer.

"You haven't … you've never kissed him?" Samuel asked, trying to make sense of her answer.

"I've never kissed *anyone*. And I didn't think he held feelings for me. We traveled together for over a month without a hint of attraction on his part," she admitted as she thought back over their journey. "He was protective—he killed two men to protect me. But he never so much as touched me if we were alone."

Sergius and Samuel looked at each other, conversing silently with only their expressions. Sergius sighed when Samuel began speaking once more.

"*Why* didn't you kiss him?" Samuel asked.

"I cannot risk his life like that," Caterina answered without hesitation. Both men looked at her with expressions begging for clarification. Caterina decided to tell them her theory. "My immortality was born out of plague. I am fairly certain that I *died* and then awoke as an immortal. I have spent the past fifty years living in fear of spreading the plague to others. I know I cannot kill another by mere proximity, but if it is somehow inside my body and he kisses me, it could kill him. I cannot know how it might affect his body, and I could never live with myself if he somehow contracted the sickness and spread it to your whole family."

"But we can't get sick. Didn't he tell you that? Do you suffer from sickness?" Samuel asked, curious at the possibility of a difference in their immortal lives.

"Well, no. I didn't want to assume, though. How can you be sure what I have inside *my* body *won't* kill him? Would you be willing to risk the life of someone you love for a kiss if you thought it might kill them?" she asked.

Samuel and Sergius sat silently, their faces clothed in surprise. She didn't understand what surprised them—until she realized she had openly admitted that she loved their brother.

"Can you please forget what I just said?" she pleaded. Sergius nodded in agreement, but Samuel's face twisted into a smile as he shook his head 'no.' "Please, Samuel!" she begged, as Sergius grabbed his arm and squeezed.

"Ow!" Samuel yelled, slapping his brother's hand away. "Fine. I won't say a word. But you should at least explain to Thomas *why* you rejected him. He deserves that."

That night, Samuel returned to the castle to bring back fresh food and a few items for him and Sergius, while Sergius kept watch over Caterina's home. She still couldn't sleep in a bed, but she had begun adding more padding to the floor each week in an attempt to become accustomed to sleeping on a bed once more.

When she fell asleep for the night, she dreamed of the way Thomas's lips might have felt against hers if she had kissed them, and when she woke the next morning, the trails of dried, salty tears remained on her cheeks. She had to see Thomas. She needed to tell him why they could never be together.

Thomas heard Samuel's heavy steps come down the hallway—even after years away, he could still identify those clumsy feet just from the sound they made. He flung open his door and found Samuel facing him with a conflicted expression.

"Where the hell did you take her?" Thomas roared, angry that his brother knew where Caterina was and he did not.

"To her family's villa in Florence," Samuel said shortly. He wasn't normally one for few words, and Thomas could immediately tell Samuel was trying to hide something.

"Why do you look guilty?" Thomas asked, more coaxing than upset in his tone.

"Why do you think I'm guilty of something? I don't look guilty!" Samuel said tensely.

Thomas grabbed Samuel's shoulder and dragged him into his bedroom, shutting the door behind him.

"What is going on? Tell me right now, or you will deeply regret it. You know how much dirt I have on you. All you need is for our brothers to find out about the Pope's assassination … they would never let you live it down," Thomas threatened.

"That's not fair!" Samuel whined. "I promised I wouldn't tell you. Sergius made me swear," he groaned.

"Now," Thomas demanded.

"She didn't kiss you because she thinks she's still carrying the plague, and she's worried it could kill you. And she accidentally admitted she loves you. That's everything I know," he spat out in one breath.

Thomas's heart leapt with joy, and he laughed as he picked up Samuel in a giant hug.

"That's wonderful! Of course she's not going to kill me! We can't get sick!" he almost sang. "Take me there. Please," he asked much more politely, as he released Samuel.

"Sergius *is* going to kill me … unless Caterina gets to me first," Samuel said as he sulked down the stairs and back outside.

Caterina took nearly an hour to climb out of bed. She opened the chest at the end of her bed and pulled out one of her old gowns. The material had deteriorated in her years of absence, but she held it tightly as she remembered how she had often worn it to take walks outside on nice days. She looked in another chest and found several new dresses that seemed to be the same size as her old gowns. She slipped into one and frowned. It hung awkwardly off her tiny frame and made her feel unattractive. She had lost so much weight during the time she spent in Tantun, the clothes that once would have fit her snugly didn't even look like they belonged to her. She tied a ribbon tightly around her waist to make the dress look like it fit a *little* better, but the extra fabric in the back would look ridiculous if anyone saw her.

She opened the door of her room, and a small yelp broke out of her mouth. Thomas leaned against the wall across from her door.

"Is it so awful to see me?" he asked with raised eyebrows.

"No. Only unexpected," she said, trying to recover as gracefully as possible. She looked left and right and listened downstairs—his brothers didn't seem to be inside the house, and she wanted to scream in annoyance at their betrayal.

"I captured Samuel last night when he came home. And I threatened him. And I gave him the option of telling me where you were or letting me embarrass him in front of the entire Family—so don't blame him for my presence," he said, his expression turning serious.

The narrow hallway didn't leave much room for maneuvering, but Caterina didn't want to slip back into her room for fear of offending Thomas. She closed the door and leaned her back against it, clasping her hands behind her back. She tried to look nonchalant, despite the fact that her heart was threatening to pound right out of her chest.

"Caterina. I am truly sorry," Thomas began. "Please do not think I was angry with *you* for one second. I was furious with myself for touching you without your permission. Especially after what you've been through ... I could not stand the thought of you picturing me as the same type of man as those sailors. I'm sorry..." his words faded at the end, emotion thick in his voice.

Caterina wanted to wrap her arms around him and comfort him. To tell him that there was no need for her to forgive him—because there was absolutely nothing to forgive. But she worried that would give him hope of a future for them, and she certainly didn't want to lead him on.

"All is forgiven, Thomas," she assured him. "There was honestly nothing to forgive," she tacked on, unwilling to speak the rest of her thoughts.

Relief washed over Thomas's face, and he took a small step toward her.

"Samuel revealed more than your location," he said in a low, quiet voice. Caterina felt an involuntary gulp in her throat as her mind braced for what was coming.

"And what did you discover?" she asked more quietly than intended.

"That you're worried about *me*," he answered as he took another small step in her direction.

She didn't know what to do—she felt sweaty and uncomfortable and awkward all at the same time. Her breathing picked up, and she could hear her heart beating wildly in her chest. She remained as still and silent as possible.

"But now you listen to me," Thomas said as he closed the gap between them and placed a hand on each of Caterina's hips. "If I kissed you and it killed me, I wouldn't care one bit. I would rather kiss you over and over for a few short days than live out the next nine hundred years worrying over what might have been." He ran his hands up her back and brushed his fingers lightly over her neck. She shivered at the lovely feeling that raced up her spine. His hands found her face, and he stroked her cheeks with his thumbs as his other fingers cupped the back of her head. "I am in love with you. And I know you love me as well. And if it somehow kills me, at least I'll die a *very* happy man," he whispered against her forehead.

Caterina thought she might melt. She wasn't quite sure how her legs had kept her standing for so long. She thought she was awake, but she worried if she moved, she might wake up from the beautiful dream. She decided to risk the heartbreak and angle her head up in order to look Thomas in the eyes. The look on his face was of absolute adoration, and she couldn't hide the smile that found her lips. She wasn't going to wake up, because this moment didn't live inside a dream—Thomas loved her.

Tears dripped down her cheeks, and he quickly wiped them away with his thumbs.

"You love me?" she asked, just to make sure.

"Caterina," he breathed. "I have lived for over nine hundred years, and never have I been capable of allowing my heart to open fully to a mortal woman. A part of me knew that the woman would someday die, whether it be after twenty or sixty years, and I would have to go on living without them. But with you," he whispered as his lips gently brushed hers, "I can share my whole heart. You are like a complex puzzle—the more I discover, the more enchanting you become. It is as if all the missing pieces in my own life weren't actually missing—they were simply waiting for you to fill their voids. And I am somehow miraculously blessed to live with my heart unbroken for the rest of time."

She kissed him, tentatively at first, but as she became familiar with the motion, she grew hungry for more. Her hands found the back of his head and her fingers wound their way through his dark brown hair. She felt his body move as chills ran up his spine. He pulled his face away from hers and looked down at her for a moment, as if studying her eyes and lips.

"You are stunningly beautiful," he said as his lips found her neck. She gasped in pleasure the moment they touched her, and she knew she didn't want him to stop. She could tell Thomas was doing his best to be gentle with her, but she didn't care if he was gentle or rough. She had waited her entire life for this moment. And though, in the back of her head, she heard herself telling her young cousin to behave the way a lady should, she finally understood the urge to push proper behavior aside and act in the way she truly wanted. She pushed Thomas away roughly and watched his eyes flood with rejection, but she followed his body, pressing her hands against his chest, forcing him against the opposite wall. She began kissing his neck just as he had done to her. She wrapped her arms around his shoulders and pulled him down to her height so she could kiss him more easily. He willingly obeyed her every command, allowing her to take the lead. Her lips found his once more, and he used the opportunity to wind his fingers through her hair again. She felt him pull the ribbon out of her braid and undo the work she had done earlier. He looked at her once more when her hair was loose and wild, and the smile on his face told her he loved what he saw.

Caterina hadn't truly felt beautiful before that moment. Her mother and father and brothers and cousins had told her time and time again that she was beautiful. Thomas had told her only moments before. But in that one look, everything snapped into place.

"You think I'm beautiful," she breathed as tears dripped from her eyes.

"No. I *know* you're beautiful. Every single part of you. And I am in love with you," he said as he kissed her forehead, her cheeks, and finally her lips.

She giggled in delight as he swept her into his arms and carried her down the stairs and out the door, his mouth forming a wide smile that matched hers.

SIXTY-ONE

CATERINA AND THOMAS were inseparable. After a few days, Caterina finally stopped fretting over Thomas's health. She could see he showed no signs of the plague, and for the first time since she had fled Paris, she felt comforted by the thought of living life without any fear of killing those around her.

They decided to wait until after the Family meeting to travel to Milan to see her family. Caterina wanted to take her time visiting with her family and didn't want the stress of the meeting looming in the back of her mind when she should be celebrating her return with her brothers. Thomas's foremost concern was that his Family was able to spend as much time with Caterina as possible before the meeting. It was important for her to have the full support of his brothers and nephews—and even more important for Priest to see her as a permanent, loved member of the Family.

Caterina and Thomas fell into an effortless relationship—they already knew the worst parts of each others' personalities—and Samuel and Sergius took it upon themselves to fill Caterina in on each and every embarrassing moment of Thomas's nine-hundred-year-old life. Thomas wasn't upset by the stories they told. He could see the joy they brought to Caterina—and his new goal in life was to bring her as much pleasure and happiness as her life could hold.

The meeting took place one week after her arrival, but in that short time, she managed to win over the majority of the Family. Thomas gave Caterina an unadorned, long, black tunic for the occasion—as was tradition for all the women of the Family during an official gathering. Thomas and the rest of the men wore brown trousers and white shirts (about which Caterina poked fun, accusing his Family of dressing in their night shirts for something so important).

He waited nervously outside her door, hoping and praying the meeting would go well. When Caterina emerged, she did not have to say a word. He embraced her tightly for a moment, and when he released her, they exchanged a smile that put his mind at ease.

As everyone filed down the stone steps into the large, underground chamber, Thomas felt Caterina's hand squeeze a little tighter. He looked at her reassuringly and escorted her to the bench at the front of the half-circle amphitheater where the other women were seated.

"You will likely be seated in either my father's or uncle's chair so everyone will be able to hear your answers, but wait here until they call you to the front. Be honest, but only disclose as much as you want—no one needs to know your full story unless you wish. I will be on the front row, and if you desire that I come and stand by you, you need only ask," he promised. He kissed her hand before releasing it to walk to his seat.

The front row of marble benches was reserved for him and his brothers. They sat in order of descending age—which he suspected Priest had concocted as a way to separate Thomas from Sergius and Samuel. The amphitheater was the first part of the castle to be dug when the Family built it in the 12th century. Priest had apparently expected far more offspring, because only the front two rows of marble benches were filled—and Thomas often observed Priest eying the back three empty rows with disappointment.

Once Priest and Saint sat in their chairs at the front of the chamber, a hush fell over the room. Saint stood, and everyone rose immediately to their feet in response. The official meetings had been the same for centuries, and Thomas loved the energy that flowed through the room each time they gathered for one.

"I call this meeting of the Family to order," Saint announced.

Though there was no one to tell the men exactly when to begin, every man breathed in at the same moment, and they spoke as one:

"We stand united, Family of Immortals. Plagued by life. Cursed by the hand of God. We pledge our lives to the Family, the Priest, and the Saint."

Everyone sat down in unison, and Thomas glanced at Caterina to see her reaction. She looked slightly startled, but that was to be expected at one's first Family meeting.

Caterina's heart raced. She soaked in every moment, not wanting to miss a single word of the meeting. She knew the meeting would determine her place in Thomas's family, and she hoped her answers would prove to them that she was, indeed, an immortal just like the rest of them.

Saint looked at the men seated before him, then back at Caterina. He winked at her, and she pushed down the urge to smile back at him, not wanting to betray the kind gesture to Priest.

"Thomas, son of Priest, you have called this meeting to discuss the nature of this woman," Saint began, extending his hand toward her. She shifted uncomfortably on the bench as every eye turned to her. "I agree that this meeting is of great import, as an immortal woman has never before been discovered. So, if I may, I would ask Caterina Galli to take my seat before us so we may question you to confirm the sincerity of your claim. Each man in the room will have the opportunity to ask his question."

Caterina stood, doing her best to hide her now-shaking hands and knees, and Saint escorted her to his seat in the front of the room. Priest rose and began the questioning.

"How can you possibly expect us to believe you are telling the truth? Be truthful, Thomas told you of his immortality to make you fall in love, and you thought it would be nice to play along. There is no proof you can bring this day to show any of us there is truth in your claim," Priest said in a disingenuously kind tone.

Caterina hated being at the front of the room with everyone staring at her, waiting for her reaction to Priest's words. But she had no intention of crying over the insulting speech. She straightened, smoothing her dress as she scooted to the edge of the chair, and smiled sweetly.

"I was born in the year 1446 in my family's home, just outside Milan. For my twentieth birthday, my parents allowed me to travel to Paris to visit my cousins. As you may recall, plague struck the city of Paris in 1466. I was stricken with the sickness, died, and awoke several weeks later, only to find myself in perfect health other than fierce hunger. How, exactly, would I concoct a story like that if Thomas had first told me he was *born* an immortal? I assure you, it is the truth," Caterina said with as much innocence as she was capable of displaying.

Priest's eyes widened a little as she told her story, but she watched as he masked his surprise behind his former annoyance. He sauntered back and forth in front of her, either to think of a question or for dramatic effect—Caterina did not know which.

"I would like for you to go into the specifics of your time in Paris. Any detail you might remember, anything at all, it could be valuable," Priest said, his tone interested and pleading rather than insulting or bothered.

Caterina started from the moment plague broke out in the city. She spared no details of the gory deaths of her family, and she fought back emotion as she told them of the letter she had written to her family in her final moments.

"I'm not actually sure I wrote that letter, though. I did not find it when I awoke," she admitted.

"My God," Thomas breathed, shattering the silence of the listeners.

"Was there something you wanted to add?" Priest asked, only slightly agitated by the interruption.

"Please allow me a moment. I do have physical evidence that Caterina is telling the truth. Please. Just one moment," he yelled as he ran up the stairs of the amphitheater and left the room.

Caterina looked around the room, happy her confusion was shared by everyone else. She looked toward Sergius and Samuel, hoping they might have an idea of why Thomas had just exited the meeting, but they only shrugged in response.

Thomas returned a few minutes later, out of breath from running. He held up a piece of parchment and smiled.

"I cannot believe this is real," Thomas whispered. "But when we were searching for survivors in Paris, Sergius and Samuel and I came across a home where everyone inside was deceased. I noticed a letter sitting on the table near one of the covered bodies, and I had a mind to deliver it to the family to whom it was addressed. But when we returned home, I found I could not part with it. I never opened it to read it, but I felt I had to keep it."

Tears dripped down Caterina's cheeks. *Surely this is an act of God. He orchestrated the entire scenario—from my writing the letter, to Thomas finding it and keeping it, to him having it still so he can prove what I am. Thank you, God. Will your graciousness never cease?*

Thomas handed the letter to Priest, who seemed incredulous over the turn of events. He broke the seal, unfolded the parchment carefully, and began to read aloud.

"My dearest family," Priest began, and Caterina's breath caught in anticipation. This truly was her letter. "I have fallen ill with plague and will not be able to return home. I wish I had the strength to write at length, but I am very tired. I wish I could have seen you all one last time. I still wear my ring every day. I still wear my brothers' gift every day as well. Thank you for being good to me all my life. I hope this letter finds its way to you. I love you forever. Caterina," he finished.

Everyone was astounded by the discovery of physical proof of her existence. Thomas beamed at Caterina, apparently feeling the same awed emotion as Caterina.

"This ink is worn with age. There is no possibility that the letter is a fake. I only ask that Caterina now show us her handwriting so I can confirm the letter was, indeed, written by her hand," Priest announced.

She was given a quill and parchment, and told to reproduce the letter without seeing the original. In a matter of seconds, Priest was satisfied that the handwriting was a match.

"I can confirm that this woman is the same Caterina who wrote this letter in 1466," Priest announced. Quiet whispers broke out all over the room until Saint looked sternly toward the men to remind them the meeting was still in session.

Neither Caterina's eyes nor mind could focus on a single point. They flitted from Priest's shock to Thomas's excitement, to Saint's look of smugness, to the other women's gazes of jealousy and sorrow. It wasn't until Priest spoke once more that she could concentrate.

"Would you permit us to inquire over the life you lived after your change?" Priest asked with genuine curiosity.

Caterina was a bit taken aback. This was the first time she had witness Priest ask a question that wasn't posed as a command or hidden threat. If she answered 'no' there would be no repercussions. But if she truly wanted to become a part of this family—and she unquestioningly did—why would she feel compelled to withhold the truth from them?

"I will answer any question to the best of my ability," she smiled tentatively at Priest. His expression softened further, and she felt her breath catch when she saw the hint of a smile play at the corners of Priest's mouth. *Perhaps there is more to this man than meets the eye*, she thought as Sergius asked the first question.

By the end of the meeting, Caterina had answered hundreds of questions. The meeting had lasted more than half the day. Thomas watched admiringly as Caterina answered each query with the poise of a true noblewoman. She was the first of her kind, and every man in the room was overjoyed by the confirmed existence of an immortal woman. As soon as the meeting was adjourned, dozens of men rushed to Priest to volunteer to search for survivors whenever the next pocket of plague broke out. Thomas didn't try to hide his amusement—he knew he was the most fortunate man in the Family. Caterina would live by his side for the rest of their lives—any man would have reason to seek for the same.

"We are blessed," he whispered as he pulled Caterina from Saint's chair and into his arms. "We are so very blessed."

Sixty-two

"I THINK IT'S TIME to take you to your family in Milan," Thomas said the morning after the meeting. Thomas had been waiting for nearly an hour when Caterina finally emerged from her room in the Family castle.

"Yes," was her only reply as her happy expression grew concerned.

"There is no need for distress. If you wish me to stay with you during your visit, I will not leave your side," he said, leaning in for a kiss.

"Thank you. I will pack my things," she answered, turning back to her room.

"The trip will take four or five days at least," he said as she gathered her belongings into a bag. He hoped she would leave a few things behind as a sign that she intended to return home with him after their visit.

"I'll meet you downstairs in a moment," Thomas said as he descended the stairs to the castle's entry.

"I don't think it's a good idea for you to grow too attached," Thomas heard Priest say as he stepped out from the dining hall. Thomas harbored enough resentment toward his father without any additional commentary on his relationship with Caterina.

"And why do you say that, father?" he asked as he rolled his eyes, unable to hide his frustration with the man.

"She's ... unnatural. I'm not sure I want her breeding with any of my sons or grandsons," Priest said with an unfamiliar gleam in his eyes. Thomas knew Priest wasn't revealing the full breadth of his opinions on the matter, but Thomas didn't want to hear them.

"Keep your thoughts to yourself, father. You do not have the right to dictate whom any of your offspring marry. I am over nine hundred years old. I'm not some child you can control," Thomas said, his voice rising in disgust.

"I'm ready, Thomas," Caterina said with a forced cheerfulness as she descended the stairs and took his arm.

"Me too," Thomas said, and they turned and left the castle. Once they were inside the stables, Thomas picked up a horse-shoe and threw it at the back wall, lodging it into a part of the wall.

"Don't allow him to upset you. I'm sure there's more to his behavior than we know," she said as she grabbed his face in her hands and placed her forehead against his. Thomas could feel his pulse calming as she spoke.

"I don't understand how he became so … twisted. He wasn't this way until recently. He had morals before—he had … a conscience. I don't know what to think. There's always an undercurrent of cynicism or anger in his words. And he's slowly withdrawing from our Family gatherings—more often than not, he dines alone in his quarters. I no longer know how to act around him. I'm sorry. It was not my intention to dampen this joyful moment with my family woes. Let's go see your family," he said with an apologetic smile.

"I'm happy you know you can speak about these things with me," she said as she mounted her horse.

Thomas could tell there was more she wanted to say, but she remained silent.

"Are you nervous about seeing your brothers?" Thomas asked as they made their way down the tree-lined path that led away from Castello San Romolo.

"I'm worried they won't be alive. I mean, I know my nieces and nephews will, but I have doubts about my brothers. I don't want to arrive home and immediately have an emotional breakdown," she admitted nervously.

"I'll be with you for whatever you need. And if you want to leave, you only have to say the word and we'll go," he promised.

"I wonder if Leo still lives in Milan," she said absentmindedly.

"Who is Leo?" Thomas asked quickly.

"The painter I told you about," she said with a far-off stare.

Thomas bristled at the mention of another man in her life. He knew she had never kissed anyone, but perhaps she had *wanted* to kiss this Leo person and hadn't out of fear.

"He was like a brother, Thomas. I can see your face. Leo was not interested in women—if you take my meaning." She raised an eyebrow at him.

Thomas breathed a sigh of relief.

"Good," he said as they rode on quietly.

Their first night was a bit awkward. The inn where they stopped consisted of one guest room only. That hadn't been an issue on the trip to Florence because Caterina and Thomas weren't *together* during that trip. Now, Caterina didn't know how to act. She had no intention of having sexual relations with Thomas until they were married … which she thought might happen sooner rather than later, after overhearing Thomas's conversation with his father earlier that day. She hoped it would happen in the very near future. All she wanted was to make love to Thomas. Thomas had finally proven to her that he was not going to become infected with the plague. After that realization hit, she gave to him all the remaining pieces of her heart she had held back in case he became sick and died.

"I'll take the floor," she said as she stole a single piece of cloth from the end of the bed and folded it so she wouldn't have to lie directly on the floor.

"Oh, no you don't," Thomas said as he scooped Caterina into his arms and laid her down on the bed. "I've been watching you add more and more covers to your bedding on the floor at the castle. You take the bed. I know you'll be able to sleep on it now. I'll be fine on the floor," he said as he kissed her forehead and walked to the corner where she had placed the cloth.

"I can sleep on the floor. I really don't mind," Caterina said, hoping to persuade him to sleep in the bed. She couldn't bear the thought of Thomas being uncomfortable on her account.

"I'll hear nothing more of it," he said as he removed his belt, shoes, and knife holster and lay down. "Sleep well," he whispered as she blew out the candle next to the bed.

Caterina did her best to fall asleep, but no matter how she lay, sleep would not come. She tossed and turned for hours, trying to make herself comfortable. There was something about knowing she was lying in a bed that made her uneasy. She took the covering from the bed, folded it, and placed it on the floor next to the bed. As soon as she lay down on it, she fell right to sleep.

"We're going to have to do something about that, aren't we?" she heard Thomas say from above. She opened her eyes and found Thomas dressed for the day, their bags in hand.

"I couldn't fall asleep on the bed," she said groggily. "I think my mind was protesting against the idea of being so high off the ground," she smiled as Thomas pulled her to her feet. He kissed her cheek and gave her a moment alone to freshen up for the day.

The night of restlessness made Caterina groggy. She felt as if she could never fully awaken, and when they stopped at an inn that night, she was too tired to finish her dinner.

"I'll be in the next room if you need anything," Thomas said as he left her for the night.

Caterina lay down on the bed—not having enough energy to take the sheet from the bed and place it on the floor. She didn't remember anything after her body landed on the bed. But a few hours later, she had a terrible nightmare about the men who attacked her on the ship. The one with the sadistic laugh was sitting on top of her, and she was once again stabbing at his side with her knife, trying to scream through the hand that covered her mouth. She didn't know how it happened, but one minute she was on the ship, and the next, she was in Thomas's arms. He cradled her tightly, shushing her sobs and drying her cheeks.

"You're safe, Caterina. I have you. I'm here," he whispered as she cried into his chest. "I'll take care of you. I'll always be here to take care of you," he promised.

"How did you know I was having a nightmare?" she asked between sobs.

"You were screaming my name," he answered, making no attempt to hide his satisfaction.

"Oh. I suppose that makes sense. I was dreaming about what happened on the ship," she explained.

"I assumed as much. I don't really want to leave you alone. Would you like me to sleep on the floor?" he asked. She was grateful that he understood and respected her feelings about their relations without her having told him. But the idea of him leaving her in the bed did not sit well with her emotions, and panic began welling up in her chest once more. "Or I could sit next to you while you sleep," he offered, sensing her emotional instability.

"Are you sure? I want you to rest as well," she worried.

"I'm positive. I'll be right here when you wake up," he promised as he kissed her cheek and placed her beside him on the bed. He made sure she was comfortable and closed his eyes.

The next morning, she woke to discover she had wrapped her arms around Thomas's leg sometime in the night, and her head was resting in his lap. She moved to look up at his face, hoping he was still asleep. But the second she moved, he ran his fingers through her hair, bent down, and placed a soft kiss on her temple.

"Good morning, beautiful," he said quietly.

"Good morning," she smiled as she sat up. "Thank you for coming to my rescue ... again."

"Any time. Day or night," he said as he brushed her lips with his thumb.

The next two nights, Thomas refused to stay in a separate room. He sat up while she slept soundly beside him—she couldn't remember the last time she slept so well. Each morning she felt refreshed while he looked miserably tired.

"I wish you would sleep on the bed. I do not like how exhausted you look," she worried, touching the circles under his eyes.

"It's worth it for you to sleep soundly. And I'm more than a little flattered that you sleep so well next to me," he said as he stole a quick kiss. "Are you ready to see your family today?"

"Yes," she answered with a deep breath. Her nerves felt raw as she thought over every possible scenario. They might not remember her. They might not be living there anymore. They might be dead. They might be afraid of her. She was worried she would not be welcome, but tried to hope for the best.

A few hours later, Caterina saw her home ahead. It was exactly as she remembered. *And it's harvesting season*, she thought with a smile. Everyone would be in the vineyards or outside in the warm summer air. As they rode closer, she saw children running around outside, playing tag and laughing. She stopped her horse abruptly.

"Are you all right?" Thomas asked with a furrowed brow.

"Everything is exactly as I remember. It's been a long time, but all of it is the same," she breathed as a tear dripped down her cheek.

"They're going to be happy to see you. And I want to meet your brothers," he said as he began trotting in the direction of her family home. She took a moment to simply take in the scene. She would paint it from memory later on. This was a moment of pure joy. She gave her horse a nudge and trotted quickly after Thomas.

As soon as they reached the house, dozens of people came over to greet their visitors. She jumped down from the saddle and smoothed her dress.

"Can I help you?" a familiar voice asked.

Caterina's mouth popped open as she spun around. There before her was Jacopo, her trusted friend and servant.

"Jacopo," she said, trying to see his face through blurry eyes. The old man walked closer and looked over Caterina's face.

"I knew you would come back," he said as he grabbed her hand and squeezed it tightly. "Caterina has returned! Gather the family!" he yelled as people began running around to sneak a better look at her face. Most of the people here were complete strangers, but a few looked familiar.

"This is my son, Niccolo. And my grandson, Piero," Jacopo said, grabbing the two grown men and holding them tightly to each side. "They are in charge of the vineyards now."

"How wonderful. It's lovely to meet you both," Caterina said as she grasped each of their hands. She felt tears dripping from her eyes, but she didn't try to dry them. Niccolo and Piero smiled courteously, and she noticed they had Jacopo's smile and Fiora's eyes.

"Caterina?" Ludovico's voice rang out.

"Ludo!" she squealed as she rushed to hug her brother's wrinkled body. He looked quite old, but she had no problem recognizing him.

"I cannot believe you are here. I dreamed of this moment so many nights," he said as he took her face in his trembling hands and kissed her forehead and cheeks.

"Giovanni and Filippo?" she asked, trying to keep a smile on her face though she already knew the answer to her question.

Ludovico shook his head with a sad look on his face.

"But I have *you*, brother," she smiled, leaning her forehead against her brother's. "I am grateful you waited for me to come home."

"Come inside. Please, please," he motioned to Thomas as he pulled Caterina into their home, tucked closely to his side.

The house was unchanged, except that every wall was covered only in Caterina's artwork. Before, her paintings had been mixed in with her mother's, but it seemed the walls were now a shrine to Caterina's life. She looked at each piece in awe, having forgotten how skilled she once was with a brush. She would need to dedicate herself to the craft once more if she would ever be capable of matching her level of talent from long ago. Memories swirled in her head as she looked around her old home.

"This feels like a dream," she said quietly as she hugged Ludo tightly.

"Please, tell me everything."

Sixty-Three

Milan, September 1519

Ludo told Caterina about the family business, city, and political changes—though he only talked of the prior few years and didn't say a word about their family. Caterina could not understand why, but she decided it would be best to ask him privately.

"Milan is under French rule now. Not much has been altered, but the changes are certainly noticeable. It is quite strange to hear French spoken regularly in an Italian city. I've had to make fewer visits to our Florentine villa because of my health, but I have it maintained—just in case you needed it someday," he smiled. "The city is growing every day. You will barely recognize it now!"

When it was time for everyone to go to sleep, Ludo arranged for Caterina to sleep in her old room. She said a silent goodnight to Thomas from across the room while Ludo took her by the hand and walked with her up the old familiar steps to the room she once called her own. She felt as if she had never left as she ascended the stairs hand-in-hand with her brother, but she found herself aiding him every few steps. He was growing old, and she felt fortunate that he was alive to tell her the stories she had missed.

When they entered the room, she heard herself gasp in delight. Everything was just as she had left it. Additions had been made to the room, but her things were still there.

"I cannot believe it is the same," she marveled as Ludo watched from the door.

"We couldn't bear to change it. It was our own personal shrine to your life … just like your artwork on the walls," Ludovico smiled.

"Will you tell me more about Italy and what happened to our family while I was away?" she asked hopefully.

"Of course. Tomorrow," Ludovico said as he walked to his sister to grasp her hands. "I am grateful you are alive and well. When you did not return after all those years away, we feared the worst."

"I am sorry to have caused you distress. But I am very well, as you see," she smiled.

"I needed to be certain you had already told Thomas about your life before I began divulging the past. If he did not know, I wasn't going to be the one to tell him," he winked.

"Oh, my dear brother. I missed you three so much," she said as a tear found her cheek. "I even missed your over-protectiveness. I could have used that a time or two," she chuckled, embracing her brother once more. "Thomas knows everything. It will be fine sharing our stories as long as you feel comfortable with him hearing them," she assured him.

Ludo promised to tell her everything over the next several days, and he headed back downstairs, leaving Caterina to her thoughts.

Thomas waited patiently for Caterina's brother to return. He didn't care where he slept during their stay—he was simply grateful to see how happy Caterina looked in her old home.

"Everyone else seems to be off to bed," Ludovico said as he entered the room where Thomas waited. "And you look as if you haven't slept in days." Ludovico poured Thomas a glass of wine and walked over to sit with him.

"I haven't," Thomas confirmed with a nod as he took the wine Ludovico offered and tried a sip. "This wine is delicious," he said as soon as he tasted the rich, complex flavor of the Galli vineyard wine.

"Good. You're a man who knows excellent wine when he tastes it. That's a decent start," Ludovico smiled. "Why is it that you haven't slept in days?" he asked with a suspicious gaze.

"Caterina," he began, Ludovico looking at him with a little more venom in his stare. Thomas found the inquisition endearing rather than upsetting, knowing that if he and his brothers were blessed with a sister, her suitors would receive the exact same treatment … or worse.

"I feel an overwhelming responsibility to keep her safe. She hasn't been sleeping soundly as of late. Three nights ago—on the first night of our trip from Florence—she was in her own room when I woke to her screams. I rushed to her room and offered to sit up with her while she slept each night. And that's exactly what I've done for the past three nights. Now I can't imagine leaving her unprotected," he finished.

Ludovico leaned forward to grasp Thomas's hand in a firm shake. Emotion seeped through every pore on Ludovico's body.

"She will never tell me what she's been through. Please. Do you know? Will you tell me the truth?" Ludovico pleaded. "I have never forgiven myself for allowing her to leave. My father and mother, my brothers, they bore the weight of our decision until the day they died. I need to know that we didn't send her to some nightmarish place. When word reached us that Colombo's crew never made it to the East Indies, we were inconsolable. And when Prospero returned with news that Caterina had fled from the crew to escape being discovered as a woman, my father's heart broke. His health deteriorated quickly, and he never recovered. I am begging you to tell me what you know."

Thomas understood Ludovico's plea. He didn't want to upset Caterina's brother, but he didn't want to break Caterina's trust.

"I will speak with Caterina about it tomorrow. I do know what she has been through, but I also believe it is not my right to tell the story, as it is not mine. I know she would never be able to tell you, but perhaps she wouldn't mind if I was to tell you in private," Thomas offered.

"I respect your loyalty," Ludovico said with a knowing smile. "My instincts are telling me you're the right man, Thomas. I don't necessarily know that you're a *good* man—you have a hardness about you that's only explained by doing difficult things. But I can see ... you are the *right* man for my sister."

There was something refreshing about an honest man, and Ludovico fit the description perfectly. His assessment of Thomas could not have been more accurate if Thomas had said it himself. Thomas smiled as Ludovico showed him to his room and bid him goodnight. Thomas was very much looking forward to the coming days he would spend in the Galli home.

SIXTY-FOUR

THE HOUSEHOLD WOKE early the next morning, and Caterina was eager to participate in the harvesting of her family's grapes. She felt like a child again as she dressed in clothes appropriate for the day's work.

"Isn't this exciting?" she asked Thomas as she opened her bedroom door. She knew he would be standing there, waiting for her to emerge. Of course, she had heard him approach the door half an hour earlier, but even if she hadn't heard him, she would still have expected him to be there.

"It seems like quite the event," he smiled.

She took his arm, and they headed down for breakfast. Everyone welcomed them when they entered the room, and Ludo eyed the two of them with a knowing grin on his face. She wasn't going to hide her affection for Thomas— there was no reason that a grown woman should not be happily situated in life.

Breakfast conversation was mostly limited to the division of labor for the harvesting of the grapes. But every once in a while, Ludo would direct a comment or two toward Caterina about the way things had changed since she last participated in a harvest.

"You do realize I was involved in the harvest for over forty years?" Caterina asked Ludo with the roll of her eyes.

"Yes, sister. I am aware. I only want you to know how things have changed! You've been gone a long time," Ludo said, defending himself.

"You know I am prepared for the task. And you know I'm not going to ruin your grapes," she told him with a smirk.

"All right, I understand. You're prepared," Ludo said with a low chuckle as he pinched her arm playfully.

Caterina could see that Thomas was listening closely to the instructions— he wanted to make a good impression on her family, and she rejoiced inwardly at his effort.

Once the harvesting began, Thomas stayed close by Caterina's side. They didn't say much as they walked from vine to vine, cutting each cluster of grapes from its vine. The work was strenuous, but as they looked over each bunch, removing any bad grapes before placing them in a basket, Caterina could see Thomas glancing at her from the corner of her eye.

"Are you planning to say whatever it is that you want to say? Or is it your intention to covertly stare at me for the rest of the day?" she asked with a raised eyebrow.

"I'm worried you won't like what I have to say," he said far too solemnly. Caterina's heart pounded in her chest. She picked up the full basket of grapes and began walking toward the end of the row to empty the basket into one of the large carts their horses would later pull to the villa. *Does he want to leave me here now that he knows I'm happy with my family? Has he lost his feelings for me? Did Ludo scare him off somehow?* The questions raced across her mind one after another.

"Caterina! Why do you look terrified? Don't fret! I'm sorry my words were careless," Thomas said, chasing after her. He grabbed her elbow and pulled her close against his body, nearly knocking the basket from her arms. He kissed her forehead and temple as his embrace calmed her racing pulse.

"Last night, your brother asked me why I looked so tired. And I didn't think before I told him I've been sitting up with you while you slept. He asked me to tell him what happened to cause such nightmares, but I know it is not my story to tell," he confessed, watching her face closely.

Caterina's panic returned a little with his admission. She didn't want Ludo to know of her struggles. She didn't want him to feel any guilt or responsibility for her troubles. She resumed her delivery of the grapes to the cart, walking slowly as she pondered the situation.

"I told him I would ask you if it would be all right for me to tell him. I know it's not what you wanted, but perhaps it wouldn't be so terrible if I told him without you present?" Thomas asked, as she poured the bunches out and turned to face him. He took the empty basket from her and held her hand, rubbing his thumb gently across her fingers.

Caterina sighed. The damage was already done. If Ludo knew she was having nightmares, he would likely assume the worst … not that her story was far from the worst. But maybe Thomas could allay some of Ludo's fears.

"You can tell him. But please … *please* make sure he does not feel responsible for my troubles. It was always my decision," she said, resting her head on Thomas's chest and hugging him tightly.

"You are not upset with me?" he asked sheepishly.

"Of course not. You answered him truthfully, and you did not reveal my story before asking if that would be all right. Thank you," she said as she gave him a small kiss and turned her attention back to the vines.

That night, Ludovico told Caterina about the lives her mother and father had lived after she left. Her father's death in 1496 caused her mother to immerse herself into the care of her many grandchildren. Caterina's brothers had fathered ten sons and four daughters. Her mother passed away six years later, but she remained heartbroken over her distance from Caterina until her final breath. She wrote a letter to Caterina for just this moment, and Ludovico promised he would find it so she could have it as her mother had intended.

Thomas watched as Caterina laughed with her brother over stories of days past. They bickered the same way he and his brothers did. He could feel how difficult it would be for an immortal in a family of mortals—the loss would be immense. But he felt jubilation in the knowledge that their future together was infinite. He could give her the immortal family she truly needed.

The next night, Ludovico told Caterina about her brothers and sisters-in-law. Giovanni and Filippo had died just a few years earlier—and only months apart. All three brothers lost their wives before their own deaths—Vittoria to a fever, Mella to consumption, and Gemma to old age. Ludovico was the only one left, and as he spoke, Caterina clung to his wrinkled hand.

All the nieces and nephews reacquainted themselves with Caterina, but Thomas could sense how foreign it felt for them to have an aunt who would always remain younger than they. Thomas was surprised that everyone already knew about her existence.

"You were always talked about. Always remembered," Ludovico explained. "And you arrived just at the right time, too, since everyone is here for the harvest."

Caterina looked around at her brothers' children and grandchildren.

"It is such a pleasure to be here," she said, fighting back tears. Thomas watched as the fight between joy and sorrow wore on Caterina—her eyes glistened with moisture while her smile stretched from one ear to the other. By the end of the night, she looked exhausted. He kissed her forehead and said his goodnight as she headed off to bed.

Ludovico stayed behind just like the first night, once again offering Thomas a glass of the Galli wine.

"Will Caterina allow you to tell me?" Ludovico asked, worry clearly showing in his wrinkled brow. Thomas could see how much Ludovico yearned to hear his sister's story, but the old man did his best to temper his hopes in case Thomas could not tell him.

"She doesn't exactly *want* you to know, but she's given me permission to tell you regardless."

Ludovico heaved a sigh of relief and leaned forward in his chair, desperate to hear the tale.

Thomas tried to condense the story down into only the most important of details. He left out the part about his own family's immortality. But it was such a long story, that by the time he was finished, the sun threatened to rise over the east vineyard.

Ludovico sat silently for the duration of the tale, only moving to readjust or wipe away an occasional tear.

"My perception of you was accurate," Ludovico finally managed to say. "You are the right man for her." He looked up at Thomas and reached out to shake his hand. "I am indebted to you, Thomas, for taking care of my baby sister. I do not know how she will live without you someday, but I hope in your years together, you will bring her enough happiness to last all her days. When my wife passed away, I had our children and grandchildren to help keep her memory alive. Hopefully Caterina will have a home full of children when you are gone."

Thomas adjusted in his chair, uncomfortable with the direction the conversation had taken. *If Ludovico has kept his sister's immortality a secret all these years, perhaps there is no harm in him knowing I am the same.*

"She will never have to lose me," Thomas said quietly.

Ludovico's eyes snapped to Thomas's face immediately.

"Are you ... are you saying you are as she?" Ludovico barely finished his question.

"I am saying that as long as Caterina lives, I will be by her side," Thomas nodded.

"How is that possible?" Ludovico asked, bewildered by Thomas's confession.

"I hope this does not offend, but I cannot reveal my story. I can only assure you that I will devote the rest of my days to bringing your sister as much happiness as is possible for one person to endure," Thomas promised.

Ludovico could not have smiled any wider if he tried. His laughter filled the room as jubilation overtook his entire being.

"Yes. The right man indeed," Ludovico said when he finally quieted again.

"There's something I want to ask you," Thomas said with a smirk.

"I was hoping you would," Ludovico admitted. "My sister is unique— which you know. She is precious. And she is priceless. No man will ever deserve her. Not even the one who does," he said with a serious gleam in his eyes.

"I completely agree," Thomas nodded, knowing Caterina was far too good for him.

"Good." Ludovico shook Thomas's hand firmly. "Then you have my blessing."

"What?" Thomas blinked in confusion. He expected quite a bit more questioning or threatening.

"I knew you were worthy of her once she told me you knew the truth about her nature. Caterina does not show vulnerability with most people. If she shared her story with you, it means she has accepted you into her heart. She is an excellent judge of character, and if she trusts you, so do I," Ludovico admitted. "Marry her. Make her happy."

"I promise. I will do everything in my power to fill her life with joy and rid it of sorrow," Thomas swore.

"Excellent. Now get some rest. We still have days of labor ahead of us."

SIXTY-FIVE

THE FINAL DAY of the harvest brought the best out of everyone, and the festivities began in the late afternoon—as soon as the last grapes were picked.

Caterina looked around at her family enjoying the celebration feast. She watched as young and old laughed and danced together. She observed Ludo slowly making his way to each table, talking to his children, grandchildren, nieces and nephews. She smiled as Jacopo did his best to herd children away from the open wine barrels. And she was happy to see the Galli household carrying on as joyfully as ever. She could see her brothers and parents living on in the faces of their offspring.

But she knew this was no longer her home. She was unable to admit it before, but to everyone in her family except Ludovico, she was more myth than real.

"We can stay for as long as you want," Thomas spoke softly into her ear from behind, as he wrapped his arms around her waist and held her tightly.

She closed her eyes and leaned back into him, feeling at home for the first time all day.

"I know," she began. "But I think I'm ready to go home," she said, turning around to look him in the eyes. The look on Thomas's face morphed into a bewildered gaze. She loved catching him off guard, and she grinned at his expression.

"Are you saying you feel more at home in Florence? At the castle?" he asked excitedly.

"Yes. Even though I'm an oddity of sorts at your home because I am a woman, at least everyone understands my nature. With your family, no one looks at me as if I'm a myth or a deity or a ghost. With you, I'm simply the woman who fell in love with you. And I think I'm ready to live a *normal* life like that."

"I can absolutely promise you that life with me will never be normal," Thomas laughed as he kissed her cheek.

She looked up and saw Ludo smiling at her from across the room. She knew it pleased him to see her so happy, but worried his heart would break when she told him they were leaving.

"My dear family," Ludo said loudly as he pounded his fist on the table. A hushed quiet fell over the party in anticipation of his toast. "We have been blessed this season with a bountiful harvest of delicious grapes. We have been blessed with health and love and joy. But most of all, we have been blessed by the return of my baby sister, Caterina."

Everyone clapped and smiled at her as Ludo continued his speech.

"Sister. May your past never have room to sully the joys of your future. May your long life never be saddened by the passing of loved ones. May your days be filled with laughter and love. And may your life be like a Galli wine—tenderly cared for, well-balanced, and even better with time. To Caterina!" Ludo finished.

"To Caterina!" everyone else said as they toasted her.

She didn't hold back her tears during the speech. She knew it was his goodbye, and she had not even told him she was leaving. She walked to her brother, pulling Thomas behind her, and embraced Ludo tightly.

"Thank you," she whispered as she kissed her brother's cheek.

He held her face in his hands and put his forehead against hers.

"You have made this the best harvest of my life. Thank you," he said as he kissed her cheeks.

Sixty-six

THE NEXT MORNING Caterina and Thomas said their goodbyes and mounted their horses. Caterina had taken a final tour of the house, complete with a stop in the chapel to say a few prayers for her brother and the rest of her family. She looked back at her family's home as they rode away, and felt the same pulling at her heart strings that she had felt each time she had left it in the past.

"We are only a few days' ride away, Caterina. We can come visit whenever you feel the need," Thomas assured her.

She grasped two letters in her hand—the one her mother had written, and a second letter Ludo told her to read when she was alone. She slid them into her saddlebag, looking forward to the moment when she would read their contents.

The ride home was much the same as their ride to Milan—the only difference was that Thomas seemed more at ease, almost as if he was happier after having met her family. She didn't quite understand the change, but she didn't mind it.

"Are you excited to return to your family?" Caterina asked on the last morning of their trip.

"I suppose. I want to speak with my brothers, to tell them about your family. I like Ludovico very much. I thought you should know that," he smiled.

"I could tell," Caterina said smugly. There was little about Thomas she did not notice.

They arrived at Castello San Romolo in time for lunch, and everyone was scrambling around the kitchen, each man trying to make a different dish for himself.

Caterina stood against the wall, giggling at the chaotic display before her.

"I'm glad to see this amuses you," Sergius said, leaning back against the wall beside her.

"I feel at home here. I think this was the reason God gave me brothers ... so I would understand this level of barbarism," she laughed.

Sergius smiled at her assessment—which seemed as good as laughter, coming from him.

"Thomas said you plan to stay?" Sergius asked.

"Yes. I think this is where I belong," she said, still watching the scene unfold in the kitchen.

"Then maybe it's time Thomas ..." Sergius was cut off by Thomas's fist making contact with his shoulder.

"Don't you have your own lunch to make?" Thomas asked his brother with a meaningful glare. Sergius walked away with a smirk on his face, all the while rubbing his sore shoulder. Caterina knew brothers were violent with one another, but she thought that might have been excessive.

"Shouldn't you apologize to him? We were talking!" Caterina scolded.

"Oh that? No. He's fine. Here—Felix made lunch," he said as he handed her a large bowl of stew.

Caterina's stomach growled at the delicious smell of the food, and her former train of thought was swept away.

Thomas spent the afternoon with a pit of fear in his stomach. He knew Caterina loved him. He knew she planned to stay with him at the Family castle. And he had already received her brother's permission to ask. But there was something terrifying about actually asking the question that was twisting his insides into knots.

"Are you all right?" she asked on the way to dinner that night. "You've been acting strange since lunch, and it really seems like something is ... off."

"I am not acting strange. If anyone is acting strange, it's you," he said, unable to think of another response.

"I am *not* acting strange," she said as she pulled her hand away from his grasp.

Excellent. Now I have to propose to an angry woman. This cannot possibly go badly, he thought sardonically.

About midway through the third course, Thomas could see Caterina was still upset with him. He waited as long as he could stand, but his heart was pounding and he felt if he waited any longer his heart might give out from the excessive pounding. He stood abruptly to his feet, his chair pushing noisily away from the table. Every eye snapped to his movement, and silence flooded the room.

"As you know, we have just arrived home this day from Caterina's family home in Milan," he began. "While on that trip, I was able to speak at length with Caterina's brother. And I am grateful to say that he approved of my attitude toward his sister," he announced, turning to Caterina. "So, my love, I would ask that you do me the honor of becoming my wife. I want to always be there for you, to keep away your nightmares. I want to comfort you whenever you feel pain. And I want to tell you how beautiful you are every day—for the rest of our lives. Please say you'll be mine forever?" he asked. The look on Caterina's face drained all the nervousness from his body.

"Of course!" she cried as she jumped up and threw her arms around his neck.

Everyone banged their fists on the table and shouted congratulations. Even Priest had a slight smile on his face as the Family celebrated the upcoming nuptials.

"You asked Ludo?" Caterina said as Thomas returned her to her room later that night.

"Not exactly. He didn't let me ask, but he gave his permission nonetheless.

I made sure it would be all right with him if we married here. Ludovico wanted to come to walk you down the aisle, but he told me he is too old and the journey too long. I promised he could host a celebration with your family as soon as possible," Thomas answered.

Caterina was disappointed that her family wouldn't be present for the wedding, but simply knowing that Ludo had given his blessing over the union comforted her.

"Since you seem to have everything planned already, have you a date for our blessed union?" she asked excitedly.

"I was hoping we could have your dress finished within a week. I don't want to wait any longer for the rest of our lives to begin."

That night, Caterina could barely stay in bed for all her excitement. She didn't know how she was going to get any sleep over the next few days. She was going to be a wife. To a man whom she loved and respected. A man who would go to any lengths to protect her and keep her happy. *This is not a dream. I cannot believe that this is not a dream!*

SIXTY-SEVEN

Castello San Romolo, October 1519

OVER THE COURSE of the next two weeks, the arrangements were made for the marriage celebration. Caterina was not surprised that her wedding gown would take longer to make than Thomas expected. She was amused by his exasperation over the extra week, but he knew she enjoyed his impatience.

Thomas felt Caterina was far too secretive with the plans, and it seemed that every single one of his brothers had a mission about which they were sworn to secrecy. Even Priest and Saint were in on the planning. Thomas was only allowed to decide on his own clothing for the event (but even that task had parameters for him to stay within).

Thomas watched as the rest of the household moved about, eying him with secretive smiles. But he was grateful that in at least two details, he would be able to surprise his bride. He smirked and walked out into the vineyard ... from which he was quickly shooed away. He laughed, rather than give into his frustration, and instead hopped on his newly-befriended horse to take a ride in his favorite part of the countryside.

He looked around as he rode, feeling joyful that in less than one day, he would have a wife—a wife for the rest of his life. He would never again be accosted by the pain of losing a mortal loved one. His wife (and hopefully their future offspring) would be immortal. He prayed Caterina would be able to bear him sons.

Several hours later, he arrived back at the castle—just in time for a feast. The Family was already in full celebration over the following day's events. Caterina was clothed in a new gown—one befitting of a noblewoman. His breath caught at the sight of her. Since they first met, she had only worn dresses and gowns that were too big for her. He had not cared or even noticed until he finally saw her in a fitted gown. She was a vision in light blue. It was still simple—the way Caterina liked—but she was stunning.

"The groom has returned!" Sergius yelled when he spotted Thomas. Cheers were yelled and cups of alcohol lifted.

Thomas could not take his eyes off Caterina. She was born for this life. She was born to be a sister-in-law to his brothers. He knew more was at work here than mere fate. Their meeting and subsequent connection was *ordained*. And he smiled that he was the lucky recipient of such a gift.

SIXTY-EIGHT

THE MOMENT Caterina's eyes opened, she was fully awake. Dawn's dim light peeked through the windows, and she knew. Today was her wedding day. This was the day she had never dared dream about. The day that only mortals were allowed to have. But by some miracle, she was going to have her very own wedding day.

She smiled as her heart began pounding. She sat up and found a note and an arrangement of wildflowers lying next to her on the bed.

By the end of this day, I will have the privilege of calling you my wife. I'll see you in the chapel.

—Thomas

She took in a deep breath as she read the note. *This is real. This is happening.*

"Thank you, God. I know you did this. I owe my happiness to you," she prayed. There was more joy in her heart than she knew what to do with.

A knock on her door brought her out of her thoughts.

"Were you awake?" Samuel asked as she cracked the door.

"Yes! I can't believe the day is here," she answered cheerfully.

"Well good, because there's a lot to do. I've asked Paulus's and Claudius's wives if they will help you prepare. I hope that's all right," Samuel said sheepishly.

"Of course!" Caterina assured him. "It has been a long time since I've had to prepare for something so formal. I don't even know if I remember how to fix my hair properly."

She opened the door wider and the two women came into view.

"Oh my goodness! Come in! I didn't realize you meant right now, Samuel," she scolded.

"Well of course. You have to be scrubbed down and put together. And you only have three hours until it's time for you to say your vows. I'll leave you to it," Samuel said as he shut the door and walked away.

Paulus's wife, Ersebet, was Hungarian but spoke excellent Italian. Claudius met his wife, Marjorie, in the south of France. She mostly spoke French, but fortunately, Caterina spoke French almost as fluently as Italian. Caterina had grown to like the women during the time she spent at Castello San Romollo, and though she knew they enjoyed her company as well, their glances were occasionally tinged with jealousy. She did her best to ignore the lapses—she couldn't imagine how they must feel, so she tried only to focus on the joy of her wedding.

They scrubbed her from top to bottom until every piece of dust and dirt was removed. They braided her hair into an intricate crown over the top of her head. They placed a vine of greenery just behind the braid, making her feel as if she was a fairy from a story. She was adamant that the majority of her hair remain down—Thomas adored her red curls.

The women carefully helped her into her gown. The chemise was made of cream silk. The kirtle was a deep-red silk with black embroidery of grapes and vines. She had asked the seamstress to embroider the vines onto the gown to represent her family. And she asked that the embroidery be done in black to represent that Thomas was a widower. She did not want to wear black on her wedding day (as was common for a woman marrying a widower), but she wanted to honor his loss nonetheless. She smiled as she looked at her dress. *It is a happy compromise, I think.* The overgown was an ornate red-and-gold silk brocade. When Ersebet finished applying Caterina's makeup and Marjorie smoothed her dress, the two women stood back and sighed, smiling at what they saw.

"Am I presentable?" Caterina asked.

"See for yourself," Marjorie said, holding out a mirror so Caterina could see herself.

It took Caterina a moment to realize that she was actually looking at her own reflection. An involuntary gasp came from her mouth, and she held in her tears, not wanting to ruin her perfect makeup.

"I can't believe I look like this again. I only saw my reflection in the water of a stream for many years, and when I returned, I didn't see a need for pampering. I look like Caterina Galli once more. Thank you for your help," she said as she hugged her soon-to-be sisters-in-law.

The women left Caterina to allow her a few moments of peace before the events began. But soon after they left, there was another knock at her door.

"Hello? You can come in," she said as she stood in the center of her room, still trying to figure out how the women had brought back the noble that she used to be.

"Caterina?" a familiar voice said from the doorway.

"Jacopo?" Caterina turned to face the voice, feeling overwhelming joy and excitement.

"Thomas told me you needed someone to walk you down the aisle. And since your brother was unable to come, he thought you might want me as a replacement. I did not think you would, but in the off-chance ... well ... here I am," Jacopo said bashfully.

Caterina could barely speak, but her day felt as if the missing piece of home had finally slid into place.

"Oh, Jacopo!" she said as she ran to embrace her old friend. "I would not have it any other way. It is only fitting that the protector of my youth gives me away to the protector of my present and future. This day is truly perfect now!"

Thomas waited anxiously at the front of the Family chapel. Saint stood next to him, ready to perform the ceremony. There was nothing left but to wait for his bride to enter from the back of the chapel. He could hardly contain his excitement.

This wedding day did not hold to the typical traditions of the church. The Family had lived for too long and seen too many traditions come and go. Now, they simply did whatever felt right for the individual couple. Caterina wished for a reverent, Catholic service, and Thomas wished for a short service that still made his bride happy. Saint had assured them he could please both parties.

The chapel was as full as Thomas had ever seen it—almost all of the Family had remained home following the meeting a few weeks earlier. He tried to distract himself from the nervousness that churned in his stomach, but nothing seemed to ease his restless anticipation.

Caterina held tightly to Jacopo's arm as they approached the Family chapel. The stones were all in their perfect places, and a wooden cross stood high over the doors to the little sanctuary. She thanked God again for his blessings as she clung even more tightly to Jacopo. She worried if she loosened her grip even a little she might faint.

"Are you ready?" her friend asked with a smile in his voice.

"I am. Thank you for keeping me upright," she answered as she kissed his weathered cheek.

When the doors opened, Thomas felt his breath catch in his throat. He had never seen anything like her. She was the most beautiful woman in the world.

And with each step, he realized he was a moment closer to calling Caterina his wife. He wanted her to move with more urgency. He wanted to hold her in his arms and kiss her perfect pink lips.

When she finally made it to the front of the small chapel, he realized that Jacopo was standing next to her. He had somehow forgotten about the presence of her old friend. Jacopo smiled, bowed, and transferred Caterina's small hand over to Thomas. And when his hand touched hers, it was as if a blasting wind swept through his being. He could only see her. Only hear her. He did not know what Saint said or how long he spoke. Thomas forgot that there were others in the chapel with them. He only knew that Caterina was finally his, and he, hers. When at last Saint told them to kiss, Thomas placed one hand on the small of Caterina's back and the other in her beautiful, red, curly hair and pulled her close.

"I cannot believe you are real," Caterina whispered as her lips grazed his. He kissed her gently at first, then more passionately. He did not want to break away for even a moment, but the cheers from his brothers and nephews grew louder and louder. When he finally pulled away, they were both breathless.

"It is I who cannot believe *you* are real," he said into her ear as he leaned down to kiss her neck.

The wedding feast lasted all day. They strategically planned for a morning wedding so the celebration could continue through lunch *and* dinner. Priest surprised everyone by insisting that a large group of cooks be brought in so no one would miss any part of the day's events.

"Thank you for my surprise," Caterina said as she sat down on Thomas's lap after lunch.

"I wished to have Ludovico walk you down the aisle, but I knew Jacopo would be almost as pleasing to you." Thomas was delighted that she was satisfied with her escort.

"Jacopo *is* my family. He is as dear to me as my own flesh and blood. And you are wonderful for arranging it," she said, placing another kiss on his lips.

By the time dinner came around, everyone was reaching the cusp of drunkenness. The wine had been flowing all day, and even the most serious in the Family were happier than usual in their alcohol-induced states.

"I have a gift for my immortal daughter-in-law," Priest said as he stood to his feet and raised his glass. Caterina felt Thomas tense next to her, and she wondered if she should be worried. The room fell silent.

"You are the first female we have ever found. You mark the beginning of a new era. And I hope for you and Thomas to always stay with us here where we can keep you safe from harm. May you always find happiness at Castello San Romolo. I would like to give you a ring. I took one of my wife's rings from long ago and had Thomas's crest etched into the top of it. You are one of us now, daughter," he finished as he walked over to hand Caterina the ring and kiss her forehead.

"Here here!" everyone cheered as they raised their glasses drunkenly toward Caterina and Thomas.

Thomas looked at Caterina with a nervous smile. Caterina loved the ring, but she had no idea that Thomas had a crest of his own.

"It is lovely. Thank you," Caterina smiled as she curtsied to her new father-in-law. Priest seemed pleased by her show of gratitude and quietly returned to his seat.

"I also have a gift for my new bride," Thomas said as he stood.

Caterina couldn't imagine what else he could possibly give her. He had given her a husband, a wedding, and brought Jacopo from Milan to walk her down the aisle. As far as she was concerned, life couldn't be any better.

"With a little help from your brother, I purchased a villa close to your family's home in Milan. We can visit whenever you would like, and if you decide you want to move there, we will make it our permanent home," he said, watching her nervously as he waited for her reaction.

"That's … that's incredible!" she whispered, in shock that she had a villa of her own. She jumped up to hug Thomas, not knowing how to process the mass amount of happiness exploding from her heart.

She smiled at everyone around the table, noting that Priest did not seem as excited about her gift as everyone else. But nothing would dampen her mood. It was the most perfect day of her life.

Most women dreamed of their wedding day their entire lives. Caterina had not thought something so blissful was even a possibility, so she had dared not dream of what it might be like. But as she looked around at her new family— who were as happy for her and Thomas as she and Thomas were for themselves —a new wave of joy poured over her. She had been floundering her entire life. When she was a girl, she was the only sister in a household of brothers. She grew into a young woman whom no men found appealing. She contracted the plague and became an immortal, forced to flee Europe to save her own life and the lives of her family. Not once had she been able to see the greater picture. Until now.

God allowed her to understand how brothers interact so she would know how to survive in a family of men. God let her think she was plain in her looks so that when the right man came into her life and told her she was beautiful, it would be clear he was made for her. God let her become an immortal so she could meet Thomas and spend an eternity at his side. Those years of pain and loneliness now seemed like a short blip compared to the unending span of time that stretched out ahead.

She was Thomas's *wife*. Forever.

Tears of joy spilled from her eyes as she kissed Thomas's lips once more.

"I love you," he whispered into her ear.

SIXTY-NINE

THOMAS WATCHED Caterina all day. She smiled and held his hand at all times, only letting go when she needed to eat something that required both hands.

Priest even seemed to be enjoying himself. Thomas certainly hadn't expected his father to give Caterina a gift—especially not one of his mother's rings. Thomas and his brothers rarely spoke of their mother out of respect for their father's pain. Thomas knew it was significant that Priest not only brought their mother up in his toast, but also gave Caterina one of his mother's few remaining possessions. He would file that away for another time, though. This was a night for celebrating.

When, at last, the festivities began to die down, Thomas picked Caterina up —with cheers and hoots from his brothers and nephews—and carried her up to his bedroom. Caterina giggled nervously as they ascended the stairs, but he felt no nervousness at all. For the first time in his life, he wanted to give another person every part of himself.

He closed the door and set Caterina on her feet in front of him.

"You are the most beautiful bride in all of history," he said as he watched her face light with a smile. "I have wanted to hold you next to me every night since we were on the journey home from Cozumel. *You* are the woman I choose for the rest of my existence—and I hope I am able to live forever, because anything less simply won't be enough time."

"I can't believe you're mine," she whispered as she tiptoed up and kissed his lips softly.

"Funny. I was thinking the same thing," he agreed as he kissed her more passionately.

Caterina moved her hands through Thomas's thick hair, along his neck, and down his shoulders. He wrapped his arms around her waist and pulled her as close as he could. She pulled away slightly to untie the string on the neck of his shirt. She tugged on the fabric where it had been tucked into his pants and yanked the shirt over his head. It was her first time seeing Thomas without a shirt on, and she drank in every detail of his muscled body. On the left side of his chest, she saw the same symbol that was engraved on her ring. Her mind could not focus on the symbol for long, and she smiled as she took a tiny step away and turned around, moving her long hair out of the way for Thomas to have unimpaired access to the back of her dress. He bent down and placed a kiss on the back of her neck before pulling a knife from his side and cutting the back of the dress down the middle.

"Thomas!" she yelled, trying to hold in her laughter, "I like this dress! I want to *keep* this dress!"

"And we'll have it mended. But for now, it's in my way," he said in a mischievous tone.

Thomas grazed Caterina's now-exposed back with his fingertips, and smiled when he heard his bride suck in a breath. He pushed the dress down over her shoulders, all the while keeping his hands on her warm skin. Every part of her was soft. He kissed her shoulders, and knelt down so his lips could easily kiss each part of her back. As her dress fell to the floor, he ran his hands down her sides and let them rest on her hips. She was perfect in every way. He stood up and turned her around—allowing himself to see his wife for the first time— and he thought he might pass out. She was the definition of 'beautiful,' and he was positive he had never seen a more perfect woman.

She smiled as he drank her in. Closing the distance between them, she removed his pants and pulled him to their bed. They had barely laid down before Thomas realized he could wait no longer. He moved as slowly and carefully as he could—worrying that any moment he might hurt her or scare her. But she never once showed any fear or concern. She was perfectly at ease in his arms. He could only take so much of her perfection—and was embarrassed when their love-making ended too quickly. But Caterina looked as if she had never been happier.

"Now it's your turn," he announced as he laid her on her back.

"Wasn't *that* my turn?" she asked, confused.

"Not even close," he smiled as he began kissing her on every part of her lovely body.

When he finished showing her what 'her turn' consisted of, she lay, unmoving, for nearly ten minutes. He watched as she recovered from the new and unfamiliar exertion, all the while tracing her body with his fingertips.

"I like my turn," she finally whispered.

"So do I," he agreed with a smirk. "And you may have as many of those turns as you would like for the rest of eternity," he said as his lips found hers once more.

Seventy

When Caterina awoke the next morning, she was sore in places that had never been sore before. She turned onto her side and saw Thomas asleep next to her—completely naked. In the candlelight the night before, she thought she had seen how handsome her husband was. But with the sun shining through the window, her breath caught at his perfection. Each muscle was defined on his chest and stomach. The design on his chest was even more beautiful than she remembered. She looked at it closely, tracing the design with her fingertip—careful not to wake her sleeping husband. It matched the design on her ring perfectly. She liked that she wore a ring with her husband's 'mark'. She found her desire to be identified as his even stronger after seeing his magnificent body splayed out before her. In a moment of humor and immaturity, she couldn't resist the urge to pull back the sheet that covered his bottom half—and yes, the rest of him was more beautiful than she remembered too. She felt a giggle escape from her mouth.

That is my husband. I am that man's wife! She repeated the words several times, and even then she had trouble believing them. She crept out of the bed, hoping she wouldn't wake Thomas, and wrapped herself in a blanket that had been knocked to the floor during their activities the night before.

That was when she saw the letters. She had completely forgotten about the letters from her mother and Ludo in the excitement of her travels home and during the wedding planning, but now she finally had a moment to read them. She opened her mother's first and sat down on the edge of the bed.

My sweet Caterina,

I am so happy you are reading this letter—it means

you are alive and hopefully well. I have spent every day since your departure regretting our decision. I have never stopped fearing that we sent you to your death. I am sorry you left us. We should have been more brave. We should have had more faith that God would protect you even if you stayed. I hope you can forgive us. Please, my daughter, forgive me.

I thought of you nearly every moment of every day, and I prayed for your joy and safety. I hope those prayers were sufficient. I hope you are well.

There was no closing, and she knew these were likely the final words her mother had written. Caterina choked down sobs as she read the letter once more. She had known her mother would be sad when she left, but she hadn't grasped the depth of her mother's devastation. Her poor mother spent her entire life bemoaning Caterina's absence. "There is nothing to forgive," she whispered as she folded the letter and kissed it. "Be at peace."

She took the second letter in her hands and unfolded the parchment. As soon as she saw the script on the page, her heart overflowed with joy. It was Leonardo's handwriting. She held the letter to her chest and cried for a few minutes before wiping her eyes and opening the parchment to read.

December 1515
Caterina Galli,

My enigma of a friend. I have missed you dearly. Each month that passes marks another month that I wish we could speak. I want to tell you about my work. I want your opinions on my inventions—I finally created that flying machine. It is incredible! You must see it when you return. I hope you will return soon. I can feel in my gut that you will.

I'm moving to France for a time to build a lion out of metal. It sounds ridiculous each time I say it, but of course that's why I accepted the commission.

I'm leaving this letter with your family so that if you return while I am away, you will have a surprise awaiting you. I've left something for you under the care of my apprentice at my old workshop in Florence. It isn't finished—which shouldn't come as any surprise—but I want you to critique the piece. I don't think the work will truly be complete until I know you approve of it.

I love you, my sister. I hope I'll see you soon,

Leonardo

This was only four years ago! Maybe he is back from France.

"What are you laughing about?" Thomas asked groggily as he stretched his long body.

"I'm sorry I woke you! I didn't realize I was laughing," she apologized.

"Leonardo wrote me this letter. And he's left something for me at his workshop in Florence. Can we go?" she asked excitedly.

"Of course, my love. Right after breakfast," he said as he grabbed her around the waist and threw her back onto the bed. "And when I say breakfast, I'm not referring to food."

Seventy-one

Florence, October 1519

CATERINA KNOCKED on the door of Leonardo's old workshop. Butterflies filled her stomach at the prospect of seeing her friend again. An old woman opened the door and stared at her in confusion.

"Hello. Is this still Leonardo's workshop?" she asked, trying to peek in through the half-closed door.

"No. He's gone," the woman said abruptly.

"Well ... he told me he left something here for me. Is there anything for Caterina Galli here?" she asked hopefully.

The old woman studied Caterina's face for a few minutes without saying a word, and Caterina didn't know if the woman was going to speak again or shut the door in her face.

"You are Caterina?" she asked.

"Yes ma'am. Did he leave anything here for me?" she said, more slowly this time.

"Follow me," the woman said as she left the door open for them and walked inside the home.

Caterina couldn't believe how different the space looked since the last time she was there. The large, open room, formerly covered in a mess of paints and papers, was now a small home, partitioned off into various rooms. This was definitely not Leonardo's space—it was far too clean and tidy to even bear a resemblance to the way Leo lived.

"Here it is," the woman said as she pulled out a rolled canvas and another folded piece of parchment. "Read the letter first," she said as she walked away to give them privacy.

Dearest Caterina,

My health is fading quickly, and I fear I will not have the chance to see you again as I long to do. I have left you a certificate of your death. The story is, you lived with me from 1493 to 1495 and died under my care. I even went to the lengths of giving you a funeral so everyone would hear of Caterina Galli's demise. I feel as if you're laughing at the idea of a fictitious funeral, and nothing would bring me more pleasure than to hear that laugh again. How I've missed you. I hope you approve of your surprise —I still feel as if something is lacking, but you can be the judge of that. Feel free to fix whatever needs fixing. I'm sure it's all wrong, but then again, you always were an enigma.

Leonardo

Tears fell down Caterina's cheeks. She knew that Leonardo would not speak of his death in such a way unless he was truly dying. She would likely never see him again.

"Are you all right, my dear?" Thomas asked as he sat next to her and wrapped his arms around her waist.

"I will be. I just thought ... I thought surely he would still be here. But I know he's gone," she said as she cried into Thomas's chest.

"What was the surprise?" he asked, obviously trying to brighten her dark mood.

She picked up the rolled canvas and opened it.

"That's incredible," Thomas said as he held two of the edges so they could look at the entire painting. "Same irritatingly adorable little smirk. But you're much thinner now."

Caterina stared at the painting of herself. She knew for a fact that every painting Leonardo had made of her had gone up in flames during his experiments.

"He did this from memory," she marveled. "Every part is flawless."

"I agree," Thomas said—and she knew he was looking at her rather than the painting.

"You can't keep it," the old woman said from behind them, causing them both to jump. "I have instructions on where it has to go. Most of his paintings were sold to a Frenchman after he died, and this is the last one that has to be delivered. I was told to keep it until you came to see it or until next May came around. Luckily, you arrived in time."

"When did he die?" Caterina whispered.

"A few months back. I have this for you, too," the woman said as she handed over an official-looking document that Caterina suspected was a copy of the church's record of her death.

"Thank you," Caterina said as she looked at her painting one last time. "Thank you for knowing me so well," she whispered, hoping that Leonardo could see how much she loved it.

"If you want to keep it, I could steal it for you. No one would ever know," Thomas offered.

"No, no. I can see his work all over Europe," she assured him.

"What was his full name? You never told me," he asked as they left the house.

"Leonardo da Vinci," she said as she watched bewilderment sweep over her husband's face.

"You studied with him? He's brilliant!" Thomas gawked. Caterina couldn't contain her laughter. She hadn't expected such a strong reaction.

"Yes," she said between laughs. "And he was my dearest friend to the end. I used to pretend I could talk to him in my hut in Tantun. I told him about you," she said, growing sad at the memory of her lost friend.

"Well I hope you only told him the good parts," Thomas smirked as they mounted their horses.

"What other parts are there?" she replied with a flirtatious smile affixed to her mouth.

Seventy-Two

Milan, Present Day

CATERINA LOOKED at herself in the mirror and sighed. Her husband had been gone for nearly a week, and she was growing tired of her alone time. Over the past centuries, she had enjoyed the days she spent by herself, but, for obvious reasons, she no longer felt that same peace when Thomas was away.

After the Family meeting two years ago—the meeting where she sat quietly by and feared for her youngest son's life at the hands of her father-in-law— every trip Thomas took was cause for worry. Priest had grown mad in his long life. His mind was like an hourglass slowly losing sand, and no one knew what to expect when the last of his sanity dripped away.

"Caterina?" she heard from below. She jumped to her feet and ran to the balcony that overlooked the foyer of her home.

"How are you home?" Caterina asked as she watched her husband and two eldest sons walk through the front door. "I did not expect you home for at least another two days! And you have brought our sons," she said as she walked down the stairs to embrace three of her favorite men.

"I finished my contract earlier than expected. And Antonio and Marcus were in Florence when I arrived—waiting for me," Thomas said with a wary look on his face.

"Why? Why were you waiting for your father?" Caterina worried. Mattia and Lissie had been traveling around the world for the past ten months, and there had been no updates from them in several weeks. Caterina did her best not to worry, but a mother's heart is never at rest unless she knows each of her children is in good health.

"Don't worry, mother. I received an email from Mattia not two days ago letting me know he and Lissie are doing well," Marcus said comfortingly.

"Then what is the matter?" Caterina turned to Thomas.

"Father has given Elias a contract of which the contents are unknown. Elias was instructed not even to share the contract with Gregorius, and now Elias walks around looking as if he is ill. He refuses to leave his room, and he won't even talk to Gregorius—his own twin brother. Whatever was contained within that contract is causing Elias more grief than he can bear. We are doing our best to coax it out of him, but we're hoping whatever it is will lead him and Gregorius to join in our views of father's madness. Honestly, I don't know how they can ignore the truth when it's staring them in the face every day. Priest is mad. My father is losing his mind," Thomas said as he pushed a hand through his dark hair.

Caterina was just as worried about Elias and Priest as the rest of her family was. But when Thomas became passionate about something, she could not help but lust after him. His defined muscles tensed under his shirt. His green eyes shone a bit brighter. And his perfectly chiseled jawline grew even more defined as he clenched his jaw shut in anger. He was a vision at six foot three inches—nearly a foot taller than Caterina, who stood at five foot four. And he had been away from her for too long.

She took his massive hand inside her tiny ones, and the tension fell away from his body.

"Come, my dear. We will discuss the situation later, over lunch. Surely you need a nap, you must be tired from the drive," she smirked. He followed her willingly as Marcus and Antonio made gagging sounds behind.

"That will never sit well with us," Antonio yelled from behind them. Caterina and Thomas snickered in unison at their sons' disgust.

Before the door was even shut behind them, Caterina pushed Thomas against the bedroom wall, yanking off his t-shirt and unbuttoning his jeans.

"You missed me, my dear?" Thomas asked as he kissed Caterina's neck and lifted her shirt over her head.

"I will always miss you. Even if you are only gone for one night," she promised as her lips found his. He picked her up in his arms and carried her to their bed. Forty-five minutes later, they emerged, both feeling a bit happier with their situation in life.

"We made lunch," Marcus called from the kitchen.

When Caterina and Thomas entered their kitchen, she smiled at the feast laid out before them. She had been adamant that their house be remodeled in a similar style to the one she grew up in. The only change she requested was that the kitchen be large enough for the entire family to cook together. Thomas designed most of the villa's interior in the old style, but the kitchen—though it looked befitting of a sixteenth-century villa—was fitted with only new appliances. Everyone had enough counter space to make their own dish without getting in the way of someone else. She loved to see the counters covered in a good mess—it meant that her sweet family was using the space she had created just for them.

"And what have you made for our feast?" she asked.

"A basil pesto crostini, beef ragu over gnocchi, and roasted vegetables," Antonio smiled.

"So you found my beef ragu in the refrigerator?" Caterina asked.

"Yes, mother," Antonio replied guiltily. "No one makes ragu as good as yours," he smiled, making him look like a little boy once more, and kissed her on the cheek.

"Well, we'd better eat before it gets cold," she said as the men each grabbed a plate and followed her to the table.

SEVENTY-THREE

CATERINA STARED at the blank canvas in front of her. She loved using art as a way to escape her troubles, but her mind was still clouded with worry over Elias's secret contract. She could hardly decide where to begin as she looked down at her paints. *Maybe I'll work on an unfinished painting*, she thought. There were at least five paintings she had deemed "rubbish" in the past few months and tossed into the corner of her art room. She didn't have any true artists to critique her work—and she worried she was losing her talent with a brush.

"Are you all right, my love?" Thomas asked softly as he crouched down beside her and took her hand.

"I don't know," she admitted. "I feel like something is off. I can't concentrate. I just keep thinking about Elias and worrying that our worst fears are coming to fruition."

"I know. I feel the same way. I was thinking maybe one of the boys should find Mattia and Lissie and bring them home. I think they should be here if something serious happens," Thomas said.

"Oh yes. Send one of them. My mind would be much more at ease if I knew my own family was safe," Caterina anxiously agreed. She knew it was foolish for her to worry about Mattia and Lissie. Mattia had been freed from the burden of fulfilling contracts over two years earlier. He spent the majority of his days traveling the world with Lissie—his fiancée—and the rest of his days at the castle, training the Family to use the latest technology. He was far more likely to be safe in this situation than any of the rest of the Family.

"Marcus? Antonio?" Thomas called.

"Are you all right, father?" Marcus asked, rushing into the room.

"Yes, I'm fine. Your mother and I were thinking maybe you should find Mattia and Lissie and bring them home … in light of recent events," he said, more as a question than an official request. Caterina loved that about their relationship with their sons. After five or six hundred years, the boys were nothing short of equals. They always showed the utmost respect to her and Thomas; but as parents, she and her husband never expected their sons to bow to their wishes.

"I think that's wise," Marcus began, "but we've just received a contract in Africa. It may take up to a month to plan and carry out. Sergius and Demetrius are joining us as well."

Caterina couldn't help but chuckle. That left one person who would eagerly help with finding her son and future daughter-in-law.

"So I suppose we should ask Samuel?" she suggested with a smirk.

"Well … I know he would be more than happy to carry out the task," Thomas said warily. "But you know how he struggles with technology. Perhaps he might find them without need of technological advancements?"

Marcus and Antonio laughed, but quickly stopped when they saw Caterina's scowl.

"He loves your brother above all others in this Family. He should be the one to find them," she said with finality.

Samuel eagerly accepted the task and was at Thomas and Caterina's home within a few hours. He was, admittedly, a walking disaster. But he was a skilled killer, a devoted uncle, and an intelligent person (when he actually used his brain). Each time Caterina heard stories about his past, she marveled over how resilient he must be to overcome so many embarrassing predicaments while maintaining such a merry outlook on life. He made those around him laugh— even if his purpose was of a different nature.

"Any idea where I should start?" Samuel asked as they sat around the dining table with a world map in the center.

"You can check China off the list. They spent over four months there last year, and Mattia was adamant about not returning for some time," Antonio began.

"Also check off Madagascar, Egypt, and Tanzania. And Kenya," Marcus said, his eyes turned upward as if he were searching for the answer somewhere on the ceiling. Caterina held back a smile. He had done the same thing since he was a small boy. He always answered questions with as much thought and focus as possible. She loved that about her eldest son.

"I know they were in Moscow earlier this year—Lissie sent me a postcard to let me know they were all right. And I think they spent time in Turkey as well. But I haven't heard from them in over a month," Caterina said, wondering how they would ever find the happy couple who were doing their best to stay hidden.

"It's ridiculous is what it is. Why do they not just keep a cell phone with them at all times?" Thomas pounded his fist on the map.

"Because they know Priest would find the number and track their every move," Caterina countered softly, placing her hand on top of Thomas's fist.

"A month ago Mattia said they had just finished exploring Lebanon," Antonio said. "But I know they've moved on since then, and he didn't give me any hints about where they were headed."

"Then I'll start in Lebanon," Samuel said with a determined look on his face. "I'll take a photo of them with me, and I'll go to all the spots I know Mattia loves. There's one hotel in particular where Mattia stays when he visits —just outside of Byblos. I know he'll have taken Lissie there."

"Excellent. If you need any help, we're all a call away," Thomas said as he embraced his youngest brother and sent him on his way.

"I hope he finds them before this Family implodes," Caterina said under her breath.

Thomas wrapped his arms around her tiny waist and held her closely. He bent down, kissed her neck and whispered, "He will, my love. He will."

SEVENTY-FOUR

Castello San Romolo, Present Day

SAMUEL BOOKED a flight from Milan to Beirut the day after he volunteered to leave. Antonio and Marcus left for Africa with Sergius and Demetrius a week after that. Thomas and Caterina decided a few days later that it would be best if they made an "impromptu" trip to the Family castle to keep a watchful eye on Elias and Priest.

"Thomas," Gregorius said as he embraced his brother in a firm hug. "You have to help me."

Thomas and Caterina were inside the castle for less than a minute when Gregorius petitioned him for help. Thomas swallowed hard. He had never maintained a close relationship with Gregorius or Elias the way he had with his other brothers—but that was mainly because the twins kept to themselves most of the time. They knew everything about each other, and only a few others were allowed into their circle. Thomas realized at that very moment just how much he longed for his twin brothers to confide in him.

"I'll come to you when I'm finished," Thomas said to Caterina, whose reassuring look told him he could take as long as he needed.

"Tell me what I should do, Gregorius. I will do anything I can to help," he promised as they walked up the stairs to Elias's room.

"Elias?" Thomas said as he knocked on the locked door. "Can I speak with you for a moment?"

Thomas heard footsteps on the other side of the door. Elias sighed heavily as he unlatched the lock on the door and opened it for Thomas and Gregorius to enter his room.

"You must tell us what is the matter, brother," Thomas pleaded as Gregorius shut and locked the door behind them. "You are troubled, and you shouldn't have to bear this burden alone."

"I have orders. And I will not lose favor with our father the way you and your son have," Elias sneered.

"I was protecting my son and his fiancée," Thomas said, hoping Elias would see the merit in his decision.

Elias breathed a single, unamused laugh.

"I'm not referring to you holding a knife to Priest's throat at Mattia's meeting," Elias said with a bewildered look. "I'm talking about when you spoke out against him at the beginning of the sixteenth century. You angered him so much, that he hired you out as a mercenary on the other side of the world. He was so furious, I was sure he was going to have you killed." His words died out at the end of his last sentence, and his face went completely white. "I cannot do it," he said, burying his face in his shaking hands.

"Do what? You need to tell us," Gregorius pleaded.

"No!" Elias screamed. "I obey Priest's commands. And I will complete the task set before me," he said as he stood, color returning to his face. "Now get out. I have to pack my things."

"He's gone," Thomas said, defeated, as he walked into his and Caterina's bedroom. Caterina had only waited for half an hour, and she didn't know what could have transpired in that short time.

"What happened?" she asked, running her hands up and down Thomas's tense arms and shoulders.

"Elias would give up nothing. Not one piece of information. He's gone off on some insane task, and none of us know where he is or why he's gone," Thomas said, frustration leaking into his tone. "Except father."

"I know that tone, Thomas. Be careful. Whatever you're thinking, make sure you've discussed it with your brothers before you do anything rash," she warned.

"I need to speak with Saint," he said as he kissed her cheek and left her alone in their room once more.

"I know you feel as betrayed by Priest as the rest of us. You cannot possibly be all right with the way this Family has been run over the past few centuries. He is *mad*, uncle. Can you not try to reason with him?" Thomas begged as Saint watched him with the infuriatingly calm look on his face that he always wore.

"I have lived side-by-side with your father for millennia. I know better than all of you how his mind works. And it is true that he has become a little 'off' in recent years. But I'm not willing to push him to a breaking point as you would have me do," Saint said calmly.

Thomas didn't know how to respond. He was furious with the avoidance in Saint's answer. *He's telling me that he doesn't want to be on father's bad side. Why? Priest would never strike out against his brother.*

"I know the way you think, Thomas. When you're upset about some wrongdoing, you cannot rest until it has been made right. But tell me something. What would you have me *do*?" Saint asked, pressing more deeply into the matter.

Thomas stopped fidgeting. What *did* he want Saint to do? If Priest was truly mad, how would they stop him? Asking clearly wouldn't make a change. Was he asking Saint to stop Priest *permanently* if he refused to comply? Could he really ask Saint to end Priest's life? Thomas swallowed hard, the lump in his throat seemingly becoming a permanent fixture there.

"I don't know. We need to stop him," Thomas whispered.

"To what lengths would Priest need to go in order to deserve a death sentence?" Saint said more intensely as he leaned toward Thomas.

"I don't know. But promise me, if we find the line and he crosses it, you'll help me do what needs to be done," Thomas begged, realizing what he was asking of his uncle.

Saint stared at his own folded hands for some time. Thomas thought Saint might be praying for the right answer, but he finally moved, looking straight into Thomas's eyes.

"I promise. If you find evidence that Priest has committed an unforgivable crime against this Family, I will help you do what needs to be done."

SEVENTY-FIVE

THOMAS SAT across from Caterina as they silently ate breakfast. Gregorius sat next to Caterina, his eyes never lifting from his plate of bread and jam. It had been a week since anyone had heard from Elias, and no one knew where he had gone. Gregorius remained at the Family castle and was doing his best to stay occupied during his brother's disappearance. But everyone knew he was worried sick.

"Samuel thinks he's found Mattia and Lissie's tracks," Thomas said, hoping to take Gregorius's mind off his brother.

"That's good," Caterina said cheerfully, understanding the hidden meaning behind the conversation. "Did he say where?"

"He said they were recently in Syria, and he has a good lead," Thomas replied, realizing Gregorius wasn't listening to a word they spoke. He hung his head, feeling the weight of Gregorius's situation, and remained silent for the rest of the meal. He knew there was nothing he could say to lighten his brother's burden.

"I was thinking of going out into the Family vineyards today to paint. Would you care to join me, Gregorius?" Caterina asked.

"Umm ... I suppose I might enjoy that," he answered quietly.

"Wonderful! I'll gather my things together after we finish breakfast. It will be nice to have someone to help me carry the canvas and easel. I find it difficult to transport everything to my favorite spot in just one trip," she smiled.

Gregorius nodded and forced a tiny smile. He and Caterina had not been close over the past centuries. They were always genial with one another, but Thomas rarely spent time with Gregorius and Elias, so Caterina had not found any opportunities to get to know them. Since Elias's leaving, she'd made quite an effort to spend time with Gregorius, and he seemed grateful for the attention.

Gregorius had only been married a handful of times over his life—twice during the reign of the Roman Empire, once during the Middle Ages, and again during the Ottoman Empire. When his wives passed away, he'd relied heavily on Elias while he grieved. Thomas had never been *needed* by either of the twins, so he'd not put in as much effort with them as he now realized he should have.

Moreover, the twins *always* stood beside Priest's decisions—regardless of how egregious they were. They were faithful sons and ruthless killers—and Priest loved them most of all.

Elias's comment about how he didn't want to end up falling out of favor with Priest like Thomas and Mattia still weighed on Thomas's mind. He wrongly assumed that all was forgiven between him and his father after he returned from Cozumel, but it seemed Priest was still holding a grudge—likely spurred on by Thomas's support for Mattia two years earlier.

"Has father never forgiven me?" Thomas asked quietly.

Gregorius's head jerked up as he looked Thomas in the eyes with a troubled look on his face.

"Would you forgive one of your sons for declaring—in front of your entire Family—that you are losing your mind? Then, centuries later, the same son holds a knife to your throat with the intent to kill you if you don't relinquish your will to his? No, Thomas. I do not think our father will ever forgive you," Gregorius said as if it was the most obvious answer in the world.

Thomas looked at Caterina, who was glaring at him angrily. His timing probably could have been better, but he hadn't stopped thinking about Elias's comment since it was spoken. He mouthed "sorry" to Caterina and finished his breakfast.

"I'm going to practice archery," he announced as he walked from the room silently. It felt like his Family was falling apart piece by piece, and he desperately needed to be alone.

Caterina and Gregorius took the art supplies out into the vineyard. The sun was still rising in the East, and the way the light reflected off the grapes was simply perfect. Caterina knew she would have to revisit the exact spot at the same time for several weeks in order to capture the moment correctly, but she didn't mind. The cool, September morning air felt relaxing against the backdrop of the Family drama. She needed time outside the walls of the castle to regain her mental stability, and she hoped Gregorius would benefit from the quiet separation in the same way.

"It's beautiful out here," he said as sat down on the ground next to her. "I haven't spent enough time in the vineyards over the past few decades. It's easy to forget how peaceful they are."

"They make me feel at home. My father and brothers grew grapes," she said, her mind taking her back to a time when she and her brothers would run through the vineyards, playing chase and laughing.

"I remember you told me that once," he said, seeming to take an interest. She went on.

"After I came back with Thomas, I kept in touch with my nieces and nephews. I maintained my distance—I didn't want their children and grandchildren to grasp that I was an immortal and tell others of my existence. The entire point of leaving in the first place was to keep my family safe—so of course that extended to future generations. But I keep track of the land. My family still owns the vineyard, and every year on the anniversary of our marriage, Thomas buys a bottle of my family's wine and takes me to Paris for a week," she finished, worried that Gregorius might not care to hear her story.

"Why Paris?" Gregorius asked, welcoming her walk down memory lane.

"To visit an old friend," she said with a smile.

After that, the conversation was kept to a minimum. She painted for two hours, getting her bearings on the horizon line, the slope of the hills, and the light. When she was finished, Gregorius teased about how little she'd accomplished.

"I'll be out here for weeks," she smiled. "You're welcome to join me whenever you want. I find the solitude of nature ... mesmerizing."

Gregorius nodded and helped her carry her supplies back to her art room. But before he left, he faced Caterina with a strange look on his face.

"Thank you," he said as he leaned down to kiss both of her cheeks. "That was the most at peace I've felt since Elias left." And with that, he walked out of the room.

SEVENTY-SIX

THOMAS PICKED UP the bottle of Galli wine he had purchased the week before. His and Caterina's anniversary was only two weeks away, and he knew they wouldn't have a chance to take their yearly trip to Paris unless they went soon.

After breakfast, he realized just how much he and Caterina needed distance from the Family—even if only for two or three days. He booked their flights and found an apartment only steps from the Louvre and Île de la Cité. They normally stayed in Montmartre—Caterina's favorite neighborhood—but with only two nights in the city, he wanted Caterina to be in the heart of the action. He grabbed the bottle of wine and walked purposefully to the castle's art room (which most of the Family referred to as Caterina's art room).

"Darling," he said as he walked through the door, hiding the wine behind his back.

"What? I know that look," she smiled flirtatiously.

"I have a surprise for you," he answered, grabbing her hand and spinning her around as if they were dancing.

"You know how I love your surprises. Do I have to wait? Or do I find out now?" she asked, trying to avoid touching his clothes with her paint-covered hands.

"Right now," he smiled widely. "I don't want to miss out on our anniversary trip this year. We leave tomorrow, and we'll only stay for two nights."

Caterina's face lit with excitement, but her expression quickly fell.

"Are you sure we can leave Gregorius alone? He's a mess," she worried.

"My lovely, caring wife—we will only be gone for two days. The flights take less than two hours, and we'll be back before Gregorius even realizes we're away. I don't want to give up this tradition. We need to have some time to ourselves before the rest of the Family starts to crumble."

"I love you," Caterina said as she tiptoed up to meet Thomas's lips in a soft kiss. His response was automatic—no matter how many times he kissed her over the past five hundred years, the feeling of longing never dissipated.

"Every day my passion for you grows. And each day you look even lovelier than the last," he said as he picked her up and pressed her body against the closest wall, his lips moving with more urgency than before.

He heard someone clear their throat outside the room, and he released his wife, smoothing his shirt before turning around to face Paulus.

"Everyone has their instructions, Thomas. If Samuel, Mattia, or Elias calls while you are in Paris, we will contact you. You will be updated immediately if anything strange happens within the castle walls. And Thomas," Paulus said as his expression shifted from dead serious to a slight smirk, "Happy anniversary. Enjoy your trip."

Caterina loved the apartment Thomas secured for their stay. It was on the top floor of a building that overlooked the Louvre. Their plane landed around four o'clock—which gave them just enough time to get the keys to their apartment, drop their things off, and head out to dinner. Thomas took her to Lapérouse—just across the Seine—for dinner. And when they were filled to the brim with food and wine, they walked along the left bank of the River Seine.

As they passed sites new and old, Caterina felt the familiarity of the city wash over her. She first walked along the exact same path when she was only twenty years of age, her cousins by her sides. The pain of her old memories had faded centuries ago—Thomas helped her see past the hardships of her old life and look forward to the joys of the life they experienced each day together. Now when she walked through the city, she rejoiced at the pain she experienced so long ago. Without that pain, she would never have been able to live an immortal life at Thomas's side.

She squeezed his arm more tightly as they turned onto the Pont Alexandre to cross back over to the right bank. They walked past the palace and its gardens, and Caterina smiled as tourists took photos in the dimming light. She didn't need photos of the places she and Thomas visited together—she stored each place in the banks of her memory. Thomas kissed the top of her head and placed a hand over hers.

"The only place I've seen you more at ease is in our own home," he smiled. "I love the way you relax when you're here."

"Well, you made it that way for me. This was once a city I could only think of in terror and pain. You changed it into something of a shrine to my past. You've made it my second home," she smiled as she placed a quick kiss on his mouth.

The next day, Caterina awoke to the smell of coffee wafting into the bedroom. Thomas had woken up early to go to the boulangerie across the street and spoil her with her favorite kind of breakfast—fresh baguettes with homemade blueberry jam.

"No one makes jam like the French," she exclaimed after sinking her teeth into the first bite. Thomas chuckled over the way she savored each nibble, but she knew he enjoyed seeing his efforts appreciated, so she continued to make a fuss over the meal until it was finished.

As she readied herself for the day, she laughed that she still felt strange wearing modern clothes when she visited Paris. She felt as if her tight jeans and long-sleeved tops were an insult to the city. She braided her hair over the crown of her head, leaving the rest of her long, tight curls down. She thought she looked wild this way, but she knew it was Thomas's favorite style. Her tan top with a scoop neck and half sleeves showed off every curve. She slipped on a pair of comfortable tan heels that added almost four inches to her height—and made it much easier to kiss her husband. Finally, she covered her face in far more makeup than she normally liked to wear, but this was a special occasion (and special occasions always called for a little something extra).

"Are you ready to visit your old friend?" he asked as he finished cleaning off the table. He looked glorious in his t-shirt and jeans. She often marveled at how Mattia successfully kept them aware of the latest fashions, and she thoroughly approved of Thomas's current look.

"Yes. I am," she smiled as she slipped on a light jacket and headed out the door.

Thomas and Caterina never waited in line at the Louvre. He had somehow secured an official pass that allowed them to enter the museum without waiting in line. They walked the exact same set of stairs each year. They rounded the exact same corners. Caterina breathed deeply as she braced herself for the room ahead.

"Are you all right?" Thomas asked—as he did each time she stopped to take a deep breath just outside the room's entry.

"I am. I'm so happy to be here," she always replied. She took his hand and walked slowly into the room.

Dozens of tourists snapped photos of the painting, walking around to capture it from every angle. She remembered a time when it wasn't enclosed behind glass—and a time before that when she could stand right in front of it without a single tourist vying for a chance to see it closer than everyone else.

"Hello, old friend," she whispered. "I miss you every day." Before her emotions could take over, a large tour group entered the room. She heard 'oohs' and 'aahs' as they beheld the small painting.

"And this is the Mona Lisa," the guide said loudly. "There has always been speculation about the subject of the piece, but it is Leonardo da Vinci's most famous work by far."

Caterina felt her cheeks blush as she buried her face in Thomas's chest.

"No one would possibly imagine you were alive even if they noticed you looked like the painting," he assured her quietly.

She knew it was foolish to worry. No one lived to be over six hundred years old.

"I always feel closest to him when I'm looking at it," she said as her eyes turned back to the painting. It didn't really look like her any more. She had been a little heavier before leaving Europe. And she never really gained the weight back after Thomas brought her home. But the expression Leo captured on her face was flawless. And she knew that, apart from Thomas, no one had ever known her better.

"It was wonderful to see you again," she said under her breath. "I'll see you next year."

SEVENTY-SEVEN

Istanbul, Turkey, Present Day

SAMUEL SEARCHED for weeks for his nephew. There were little clues of Mattia and Lissie's whereabouts scattered across the Middle East, but Samuel still had no idea where they were. He only knew for sure that they had been through Jordan, Lebanon, Syria, and Turkey. He sat in his small hotel room in Istanbul and looked over the map. The route his nephew had taken was enough evidence to suggest they were driving. So his next step was to figure out where the car rental originated. If he could determine that, he would be able to track the car's GPS to find Mattia's current location.

He chuckled a little, finding humor in the idea that Mattia himself had taught the skill to Samuel earlier that year. Samuel's knowledge of computers had grown exponentially since Mattia saw fit to take Samuel under his wing and train him privately. No one else in the Family knew about their arrangement, but Samuel now considered himself at least as skilled with technology as any of the rest of the Family—if not more.

He once again dialed the number Mattia gave him to use in case of an emergency. There was still no answer. Mattia was the one person Samuel knew he could always rely on. If Samuel was in trouble, Mattia always seemed to find a way to bail him out. But Samuel was *not* in trouble, and it seemed Mattia somehow knew.

Samuel would have to dig deeper if he was going to find his nephew.

SEVENTY-EIGHT

Castello San Romolo, Present Day

CATERINA AND THOMAS'S short trip had proven to be exactly the right amount of time away. When they arrived back at the castle, word had reached Paulus that Sergius, Antonio and Marcus had completed their contract and were on a plane back to Florence. There was still no word of Elias's whereabouts, and no one had spoken to Priest since Elias left.

"I do not feel we should worry so much," Paulus said in a failed attempt to allay his brothers' fears. "There are any number of reasons Elias might be away."

But Thomas knew better. And he knew Paulus's words were only for Gregorius's comfort—Paulus's expression was incredulous even as the words flowed from his own mouth.

"I have never seen Elias fret over a contract. Over women? Yes. But never over our work. That is … deeply concerning," Gregorius snapped at Paulus.

All day Caterina kept the men full of food and wine. And when Sergius, Marcus, and Antonio arrived home that night, the atmosphere was silent and still. Everyone waited for a phone to ring. Thomas could feel the buzz in the air.

SEVENTY-NINE

Taşucu, Turkey, Present Day

SAMUEL BOARDED the ferry to Cyprus with a smug look of satisfaction on his face. He had traced Mattia and Lissie all the way to the island, and he would find them in a matter of days.

Not once had he needed help from anyone in the Family. He used his new skills to hack into each car rental company's system, search all of Mattia's known aliases for a rental agreement, and locate the exact vehicle's GPS. Once he saw the trip the GPS had recorded, he confirmed that it was, in fact, the correct vehicle. Only two days earlier, Mattia, Lissie and their rental car boarded a ferry in Taşucu, bound for Girne, Cyprus.

Samuel was quite pleased with himself. He wished he could call everyone in the Family and brag about his ingenuity—but he knew better. He would wait until he had Mattia and Lissie at his side. *Then* he would call everyone in the Family and brag.

Samuel looked at the car's current GPS. They were somewhere in the city of Paphos. As soon as his ferry docked in Girne, Samuel hopped into a taxi and lay back to take a short nap during the two-hour drive.

Once the driver dropped him off in the heart of Paphos, Samuel checked into the closest hotel and turned on his laptop once more. It seemed Mattia's car was near the Tomb of the Kings—only a few kilometers from where Samuel sat. He put his laptop back into his bag, threw the bag over his shoulder, and headed out on the short walk to where Mattia and Lissie surely were.

The Mediterranean air blew around him in strong gusts as he walked—almost throwing him off balance once or twice. He felt urgency pushing him onward. He was so close to his bragging rights.

He turned right onto Tombs of the Kings Avenue and felt the need to jog. It was as if the wind behind him was pushing him to move faster. He came to a halt when he saw the black Range Rover with rental plates parked in a small lot. *I found them*, he thought jubilantly.

He began walking—at a normal pace again—toward the ruins he knew Mattia and Lissie were exploring. He saw them, laughing and holding hands, heading right toward him. As he opened his mouth to speak, a swift movement caught his eye. A man, dressed in desert camouflage, was running toward the pair quickly. Samuel couldn't see who the man was, but his gut told him there were ill intentions in his posture.

"Get down!" Samuel screamed as he sprinted toward his nephew. He closed the distance as quickly as he could, hoping to beat the camouflaged man to them. Samuel watched shock flash in Mattia's eyes, and he watched his nephew turn and scan the area while pushing Lissie behind his back. In the time it took Samuel to blink, Mattia's hands were each equipped with a knife. Samuel was only a few yards from Mattia now, but so was the attacker—Samuel could categorically list the man as an attacker now that his course continued directly toward Mattia and Lissie. He saw the reflection of the sun off a knife that was carefully hidden in the man's sleeve. Samuel pulled a knife from the pocket of his bag and swung his arm at the attacker. The man was prepared for the move, and countered far more quickly than Samuel expected. As he swung again for the man, he felt a sting in his chest and heard an echoing that sounded eerily like a scream come from behind him. Samuel looked down and saw a wound— at least six inches long—across his chest. The attacker lay dead on the ground in front of him—though Samuel couldn't remember making contact with his own knife.

"Uncle!" Mattia screamed as he laid Samuel gently on the ground. "Uncle, stay awake. We'll have you stitched up in no time. You'll be fine. You'll be fine."

"I'll be fine," Samuel whispered as he succumbed to the darkness.

EIGHTY

Castello San Romolo, Present Day

THE PHONE RANG at 4:53PM.

"It's Samuel!" Thomas called to Caterina. "Please tell me you've found them," Thomas said the moment he answered the phone. Antonio and Marcus tensed next to him.

"Father," he heard a voice choke out on the other end of the call.

"Mattia?" Thomas asked as a feeling of fear buried itself deep within his chest.

"Yes. Samuel found us. He ... I don't even know where to begin," Mattia said on the other line, sobs breaking up his sentences.

"What's going on?" Thomas asked.

"We were attacked. Samuel alerted us to the attacker, but he ... the attacker killed Samuel before I could stop him. Father ..."

Thomas felt tears run down his cheeks, and his breath caught each time he inhaled.

"Did he find them?" Caterina asked as she emerged from the bathroom. Thomas made eye contact with her, and as soon as she saw the expression on his face, she ran to the phone and ripped it from his hands.

"Where is my son?" she yelled.

"I'm here mother. But Samuel ... he's gone."

Caterina put her hand over her mouth and bent over, weeping uncontrollably. Thomas couldn't console her. He couldn't even console himself. He took the phone back from her limp hand and tried to take a deep breath while Antonio and Marcus rushed to keep Caterina from falling onto the floor in her fit of grief.

"Who was the attacker? Is he dead? Do you have any idea why someone was after you?" Thomas asked rapidly, his mind kicking into work mode.

"Yes. He's dead," Mattia said, his voice full of grief. "I killed him."

"And you're sad about this?" Thomas roared. "I know it was your first kill, but surely the situation provides enough justification," he growled, upset that his son was worried over taking a life to protect himself and avenge his uncle.

"Of course it was justified, but I'm devastated. It … it was Elias," Mattia sobbed once more. "We didn't know. His face was covered. Father … I don't understand."

Thomas dropped the phone on the ground without ending the call and walked out of the room. Marcus and Antonio flanked his sides closely, having heard enough of the conversation to understand that battle was upon them, and they needed to remain close to their father. Thomas's brothers and nephews had gathered at the bedroom door to see what the commotion was about. They asked him what was the matter as he strode past them silently, and they followed him down the stairs and across the house when he gave no answer.

He did not stop or deviate from his warpath. He walked straight into Saint's room without so much as a knock. He stood, staring at Saint for a few silent moments.

"What is the matter, Thomas?" Saint asked, concern thick in his voice.

"Priest sent my brother to *kill* my son. But instead, two of my brothers have died this day. What further proof do you need? Priest is a psychopathic killer. And if you cannot see the truth of that now, I will end your life the moment after I end his."

ACKNOWLEDGEMENTS

Once again, I have to first thank my partner, Caleb—you are the most loving and gracious partner a person cold ask for. Thank you for supporting my dreams, editing my words, encouraging my passions, and pushing me to be better at everything I do.

Melissa—you are the best editor I could ask for. Your brutality is exactly what I need to have my butt kicked into gear. Thank you for not letting me get away with any laziness. You make my stories SO much better.

Bri—thank you for the hours you spent teaching me about costuming and textiles. I would have been lost without your guidance!

Jake—thank you for being my first reader! Your feedback is more valuable to me than you know.

Stacey—once again, your consultations over the cover design made it as beautiful as it is! Thank you!

Special thanks to Giovanni Tamponi for the perfect hourglasses that grace Ghost's cover. You're a graphic design genius.

Finally, thank you to my incredible readers for your unending support and excitement. Every time I write, edit, or design a cover, I'm thinking of you! You are the reason I'm excited each time my fingers touch the keyboard.

KEEP READING FOR A SNEAK PEEK OF PLAGUE, THE EPIC CONCLUSION TO THE PLAGUED TRILOGY...

ONE

AHUZZAN'S EYES popped open, and he tried to inhale a deep breath. But there was little air to be found. The darkness that surrounded him was blacker than night. Panic filled his mind.

What has happened? Is this a tomb? Am I buried under the earth? This enclosure presses too closely. I do not remember being in such a place, he thought frantically, trying to push at the substance which restrained him from movement.

He had not been confined before in any fashion. For he was Ahuzzan—the great leader of soldiers. He could not be defeated—he won every battle of which he was leader. His reputation for swift and deadly retaliation kept his enemies at bay and his allies in the palm of his hand. *This cannot be imprisonment*, he decided. *None would risk my wrath. But where am I?* he wondered again as he tried to move his limbs more vigorously. He could not tell which direction was up and which was down. His body was in a fixed state —smashed.

He calmed his racing mind and pounding heart for a moment, pressing his eyes shut and focusing solely on his weight distribution. When he realized he was lying face down, his determination faltered. It would be more difficult to maneuver from his position if he first had to turn over.

He began to work his arms, legs and waist a little at a time, doing everything in his power to take short breaths. He was going to run out of air soon. Whatever he was surrounded by was clingy and soft—but there were alternately fragments of hard, staff-like objects mixed with the gooey substance. He kicked his feet forcefully away from his torso, and everything crumbled, dry and dusty, where they touched. He did not let his mind concentrate on the confusing blend of the surrounding elements. He only focused on a plan to escape his confinement.

The materials around him shifted as he kicked, allowing his arms to move a little. He did his best to clear the area around his face, but the weight of the objects pressing down on his back was substantial. He knew he must be buried deep in the earth. Every movement was labored, the ground crumbling around him wherever he made space. After a laborious battle against the earth, his body was finally on its back. He needed to begin his climb to the surface. *How did I get here?* he worried, not understanding what led to a complete memory lapse of the events leading to a burial.

He pushed his legs upward hard, feeling the surrounding substances give way at his forceful movements. As the ground at his feet moved, he used his hands and torso to move the earth above his head into the area his feet had cleared. After several attempts, he was able to sit up. The dust covered his face, and with each breath he took, more dust entered his lungs. *Do not think of the dust. Think only of the escape.* He thrust his body upward, pulling his feet beneath him, and though it was painful to stand on … whatever he was standing on … he used the same earth-clearing technique to push the dirt around his body and pull himself closer to the surface—closer to the fresh air he longed to breathe. He moved one lump of material from over his head, and when he inhaled, his mind registered the stench that surrounded him. It smelled like the aftermath of a battle. It smelled like death.

Was I on the battlefield? Has someone thrown me in with the dead? Should I not remember fighting? His mind protested as his body worked tirelessly to free itself from what he now recognized as a trench dug for the bodies of the deceased.

He was swimming toward the surface of a mass grave. The decaying flesh and entrails of the dead around him made up the tacky, soft earth he had pushed aside. The fragmented sticks were bones. He swallowed the bile that rose in his throat, threatening to add to the stench of his surroundings.

Get me out, he commanded his tired limbs. They struggled harder. His hands grabbed at the putrid flesh of the decaying bodies that kept him underground. Now that he understood what blocked his escape, he felt skin and muscle slide from the bone as he pushed against them with his shaking hands. The weight and effort lessened the further he pushed upward.

He risked opening his eyes for a moment after he cleared a small gap in the earth surrounding his face. The faintest glow of light seeped through a space above, and it was enough to make him move with even more ferocity.

He shut his eyes tightly again and refused to think about the bodies around him. As he ascended higher, the bodies became less gooey. They felt more like the crumbling bark of a tree. He felt a glimmer of hope—he was close to the surface where the maggots and carrion-eaters had already picked the bodies clean. He felt like he could lose consciousness at any moment—he was starving for a bite of food, and his mouth begged for just one drop of water.

He opened his eyes again and saw light coming in from multiple locations. He was almost there. Almost to the surface. He would emerge with just a few more pulls from his arms and pushes from his legs.

He could feel freedom in his grasp, but his breaths became more labored with each effort. The air around him was dusty with the cracking remains of the deceased. He coughed after each breath, which caused him to inhale more dust. Hope was slipping from his grasp as he felt his mind begin to darken once more.

He bent his knees as much as he could, and his feet searched to find purchase on anything solid. He thrust one last time with all his might, his hands plunging up toward the sun above.

Stay awake, he begged his failing mind. *Just for a few more seconds*, as he coughed too hard and sucked in too much dust. *Stay ...*

Priest sat up in bed, his eyes searching for the light he always kept on beside his bed. His lungs breathed in greedily the fresh air in the room. He had dreamed that dream too many times. He had awoken in terror for far too long.

"Enough," he whispered wearily. "Please. I have had enough."

KARI NICHOLS

was inspired to write after moving from Arkansas to the colorful and energetic city of New York. Her passion for creating art was developed from the time she was a child. Her artistic endeavors have ranged from music composition to photography to fashion design, but writing novels is far and away her favorite artistic outlet. She can often be found wrapped up in her favorite blanket, writing her next novel with a cup of hot tea in hand. She is a self-professed nerd, and when she isn't writing, she loves to play video games, read romance novels, and go on international adventures with her charming husband.

You can visit her online at

www.KariNichols.com

or on Twitter (@TheKariNichols)

www.ingramcontent.com/pod-product-compliance
Lightning Source LLC
Chambersburg PA
CBHW051324250626
47155CB00007B/2447